PENGUIN BOOKS

The Murder Room

'Vintage P. D. James' *Spectator*

'Elegant . . . James creates a pervasive atmosphere of
claustrophobia' *The Times*

'An absorbing delight from start to finish' *Scotsman*

'Fascinating . . . It's never a mistake to read P. D. James'
Sunday Telegraph

'James is the last of the great Golden Age crime writers'
Independent

'A thoroughly satisfying whodunit' *Mail on Sunday*

'A classic piece of crime fiction by James with plenty of
meat on its bones to satisfy the hungriest crime fan'
Sunday Herald

'An intricate, carefully laid plot' *Irish Times*

'Crime writing for the connoisseur'
The Times Literary Supplement

P. D. James was born in Oxford in 1920 and educated at Cambridge High School. From 1949 to 1968 she worked in the National Health Service as an administrator, and the experience she gained from her job helped her with the background for *Shroud for a Nightingale*, *The Black Tower* and *A Mind to Murder*. In 1968 she entered the Home Office as Principal, working first in the police department concerned with the forensic science service, and later in the criminal policy department. She retired in 1979. She is a Fellow of the Royal Society of Literature and a Fellow of the Royal Society of Arts. She was a Governor of the BBC from 1988 to 1993 and was a member of the Board of the British Council from 1988 to 1993. She served on the Arts Council and was Chairman of its Literary Advisory Panel from 1988 to 1992. She has served as a magistrate in Middlesex and London. She has won awards for crime writing in Britain, America, Italy and Scandinavia, and has received honorary degrees from six universities. In 1983 she received the OBE and she was created a life peer in 1991. In 1997 she was elected President of the Society of Authors. She has been a widow for over thirty-five years and has two children and five grandchildren.

Her novels include *An Unsuitable Job for a Woman*, *Innocent Blood*, *The Skull Beneath the Skin*, *Death of an Expert Witness*, *A Taste for Death*, *Devices and Desires*, *Cover Her Face*. *Unnatural Causes*, *The Children of Men*, *Original Sin*, *A Certain Justice* and *Death in Holy Orders*, several of which are published by Penguin. She is co-author, with T. A. Critchley, of *The Maul and the Pear Tree*.

The Murder Room

P. D. JAMES

PENGUIN BOOKS

IN ASSOCIATION WITH FABER AND FABER

PENGUIN BOOKS

Published by the Penguin Group

Penguin Books Ltd, 80 Strand, London WC2R ORL, England

Penguin Group (USA) Inc., 375 Hudson Street, New York, New York 10014, USA

Penguin Books Australia Ltd, 250 Camberwell Road, Camberwell, Victoria 3124, Australia

Penguin Books Canada Ltd, 10 Alcorn Avenue, Toronto, Ontario, Canada M4V 3B2

Penguin Books India (P) Ltd, 11 Community Centre, Panchsheel Park, New Delhi – 110 017, India

Penguin Group (NZ), cnr Airborne and Rosedale Roads, Albany, Auckland 1310, New Zealand

Penguin Books (South Africa) (Pty) Ltd, 24 Sturdee Avenue, Rosebank 2196, South Africa

Penguin Books Ltd, Registered Offices: 80 Strand, London WC2R ORL, England

www.penguin.com

First published by Faber and Faber Limited 2003
Published in Penguin Books 2004

6

Set in 11/13 pt Monotype Dante
Typeset by Rowland Phototypesetting Ltd, Bury St Edmunds, Suffolk
Printed in England by Clays Ltd, St Ives plc

To my two sons-in-law
Lyn Flook
Peter Duncan McLeod

Time present and time past
Are both perhaps present in time future,
And time future contained in time past.

T. S. Eliot, *Burnt Norton*

Contents

Author's Note

I must apologize to all lovers of Hampstead Heath and to the Corporation of London for my temerity in erecting the fictional Dupayne Museum on the fringes of these beautiful and well-loved acres. Some other locations mentioned in the novel are also real and the notorious cases of murder exhibited in the Murder Room at the Museum were real crimes. It is the more important to emphasize that the Dupayne Museum, its trustees, staff, volunteers and visitors exist only in my imagination, as does Swathling's College and all other characters in the story. I should also apologize for arranging temporary breakdowns of service to the London Underground and the rail link between Cambridge and London, but travellers by public transport may feel that this is a fictional device which imposes no great strain on their credulity.

As usual I am grateful to Dr Ann Priston OBE of the Forensic Science Service and to my secretary, Mrs Joyce McLennan. I also owe particular thanks to Fire Investigation Officer Mr Andrew Douglas of the Forensic Science Service, for his invaluable help in educating me in the procedure for the investigation of suspicious fires.

P. D. James

BOOK ONE

The People and the Place

Friday 25 October – Friday 1 November

I

On Friday 25 October, exactly one week before the first body was discovered at the Dupayne Museum, Adam Dalgliesh visited the museum for the first time. The visit was fortuitous, the decision impulsive and he was later to look back on that afternoon as one of life's bizarre coincidences which, although occurring more frequently than reason would expect, never fail to surprise.

He had left the Home Office building in Queen Anne's Gate at two-thirty after a long morning meeting only briefly interrupted by the usual break for brought-in sandwiches and indifferent coffee, and was walking the short distance back to his New Scotland Yard office. He was alone; that too was fortuitous. The police representation at the meeting had been strong and Dalgliesh would normally have left with the Assistant Commissioner, but one of the Under Secretaries in the Criminal Policy Department had asked him to look in at his office to discuss a query unrelated to the morning's business, and he walked unaccompanied. The meeting had produced the expected imposition of paperwork and as he cut through St James's Park Underground station into Broadway he debated whether to return to his office and risk an afternoon of interruptions or to take the papers home to his Thames-side flat and work in peace.

There had been no smoking at the meeting but the room had seemed musty with spent breath and now he took pleasure in breathing fresh air, however briefly. It was a blustery day but unseasonably mild. The bunched clouds were tumbling across a sky of translucent blue and he could have imagined that this was spring except for the autumnal sea-tang of the river – surely half imagined – and the keenness of the buffeting wind as he came out of the station.

Seconds later he saw Conrad Ackroyd standing on the kerb at the corner of Dacre Street and glancing from left to right with that air of mingled anxiety and hope typical of a man waiting to hail a taxi. Almost immediately Ackroyd saw him and came towards him, both arms outstretched, his face beaming under a wide-brimmed hat. It was an encounter Dalgliesh couldn't now avoid and had no real wish to. Few people were unwilling to see Conrad Ackroyd. His perpetual good humour, his interest in the minutiae of life, his love of gossip and above all his apparent agelessness were reassuring. He looked exactly the same now as he had when Dalgliesh and he had first met decades earlier. It was difficult to think of Ackroyd succumbing to serious illness or facing personal tragedy, while the news that he had died would have seemed to his friends a reversal of the natural order. Perhaps, thought Dalgliesh, that was the secret of his popularity; he gave his friends the comforting illusion that fate was beneficent. As always, he was dressed with an endearing eccentricity. The fedora hat was worn at a rakish angle, the stout little body was encased in a plaid tweed cloak patterned in purple and green. He was the only man Dalgliesh knew who wore spats. He was wearing them now.

'Adam, lovely to see you. I wondered whether you might be in your office but I didn't like to call. Too intimidating, my dear. I'm not sure they'd let me in, or if I'd get out if they did. I've been lunching at a hotel in Petty France with my brother. He comes to London once a year and always stays there. He's a devout Roman Catholic and the hotel is convenient for Westminster Cathedral. They know him and are very tolerant.'

Tolerant of what? wondered Dalgliesh. And was Ackroyd referring to the hotel, the Cathedral, or both? He said, 'I didn't know you had a brother, Conrad.'

'I hardly know it myself, we meet so seldom. He's something of a recluse.' He added, 'He lives in Kidderminster,' as if that fact explained all.

Dalgliesh was on the point of making tactful murmurings of imminent departure when his companion said, 'I suppose, dear boy, I couldn't bend you to my will? I want to spend a couple of hours at the Dupayne Museum in Hampstead. Why not join me? You know the Dupayne of course?'

'I've heard of it but never visited.'

'But you should, you should. It's a fascinating place. Dedicated to the inter-war years, 1919–1938. Small but comprehensive. They have some good pictures: Nash, Wyndham Lewis, Ivon Hitchens, Ben Nicholson. You'd be particularly interested in the library. First editions and some holographs and, of course, the inter-war poets. Do come.'

'Another time, perhaps.'

'You never manage another time, do you? But now I've caught you, regard it as fate. I'm sure you have your Jag tucked up somewhere in the Met's underground garage. We can drive.'

'You mean I can drive.'

'And you'll come back to Swiss Cottage for tea, won't you? Nellie will never forgive me if you don't.'

'How is Nellie?'

'Bonny, thank you. Our doctor retired last month. After twenty years together it was a sad parting. Still, his successor seems to understand our constitutions and it might be as well to have a younger man.'

Conrad and Nellie Ackroyd's marriage was so well established that few people now bothered to wonder at its incongruity or to indulge in prurient speculation about its possible consummation. Physically they could hardly have been more different. Conrad was plump, short and dark with inquisitive bright eyes and moved as sprightly as a dancer on small nimble feet. Nellie was at least three inches taller, pale-skinned and flat-chested, and wore her fading blonde hair curled in plaits on each side of her head like earphones. Her hobby was collecting first editions of 1920s and 1930s girls' school stories. Her collection of Angela Brazils was regarded as unique. Conrad and Nellie's enthusiasms were their house and garden, meals – Nellie was a superb cook – their two Siamese cats and the indulgence of Conrad's mild hypochondria. Conrad still owned and edited *The Paternoster Review*, notable for the virulence of its unsigned reviews and articles. In private life he was the kindest of Jekylls, in his editorial role an unrepentant Hyde.

A number of his friends whose wilfully overburdened lives inhibited the enjoyment of all but necessary pleasures somehow found time to take afternoon tea with the Ackroyds in their neat Edwardian villa in Swiss Cottage with its comfortable sitting-room and atmosphere of timeless indulgence. Dalgliesh was occasionally among them. The meal was a nostalgic and unhurried ritual. The delicate cups with their handles aligned, the thin brown bread and butter, bite-size cucumber sandwiches and homemade sponge and fruit cakes made their expected appearance, brought in by an elderly maid who would have been a gift to a casting agent recruiting actors for an Edwardian soap opera. To older visitors the tea brought back memories of a more leisurely age and, to all, the temporary illusion that the dangerous world was as susceptible as was this domesticity to order, reason, comfort and peace. To spend the early evening gossiping with the Ackroyds would, today, be unduly self-indulgent. All the same, Dalgliesh could see that it wouldn't be easy to find a valid excuse for refusing to drive his friend to Hampstead.

He said, 'I'll drive you to the Dupayne with pleasure, but I might not be able to stay if you plan a long visit.'

'Don't worry, dear boy. I'll get a cab back.'

It took Dalgliesh only a few minutes to collect the papers he needed from his office, hear from his PA what had happened during his absence and drive his Jaguar from the underground car-park. Ackroyd was standing near the revolving sign looking like a child obediently waiting for the grown-ups to collect him. He wrapped his cloak carefully around him, climbed into the car with grunts of satisfaction, struggled impotently with the seatbelt and allowed Dalgliesh to strap him in. They were travelling along Birdcage Walk before he spoke.

'I saw you at the South Bank last Saturday. You were standing by the window on Level Two looking out at the river with, I might say, a remarkably beautiful young woman.'

Without looking at him, Dalgliesh said evenly, 'You should have come up and been introduced.'

'It did occur to me until I realized that I would be *de trop*. So I contented myself with looking at your two profiles – hers more than yours – with more curiosity than might have been considered polite. Was I wrong in detecting a certain constraint, or should I say restraint?'

Dalgliesh did not reply and, glancing at his face, at the sensitive hands for a second tightening on the wheel, Ackroyd thought it prudent to change the subject. He said, 'I've rather given up the gossip in the *Review*. It isn't worth printing unless it's fresh, accurate and scurrilous, and then you risk the chance of being sued. People are so litigious. I'm trying to diversify somewhat. That's what this visit to the Dupayne is all about. I'm writing a series of articles on murder as a symbol of its age. Murder as social history, if you like. Nellie thinks I could be on to a winner with this one, Adam. She's very excited. Take the most notorious Victorian crimes, for example. They couldn't have happened in any other century. Those cluttered claustrophobic drawing-rooms, the outward respectability, the female subservience. And divorce – if a wife could find grounds for it, which was difficult enough – made her a social pariah. No wonder the poor dears started soaking the arsenical flypapers. But those are the easiest years. The inter-war years are more interesting. They have a room at the Dupayne dedicated entirely to the most notorious murder cases of the 1920s and 30s. Not, I assure you, to titillate public interest – it's not that kind of museum – but to prove my point. Murder, the unique crime, is a paradigm of its age.'

He paused and looked at Dalgliesh intensely for the first time. 'You're looking a little worn, dear boy. Is everything all right? You're not ill?'

'No, Conrad, I'm not ill.'

'Nellie said only yesterday that we never see you. You're too busy heading that innocuously-named squad set up to take over murders of a sensitive nature. "Sensitive nature" sounds oddly bureaucratic – how does one define a murder of an insensitive nature? Still, we all know what it means. If the Lord Chancellor is found in his robes and wig brutally battered to death on the Woolsack, call in Adam Dalgliesh.'

'I trust not. Do you envisage a brutal battering while the House is sitting, no doubt with some of their Lordships looking on with satisfaction?'

'Of course not. It would happen after the House had risen.'

'Then why would he be sitting on the Woolsack?'

'He would have been murdered somewhere else and the body moved. You should read detective fiction, Adam. Real-life murder today, apart from being commonplace and – forgive me – a little vulgar, is inhibiting of the imagination. Still, moving the body would be a problem. It would need considerable thought. I can see that it might not work.'

Ackroyd spoke with regret. Dalgliesh wondered if his next enthusiasm would be writing detective fiction. If so, it was one that should be discouraged. Murder, real or fictional, and in any of its manifestations, was on the face of it an unlikely enthusiasm for Ackroyd. But his curiosity had always ranged widely and once seized by an idea he pursued it with the dedicated enthusiasm of a lifelong expert.

And the idea seemed likely to persist. He went on, 'And isn't there a convention that no one dies in the Palace of Westminster? Don't they shove the corpse into the ambulance with indecent haste and later state that he died on the way to hospital? Now that would create some interesting clues about the actual time of death. If it were a question of inheritance, for example, timing could be important. I've got the title, of course. *Death on the Woolsack.*'

Dalgliesh said, 'It would be very time-consuming. I should stick to murder as a paradigm of its age. What are you expecting to get from the Dupayne?'

'Inspiration perhaps, but mostly information. The Murder Room is remarkable. That's not its official name, by the way, but it's how we all refer to it. There are contemporary newspaper reports of the crime and the trial, fascinating photographs including some originals, and actual exhibits from the scene of the murder. I can't think how old Max Dupayne got his hands on those, but I believe he wasn't always scrupulous when it came to acquiring what he wanted. And of course the museum's interest in murder coincides with mine. The only reason the old man set up the Murder Room was to relate the crime to its age, otherwise he would have seen the room as pandering to depraved popular taste. I've already selected my first case. It's the obvious one, Mrs Edith Thompson. You know it, of course.'

'Yes, I know it.'

Everyone interested in real-life murder, the defects of the criminal justice system, or the horror and anomalies of capital punishment knew of the Thompson–Bywaters case. It had spawned novels, plays, films, and its share of the journalism of moral outrage.

Apparently oblivious of his companion's silence, Ackroyd prattled happily on. 'Consider the facts. Here we have an attractive young woman of twenty-eight married to a dull shipping clerk four years her senior and living in a dull street in a drab east London suburb. Do you wonder she found relief in a fantasy life?'

'We have no evidence that Thompson was dull. You're not suggesting dullness is a justification for murder?'

'I can think of less credible motives, dear boy. Edith Thompson is intelligent as well as attractive. She's holding down a job as the manageress of a millinery firm in the City and in those days that meant something. She goes on holiday with her husband and his sister, meets Frederick Bywaters, a P&O Line steward eight years her junior, and falls desperately in love. When he's at sea she writes him passionate letters which, to the unimaginative mind, could certainly be interpreted as an incitement to murder. She claims that she's put ground electric light bulbs in Percy's porridge, the probability of which the forensic pathologist, Bernard Spilsbury, discounted at the trial. And then on 3 October 1922, after an evening at the Criterion Theatre in London, when they're walking home, Bywaters springs out and stabs Percy Thompson to death. Edith Thompson is heard crying out "Don't – oh don't!" But the letters damned her, of course. If Bywaters had destroyed them she'd be alive today.'

Dalgliesh said, 'Hardly. She'd be a hundred and eight. But could you justify this as a specifically mid twentieth-century crime? The jealous husband, the young lover, the sexual enslavement. It could have happened fifty or a hundred years earlier. It could happen today.'

'But not in exactly the same way. Fifty years earlier she wouldn't have had the chance of working in the City for one thing. It's unlikely she'd ever have met Bywaters. Today, of course, she would have gone to university, found an outlet for her intelligence, disciplined her seething imagination and probably ended up rich and successful. I see her as a romantic novelist. She certainly wouldn't have married Percy Thompson and if she did go in for murder, psychiatrists today would be able to diagnose a fantasist; the jury would take a different view of extra-marital sex and the judge wouldn't indulge his deep prejudice against married women who took lovers eight years their junior, a prejudice undoubtedly shared by a 1922 jury.'

Dalgliesh was silent. Ever since, as an eleven-year-old, he had read of that distraught and drugged woman being half-dragged to her execution, the case had lain at the back of memory, heavy as a coiled snake. Poor dull Percy

Thompson had not deserved to die, but did anyone deserve what his widow had suffered during those last days in the condemned cell when she finally realized that there was a real world outside even more dangerous than her fantasies and that there were men in it who, on a precise day at a precise hour, would take her out and judicially break her neck? Even as a boy the case had confirmed him as an abolitionist; had it, he wondered, exerted a subtler and more persuasive influence, the conviction, never spoken but increasingly rooted in his comprehension, that strong passions had to be subject to the will, that a completely self-absorbed love could be dangerous and the price too high to pay? Wasn't that what he had been taught as a young recruit to the CID by the older experienced sergeant now long retired? 'All the motives for murder are covered by four Ls: Love, Lust, Lucre and Loathing. They'll tell you, laddie, that the most dangerous is loathing. Don't you believe it. The most dangerous is love.'

He put the Thompson–Bywaters case resolutely out of mind and listened again to Ackroyd.

'I've found my most interesting case. Still unsolved, fascinating in its permutations, absolutely typical of the 1930s. Couldn't have happened at any other time, not in precisely the way it did happen. I expect you know it, the Wallace case? It's been written about extensively. The Dupayne has all the literature.'

Dalgliesh said, 'It was once featured on a training course at Bramshill when I was a newly-appointed Detective Inspector. How not to conduct a murder investigation. I don't suppose it's included now. They'll choose more recent, more relevant cases. They're not short of examples.'

'So you know the facts.' Ackroyd's disappointment was so evident that it was impossible not to indulge him.

'Remind me.'

'The year was 1931. Internationally the year that Japan invaded Manchuria, Spain was declared a republic, there were riots in India and Cawnpore was swept by one of the worst outbreaks of inter-communal violence in the country's history, Anna Pavlova and Thomas Edison died and Professor Auguste Piccard became the first man to reach the stratosphere in a balloon. At home the new National Government was returned in the election in October, Sir Oswald Mosley concluded the formation of his New Party, and two and three-quarter million were unemployed. Not a good year. You see, Adam, I've done my research. Aren't you impressed?'

'Very. That's a formidable feat of memory. I don't see its relevance to a very English murder in a suburb of Liverpool.'

'It puts it in a wider context. Still, I may not use it when I come to write. Shall I go on? I'm not boring you?'

'Please do. And you're not boring me.'

'The dates: Monday the nineteenth and Tuesday the twentieth of January. The alleged murderer: William Herbert Wallace, fifty-two years old, Prudential Company insurance agent, a bespectacled, slightly stooping, undistinguished looking man living with his wife Julia at twenty-nine Wolverton Street in Anfield. He spent the days going from house to house collecting insurance money. A shilling here, a shilling there against a rainy day and the inevitable end. Typical of the time. You might have barely enough to feed yourself but you still put by a bit each week to ensure you could pay for a decent funeral. You might live in squalor, but at least you could make something of a show at the end. No quick dash to the crematorium and out again in fifteen minutes or the next lot of mourners will be hammering on the door.

'Wife Julia, fifty-two, socially a little superior, gentle-faced, a good pianist. Wallace played the violin and sometimes accompanied her in the front parlour. Apparently he wasn't very good. If he was enthusiastically scraping away while she was playing, you have a motive for murder but with a different victim. Anyway, they were reputed to be a devoted couple, but who's to know? I'm not distracting you from the driving, am I?'

Dalgliesh recalled that Ackroyd, a non-driver, had always been a nervous passenger. 'Not in the least.'

'We come to the evening of nineteenth January. Wallace was a chess player and was due to play at the Central Chess Club which met at a café in the centre of the city on Monday and Thursday evenings. On that Monday a call was received asking for him. A waitress took it and called the captain of the club, Samuel Beattie, to speak to the caller. He suggested that as Wallace was due to play but had not yet arrived, the man should try again later. The caller said he couldn't, he had his girl's twenty-first birthday on, but would Wallace come round tomorrow at seven-thirty to discuss a business proposition. He gave the name R.M. Qualtrough, the address twenty-five Menlove Gardens East, Mossley Hill. What is interesting and important is that the caller had some difficulty getting through, either genuine or contrived. As a result we know the operator reported the time of the call: twenty minutes past seven.

'So the next day Wallace set off to find Menlove Gardens East which, as you already know, doesn't exist. He needed to take three trams to get to the Menlove Gardens area, searched for about half an hour and enquired about the address from at least four people including a policeman. Eventually he gave up and went home. The next-door neighbours, the Johnstons, were getting ready to go out when they heard knocking at the back door of number twenty-nine. They went to investigate and saw Wallace, who said that he couldn't get in. While they were there he tried again and this time the door handle turned. The three of them went in. Julia Wallace's body was in the front room lying face down on the hearthrug with Wallace's bloodied mackintosh lying against her. She had been battered to death in a frenzied attack. The skull had been fractured by eleven blows delivered with terrific force.

'On Monday second February, thirteen days after the murder, Wallace was arrested. All the evidence was circumstantial, no blood was found on his clothes, the weapon was missing. There was no physical evidence linking him with the crime. What is interesting is that the evidence, such as it was, could support either the prosecution or the defence depending on how you chose to look at it. The call to the café was made from a phone box close to Wolverton Street at the time Wallace would have been passing. Was that because he made it himself, or because the murderer was waiting to ensure Wallace was on his way to the club? In the view of the police he was preternaturally calm during investigation, sitting in the kitchen with the cat on his knee and stroking it. Was that because he was uncaring, or because he was a stoic, a man who concealed emotion? And then the repeated enquiries about the address, was that to establish an alibi or because he was a conscientious agent who needed business and didn't give up easily?'

Dalgliesh waited in the queue at yet another traffic light as he was recalling the case more clearly. If the investigation had been a shambles, so had been the trial. The judge had summed up in Wallace's favour, but the jury had convicted, taking only an hour to reach their verdict. Wallace appealed and the case again made history when the appeal was allowed on the grounds that the case was not proved with that certainty which is necessary in order to justify a verdict of guilty; in effect, that the jury had been wrong.

Ackroyd prattled on happily while Dalgliesh gave his attention to the road. He had expected the traffic to be heavy; the homeward journey on a Friday began earlier each year, the congestion exacerbated by families leaving London for their weekend cottages. Before they reached Hampstead, Dalgliesh was already regretting his impulse to see the museum and mentally calculating the lost hours. He told himself to stop fretting. His life was already overburdened; why spoil this pleasant respite with regrets? Before they reached Jack Straw's Castle the traffic was at a standstill and it took minutes before he could join the thinner stream of cars moving down

Spaniards Road, which ran in a straight line across the Heath. Here the bushes and trees grew close to the tarmac, giving the illusion that they were in deep country.

Ackroyd said, 'Slow down here, Adam, or we'll miss the turning. It's not easy to spot. We're coming to it now, about thirty yards to the right.'

It was certainly not easy to find and, since it meant turning right across the traffic, not easy to enter. Dalgliesh saw an open gate and beyond it a drive with thickly entwined bushes and trees on either side. To the left of the entrance was a black board fixed to the wall with a notice painted in white. THE DUPAYNE MUSEUM. PLEASE DRIVE SLOWLY.

Dalgliesh said, 'Hardly an invitation. Don't they want visitors?'

'I'm not sure that they do, not in large numbers. Max Dupayne, who founded the place in 1961, saw it as something of a private hobby. He was fascinated – one might say obsessed – by the inter-war years. He was collecting in the 1920s and 30s, which accounts for some of the pictures; he was able to buy before the artist attracted big money. He also acquired first editions of every major novelist and those he thought worth collecting. The library is pretty valuable now. The museum was intended for people who shared his passion and that view of the place has influenced the present generation. Things may change now that Marcus Dupayne is taking control. He's just retiring from the Civil Service. He may well see the museum as a challenge.'

Dalgliesh drove down a tarmacked drive so narrow

that two cars would have difficulty in passing. On each side was a narrow strip of turf with, beyond it, a thick hedge of rhododendron bushes. Behind them spindly trees, their leaves just fading to yellow, added to the dimness of the road. They passed a young man kneeling on the turf with an elderly angular woman standing over him as if directing his work. There was a wooden basket between them and it looked as if they were planting bulbs. The boy looked up and stared at them as they passed but, beyond a fleeting glance, the woman took no notice.

There was a bend to the left and then the lane straightened out and the museum was suddenly before them. Dalgliesh stopped the car and they gazed in silence. The path divided to curve round a circular lawn with a central bed of shrubs, and beyond it stood a symmetrical red brick house, elegant, architecturally impressive and larger than he had expected. There were five bays, the central one brought well forward with two windows, one above the other, four identical windows in the two lower storeys on each side of the central bay and two more in the hipped roof. A white-painted door, glass-panelled, was set in an intricate pattern of brickwork. The restraint and complete symmetry of the building gave the house a slightly forbidding air, more institutional than domestic. But there was one unusual feature: where one might have expected pilasters there was a set of recessed panels with capitals in ornate brickwork. They gave a note of eccentricity to a façade which might otherwise have been formidably uniform.

Ackroyd said, 'Do you recognize it, the house?'

'No. Should I?'

'Not unless you've visited Pendell House near Bletch-ingley. It's an eccentric Inigo Jones dated 1636. The prosperous Victorian factory owner who built this in 1894 saw Pendell, liked it and didn't see why he shouldn't have a copy. After all, the original architect wasn't there to object. However, he didn't go as far as duplicating the interior. Just as well; the interior of Pendell House is a bit suspect. Do you like it?'

He looked as naïvely anxious as a child, hoping his offering wouldn't disappoint.

'It's interesting, but I wouldn't have known it was copied from Inigo Jones. I like it, but I'm not sure I'd want to live in it. Too much symmetry makes me uneasy. I've never seen recessed brickwork panels before.'

'Nor has anyone, according to Pevsner. They're said to be unique. I approve. The façade would be too restrained without them. Anyway, come and see inside. That's what we're here for. The car-park is behind those laurel bushes to the right. Max Dupayne hated to see cars in front of the house. In fact, he hated most manifestations of modern life.'

Dalgliesh restarted the engine. A white arrow on a wooden sign directed him to the car-park. It was a gravelled area of some fifty yards by thirty with the entrance to the south. There were already twelve cars neatly parked in two rows. Dalgliesh found a space at the end. He said, 'Not a lot of space. What do they do on a popular day?'

'I suppose visitors try the other side of the house. There's a garage there but that's used by Neville

Dupayne to house his E-type Jag. But I've never seen the parking spaces full, or the museum particularly busy for that matter. This looks about normal for a Friday afternoon. Some of the cars belong to the staff anyway.'

There was certainly no sign of life as they made their way to the front door. It was, thought Dalgliesh, a somewhat intimidating door for the casual visitor, but Ackroyd seized the brass knob confidently, turned it and thrust the door open. He said, 'It's usually kept open in summer. You'd think with this sun it's safe to risk it today. Anyway, here we are. Welcome to the Dupayne Museum.'

2

Dalgliesh followed Ackroyd into a wide hall with its chequered floor in black and white marble. Facing him was an elegant staircase which, after some twenty steps, divided, the stairs running east and west to the wide gallery. On each side of the hall were three mahogany doors with similar but smaller doors leading from the gallery above. There was a row of coat hooks on the left wall with two long umbrella stands beneath them. To the right was a curved mahogany reception desk with an antiquated telephone switchboard mounted on the wall behind, and a door marked PRIVATE which Dalgliesh supposed led to the office. The only sign of life was a woman seated at the desk. She looked up as Ackroyd and Dalgliesh moved towards her.

Ackroyd said, 'Good afternoon, Miss Godby.' Then, turning to Dalgliesh, 'This is Miss Muriel Godby who presides over admissions and keeps us all in order. This is a friend of mine. Mr Dalgliesh. Does he have to pay?'

Dalgliesh said, 'Of course I have to pay.'

Miss Godby looked up at him. He saw a sallow, rather heavy face and a pair of remarkable eyes behind narrow horn-rimmed spectacles. The irises were a greenish-yellow with a bright centre, the whole iris darkly ringed. The hair, an unusual colour between rich russet and gold, was thick and straight, brushed to the side and clipped back from the face with a tortoiseshell slide. Her mouth was small but firm above a chin which belied her apparent age. She could surely not be much above forty, but her chin and her upper neck had some of the sagging fleshiness of old age. Although she had smiled at Ackroyd, it had been little more than a relaxing of her mouth, giving her a look that was both wary and slightly intimidating. She was wearing a twin set in fine blue wool and a pearl necklace. It made her look as old-fashioned as some of the photographs of English débutantes seen in old copies of *Country Life*. Perhaps, he thought, she was deliberately dressing to conform to the decades of the museum. There was certainly nothing either girlish or naïvely pretty about Miss Godby.

A framed notice on the desk gave the admission charges as £5 for adults, £3.50 for senior citizens and students, free for the under-tens and those on jobseekers' allowance. Dalgliesh handed over his £10 note and received with his change a round blue sticky label. Ackroyd, receiving his, protested: 'Do we really have to wear these? I'm a Friend, I've signed in.'

Miss Godby was adamant. 'It's a new system, Mr Ackroyd. Blue for men, pink for women and green for the children. It's a simple way of reconciling takings with the number of visitors and providing information on the people we're serving. And, of course, it means that the staff can see at a glance that people have paid.'

They moved away. Ackroyd said, 'She's an efficient woman who's done a great deal to put the place in order, but I wish she knew where to stop. You can see the general layout. That first room on the left is the picture gallery, the next is Sport and Entertainment, the third is the history room. And there on the right we have Costumes, Theatre and Cinema. The library is on the floor above and so is the Murder Room. Obviously you'll be interested to see the pictures and the library, and perhaps the rest of the rooms, and I'd like to come with you. Still, I need to work. We'd better start with the Murder Room.'

Ignoring the lift, he led the way up the central staircase, sprightly as ever. Dalgliesh followed, aware that Muriel Godby was watching at her desk as if still uncertain whether they were safe to be left unescorted. They had reached the Murder Room on the east side and at the back of the house when a door at the top of the stairs opened. There was the sound of raised voices suddenly cut off and a man came hurriedly out, hesitated briefly when he saw Dalgliesh and Ackroyd, then gave them a nod of acknowledgement and made for the stairs, his long coat flapping as if caught in the vehemence of his exit. Dalgliesh had a fleeting impression of an undisciplined thatch of dark hair and angry eyes in a flushed face. Almost at once another figure appeared standing in the doorway. He showed no surprise at encountering visitors but spoke directly to Ackroyd.

'What's it for, the museum? That's what Neville Dupayne has just asked. What's it for? It makes me wonder if he's his father's son, except that poor Madeleine was so boringly virtuous. Not enough vitality for sexual capers. Good to see you here again.'

He looked at Dalgliesh. 'Who's this?'

The question could have sounded offensive if it had

not been asked in a voice of genuine puzzlement and interest, as if he were faced with a new if not particularly interesting acquisition.

Ackroyd said, 'Good afternoon, James. This is a friend of mine, Adam Dalgliesh. Adam, meet James Calder-Hale, curator and presiding genius of the Dupayne Museum.'

Calder-Hale was tall and thin almost to the point of emaciation, with a long bony face and a wide, precisely shaped mouth. His hair, falling across a high forehead, was greying erratically with strands of pale gold streaked with white, giving him a touch of theatricality. His eyes, under brows so defined that they could have been plucked, were intelligent, giving strength to a face which otherwise could have been described as gentle. Dalgliesh was not deceived by this seeming sensitivity; he had known men of force and physical action with the faces of unworldly scholars. Calder-Hale was wearing narrow and creased trousers, a striped shirt with a pale blue tie unusually wide and loosely tied, checked carpet slippers and a long grey cardigan reaching almost to his knees. His apparent anger had been expressed in a high falsetto of irritation which Dalgliesh suspected might be more histrionic than genuine.

'Adam Dalgliesh? I've heard of you.' He made it sound rather like an accusation. '*A Case to Answer and Other Poems*. I don't read much modern poetry, having an unfashionable preference for verses which occasionally scan and rhyme, but at least yours aren't prose re-arranged on the page. I take it Muriel knows you're here?'

Ackroyd said, 'I signed in. And look, we've got our little stick-on labels.'

'So you have. Silly question. Even you, Ackroyd, wouldn't get beyond the entrance hall if you hadn't. A tyrant of a woman, but conscientious and, I'm told, necessary. Excuse my vehemence just now. I don't usually lose my temper. With any of the Dupaynes it's a waste of energy. Well, don't let me interrupt whatever you're here for.'

He turned to re-enter what was obviously his office. Ackroyd called after him, 'What did you tell him, Neville Dupayne? What did you say the museum was for?'

Calder-Hale hesitated and turned. 'I told him what he already knew. The Dupayne, like any reputable museum, provides for the safe custody, preservation, recording and display of items of interest from the past for the benefit of scholars and others interested enough to visit. Dupayne seemed to think it should have some kind of social or missionary function. Extraordinary!'

He turned to Ackroyd. 'Glad to see you,' and then nodded to Dalgliesh. 'And you, of course. There's an acquisition in the picture gallery which might interest you. A small but agreeable water-colour by Roger Fry, bequeathed by one of our regular visitors. Let's hope we're able to keep it.'

Ackroyd asked, 'What do you mean by that, James?'

'Oh, you couldn't know, of course. The whole future of this place is in doubt. The lease runs out next month and a new one has been negotiated. The old man drew up a curious family trust. From what I gather, the museum can only continue if all three of his children agree to sign the lease. If it closes it will be a tragedy, but one which I personally have been given no authority to prevent. I'm not a trustee.'

Without another word he turned, went into his office and shut the door firmly.

Ackroyd said, 'It will be something of a tragedy for him, I imagine. He's worked here ever since his retirement from the Diplomatic Service. Unpaid, of course, but he gets the use of the office and conducts the favoured few round the galleries. His father and old Max Dupayne had been friends from university. For the old man the museum was a private indulgence, as of course museums tend to be for some of their curators. He didn't exactly resent visitors – some were actually welcomed – but he thought one genuine enquirer was worth fifty casual visitors and acted accordingly. If you didn't know what the Dupayne was and the opening hours, then you didn't need to know. More information might attract casual passers-by wanting to come in out of the rain, hoping they might find something to keep the children quiet for half an hour.'

Dalgliesh said, 'But a casual uninformed visitor could enjoy the experience, get a taste for it, discover the fascination of what in deplorable contemporary jargon we are encouraged to call "the museum experience". To that extent a museum is educational. Wouldn't the Dupayne welcome that?'

'In theory, I suppose. If the heirs keep it on they may go down that path, but they haven't got a lot to offer here, have they? The Dupayne is hardly the V&A or the British Museum. If you're interested in the inter-war years – and I am – the Dupayne offers practically all you need. But the 1920s and 30s have limited attraction for the general public. Spend a day and you've seen it all. I think the old man always resented the fact that the most popular room was the Murder Room. Now a museum devoted entirely to murder would do well. I'm surprised someone hasn't set it up. There's the Black Museum at New Scotland Yard and that interesting little collection the River Police have at Wapping, but I can't see either of them being opened to the general public. Admissions strictly by application.'

The Murder Room was large, at least thirty feet long and well lit by three pendant lights, but for Dalgliesh the immediate impression was darkly claustrophobic, despite the two easterly and the single south-facing windows. To the right of the ornate fireplace was a second and plain door, obviously permanently shut since it was without either door knob or handle.

There were glass-fronted display cases along each wall with, below them, shelves for books, presumably dealing with each case, and drawers for relevant papers and reports. Above the cabinets were rows of sepia and black and white photographs, many enlarged, some obviously original and starkly explicit. The impression was of a collage of blood and blank dead faces, of murderers and victims united now in death, staring into nothingness.

Together Dalgliesh and Ackroyd made a tour of the room. Here displayed, illustrated and examined, were the most notorious murder cases of the inter-war years. Names, faces and facts swam into Dalgliesh's memory.

William Herbert Wallace, younger, surely, than at the time of the trial, an unmemorable but not unappealing head rising from the high stiff collar with its tie knotted like a noose, the mouth a little loose under the moustache, the eyes mild behind steel-rimmed spectacles. Beside it was a press photograph of him shaking hands with his counsel after the appeal, his brother at his side, both rather taller than anyone in the group, Wallace a little stooped. He had dressed carefully for the most appalling ordeal of his life, in a dark suit and the same high collar and narrow tie. The sparse hair, carefully parted, gleamed with brushing. It was a face somehow typical of the meticulous over-conscientious bureaucrat, not perhaps a man whom housewives, paying over their weekly pittance, would invite into the back room for a chat and a cup of tea.

Ackroyd said, 'And here's the beautiful Marie-Marguerite Fahmy, who shot her Egyptian playboy husband, in the Savoy Hotel of all places, in 1923. It's remarkable for Edward Marshall Hall's defence. He brought it to a crashing conclusion by pointing the actual gun at the jury, then letting it fall with a clatter while he demanded a not guilty verdict. She did it, of course, but thanks to him she got away with it. He also delivered an objectionably racist speech suggesting that women who marry what he called "the oriental" could expect the kind of treatment she received. Nowadays he'd be in trouble with the judge, the Lord Chancellor and the press. Again, you see, dear boy, we have a crime typical of its age.'

Dalgliesh said, 'I thought you were depending for

your thesis on the commission of the crime, not the workings of the then criminal justice system.'

'I'm relying on all the circumstances. And here's another example of a successful defence, the Brighton Trunk Murder in 1934. This, my dear Adam, is supposed to be the actual trunk in which Tony Mancini, a twenty-six-year-old waiter and convicted thief, stuffed the body of his prostitute mistress, Violette Kaye. This was the second Brighton trunk murder. The first body, a woman without head and legs, had been found at Brighton railway station eleven days earlier. No one was ever arrested for that crime. Mancini was tried at Lewes Assize Court in December and brilliantly defended by Norman Birkett. Birkett saved his life. The jury returned a verdict of not guilty but in 1976 Mancini confessed. This trunk seems to exert a morbid fascination on visitors.'

It held no fascination for Dalgliesh. Suddenly he felt the need to look at the outside world and walked over to one of the two easterly windows. Below, set among saplings, was a wooden garage and, within eight yards, a small garden shed with a water tap. The boy he had seen in the drive was washing his hands and then rubbing them dry on the side of his trousers. He was recalled to the room by Ackroyd, anxious to demonstrate his last case.

Leading Dalgliesh to the second of the display cabinets, he said, 'The Blazing Car Murder, 1930. This is certainly a candidate for my article. You must have heard of it. Alfred Arthur Rouse, a thirty-seven-year-old commercial traveller living in London, was a compulsive womanizer. Apart from committing bigamy, he is supposed to have seduced some eighty women during the course of his travels. He needed permanently to disappear, preferably to be thought dead, so on sixth November he picked up a tramp and on a lonely road in Northamptonshire killed him, threw petrol over him, set the car alight and made off. Unfortunately for him, two young men walking home to their local village saw him and asked him about the blaze. He went on his way, calling out, "It looks as though someone is having a bonfire". That encounter helped to get him arrested. If he'd hidden in the ditch and let them go by he might have got away with it.'

Dalgliesh said, 'And what makes it specific to its age?'

'Rouse had served in the war and was badly injured in the head. His behaviour at the scene and at the trial was exceptionally stupid. I see Rouse as a casualty of the First World War.'

He might well have been, thought Dalgliesh. Certainly his behaviour after the murder and his extraordinary arrogance in the witness-box had done more than the prosecuting counsel to put the rope around his neck. It would have been interesting to know the extent of his war service and how he had been wounded. Few men who had served long in Flanders could have returned home completely normal.

He left Ackroyd to his researches and went in search of the library. It was on the west side of the same floor, a long room with two windows facing the car-park and a third overlooking the drive. The walls were lined with mahogany bookcases with three jutting bays and there was a long rectangular table in the middle of the room. At a smaller table near the window there was a photo-copying machine with a notice saying that copies were ten pence per sheet. Beside it sat an elderly woman writing labels for exhibits. The room wasn't cold but she wore a muffler and mittens. As Dalgliesh entered, she said in a mellifluous, educated voice, 'Some of the glass cabinets are locked but I have the key if you want to handle the books. Copies of *The Times* and other newspapers are in the basement.'

Dalgliesh had some difficulty in knowing how to reply. With the picture gallery still to see, he had no time to examine the books at leisure, but he didn't wish his visit to seem peremptory, the mere indulgence of a whim. He said, 'It's my first visit so I'm just making a prelimi-nary tour. But thank you.'

He walked slowly along the bookcases. Here, the majority in first editions, were the major novelists of the inter-war years and some whose names were un-known to him. The obvious names were represented: D. H. Lawrence, Virginia Woolf, James Joyce, George Orwell, Graham Greene, Wyndham Lewis, Rosamond Lehmann, a roll-call of the variety and richness of those turbulent years. The poetry section had a case of its own which contained first editions of Yeats, Eliot, Pound, Auden and Louis MacNeice. There were also, he saw, the war poets published in the 1920s: Wilfred Owen, Robert Graves, Siegfried Sassoon. He wished that he had hours at his disposal in which the books could be handled and read. But even had there been time, the presence of that silent working woman, her cramped mittened hands moving laboriously, would have inhibited him. He liked to be alone when he was reading.

He moved to the end of the central table where half a dozen copies of *The Strand Magazine* were fanned out, their covers, differently coloured, all showing pictures of the Strand, the scene slightly varying with each copy. Dalgliesh picked up the magazine for May 1922. The cover advertised stories by P.G. Wodehouse, Gilbert Frankau and E. Phillips Oppenheim and a special article by Arnold Bennett. But it was in the preliminary pages of advertisements that the early 1920s most came alive. The cigarettes at five shillings and sixpence per hundred, the bedroom that could be furnished for £36 and the concerned husband, worried about what was obviously his wife's lack of libido, restoring her to her usual good spirits with a surreptitious pinch of liver salts in the early morning tea.

And now he went down to the picture gallery. It was at once apparent that it had been designed for the serious student. Each picture had beside it a framed card which listed the main galleries where other examples of the artist's work could be seen and display cabinets on each side of the fireplace contained letters, manuscripts and catalogues. They drew Dalgliesh's mind back to the library. It was on these shelves, surely, that the 1920s and 30s were better represented. It was the writers – Joyce, Waugh, Huxley – not the artists who had most forcibly interpreted and influenced those confused inter-war years. Moving slowly past the landscapes of Paul and John Nash, it seemed to him that the 1914–18 cataclysm of blood and death had bred a nostalgic yearning for an

England of rural peace. Here was a prelapsarian land-scape recreated in tranquillity and painted in a style which, for all its diversity and originality, was strongly traditional. It was a landscape without figures; the neatly piled logs against farmhouse walls, the tilled fields under unthreatening skies, the empty stretch of beach, were all poignant reminders of the dead generation. He could believe that they had done their day's work, hung up their tools and gently taken their leave of life. Yet surely no landscape was so precise, so perfectly ordered. These fields had been tilled, not for posterity, but for a barren changelessness. In Flanders nature had been riven apart, violated and corrupted. Here all had been restored to an imaginary and eternal placidity. He had not expected to find traditional landscape painting so unsettling.

It was with a sense of relief that he moved to the religious anomalies of Stanley Spencer, the idiosyncratic portraits of Percy Wyndham Lewis and the more tremulous, casually painted portraits of Duncan Grant. Most of the painters were familiar to Dalgliesh. Nearly all gave pleasure, although he felt that these were artists strongly influenced by continental and far greater painters. Max Dupayne had not been able to acquire the most notably impressive of each artist's work but he had succeeded in putting together a collection which, in its diversity, was representative of the art of the inter-war years, and this, after all, had been his aim.

When he entered the gallery, there was one other visitor already there: a thin young man wearing jeans, worn trainers and a thick anorak. Beneath its bulky weight, his legs looked as thin as sticks. Moving closer to him, Dalgliesh saw a pale, delicate face. His hair was obscured by a woollen cap drawn over the ears. Ever since Dalgliesh had entered the room the boy had been standing motionless in front of a war painting by Paul Nash. It was one Dalgliesh also wanted to study and they stood for a minute silently, side by side.

The painting, which was named *Passchendaele 2*, was unknown to him. It was all there, the horror, the futility and the pain, fixed in the bodies of those unknown ungainly dead. Here at last was a picture which spoke with a more powerful resonance than any words. It was not his war, nor his father's. It was now almost beyond the memory of living men and women. Yet had any modern conflict produced such universal grieving?

They stood together in silent contemplation. Dalgliesh was about to move away when the young man said, 'Do you think this is a good picture?'

It was a serious question but it provoked in Dalgliesh a wariness, a reluctance to appear knowledgeable. He said, 'I'm not an artist, nor an art historian. I think it's a very good picture. I'd like it on my wall.'

And for all its darkness it would, he thought, find its place in that uncluttered flat above the Thames. Emma would be happy for it to be there, would share what he was feeling now.

The young man said, 'It used to hang on my grandad's wall in Suffolk. He bought it to remember his dad, my great-grandad. He was killed at Passchendaele.'

'How did it get here?'

'Max Dupayne wanted it. He waited until Grandad

was desperate for money and then he bought it. He got it cheap.'

Dalgliesh could think of no appropriate response, and after a minute he said, 'Do you come to look at it often?'

'Yes. They can't stop me doing that. When I'm on jobseekers' allowance I don't have to pay.' Then, turning aside, he said, 'Please forget what I've said. I've never told anyone before. I'm glad you like it.'

And then he was gone. Was it perhaps that moment of unspoken communication before the picture which had provoked such an unexpected confidence? He might, of course, be lying, but Dalgliesh didn't think so. It made him wonder how scrupulous Max Dupayne had been in pursuit of his obsession. He decided to say nothing to Ackroyd about the encounter and after one more slow circuit of the room took the wide staircase up from the hall back to the Murder Room.

Conrad, seated in one of the armchairs beside the fireplace and with a number of books and periodicals spread out on the table before him, was not yet ready to leave. He said, 'Did you know that there's now another suspect for the Wallace murder? He didn't come to light until recently.'

'Yes,' said Dalgliesh, 'I had heard. He was called Parry, wasn't he? But he's dead too. You're not going to solve the crime now, Conrad. And I thought that it was murder related to its time not the solution which interested you.'

'One gets drawn in deeper, dear boy. Still, you're quite right. I mustn't allow myself to be diverted. Don't worry if you have to leave. I'm just going to the library to make some copies and I'll be here until the place closes at five. Miss Godby has kindly offered me a lift as far as Hampstead tube station. A kind heart beats in that formidable bosom.'

A few minutes later Dalgliesh was on his way, his mind preoccupied with what he'd seen. Those inter-war years in which England, her memory seared by the horrors of Flanders and a generation lost, had stumbled through near dishonour to confront and overcome a greater danger, had been two decades of extraordinary social change and diversity. But he wondered why Max Dupayne had found them fascinating enough to dedicate his life to recording them. It had, after all, been his own time he was memorializing. He would have bought the first-edition fiction and preserved the papers and the journals as they appeared. *These fragments I have shored against my ruins.* Was that the reason? Was it he himself that he needed to immortalize? Was this museum, founded by him and in his name, his personal alms to oblivion? Perhaps this was one attraction of all museums. The generations die, but what they made, what they painted and wrote, strove for and achieved, was still here, at least in part. In making memorials, not only to the famous but to the legions of the anonymous dead, were we hoping to ensure our own vicarious immortality?

But he was in no mood now to indulge in thoughts of the past. This coming weekend would be one of sustained writing and in the week ahead he would be working a twelve-hour day. But next Saturday and Sunday were free and nothing was going to interfere with that. He would see Emma and the thought of her would illuminate the whole week as it now filled him with hope. He felt as vulnerable as a boy in love for the first time and knew that he faced the same terror; that once the word was spoken she would reject him. But they could not go on as they were. Somehow he had to find the courage to risk that rejection, to accept the momentous presumption that Emma might love him. Next weekend he would find the time, the place, and most importantly the words which would part them or bring them together at last.

Suddenly he noticed that the blue label was still stuck to his jacket. He ripped it off, crumpled it into a ball and slipped it into his pocket. He was glad to have visited the museum. He had enjoyed a new experience and had admired much that he had seen. But he told himself that he would not return.

3

In his office overlooking St James's Park, the eldest of
the Dupaynes was clearing his desk. He did it as he had
done everything in his official life, methodically, with
thought and without hurry. There was little to dispose
of, less to take away with him; almost all record of his
official life had already been removed. An hour earlier
the last file, containing his final minutes, had been collected by the uniformed messenger as quietly and unceremoniously as if this final emptying of his out-tray had
been no different from any other. His few personal books
had been gradually removed from the book-case which
now held only official publications, the criminal statistics,
white papers, Archbold and copies of recent legislation.
Other hands would be placing personal volumes on the
empty shelves. He thought he knew whose. In his view
it was an unmerited promotion, premature, not yet
earned, but then his successor had earlier been marked
out as one of the fortunate ones who, in the jargon of
the Service, were the designated high flyers.

So once had he been marked. By the time he had
reached the rank of Assistant Secretary, he had been
spoken of as a possible Head of Department. If all had
gone well he would be leaving now with his K, Sir
Marcus Dupayne, with a string of City companies ready
to offer him directorships. That was what he had

expected, what Alison had expected. His own professional ambition had been strong but disciplined, aware always of the unpredictability of success. His wife's had been rampant, embarrassingly public. Sometimes he thought that this was why she had married him. Every social occasion had been arranged with his success in view. A dinner party wasn't a meeting of friends, it was a ploy in a carefully thought-out campaign. The fact that nothing she could do would ever influence his career, that his life outside the office was of no importance provided it was not publicly disgraceful, never entered her consciousness. He would occasionally say, 'I'm not aiming to end up as a bishop, a headmaster or a Minister. I'm not going to be damned or demoted because the claret was corked.'

He had come with a duster in his briefcase and now checked that all the drawers of the desk had been cleared. In the bottom left-hand drawer his exploring hand found a stub of pencil. How many years, he wondered, had that lain there? He examined his fingers, crusted with grey dust, and wiped them on the duster which he folded carefully over the dirt and placed in his canvas bag. His briefcase he would leave on his desk. The gold royal insignia on the case had faded now, but it brought a memory: the day when he had first been issued with an official black briefcase, its insignia bright as a badge of office.

He had held the obligatory farewell drinks party before luncheon. The Permanent Secretary had paid the expected compliments with a suspicious fluency; he had done this before. A Minister had put in an appearance and only once had glanced discreetly at his watch. There had been an atmosphere of spurious conviviality interspersed with moments of silent constraint. By one-thirty people had begun to drift unobtrusively away. It was, after all, Friday. Their weekend arrangements beckoned.

Closing his office door for the last time and entering the empty corridor, he was surprised and a little concerned at his lack of emotion. Surely he should be feeling something – regret, mild satisfaction, a small surge of nostalgia, the mental acknowledgement of a rite of passage? He felt nothing. There were the usual officials at the reception desk in the entrance hall and both were busy. It relieved him of the obligation to say some embarrassed words of farewell. He decided to take his favourite route to Waterloo, across St James's Park, down Northumberland Avenue and across Hungerford footbridge. He went through the swing doors for the last time and made his way across Birdcage Walk and into the sweet autumnal dishevelment of the Park. In the middle of the bridge over the lake he paused as he always did to contemplate one of London's most beautiful views, across the water and the island to the towers and roofs of Whitehall. Beside him was a mother with a swaddled baby in a three-wheeled pram. Next to her was a toddler throwing bread to the ducks. The air became acrimonious as the birds jostled and scrabbled in a swirl of water. It was a scene which, on his lunchtime walks, he had watched for over twenty years, but now it brought back a recent and disagreeable memory.

A week ago he had taken the same path. There had

been a solitary woman feeding the ducks with crusts from her sandwiches. She was short, her sturdy body enveloped in a thick tweed coat, a woollen cap drawn down over her ears. The last crumb tossed, she turned and, seeing him, had smiled a little tentatively. From boyhood he had found unexpected intimacies from strangers repellent, almost threatening, and he had nodded unsmiling and walked quickly away. It had been as curtly dismissive as if she had been propositioning him. He had reached the steps of the Duke of York column before sudden realization came. She had been no stranger but Tally Clutton, the housekeeper at the museum. He had failed to recognize her in other than the brown button-up overall that she normally wore. Now the memory provoked a spurt of irritation, as much against her as against himself. It was an embarrassing mistake to have made and one that he would have to put right when they next met. That would be the more difficult as they could be discussing her future. The cottage she lived in rent-free must be worth at least three hundred and fifty pounds a week in rent. Hampstead wasn't cheap, particularly Hampstead with a view of the Heath. If he decided to replace her, the free accommodation would be an inducement. They might be able to attract a married couple, the wife to do the house cleaning, the man to take over the garden. On the other hand, Tally Clutton was hard working and well liked. It might be imprudent to unsettle the domestic arrangements when there were so many other changes to be put in hand. Caroline, of course, would fight to keep both Clutton and Godby and he was anxious to avoid a fight with

Caroline. There was no problem with Muriel Godby. The woman was cheap and remarkably competent, qualities rare today. There might later be difficulties about the chain of command. Godby obviously saw herself as responsible to Caroline, not unreasonably since it was his sister who had given her the job. But the allocation of duties and responsibilities could wait until the new lease had been signed. He would retain both women. The boy, Ryan Archer, wouldn't stick at the job for long, the young never did.

He thought, *if only I could feel passionately, even strongly about anything*. His career had long since failed to provide emotional satisfaction. Even music was losing its power. He remembered the last time, only three weeks ago, when he had played Bach's Double Violin Concerto with a teacher of the instrument. His performance had been accurate, even sensitive, but it had not come from the heart. Perhaps half a lifetime of conscientious political neutrality, of the careful documentation of both sides of any argument, had bred a debilitating caution of the spirit. But now there was hope. He might find the enthusiasm and fulfilment he craved in taking over the museum that bore his name. He thought, *I need this. I can make a success of it. I'm not going to let Neville take it away from me*. Already crossing the road at the Athenaeum, his mind was disengaging from the recent past. The revitalizing of the museum would provide an interest which would replace and redeem the dead undistinguished years.

His homecoming to the detached, boringly conventional house in a leafy road on the outskirts of

Wimbledon was no different from any other home-coming. The drawing-room was, as usual, immaculate. There came from the kitchen a faint but not obtrusive smell of dinner. Alison was sitting before the fire reading the *Evening Standard*. At his entrance she folded it carefully and rose to greet him.

'Did the Home Secretary turn up?'

'No, it wouldn't be expected. The Minister did.'

'Oh well, they've always made it plain what they think of you. You've never been given the respect you deserve.'

But she spoke with less rancour than he had expected. Watching her, he thought he detected in her voice a suppressed excitement, half guilty and half defiant.

She said, 'See to the sherry, will you, darling? There's a new bottle of the Fino in the fridge.'

The endearment was a matter of habit. The persona she had presented to the world for the thirty-two years of their marriage was that of a happy and fortunate wife; other marriages might humiliatingly fail, hers was secure.

As he set down the tray of drinks, she said, 'I had lunch with Jim and Mavis. They're planning to go out to Australia for Christmas to see Moira. She and her husband are in Sydney now. I thought I might go with them.'

'Jim and Mavis?'

'The Calverts. You must remember. She's on the Help the Aged committee with me. They had dinner here a month ago.'

'The redhead with the halitosis?'

44

'Oh, that isn't normal. It must have been some-thing she'd eaten. You know how Stephen and Susie have been urging us to visit. The grandchildren too. It seems too good an opportunity to miss, having com-pany on the flight. I must say I'm rather dreading that part of it. Jim is so competent he'll probably get us an upgrade.'

He said, 'I can't possibly go to Australia this year or next. There's the museum. I'm taking it over. I thought I'd explained all that to you. It's going to be a full-time job, at least at first.'

'I realize that, darling, but you can come out and visit for a couple of weeks while I'm there. Escape the winter.'

'How long are you thinking of staying?'

'Six months, a year maybe. There's no point in going that far just for a short stay. I'd hardly have got over the jet lag. I won't be staying with Stephen and Susie all the time. No one wants a mother-in-law moving in for months. Jim and Mavis plan to travel. Jack, Mavis's brother, will be with us, so we'll be four, and I won't feel *de trop*. A party of three never works.'

He thought, I'm listening to the break-up of my marriage. He was surprised how little he cared.

She went on, 'We can afford it, can't we? You'll have your retirement lump sum?'

'Yes, it can be afforded.'

He looked at her as dispassionately as he might have studied a stranger. At fifty-two she was still handsome with a carefully preserved, almost clinical elegance. She was still desirable to him, if not often and then not

45

passionately. They made love infrequently, usually after a period when drink and habit induced an insistent sexuality soon satisfied. They had nothing new to learn about each other, nothing they wanted to learn. He knew that, for her, these occasional joyless couplings were her affirmation that the marriage still existed. She might be unfaithful but she was always conventional. Her love-affairs were discreet rather than furtive. She pretended that they didn't happen; he pretended that he didn't know. Their marriage was regulated by a concordat never ratified in words. He provided the income, she ensured that his life was comfortable, his preferences indulged, his meals excellently cooked, that he was spared even the minor inconvenience of housekeeping. They each respected the limits of the other's tolerance in what was essentially a marriage of convenience. She had been a good mother to Stephen, their only child, and was a doting grandmother to his and Susie's children. She would be more warmly welcomed in Australia than he would have been.

She had relaxed now, the news given. She said, 'What will you do about this house? You won't want a place this size. It's probably worth close to three-quarters of a million. The Rawlinsons got six hundred thousand for *High Trees* and it needed a lot doing to it. If you want to sell before I get back, that's all right by me. I'm sorry I won't be here to help but all you need is a reliable firm of removers. Leave it to them.'

So she was thinking of coming back, even if temporarily. Perhaps this new adventure would be no different from the others except in being more prolonged. And then there would be matters to arrange, including her share of that three-quarters of a million.

He said, 'Yes, I'll probably sell, but there's no hurry.'

'Can't you move into the flat at the museum? That's the obvious plan.'

'Caroline wouldn't agree. She sees the flat as her home since she took it over after Father died.'

'But she doesn't actually live there, not all the time. She's got her rooms in the school. You'd be there permanently, able to keep an eye on security. As I remember it, it's an agreeable enough place, plenty of room. I think you would be very comfortable there.'

'Caroline needs to get away from the school occasionally. Keeping the flat will be her price for co-operating in keeping the museum open. I need her vote. You know about the Trust deed.'

'I've never understood it.'

'It's simple enough. Any major decision regarding the museum, including the negotiation of a new lease, requires the consent of the three trustees. If Neville won't sign, we're finished.'

And now she was roused to genuine indignation. She might be planning to leave him for a lover, to stay away or return as the whim took her, but in any dispute with the family she would be on his side. She was capable of fighting ruthlessly for what she thought he wanted.

She cried, 'Then you and Caroline must make him! What's it to him anyway? He's got his own job. He's never cared a damn about the museum. You can't have your whole future life ruined because Neville won't sign a piece of paper. You must put a stop to that nonsense.'

He took up the sherry bottle and, moving over to her, refilled both their glasses. They raised them simultaneously as if in a pledge.

'Yes,' he said gravely, 'If necessary I must put a stop to Neville.'

4

On Saturday morning in the Principal's room at Swathling's, Lady Swathling and Caroline Dupayne settled down at precisely ten o'clock for their weekly conference. That this should be a semi-formal occasion, cancelled only for a personal emergency and interrupted only for the arrival of coffee at eleven, was typical of their relationship. So was the arrangement of the room. They sat facing each other in identical armchairs at a mahogany partner's desk set in front of the wide south-facing window which gave a view of the lawn, its carefully tended rose-bushes showing their bare prickly stems above the crumbly weed-less soil. Beyond the lawn the Thames was a glimpse of dull silver under the morning sky.

The Richmond house was the main asset Lady Swathling brought to their joint enterprise. Her mother-in-law had established the school and it had passed on to her son and now to her daughter-in-law. Until the arrival of Caroline Dupayne, neither school nor house had improved during her stewardship, but the house, through good times and bad, remained beautiful. And so, in the opinion of herself and of others, did its owner.

Lady Swathling had never asked herself whether she liked her partner. It was not a question she asked herself

49

of anyone. People were useful or not useful, agreeable to be with or bores to be avoided. She liked her acquaintances to be good looking or, if their genes and fate hadn't favoured them, at least to be well groomed and to make the most of what they had. She never entered the Principal's room for the weekly conference without a glance in the large oval mirror which hung beside the door. The look was by now automatic, the reassurance it gave unnecessary. No smoothing was ever needed of the grey silver-streaked hair, expensively styled but not so rigidly disciplined as to suggest an obsessive concern with externals. The well-cut skirt reached mid-calf, a length she adhered to through changing fashions. A cashmere cardigan was slung with apparent carelessness over the cream silk shirt. She knew that she was seen as a distinguished and successful woman in control of her life; that was precisely how she saw herself. What mattered at fifty-eight was what had mattered at eighteen: breeding and good bone structure. She recognized that her appearance was an asset to the school, as was her title. Admittedly it had originally been a 'Lloyd George' barony, which the *cognoscenti* well knew had been bestowed for favours to the Prime Minister and Party rather than to the country, but today only the naïve or the innocent worried about – or indeed were surprised at – that kind of patronage; a title was a title.

She loved the house with a passion she felt for no human being. She never entered it without a small physical surge of satisfaction that it was hers. The school which bore her name was at last successful and there was enough money to maintain the house and garden with some to spare. She knew that she owed this success to Caroline Dupayne. She could recall almost every word of that conversation seven years earlier when Caroline, who had been working for seven months as her personal assistant, had put forward her plan for reform, boldly and without invitation, and seemingly motivated more by her abhorrence of muddle and failure than by personal ambition.

'Unless we change, the numbers will continue to fall. Frankly there are two problems: we're not giving value for money and we don't know what we're for. Both are fatal. We can't go on living in the past and the present political set-up is on our side. There is no advantage for parents in sending girls abroad now – this generation of rich kids skis at Klosters every winter and they've been travelling since childhood. The world is a dangerous place and it's likely to become more dangerous. Parents will become increasingly anxious to have their daughters finished in England. And what do we mean by being finished? The concept is out of date, almost risible to the young. It's no use offering the usual regime of cooking, flower arranging, childcare, deportment, with a little culture thrown in. They can get most of that, if they want it, free from local authority evening classes. And we need to be seen as discriminating. No more automatic entrance just because Daddy can pay the fees. No more morons; they aren't teachable and they don't want to learn. They pull down and irritate the rest. No more psychological misfits – this isn't an expensive psychiatric unit. And no more delinquents. Shop-lifting from Harrods or Harvey Nicks is no different from stealing from Woolworth's, even if Mummy has an account and Daddy can pay off the police.'

Lady Swathling had sighed. 'There was a time when one could rely on people from a certain background to behave in a certain way.'

'Could one? I hadn't noticed it.' She had gone on inexorably: 'Above all we need to give value for money. At the end of the year or eighteen-month course the students should have something to show for their efforts. We have to justify our fees – God knows they're high enough. First of all they need to be computer-literate. Secretarial and administrative skills will always have value. Then we need to ensure they're fluent in one foreign language. If they already are, we teach them a second. Cooking should be included; it's popular, useful and socially fashionable, and it should be taught to cordon bleu standards. The other subjects – social skills, childcare, deportment – are matters of choice. There will be no problem with the Arts. We have access to private collections and London is on our doorstep. I thought we might arrange exchanges with schools in Paris, Madrid and Rome.'

Lady Swathling had said, 'Can we afford it?'

'It will be a struggle for the first two years, but after that the reforms will begin to pay. When a girl says, "I had a year at Swathling's", that should mean something, and something marketable. Once we achieve the prestige, the numbers will follow.'

And they had followed. Swathling's became what Caroline Dupayne had planned it to be. Lady Swathling, who never forgot an injury, also never forgot a benefit.

Caroline Dupayne had become at first joint Principal and then partner. Lady Swathling knew that the school would flourish without her, but not without her colleague. There was still the final acknowledgement of her debt of gratitude. She could bequeath both house and school to Caroline. She herself had no children and no close relatives; there would be no one to challenge the will. And now that Caroline was a widow – Raymond Pratt had smashed himself into a tree in his Mercedes in 1998 – no husband to grab his share. She hadn't yet spoken to Caroline. There was, after all, no hurry. They were doing very well as they were. And she enjoyed the knowledge that, in this one thing at least, she held the power.

They went methodically through the business of the morning. Lady Swathling said, 'You're happy about this new girl, Marcia Collinson?'

'Perfectly. Her mother's a fool, but she isn't. She tried for Oxford but didn't make it. There's no point in her going to a crammer, she already has four top-grade A levels. She'll try again next year in the hope that persistence will be rewarded. Apparently it's Oxford or nowhere, which is hardly rational given the competition. She'd have a better chance, of course, if she came from the state system, and I don't suppose a year here will help much. Naturally I didn't point that out. She wants to become proficient on a computer, that's her top priority. And her language choice is Chinese.'

'Won't that present a problem?'

'I don't think so. I know a postgraduate in London who would be glad to take individual sessions. The girl has no interest in a gap year abroad. She seems devoid of a social conscience. She said she had enough of that at school, and in any case service abroad was only a form of charitable imperialism. She mouths the fashionable shibboleths, but she has a brain.'

'Oh well, if her parents can pay the fees.'

They moved on. During the break for coffee, Lady Swathling said, 'I met Celia Mellock in Harvey Nichols last week. She brought up the Dupayne Museum in the conversation. I can't think why. After all, she was only with us for two terms. She said it was odd the students never visited it.'

Caroline said, 'The art of the inter-war years isn't on the syllabus. The modern girl isn't much interested in the 1920s and 30s. As you know, we are specializing this term in modern art. A visit to the Dupayne could be arranged, but the time would be more profitably spent at Tate Modern.'

Lady Swathling said, 'She said one curious thing as she left – that the Dupayne would certainly repay a visit, and that she was grateful to you for 1996. She didn't explain. I was wondering what she meant.'

Lady Swathling's memory could be erratic, but never about figures or dates. Caroline reached to refill her coffee cup. 'Nothing, I imagine. I'd never even heard of her in 1996. She was always an attention-seeker. The usual story: an only child with wealthy parents who gave her everything except their time.'

'Do you intend to keep the museum on? Isn't there some problem about the lease?'

The question sounded no more than an innocuous

enquiry. Caroline Dupayne knew that it was more than that. Lady Swathling had always valued the school's tenuous relationship with a prestigious if small museum. It was one reason why she had strongly approved of her partner's decision to revert to her family name.

Caroline said, 'There's no trouble over the lease. My elder brother and I are determined. The Dupayne Museum will continue.'

Lady Swathling was persistent. 'And your younger brother?'

'Neville will, of course, agree. The new lease will be signed.'

5

The time was five o'clock on Sunday 27 October, the place Cambridge. Under Garrett Hostel Bridge the willows dragged their frail wands in the deep ochre of the stream. Looking over the bridge, Emma Lavenham, Lecturer in English Literature, and her friend Clara Beckwith watched as the yellow leaves drifted downstream like the last remnant of autumn. Emma could never pass over a footbridge without pausing to gaze down at the water, but now Clara straightened up.

'Better keep going. That last haul up Station Road always takes longer than one expects.'

She had come from London to spend the day with Emma in Cambridge. It had been a time of talking, eating and strolling in the Fellows' garden. By mid-afternoon they had felt the need of more vigorous exercise and had decided to walk to the station by the longest route, along the backs of the colleges then through the city. Emma loved Cambridge at the start of the academic year. Her mental picture of summer was of shimmering stones seen through a haze of heat, of shadowed lawns, flowers casting their scent against sun-burnished walls, of punts being driven with practised energy through sparkling water or rocking gently under laden boughs, of distant dance music and calling voices. But it was not her favourite term; there was something frenetic, self-consciously youthful and deeply anxiety-making about those summer weeks. There was the trauma of tripos and feverish last-minute revision, the ruthless seeking after pleasures soon to be relinquished and the melancholy knowledge of imminent partings. She preferred the first term of the academic year with the interest of getting to know the new entrants, the drawing of curtains shutting out the darkening evenings and the first stars, the distant jangle of discordant bells and, as now, the Cambridge smell of river, mist and loamy soil. The fall had come late this year and after one of the most beautiful autumns she could remember. But it had begun at last. The streetlights shone on a thin golden brown carpet of leaves. She felt the crunch of them under her feet and could taste it in the air, the first sour-sweet smell of winter.

Emma was wearing a long tweed coat, high leather boots and was hatless, the coat's upturned collar framing her face. Clara, three inches shorter, stumped along beside her friend. She wore a short fleece lined jacket and had a striped woollen cap drawn down over the fringe of straight dark hair. Her weekend bag was slung over her shoulder. It held books she had bought in Cambridge, but she carried it as easily as if it were weightless.

Clara had fallen in love with Emma during their first term. It was not the first time she had been strongly attracted to a woman obviously heterosexual, but she had accepted disappointment with her usual wry stoicism and set herself to win Emma's friendship. She had read mathematics and had achieved her first class degree, saying that a second was too boring to be contemplated and only a first or a third were worth enduring three years' hard labour in the damp city of the plains. Since in modern Cambridge it was impossible to avoid being seriously overworked, one might as well make the extra effort and get a first. She had no wish for an academic career, asserting that academe, if persisted in, made the men either sour or pompous while the women, unless other interests supervened, became more than eccentric. After university she had moved promptly to London where, to Emma's surprise and a little to her own, she was pursuing a successful and highly profitable career as a fund manager in the City. The full tide of prosperity had ebbed, throwing up its human jetsam of failure and disillusionment, but Clara had survived. She had earlier explained to Emma her unexpected choice of career.

'I earn this totally unreasonable salary but I live comfortably on a third of it and invest the rest. The chaps get stressed because they're handed half-million-pound bonuses and begin to live like someone who earns close on a million a year – the expensive house, the expensive car, the expensive clothes, the expensive woman, the drinking. Then of course they're terrified of being sacked. The company can fire me tomorrow and I wouldn't particularly care. I aim to make three million and then I'll get out and do something I really want to do.'

'Such as?'

'Annie and I thought we might open a restaurant close to the campus of one of the modern universities. There you've got a captive group of customers desperate for decent food at prices they can afford; homemade soup, salads that are more than some chopped lettuce and half a tomato. Mostly vegetarian, of course, but imaginative vegetarian. I thought maybe in Sussex, on the downs outside Falmer. It's an idea. Annie's quite keen except that she feels we should do something socially useful.'

'Surely few things are more socially useful than providing the young with decent food at reasonable prices.'

'When it comes to spending a million, Annie thinks internationally. She has something of a Mother Theresa complex.'

They walked on in companionable silence. Then Clara asked, 'How did Giles take your defection?'

'As you'd expect, badly. His face showed a succession of emotions – surprise, disbelief, self-pity and anger. He looked like an actor trying out facial expressions in front of a mirror. I wondered how on earth I could have fancied him.'

'But you did.'

'Oh yes, that wasn't the problem.'

'He thought you loved him.'

'No he didn't. He thought I found him as fascinating as he found himself and that I wouldn't be able to resist marrying him if he condescended to ask me.'

Clara laughed. 'Careful, Emma, that sounds like bitterness.'

'No, only honesty. Neither of us has anything to be proud of. We used each other. He was my defence. I was Giles's girl; that made me untouchable. The primacy of the dominant male is accepted even in the academic jungle. I was left in peace to concentrate on what really mattered – my work. It wasn't admirable but it wasn't dishonest. I never told him I loved him. I've never spoken those words to anyone.'

'And now you want to speak them and to hear them, and from a police officer and a poet of all people. I suppose the poet is the more understandable. But what sort of life would you have? How much time have you spent together since that first meeting? Seven dates arranged, four actually achieved. Adam Dalgliesh might be happy to be at the call of the Home Secretary, the Commissioner and the senior officials at the Home Office, but I don't see why you should be. His life is in London, yours is here.'

Emma said, 'It isn't only Adam. I had to cancel once.'

'Four dates, apart from that disorienting business when you first met. Murder is hardly an orthodox introduction. You can't possibly know him.'

'I can know enough. I can't know everything, no one can. Loving him doesn't give me the right to walk in and out of his mind as if it were my room at college. He's the most private person I've ever met. But I know the things about him that matter.'

But did she? Emma asked herself. He was intimate with those dark crevices of the human mind where horrors lurked which she couldn't begin to comprehend. Not even that appalling scene in the church at St Anselm's had shown her the worst that human beings could do to each other. She knew about those horrors from literature; he explored them daily in his work. Sometimes, waking from sleep in the early hours, the vision she had of him was of the dark face masked, the hands smooth and impersonal in the sleek latex gloves.

What hadn't those hands touched? She rehearsed the questions she wondered if she would ever be able to ask. Why do you do it? Is it necessary to your poetry? Why did you choose this job? Or did it choose you?

She said, 'There's this woman detective who works with him. Kate Miskin. She's on his team. I watched them together. All right, he was her senior, she called him sir, but there was a companionship, an intimacy which seemed to exclude everyone who wasn't a police officer. That's his world. I'm not part of it. I won't ever be.'

'I don't know why you should want to be. It's a pretty murky world, and he's not part of yours.'

'But he could be. He's a poet. He understands my world. We can talk about it – we *do* talk about it. But we don't talk about his. I haven't even been in his flat. I know he lives in Queenhithe above the Thames, but I haven't seen it. I can only imagine it. That's part of his world too. If ever he asks me there I know everything will be all right, that he wants me to be part of his life.'

'Perhaps he'll ask you next Friday night. When are you thinking of coming up, by the way?'

'I thought I'd take an afternoon train and arrive at Putney at about six if you'll be home by then. Adam says he'll call for me at eight-fifteen, if that's all right by you.'

'To save you the hassle of getting across London to the restaurant on your own. He's been well brought up. Will he arrive with a propitiatory bunch of red roses?'

Emma laughed. 'No, he won't arrive with flowers, and if he did they wouldn't be red roses.'

They had reached the war memorial at the end of

Station Road. On his decorated plinth the statue of the young warrior strode with magnificent insouciance to his death. When Emma's father had been Master of his college, her nurse would take her and her sister for walks in the nearby botanical garden. On the way home they would make a short diversion so that the children could obey the nurse's injunction to wave to the soldier. The nurse, a widow of the Second World War, had long been dead, as were Emma's mother and sister. Only her father, living his solitary life among his books in a mansion flat in Marylebone, remained of the family. But Emma never passed the memorial without the pang of guilt that she no longer waved. Irrationally it seemed a wilful disrespect for more than the war dead generations.

On the station platform lovers were already indulging in their protracted goodbyes. Several couples strolled hand in hand. Another, the girl pressed hard against the waiting-room wall, looked as motionless as if they had been glued together.

Emma said suddenly, 'Doesn't the very thought of it bore you, the sexual merry-go-round?'

'Meaning?'

'The modern mating ritual. You know how it is. You've probably seen more of it in London than I have here. Girl meets boy. They fancy each other. They go to bed, sometimes after the first date. It either works out and they become a recognized couple or it doesn't. Sometimes it ends the following morning when she sees the state of the bathroom, the difficulty of getting him out of bed to go to work and his obvious acceptance that she'll be the one to squeeze the oranges and make the coffee. If it works out he eventually moves in with her. It's usually that way round, isn't it? Have you ever met a case where she moves in with him?'

Clara said, 'Maggie Foster moved in with her chap. You probably don't know her. Read maths at King's and got a two-one. But it's generally believed that Greg's flat was more convenient for his work and he couldn't be bothered to rehang his eighteenth-century water-colours.'

'All right, I'll give you Maggie Foster. So they move in together. That too either works out or it doesn't, only the split, of course, is messier, more expensive and invariably bitter. It's usually because one of them wants a commitment the other can't give. Or it does work out. They decide on a recognized partnership or a marriage, usually because the woman gets broody. Mother starts planning the wedding, father calculates the cost, auntie buys a new hat. General relief all round. One more successful skirmish against moral and social chaos.'

Clara laughed. 'Well, it's better than the mating ritual of our grandmothers' generation. My grandmother kept a diary and it's all there. She was the daughter of a highly successful solicitor living in Leamington Spa. There wasn't any question of a job for her, of course. After school she lived at home doing the kind of things daughters did while their brothers were at university: arranging the flowers, handing round the cups at tea-parties, a little respectable charity work but not the kind that brought her into touch with the more sordid reality of poverty, answering the boring family letters her mother couldn't be bothered with, helping with the garden fête. Meanwhile all the mothers organized a social life to ensure their daughters met the right men. Tennis parties, small private dances, garden parties. At twenty-eight a girl started getting anxious; at thirty she was on the shelf. God help the ones who were plain or awkward or shy.'

Emma said, 'God help them today for that matter. The system's as brutal in its own way, isn't it? It's just that at least we can organize it ourselves, and there is an alternative.'

Clara laughed, 'I don't see what you've got to complain of. You'll hardly be hopping on and off the carousel. You'll be sitting up there on your gleaming steed repelling all boarders. And why make it sound as if the merry-go-round is always heterosexual? We're all looking. Some of us get lucky, and those who don't generally settle for second best. And sometimes second best turns out to be the best after all.'

'I don't want to settle for second best. I know who I want and what I want, and it isn't a temporary affair. I know that if I go to bed with him it will cost me too much if he breaks it off. Bed can't make me more committed than I am now.'

The London train rumbled into platform one. Clara put down her duffle-bag and they hugged briefly.

Emma said, 'Until Friday, then.'

Impulsively Clara clasped her arms round her friend again. She said, 'If he chucks you on Friday, I think you should consider whether there's any future for the two of you.'

64

'If he chucks me on Friday, perhaps I shall.'

She stood, watching but not waving, until the train was out of sight.

6

From childhood the word 'London' had conjured up for Tallulah Clutton a vision of a fabled city, a world of mystery and excitement. She told herself that the almost physical yearning of her childhood and youth was neither irrational nor obsessive; it had its roots in reality. She was, after all, a Londoner by birth, born in a two-storey terraced house in a narrow street in Stepney; her parents, grandparents and the maternal grandmother after whom she had been named had been born in the East End. The city was her birthright. Her very survival had been fortuitous and in her more imaginative moods she saw it as magical. When the street was destroyed in a bombing raid in 1942 only she, four years old, had been lifted from the rubble alive. It seemed to her that she had a memory of that moment, rooted perhaps in her aunt's account of the rescue. As the years passed she was uncertain whether she remembered her aunt's words or the event itself; how she was lifted into the light, grey with dust but laughing and spreading out both arms as if to embrace the whole street.

Exiled in childhood to a corner shop in a suburb of Leeds to be brought up by her mother's sister and her husband, a part of her spirit had been left in that ruined street. She had been conscientiously and dutifully brought up, and perhaps loved, but as neither her aunt nor uncle were demonstrative or articulate, love was something she neither expected nor understood. She had left school at fifteen, her intelligence recognized by some of the teachers, but there was nothing they could do about it. They knew that the shop awaited her.

When the young gentle-faced accountant who came regularly to audit the books with her uncle began to appear more often than was necessary and to show his interest in her, it seemed natural to accept his eventual and somewhat tentative offer of marriage. There was, after all, enough room in the flat above the shop and room enough in her bed. She was nineteen. Her aunt and uncle made plain their relief. Terence no longer charged for his services. He helped part-time in the shop and life became easier. Tally enjoyed his regular if unimaginative lovemaking and supposed that she was happy. But he had died of a heart attack nine months after the birth of their daughter and the old life was resumed: the long hours, the constant financial anxiety, the welcome yet tyrannical jangle of the bell on the shop door, the ineffectual struggle to compete with the new supermarkets. Her heart would be torn with a desperate pity as she saw her aunt's futile efforts to entice back the old customers; the outer leaves shredded from cabbages and lettuces to make them look less wilted, the advertised bargains which could deceive no one, the willingness to give credit in the hope that the bill would eventually be paid. It seemed to her that her youth had been dominated by the smell of rotting fruit and the jangle of the bell.

Her aunt and uncle had willed her the shop and when they died, within a month of each other, she put it on the market. It sold badly; only masochists or unworldly idealists were interested in saving a failing corner shop. But it did sell. She kept £10,000 of the proceeds, handed over the remainder to her daughter who had long since left home, and set out for London and a job. She had found it at the Dupayne Museum within a week and had known, when first being shown round the cottage by Caroline Dupayne and seeing the Heath from her bedroom window, that she had come home.

Through the overburdened and stringent years of childhood, her brief marriage, her failure as a mother, the dream of London had remained. In adolescence and later it had strengthened and had taken on the solidity of brick and stone, the sheen of sunlight on the river, the wide ceremonial avenues and narrow byways leading to half-hidden courtyards. History and myth were given a local habitation and a name and imagined people made flesh. London had received her back as one of its own and she had not been disappointed. She had no naïve expectations that she walked always in safety. The depiction in the museum of life between the wars told what she already knew, that this London was not the capital her parents had known. Theirs had been a more peaceable city and a gentler England. She thought of London as a mariner might think of the sea; it was her natural element but its power was awesome and she encountered it with wariness and respect. On her weekday and Sunday excursions she had devised her protective strategies. Her money, just sufficient for the day, was carried in a money-bag worn under her winter coat or lighter summer jacket. The food she needed, her bus map and a bottle of water were carried in a small rucksack on her back. She wore comfortable stout walking shoes and, if her plans included a long visit to a gallery or museum, carried a light folding canvas stool. With these she moved from picture to picture, one of a small group which followed the lectures at the National Gallery or the Tate, taking in information like gulps of wine, intoxicated with the richness of the bounty on offer.

On most Sundays she would attend a church, quietly enjoying the music, the architecture and the liturgy, taking from each an aesthetic rather than a religious experience, but finding in the order and ritual the fulfilment of some unidentified need. She had been brought up as a member of the Church of England, sent to the local parish church every Sunday morning and evening. She went alone. Her aunt and uncle worked fifteen hours a day in their desperate attempt to keep the corner shop in profit, and their Sundays were marked by exhaustion. The moral code by which they lived was that of cleanliness, respectability and prudence. Religion was for those who had the time for it, a middle-class indulgence. Now Tally entered London's churches with the same curiosity and expectation of new experience as she entered the museums. She had always believed – somewhat to her surprise – that God existed but was unconvinced that He was moved by the worship of man or by the tribulations and extraordinary vagaries and antics of the creation He had set in being.

Each evening she would return to the cottage on the edge of the Heath. It was her sanctuary, the place from which she ventured out and to which she returned, tired but satisfied. She could never close the door without an uplifting of the spirits. Such religion as she practised, the nightly prayers she still said, were rooted in gratitude. Until now she had been lonely but not solitary; now she was solitary but never lonely.

Even if the worst happened and she was homeless, she was determined not to seek a home with her daughter. Roger and Jennifer Crawford lived just outside Basingstoke in a modern four-bedroomed house which was part of what the developers had described as 'two crescents of executive houses'. The crescents were cut off from the contamination of non-executive housing by steel gates. Their installation, fiercely fought for by householders, was regarded by her daughter and son-in-law as a victory for law and order, the protection and enhancement of property values and a validation of social distinction. There was a council estate hardly half a mile down the road, the inhabitants of which were considered to be inadequately controlled barbarians.

Sometimes Tally thought that the success of her daughter's marriage rested not only on shared ambition, but on their common willingness to tolerate, even to sympathize with, the other's grievances. Behind these reiterated complaints lay, she realized, mutual self-satisfaction. They thought that they had done very well for themselves and would have been deeply chagrined had any of their friends thought otherwise. If they had a genuine worry it was, she knew, the uncertainty of her future, the fact that they might one day be required to give her a home. It was a worry she understood and shared.

She hadn't visited her family for five years except for three days at Christmas, that annual ritual of consanguinity which she had always dreaded. She was received with a scrupulous politeness and a strict adherence to accepted social norms which didn't hide the absence of real warmth or genuine affection. She didn't resent this – whatever she herself was bringing to the family, it wasn't love – but she wished there was some acceptable way of excusing herself from the visit. She suspected that the others felt the same but were inhibited by the need to observe social conventions. To have one's widowed and solitary mother for Christmas was accepted as a duty and, once established, couldn't be avoided without the risk of sly gossip or mild scandal. So punctiliously on Christmas Eve, by a train they had suggested as convenient, she would arrive at Basingstoke station to be met by Roger or Jennifer, her over-heavy case taken from her like the burden it was, and the annual ordeal would get underway.

Christmas at Basingstoke was not peaceful. Friends arrived, smart, vivacious, effusive. Visits were returned. She had an impression of a succession of overheated rooms, flushed faces, yelling voices and raucous conviviality underlined with sexuality. People greeted her, some she felt with genuine kindness, and she would smile and respond before Jennifer tactfully moved her away. She didn't wish her guests to be bored. Tally was relieved rather than mortified. She had nothing to contribute to the conversations about cars, holidays abroad, the difficulty of finding a suitable au pair, the ineffectiveness of the local council, the machinations of the golf club committee, their neighbours' carelessness over locking the gates. She hardly saw her grandchildren except at Christmas dinner. Clive spent most of the day in his room, which held the necessities of his seventeen-year-old life: the television, video and DVD player, computer and printer, stereo equipment and speakers. Samantha, two years younger and apparently in a permanent state of disgruntlement, was rarely at home and, when she was, spent hours secreted with her mobile phone.

But now all this was finished. Ten days ago, after careful thought and three or four rough drafts, Tally had composed the letter. Would they mind very much if she didn't come this year? Miss Caroline wouldn't be in her flat over the holiday and if she, too, went away there would be no one to keep an eye on things generally. She wouldn't be spending the day alone. There were a number of friends who had issued invitations. Of course it wouldn't be the same as coming to the family, but she was sure they would understand. She would post her presents in early December.

She had felt some guilt at the dishonesty of the letter, but it had produced a reply within days. There was a touch of grievance, a suggestion that Tally was allowing herself to be exploited, but she sensed their relief. Her excuse had been valid enough; her absence could safely be explained to their friends. This Christmas she would spend alone in the cottage and already she had been planning how she would pass the day. The morning walk to a local church and the satisfaction of being one of a crowd and yet apart, which she enjoyed, a poussin for lunch with, perhaps, one of those miniature Christmas puddings to follow and a half-bottle of wine, hired videos, library books and, whatever the weather, a walk on the Heath.

But these plans were now less certain. The day after her daughter's letter arrived, Ryan Archer, coming in after his stint in the garden, had hinted that he might be alone for Christmas. The Major was thinking of going abroad. Tally had said impulsively, 'You can't spend Christmas in the squat, Ryan. You can come here for dinner if you like. But give me a few days notice because of getting in the food.'

He had accepted, but tentatively, and she doubted whether he would choose to exchange the camaraderie of the squat for the placid tedium of the cottage. But the invitation had been given. If he came she would at least ensure that he was properly fed. For the first time in years she was looking forward to Christmas.

But now all her plans were overlaid with a fresh and more acute anxiety. Would this coming Christmas be the last she would spend in the cottage?

7

The cancer had returned and this time it was a death sentence. That was James Calder-Hale's personal prognosis and he accepted it without fear and with only one regret: he needed time to finish his book on the inter-war years. He didn't need long; it would be finished in four to six months even if his pace slowed. Time might still be granted, but even as the word came into his mind he rejected it. 'Granted' implied the conferment of a benefit. Conferred by whom? Whether he died sooner or later was a matter of pathology. The tumour would take its own time. Or, if you wanted to describe it even more simply, he would be lucky or unlucky. But in the end the cancer would win.

He found himself unable to believe that anything he did, anything done to him, his mental attitude, his courage or his faith in his doctors, could alter that inevitable victory. Others might prepare to live in hope, to earn that posthumous tribute, 'after a gallant fight'. He hadn't the stomach for a fight, not with an enemy already so entrenched.

An hour earlier his oncologist had broken the news that he was no longer in remission with professional tact; after all, he had had plenty of experience. He had set out the options for further treatments, and the results which might reasonably be hoped for, with admirable lucidity. Calder-Hale agreed to the recommended course after spending a little time pretending to consider the options, but not too much time. The consultation was taking place at the consultant's Harley Street rooms, not at the hospital, and, despite the fact that his was the first appointment, the waiting-room was already beginning to fill up by the time he was called. To speak his own prognosis, his complete conviction of failure, would be an ingratitude amounting to bad manners when the consultant had taken so much trouble. He felt that it was he who was bestowing the illusion of hope.

Coming out into Harley Street, he decided to take a taxi to Hampstead Heath station and walk across the Heath past Hampstead Ponds and the viaduct to Spaniards Road and the museum. He found himself mentally summing up his life with a detached wonder that fifty-five years which had seemed so momentous could have left him with so meagre a legacy. The facts came into his mind in short staccato statements. Only son of a prosperous Cheltenham solicitor. Father unfrightening, if remote. Mother extravagant, fussily conventional, but no trouble to anyone except her husband. Education at his father's old school, and then Oxford. The Foreign Office and a career, chiefly in the Middle East, which had never progressed beyond the unexceptional. He could have climbed higher but he had demonstrated those two fatal defects: lack of ambition and the impression of taking the Service with insufficient seriousness. A good Arabic speaker with the ability to attract friendship but not love. A brief marriage to the daughter of an Egyptian diplomat who had thought she would like an English husband but had quickly decided that he was not the one. No children. Early retirement following the diagnosis of a malignancy which had unexpectedly and disconcertingly gone into remission.

Gradually, since the diagnosis of his illness, he had dissociated himself from the expectations of life. But hadn't this happened years before? When he had wanted the relief of sex he had paid for it, discreetly, expensively and with the minimum expenditure of time and emotion. He couldn't now remember when he had finally decided that the trouble and expense were no longer worthwhile, not so much an expense of spirit in a waste of shame as a waste of money in an expanse of boredom. The emotions, excitements, triumphs, failures, pleasures and pains which had filled the interstices of this outline of a life had no power to disturb him. It was difficult to believe that they ever had.

Wasn't accidie, that lethargy of the spirit, one of the deadly sins? To the religious there must seem a wilful blasphemy in the rejection of all joy. His ennui was less dramatic. It was more a placid non-caring in which his only emotions, even the occasional outbursts of irritation, were mere play-acting. And the real play-acting, that boys' game which he had got drawn into more from a good-natured compliance than from commitment, was as uninvolving as the rest of his non-writing existence. He recognized its importance but felt himself less a participant than the detached observer of other men's endeavours, other men's follies.

And now he was left with the one unfinished business, the one task capable of enthusing his life. He wanted to complete his history of the inter-war years. He had been working on it for eight years now, since old Max Dupayne, a friend of his father, had introduced him to the museum. He had been enthralled by it and an idea which had lain dormant at the back of his mind had sprung into life. When Dupayne had offered him the job of curator, unpaid but with the use of an office, it had been a propitious encouragement to begin writing. He had given a dedication and enthusiasm to the work which no other job had evoked. The prospect of dying with it unfinished was intolerable. No one would care to publish an incomplete history. He would die with the one task to which he had given heart and mind reduced to files of half-legible notes and reams of unedited typescript which would be bundled into plastic bags and collected for salvage. Sometimes the strength of his need to complete the book perturbed him. He wasn't a professional historian; those who were were unlikely to be merciful in judgement. But the book would not go unnoticed. He had interviewed an interesting variety of the over-eighties; personal testimonies had been skilfully interspersed with historical events. He was putting forward original, sometimes maverick views which would command respect. But he was ministering to his own need, not that of others. For reasons which he couldn't satisfactorily explain he saw the history as a justification for his life.

If the museum closed before the book was finished, it would be the end. He thought he knew the minds of the three trustees, and the knowledge was bitter. Marcus Dupayne was looking for employment that would confer prestige and relieve the boredom of retirement. If the man had been more successful, had achieved his K, the City directorships, the official commissions and committees, would be waiting. Calder-Hale wondered what had gone wrong. Probably nothing which Dupayne could have prevented; a change of government, a new Secretary of State's preferences, a change in the pecking order. Who in the end got the top job was often a matter of luck.

He was less certain why Caroline Dupayne wanted the museum to continue. Preserving the family name probably had something to do with it. Then there was her use of the flat which got her away from the school. And she would always oppose Neville. As long as he could remember the siblings had been antagonistic. Knowing nothing of their childhood, he could only guess at the roots of this mutual irritation. It was exacerbated by their attitudes to each other's job. Neville made no secret of his contempt for everything Swathling's stood for; his sister openly voiced her disparagement of psychiatry. 'It isn't even a scientific discipline, just the last resort of the desperate or the indulgence of fashionable neuroses. You can't even describe the difference between mind and brain in any way which makes sense. You've probably done more harm in the last fifty years than any other branch of medicine and you can only help patients today because the neuroscientists and the drug companies have given you the tools. Without their little tablets you would be back where you were twenty years ago.'

There would be no consensus between Neville and

Caroline Dupayne about the future of the museum and he thought he knew whose will would be the stronger. Not that they would do much of the work of closing down the place. If the new tenant wanted quick possession, it would be a formidable task undertaken against time, fraught with arguments and financial complications. He was the curator; he would be expected to bear most of the brunt. It would be the end of any hope of finishing the history.

England had rejoiced in a beautiful October more typical of spring's tender vicissitudes than of the year's slow decline into this multicoloured decrepitude. Now suddenly the sky, which had been an expanse of clear azure blue, was darkened by a rolling cloud as grimy as factory smoke. The first drops of rain fell and he had hardly time to push open his umbrella before he was deluged by a squall. It felt as if the accumulated weight of the cloud's precarious burden had emptied itself over his head. There was a clump of trees within yards and he took refuge under a horse chestnut, prepared to wait patiently for the sky to clear. Above him the dark sinews of the tree were becoming visible among the yellowing leaves and, looking up, he felt the slow drops falling on his face. He wondered why it was pleasurable to feel these small erratic splashes on skin already drying from the rain's first assault. Perhaps it was no more than the comfort of knowing that he could still take pleasure in the unsolicited benisons of existence. The more intense, the grosser, the urgent physicalities had long lost their edge. Now that appetite had become fastidious and sex rarely urgent, a relief he could provide for himself, at least he could still relish the fall of a raindrop on his cheek.

And now Tally Clutton's cottage came into view. He had paced up this narrow path from the Heath innumerable times during the last four years but always he came upon the cottage with a shock of surprise. It looked comfortably at home among the fringe of trees, and yet it was an anachronism. Perhaps the architect of the museum, forced by his employer's whim to produce exactly an eighteenth-century replica for the main house, had indulged his preference when designing the cottage. Situated as it was, at the back of the museum and out of sight, his client may not have been greatly troubled that it was discordant. It looked like a picture from a child's storybook with its two ground-floor bay windows each side of a jutting porch, the two plain windows above under a pantile roof, its neat front garden with the paved stone path leading to the front door and a lawn each side bound by a low privet hedge. There was an oblong slightly raised bed in the middle of each lawn and here Tally Clutton had planted her usual white cyclamen and purple and white winter pansies.

As he approached the gate of the garden, Tally appeared from among the trees. She was wearing the old mackintosh that she usually donned for gardening and carrying a wooden basket and holding a trowel. She had told him, although he couldn't remember when, that she was sixty-four, but she looked younger. Her face, the skin a little roughened, was beginning to show the clefts and lines of age, but it was a good face, keen-eyed behind the spectacles, a calm face. She was a contented woman, but not, thank God, given to that resolute and desperate cheerfulness with which some of the ageing attempted to defy the attrition of the years.

Whenever he re-entered the museum grounds after walking on the Heath he would call at the cottage to see if Tally was at home. If it were the morning there would be coffee and in the afternoon there was tea and fruit cake. This routine had begun some three years earlier when he had been caught in a heavy storm without an umbrella and had arrived with soaking jacket and sodden trousers clinging to his legs. She had seen him from the window and had come out, offering him a chance to dry his clothes and have a warm drink. Her anxiety at his appearance had overcome any shyness she must have felt and he remembered gratefully the warmth of the imitation coal fire and the hot coffee laced with a little whisky which she had provided. But she hadn't repeated the invitation to come in, and he sensed that she was anxious that he should not think she was lonely for company or somehow imposing on him an obligation. It was always he who knocked or called out, but he had no doubt that she welcomed his visits.

Now, waiting for her, he said, 'Am I too late for coffee?'

'Of course not, Mr Calder-Hale. I've just been planting daffodil bulbs between the showers. I think they look better under the trees. I've tried them in the middle beds but they look so depressing after the flowers have died. Mrs Faraday says that we must leave the leaves until they're absolutely yellow and can be pulled out or we won't get flowers next year. But that takes so long.'

81

He followed her into the porch, helped her off with the raincoat and waited while she sat on the narrow bench, tugged off her Wellington boots and put on her house slippers. Then he followed her down the narrow hall and into the sitting-room.

Switching on the fire, she said, 'Your trousers look rather damp. Better sit here and dry off. I won't be long with the coffee.'

He waited, resting his head against the high back of the chair and stretching out his legs to the heat. He had overestimated his strength and the walk had been too long. And now his tiredness was almost pleasurable. This room was one of the few, apart from his own office, where he could sit totally without strain. And how pleasant she had made it. It was unostentatiously comfortable without being cluttered, over-prettified or self-consciously feminine. The fireplace was the original Victorian with a blue Delft tiled surround and an ornamental iron hood. The leather chair in which he rested, with its high-buttoned back and comfortable armrests, was just right for his height. Opposite was a similar but smaller chair in which Tally usually sat. The alcoves on each side of the fireplace had been fitted with shelves holding her books on history and London. He knew that the city was her passion. He knew from previous conversations that she also liked biography and autobiography but the few novels were all leather-bound copies of the classics. In the middle of the room was a small circular table with two high-backed Windsor chairs. There, he knew, was where she usually ate. He had glimpsed through the half-open door on the right of the hall a square wooden table with four upright chairs in what was obviously the dining-room. He wondered how often that room was used. He had never met a stranger in her cottage and it seemed to him that her life was contained within the four walls of this sitting-room. The south window had a wide sill and on it was her collection of African violets, pale and deep purple and white.

The coffee and biscuits arrived and he got up with some effort and moved across to take the tray from her. Smelling the comforting aroma, he was surprised to find himself so thirsty.

When together, he usually spoke of whatever came into his mind. He suspected that only cruelty and stupidity shocked her, as they did him. There was nothing he felt he couldn't say. Sometimes his conversation seemed a soliloquy, but one in which her responses were always welcome and often surprising. Now he asked, 'Does it depress you, cleaning and dusting the Murder Room, those dead eyes in dead photographs, the dead faces?'

She said, 'I suppose I've got used to them. I don't mean I think of them as friends. That would be silly. But they are part of the museum. When I first came I used to imagine what their victims suffered, or what they themselves suffered, but they don't depress me. It's all over for them, isn't it? They did what they did, they paid for it and they've gone. They aren't suffering now. There's so much to grieve over in our world that it would be pointless to grieve over ancient wrongs. But I sometimes wonder where they've all gone – not just the murderers and their victims, but all the people photographed in the museum. Do you wonder about that?'

'No, I don't wonder. That's because I know. We die like animals and from much the same causes and, except for the lucky few, in much the same pain.'

'And that's the end?'

'Yes. It's a relief, isn't it?'

She said, 'So what we do, how we act, doesn't matter except in this life?'

'Where else could it matter, Tally? I find it difficult enough to behave with reasonable decency here and now without agonizing to acquire celestial brownie points for some fabled hereafter.'

She took his cup to refill it. She said, 'I suppose it's all that Sunday school attendance and church twice every Sunday. My generation still half-believes we might be called to account.'

'So we may, but the tribunal will be here in the Crown Court with the judge wearing a wig. And with a modicum of intelligence most of us can usually avoid it. But what did you envisage, a big account book with debit and credit columns and the Recording Angel noting it all down?'

He spoke gently, but then he always did to Tally Clutton. She smiled. 'Something like that. When I was about eight I thought the book was like the very large red account book which my uncle had for his business. It had *Accounts* written on the cover in black and the pages had red margins.'

He said, 'Well, belief had its social uses. We haven't exactly found an effective substitute. Now we construct our own morality. "What I want is right and I'm entitled to have it." The older generation may still be encumbered by some folk memory of Judeo-Christian guilt, but that will be gone by the next generation.'

'I'm glad I shan't be here to live through it.'

She was not, he knew, naïve, but now she was smiling, her face untroubled. Whatever her private morality, if it went no further than kindness and common sense – and why the hell should it? – what else did she or anyone else need?

She said, 'I suppose a museum is a celebration of death. Dead people's lives, the objects they made, the things they thought important, their clothes, their houses, their daily comforts, their art.'

'No. A museum is about life. It's about the individual life, how it was lived. It's about the corporate life of the times, men and women organizing their societies. It's about the continuing life of the species *Homo sapiens*. No one with any human curiosity can dislike a museum.'

She said softly, 'I love it, but then I think I live in the past. Not my own past, that's very unexciting and ordinary – but the past of all the people who have been Londoners before me. I never walk there alone, no one can.'

He thought, even walking across the Heath is different for each of us. He noticed the changing trees, the sky, enjoyed the softness of turf under his feet. She imagined the Tudor washerwomen taking advantage of the clear springs, hanging their clothes over the gorse bushes to dry, the coaches and carts lumbering up from the stews of the city at the time of the plague and the great fire to take refuge in London's high village, Dick Turpin waiting on his horse in the shelter of the trees.

And now she was rising to take the tray into the kitchen. He got up and lifted it from her hands. Her face looking into his was, for the first time, troubled.

She said, 'Will you be at the meeting on Wednesday, the one when the future of the museum will be decided?'

'No, Tally, I shan't be there. I'm not a trustee. There are only three trustees, the Dupaynes. None of us has been told anything. It's all rumour.'

'But can it really be closed?'

'It will be if Neville Dupayne has his way.'

'But why? He doesn't work here. He's hardly ever in the museum except occasionally on a Friday when he collects his car. He isn't interested, so why should he care?'

'Because he hates what he sees as our national obsession with the past. He's too involved with the problems of the present. The museum is a convenient focus for that hatred. His father founded it, spent a fortune on it, it bears his family name. He wants to get shot of more than the museum.'

'Can he?'

'Oh yes, if he won't sign the new lease, the museum will close. But I shouldn't worry. Caroline Dupayne is a very strong-minded woman. I doubt whether Neville will be able to stand up to her. All that he's required to do is to sign a piece of paper.'

The idiocy of the words struck him as soon as he had spoken them. When had signing one's name been unimportant? People had been condemned or reprieved through the signing of a name. A signature could disinherit or confer a fortune. A signature written or withheld

86

could make the difference between life and death. But that was unlikely to be true of Neville Dupayne's signature on the new lease. Carrying the tray into the kitchen, he was glad to turn away from the sight of her troubled face. He had never seen Tally looking like that before. The enormity of what faced her suddenly struck him. This cottage, that sitting-room, was as important to her as his book was to him. And she was over sixty. Admittedly that didn't count as old today, but it wasn't an age for seeking a new job and a new home. There were plenty of vacancies; reliable housekeepers had never been easy to find. But this job and this place were perfect for her.

He was visited by an uncomfortable pity and then by a moment of physical weakness so sudden that he had to put down the tray quickly on the table and rest for a moment. And with it came the wish that there was something he could do, some magnificent gift which he could lay at her feet which would make everything right. He toyed for a moment with the ridiculous thought that he might make her the beneficiary of his will. But he knew that such an act of eccentric liberality was beyond him – he could hardly call it generosity since by then he would no longer have need of money. He had always spent up to his income and the capital remaining was family money left in his will, carefully drawn up by the family solicitor some fifteen years ago, to his three nephews. It was odd that he who cared so little what his nephews thought of him, and only rarely saw them, should be concerned for their good opinion after death. He had lived his life comfortably and mostly in safety.

What if he could find the strength to do one last eccentric, magnificent thing which would make a difference to someone else?

Then he heard her voice. 'Are you all right, Mr Calder-Hale?'

'Yes,' he said. 'I'm perfectly all right, Tally. Thank you for the coffee. And don't worry about Wednesday. I have a feeling it will be all right.'

8

It was now eleven-thirty. As usual, Tally had cleaned the museum before it opened in the morning and now, unless she was wanted, she had no duties except to make a final check with Muriel Godby before it closed at five o'clock. But there was work to do in the cottage and she had spent longer than usual with Mr Calder-Hale. Ryan, the boy who helped with the heavy cleaning and in the garden, would arrive with his sandwiches at one o'clock.

Since the first bite of the colder autumn days Tally had suggested to Ryan that he should eat his lunch in the cottage. During the summer she would see him resting with his back against one of the trees, the open bag at his side. But as the days grew colder he had taken to eating in the shed where he kept the lawn-mower, sitting on an upturned crate. It seemed to her wrong that his comfort should be so disregarded, but she had made her offer tentatively, not wishing to impose an obligation or to make it difficult for him to refuse. But he had accepted with alacrity and from that morning onwards he would arrive promptly at one o'clock with his paper bag and his can of Coca-Cola.

She had no wish to eat with him – that would have seemed an invasion of her own essential privacy – so she had taken to having her light lunch at twelve o'clock so that everything was cleared and out of sight by the time he arrived. If she had made soup she would leave some for him, particularly if the day were cold, and he seemed to welcome it. Afterwards, taught by her, he would make coffee for them both – real coffee, not granules out of a jar – and would bring it in to her. He never stayed longer than an hour and she had become used to hearing his feet on the path every Monday, Wednesday and Friday, his working days. She had never regretted that first invitation but was always half guiltily relieved on Tuesdays and Thursdays that the morning was entirely her own.

As she had gently asked him on the first day, he removed his working boots in the porch, hung up his jacket and went on stockinged feet into the bathroom to wash before joining her. He brought with him the smell of earth and grass and a faint masculine smell which she liked. She was amazed how clean he always seemed, how fragile. His hands looked as delicately boned as a girl's, strangely discordant with the brown muscled arms.

His face was round, firm-cheeked, the skin faintly pink and looking soft as suede. His large brown eyes were wide-spaced, the upper lids heavy, above a retroussé nose and a cleft chin. His hair was cut very short, showing the shape of the rounded head. Tally saw it as a baby face which the years had enlarged, but without any imprint of adult experience. Only his eyes belied this apparent untouched innocence. He could raise the lids and gaze at the world with a wide-eyed and disarming insouciance, or disconcertingly dart a sudden glance, both sly and knowledgeable. This dichotomy mirrored what he knew; odd snippets of sophistication which he picked up as he might fragments of litter from the drive, combined with astonishing ignorance of wide areas of knowledge which her generation acquired before they left school.

She had found him by placing a card on the vacant jobs board of a local newsagent. Mrs Faraday, the volunteer responsible for the garden, had pointed out that the sweeping up of leaves and some of the heavier pruning of shrubs and young trees had become too much for her. It was she who had suggested the card rather than an approach to the local job centre. Tally had given the telephone number of the cottage and had made no mention of the museum. When Ryan phoned, she had interviewed him with Mrs Faraday and they had been inclined to take him on for a month's trial. Before he left she had asked for a reference.

'Is there anyone, Ryan, someone you have worked for, who could write and recommend you?'

'I work for the Major. I clean his silver and do odd jobs about the flat. I'll ask him.'

He had given no further information, but a letter had arrived from an address in Maida Vale within two days:

Dear Madam. Ryan Archer tells me you are thinking of offering him the job of handyman/gardener's boy. He is not particularly handy but has done some household chores for me satisfactorily and shows willingness to learn if interested. I have no experience of his gardening ability, if any, but I doubt whether he can distinguish a pansy from a

petunia. His timekeeping is erratic but when he arrives he is
capable of hard work under supervision. In my experience
people are either honest or dishonest and either way there is
nothing to be done about it. The boy is honest.

On this less than enthusiastic recommendation, and with Mrs Faraday's endorsement, she had taken him on.

Miss Caroline had shown little interest and Muriel had disclaimed all responsibility. 'The domestic arrangements are for you, Tally. I don't wish to interfere. Miss Caroline has agreed that he'll receive the national minimum wage and I will pay him from my petty cash each day before he leaves. I shall, of course, require a receipt. If he needs protective clothing, that can come out of petty cash too, but you'd better buy it and not leave it to him. He can do the heavy cleaning of the floor here, including the stairs, but I don't want him in any other part of the museum except under supervision.'

Tally had explained, 'Major Arkwright, who provided his reference, says he's honest.'

'So he may be, but he could be a talker, and we've no way of knowing whether his friends are honest. I think Mrs Faraday and you had better make a formal report on his progress after his month's trial.'

Tally had reflected that, for someone who had no wish to interfere in domestic affairs, Muriel was behaving true to form. But the experiment had worked. Ryan was certainly unpredictable – she could never be sure whether he would turn up when expected – but he had become more reliable as the months passed, no doubt because he needed cash in hand at the end of the day. If not an enthusiastic worker, he certainly wasn't a slacker and Mrs Faraday, never easy to please, seemed to like him.

This morning she had made chicken soup from the bones she had boiled up from last night's supper, and now he was sipping it with evident enjoyment, thin fingers warming on the mug.

He said, 'Does it take a lot of courage to kill someone?'

'I've never thought of murderers as courageous, Ryan. They're more likely to be cowards. Sometimes it can take more courage not to murder.'

'I don't know what you mean, Mrs Tally.'

'Nor do I. It was just a remark. Rather a silly one now I come to think of it. Murder isn't a pleasant subject.'

'No, but it's interesting. Did I tell you that Mr Calder-Hale took me round the museum last Friday morning?'

'No you didn't, Ryan.'

'He saw me weeding the front bed when he arrived. He said good morning, so I asked him, "Can I see the museum?" He said, "You can, but it's a question of whether you may. I don't see why not." So he told me to clean up and join him in the front hall. I don't think Miss Godby liked it from the look she gave me.'

Tally said, 'It was good of Mr Calder-Hale to take you round. Working here – well, it was right that you had a chance to see it.'

'Why couldn't I see it before and on my own? Don't they trust me?'

'You're not kept out because we don't trust you. It's just that Miss Godby doesn't like people who haven't paid wandering about at will. It's the same for everyone.'

'Not for you.'

'Well, it can't be, Ryan. I have to dust and clean.'

'Or for Miss Godby.'

'But she's the secretary–receptionist. She has to be free to go where she likes. The museum couldn't be run otherwise. Sometimes she has to escort visitors when Mr Calder-Hale isn't here.'

She thought but didn't say, *Or doesn't think they're important enough.* Instead she asked, 'Did you enjoy the museum?'

'I liked the Murder Room.'

Oh dear, she thought. Well, perhaps it wasn't so surprising. He wouldn't be the only visitor who had lingered longest in the Murder Room.

He said, 'That tin trunk – do you think it really is the one Violette's body was put in?'

'I suppose so. Old Mr Dupayne was very particular about provenance – where the objects come from. I don't know how he got hold of some of them but I expect he had contacts.'

He had finished his soup now and took his sandwiches from the bag: thick slices of white bread with what looked like salami between them.

He said, 'So if I lifted the lid I'd see her bloodstains?'

'You're not allowed to open the lid, Ryan. The exhibits mustn't be touched.'

'But if I did?'

'You would probably see a stain, but no one can be sure it's Violette's blood.'

'But it could be tested.'

'I think it was. But even if it's human blood that

doesn't mean it's her blood. They didn't know about DNA in those days. Ryan, isn't this rather a morbid conversation?'

'I wonder where she is now.'

'Probably in a Brighton churchyard. I'm not sure anyone knows. She was a prostitute, poor woman, and perhaps there wasn't any money for a proper funeral. She may have been buried in what they call a pauper's grave.'

But had she? Tally wondered. Perhaps celebrity had elevated her to the rank of those who are dignified in death. Perhaps there had been a lavish funeral, horses with black plumes, crowds of gawpers following the cortège, photographs in the local newspapers, perhaps even in the national press. How ridiculous it would have seemed to Violette when she was young, years before she was murdered, if someone had prophesied that she would be more famous in death than in life, that nearly seventy years after her murder a woman and a boy in a world unimaginably different would be talking about her funeral.

She raised her eyes and heard Ryan speaking. 'I think Mr Calder-Hale only asked me because he wanted to know what I'm doing here.'

'But Ryan, he knows what you're doing. You're the part-time gardener.'

'He wanted to know what I did on the other days.'

'And what did you tell him?'

'I told him that I work in a bar near King's Cross.'

'But Ryan, is that true? I thought you worked for the Major.'

95

'I do work for the Major, but I don't tell everyone my business.'

Five minutes later, watching as he put on his outdoor shoes, she realized again how little she knew about him. He had told her that he had been in care, but not why or where. Sometimes he told her that he lived in a squat, sometimes that he was staying with the Major. But if he was private, so was she – and so was everyone at the Dupayne. She thought, *We work together, we see each other frequently, sometimes every day, we talk, we confer, we have a common purpose. And at the heart of each of us is the unknowable self.*

9

It was Dr Neville Dupayne's last domiciliary visit of the day and the one he most dreaded. Even before he had parked and locked the car he had begun to steel himself for the ordeal of meeting Ada Gearing's eyes, eyes that would gaze into his with mute appeal as soon as she opened the door. The few steps up to the first-floor walkway seemed as wearying as if he were mounting to the top storey. There would be a wait at the door; there always was a wait. Albert, even in his catatonic phase, responded to the sound of the front doorbell, sometimes with a terror which held him shaking in his armchair, sometimes by rising from it with surprising speed, shoving his wife aside to get to the door first. Then it would be Albert's eyes which would meet his; old eyes which yet were able to blaze with such differing emotions as fear, hatred, suspicion, hopelessness.

Tonight he almost wished it would be Albert. He passed down the walkway to the middle door. There was a peephole in it, two security locks and a metal mesh nailed to the outside of the single window. He supposed that this was the cheapest way of ensuring protection but it had always worried him. If Albert set the place on fire, the door would be the only exit. He paused before ringing. It was darkening into evening. How quickly, once the clocks were put back, the daylight hours faded and darkness stealthily took over. The lights had come on along the walkways and, looking up, he saw the huge block towering like a great cruise ship anchored in darkness.

He knew that it wasn't possible to ring quietly; even so his finger was gentle on the bell. This evening's wait wasn't longer than usual. She would have to ensure that Albert was settled in his chair, calmed after the shock of the ring. After a minute he heard the rasp of the bolts and she opened the door to him. At once he gave her an almost imperceptible shake of the head and stepped inside. She relocked and bolted the door.

Following her down the short passage, he said, 'I'm sorry. I rang the hospital before I left and there's no vacancy yet in the special unit. But Albert is top of the waiting list.'

She said, 'He's been there, Doctor, for eight months now. I suppose we're waiting for someone to die.'

'Yes,' he said. 'For someone to die.'

It was the same conversation they had had for the last six months. Before going into the sitting-room, and with her hand on the doorknob, he asked, 'How are things?'

She had always had this reluctance to discuss her husband while he sat there, apparently either not hearing or not caring. She said, 'Quiet today. Been quiet all the week. But last Wednesday he got out, the day the woman social worker called, and he was through the door before I could lay a hand on him. He's quick on his feet when the mood takes him. He was down the steps and off down the high street before we could catch him. And then there was a struggle. People look at you. They don't know what you're doing hauling an old man about like that. The social worker tried to persuade him, talking gentle like, but he wasn't going to listen to her. That's what terrifies me, that one day he'll get out on the road and be killed.'

And that, he thought, was exactly what she did fear. The irrationality of it provoked in him a mixture of sadness and irritation. Her husband was being sucked deep into the quagmire of Alzheimer's. The man she had married had become a confused and sometimes violent stranger, unable to give her either companionship or support. She was physically exhausted with trying to care for him. But he was her husband. She was terrified by the worry that he might get out on the road and be killed.

The small sitting-room with the flowered curtains with the patterned side hung against the panes, the shabby furniture, the solid old-fashioned gas fire, would have looked much the same when the Gearings first took the flat. But now there was a television set in the corner with a wide screen and a video recorder beneath it. And he knew that the bulge in Mrs Gearing's apron pocket was her mobile phone.

He drew up his customary chair between them. He had allocated the usual half hour to spend with them. He had brought no good news and there was nothing he could offer to help them other than that which was already being done, but at least he could give them his time. He would do what he always did, sit quietly as if he had hours to spend, and listen. The room was uncomfortably hot. The gas fire hissed out a fierce heat, scorching his legs and drying his throat. The air smelt, a sour-sweet stink compounded of stale perspiration, fried food, unwashed clothes and urine. Breathing it he could imagine that he detected each separate smell.

Albert was sitting motionless in his chair. The gnarled hands were clenched tightly over the edges of the arm-rests. The eyes looking into his were narrowed with an extraordinary malevolence. He was wearing carpet slippers, baggy tracksuit trousers in navy blue with a white stripe down each leg, and a pyjama jacket covered with a long grey cardigan. He wondered how long it had taken Ada and the daily helper to get him into his clothes.

He said, knowing the futility of the question, 'How are you managing? Does Mrs Nugent still come?'

And now she was talking freely, no longer worrying whether her husband could understand. Perhaps she was beginning to realize at last how pointless were those whispered consultations outside the door.

'Oh yes, she comes. It's every day now. I couldn't do without her. It's a worry, Doctor. When Albert is difficult he says terrible things to her, hurtful things about her being black. They're horrible really. I know he doesn't mean it, I know it's because he's ill, but she shouldn't have to hear it. He never used to be like that. And she's so good, she doesn't take it amiss. But it upsets me. And now that woman next door, Mrs Morris, has heard him carrying on. She said, if the welfare get to hear about it, we'll be taken to court for being racist and fined. She says they'll take Mrs Nugent away and they'll see we don't get anyone else, black or white. And perhaps Mrs Nugent'll get fed up anyway and go somewhere where she doesn't have to hear such things. I can't say as how I'd blame her. And Ivy Morris is right. You can get taken to court for being a racist. It's in the papers. How am I going to pay the fine? The money's tight enough as it is.'

People of her age and class were too proud to complain of their poverty. The fact that, for the first time, she had mentioned money showed the depth of her anxiety. He said firmly, 'No one's going to take you to court. Mrs Nugent's a sensible and experienced woman. She knows that Albert's ill. Would you like me to have a word with Social Services?'

'Would you, Doctor? It might be better coming from you. I've got so nervous about it now. Every time I hear a knock on the door I think it's the police.'

'It won't be the police.'

He stayed for another twenty minutes. He listened, as he had so many times before, to her distress that Albert would be taken from her care. She knew that she couldn't manage, but something – perhaps the memory of her marriage vows – was even stronger than the need for relief. He tried again to reassure her that life in the hospital special unit would be better for Albert, that he would receive care that couldn't be given at home, that she would be able to visit him whenever she wanted, that if he had been capable of understanding he would understand.

'Maybe,' she said. 'But would he forgive?'

What was the use, he thought, of trying to persuade her that she need feel no guilt? She was gripped always by those two dominant emotions, love and guilt. What power had he, bringing his secular and imperfect wisdom, to purge her of something so deep-seated, so elemental?

She made him tea before he left. She always made him tea. He didn't want it and he had to fight down impatience while she tried to persuade Albert to drink, coaxing him like a child. But at last he felt able to go.

He said, 'I'll ring the hospital tomorrow and let you know if there's any news.'

At the door she looked at him and said, 'Doctor, I don't think I can go on.'

They were the final words she spoke as the door closed between them. He stepped out into the chill of the evening and heard for the last time the rasp of the bolts.

IO

It was just after seven o'clock and in her small but immaculate kitchen Muriel Godby was baking biscuits. It had been her practice ever since taking up her post at the Dupayne to provide biscuits for Miss Caroline's tea when she was at the museum, and for the monthly meetings of the trustees. Tomorrow's meeting, she knew, was to be crucial, but that was no reason to vary her routine. Caroline Dupayne liked spiced biscuits made with butter, delicately crisp and baked to the palest brown. They had already been made and were now cooling on the rack. She began preparations for the florentines. These, she felt, were less appropriate for the trustees' tea; Dr Neville tended to prop his against his teacup so that the chocolate melted. But Mr Marcus liked them and would be disappointed if they didn't appear.

She set out the ingredients as carefully as if this were a televised demonstration: hazelnuts, blanched almonds, glacé cherries, mixed peel and sultanas, a block of butter, caster sugar, single cream and a bar of the best plain chocolate. As she chopped, she was visited by a mysterious and fugitive sensation, an agreeable fusion of mind and body which she had never experienced before coming to the Dupayne. It came rarely and unexpectedly and was felt as a gentle tingling of the blood. She supposed that this was happiness. She paused, her knife poised above the hazelnuts, and for a moment let it run its course. Was this, she wondered, what most people felt for most of their lives, even for part of their childhood? It had never been part of hers. The feeling passed and, smiling, she set again to work.

For Muriel Godby the childhood years up to the age of sixteen had been a confinement in an open prison, a sentence against which there was no appeal and for some offence never precisely explained. She accepted the parameters, mental and physical, of her incarceration; the semi-detached 1930s house in an insalubrious suburb of Birmingham, with its black mock-Tudor criss-cross of beams, its small patch of back garden, its high fences shielding the garden from the curiosity of neighbours. The limits extended to the comprehensive school to which she could walk in ten minutes through the municipal park with its mathematically precise flowerbeds, its predictable changes of plants: the spring daffodils, the summer geraniums, the dahlias of autumn. She had early learned the prison survival law of lying low and avoiding trouble.

Her father was the gaoler. That undersized precise little man with his self-important gait and the mild half-shameful sadism which prudence made him keep within bearable limits for his victims. She had seen her mother as a fellow inmate, but common misfortune hadn't bred either sympathy or compassion. There were things best left unsaid, silences which, both recognized, it would be catastrophic to break. Each cupped her misery in careful hands, each kept her distance as if fearful of contamination by the other's unspecified delinquency. Muriel survived by courage, silence and by her hidden inner life. The triumphs of her nightly fantasies were dramatic and exotic but she never pretended to herself that they were other than make-believe, useful expedients to make life more tolerable, but not indulgences to be confused with reality. There was a real world outside her prison and one day she would break free and inherit it.

She grew up knowing that her father loved only his elder daughter. By the time Simone was fourteen their mutual obsession had become so established that neither Muriel nor her mother questioned its primacy. Simone had the presents, the treats, the new clothes, the weekend outings she and her father took together. When Muriel had gone to bed in her small room at the back of the house, she would still hear the murmur of their voices, Simone's high half-hysterical laughter. Her mother was their servant, but without a servant's wage. Perhaps she too had ministered to their needs by her involuntary voyeurism.

Muriel was neither envious nor resentful. Simone had nothing she wanted. By the time she was fourteen Muriel knew the date of her release: her sixteenth birthday. She had then only to ensure that she could support herself adequately and no law could compel her to return home. Her mother, perhaps at last realizing that she had no life, slipped out of it with the unobtrusive incompetence which had characterized her role as housewife and mother. Mild pneumonia need not be a killer except to those who have no wish to fight it. Seeing her mother coffined in the undertaker's chapel of rest – a euphemism which filled Muriel with an impotent fury – she had looked down on the face of an unknown woman. It wore, to her eyes, a smile of secret content. Well, that was one way of breaking free, but it wouldn't be hers.

Nine months later, on her sixteenth birthday, she left, leaving Simone and her father to their self-indulgent symbiotic world of conspiratorial glances, brief touches and childhood treats. She suspected, but neither knew nor cared, what they did together. She gave no warning of her intention. The note she left for her father, placed carefully in the centre of the mantelpiece, merely stated that she had left home to get a job and look after herself. She knew her assets but was less perceptive about her disabilities. She offered to the market her six respectable O levels, her high skills in shorthand and typing, a brain open to developing technology, intelligence and an orderly mind. She went to London with money she had been hoarding since her fourteenth birthday, found a bed-sitting-room she could afford, and looked for a job. She was prepared to offer loyalty, dedication and energy and was aggrieved when these attributes were less valued than more enticing gifts – physical attractiveness, gregarious good humour and a will to please. She obtained work easily but no job lasted long. Invariably she left by common consent, too proud to protest or seek redress when the not unexpected interview took place and her employer suggested that she would be happier in a post which made better use of her qualifications. Employers gave her good references, particularly lauding her virtues. The reasons for her leaving were tactfully obscured; indeed they hardly knew quite what they were.

She never saw or heard from her father or sister again. Twelve years after she had left home both were dead, Simone by suicide and her father two weeks later from a heart attack. The news, in a letter from her father's solicitor, had taken six weeks to reach her. She felt only the vague and painless regret that the tragedy of others can occasionally induce. That Simone should choose to die so dramatically evoked only surprise that her sister had found the necessary courage. But their deaths changed her life. There was no other living relation and she inherited the family house. She didn't return to it, but instructed an estate agent to sell the property and everything in it.

And now she was free of her life in bed-sitting rooms. She found a square brick-built cottage in South Finchley, down one of those half-rural lanes which still persist, even in the inner suburbs. With its small ugly windows under a high roof, it was unattractive but solidly built and reasonably private. In front there was parking space for the car she was now able to afford. At first she camped in the property while, week by week, she sought items of furniture from second-hand shops, painted the rooms and made curtains.

Her life at work was less satisfactory, but she met the bad times with courage. It was a virtue she had never lacked. Her penultimate job, that of typist–receptionist at Swathling's, had been a comedown in status. But the job offered possibilities and she had been interviewed by Miss Dupayne who had hinted that she might in time need a personal assistant. The job had been a disaster. She despised the students, castigating them as stupid, arrogant and mannerless, the spoilt brats of the *nouveaux riches*. Once they had taken the trouble to notice her, the dislike had been quickly returned. They found her officious, disagreeably plain and lacking the deference they expected from an inferior. It was convenient to have a focus for their discontents and a butt for their jokes. Few of them were naturally malicious, some even treated her with courtesy, but none stood out against the universal disparagement. Even the kindlier got used to referring to her as GG. It stood for Ghastly Godby.

Two years ago matters had come to a crisis. Muriel had found one of the students' pocket diary and had placed it in a drawer of the reception desk waiting to hand it over when the girl next called for her post. She had seen no reason to seek the owner out. The girl had accused her of deliberately withholding it. She had started screaming at her. Muriel had gazed at her with cold contempt; the dyed red hair sticking out in spikes, the gold stud at the side of the nose, the lipsticked mouth screaming obscenities. Snatching up the diary she had hissed her final words.

'Lady Swathling asked me to tell you she wants you in her office. I can tell you what for. You're due for the sack. You're not the kind of person the college wants on the reception desk. You're ugly and you're stupid and we'll be glad to see you go.'

Muriel had sat in silence and had then reached for her handbag. It was to be one more rejection. She had been aware of the approach of Caroline Dupayne. Now, looking up, she said nothing. It was the elder woman who spoke.

'I've just been with Lady Swathling. I think it's quite right for you to make a move. You're wasted in this job. I need a secretary–receptionist at the Dupayne Museum. The money won't be any more, I'm afraid, but there are real prospects. If you're interested I suggest you go to the office now and give in your notice before Lady Swathling speaks.'

And that is what Muriel had done. She had at last found a job in which she felt valued. She had done well. She had found her freedom. Without realizing it, she had also found love.

II

It was after nine o'clock before Neville Dupayne's last visit was completed and he drove to his flat overlooking Kensington High Street. In London he used a Rover when widely spaced appointments or a complicated journey by public transport made a car necessary. The one he loved, his red 1963 E-type Jaguar, was kept in the lock-up garage at the museum to be collected as usual at six o'clock on Friday night. It was his practice to work late from Monday to Thursday if necessary so that he could be free for the weekend out of London, which had become essential to him. He had a resident's parking permit for the Rover but there was the usual frustrating drive round the block before he was able to edge the car into a vacant space. The erratic weather had changed again during the afternoon and now he walked the hundred yards to his flat through a steady drizzle of rain.

He lived on the top floor of a large post-war block, architecturally undistinguished but well maintained and convenient; its size and bland conformity, even the serried rows of identical windows like blank anonymous faces, seemed to guarantee the privacy he craved. He never thought of the flat as home, a word which held no particular associations for him and which he would have found it difficult to define. But he accepted that it was a refuge, its essential peace emphasized by the constant muted rumble of the busy street five storeys below which came to him, not disagreeably, as the rhythmic moaning of a distant sea. Relocking the door behind him and resetting the alarm, he scooped up the scattered letters on the carpet, hung up his damp coat, dumped his briefcase and, entering the sitting room, drew down the wooden slatted blinds against the lights of Kensington.

The flat was comfortable. When he had bought it some fifteen years previously, after his move to London from the Midlands following the final breakdown of his marriage, he had taken trouble selecting the minimum items necessary of well-designed modern furniture and subsequently had found no need to change his initial choice. Occasionally he liked to listen to music and the stereo equipment was up-to-date and expensive. He had no great interest in technology, requiring only that it should work efficiently. If a machine broke down he replaced it with a different model since money was less important than saving time and avoiding the frustration of argument. The telephone he hated. It was in the hall and he seldom answered it, preferring to listen to the recorded messages every evening. Those who might need him urgently, including his secretary at the hospital, had his mobile number. No one else did, not even his daughter and his siblings. The significance of these exclusions, when it occurred to him, left him unworried. They knew where to find him.

The kitchen was as unused as when it was first re-modelled after he bought the flat. He fed himself con-scientiously but took little pleasure in cooking and depended largely on made-up meals bought from the high street supermarkets. He had opened the refrigerator and was deciding whether he would prefer fish pie with frozen peas to moussaka, when the doorbell rang. The sound, loud and consistent, came so rarely that he felt as shocked as if there had been a hammering on his door. Few people knew where he lived and none would arrive without warning. He went to the door and pressed the intercom button, hoping that this was a stranger who had selected the wrong bell. It was with a sinking of his spirits that he heard his daughter's loud peremptory voice.

'Dad, it's Sarah. I've been ringing you. I've got to see you. Didn't you get the messages?'

'No, I'm sorry. I'm just in. I haven't listened to the answerphone. Come on up.'

He released the front door and waited for the whine of the lift. It had been a difficult day and tomorrow he would be faced with a different but equally intractable problem, the future of the Dupayne Museum. He needed time to rehearse his tactics, the justification for his reluctance to sign the new lease, the arguments he would have to muster effectively to combat the resolution of his brother and sister. He had hoped for a peaceful evening in which he might find the will to reach a final decision, but he was unlikely to get that peace now. Sarah wouldn't be here if she were not in trouble.

As soon as he opened the door and took her umbrella and raincoat from her, he saw that the trouble was serious. From childhood Sarah had never been able to control, let alone disguise, the intensity of her feelings.

Her rages from her babyhood had been passionate and exhausting, her moments of happiness and excitement were frenetic, her despairs infected both parents with her gloom. Always how she looked, what she wore, betrayed the tumult of her inner life. He remembered one evening – was it five years ago? – when she had found it convenient for her latest lover to call for her at this address. She had stood where she stood now, her dark hair intricately piled, her cheeks flushed with joy. Looking at her he had been surprised to find her beautiful. Now her body seemed to have slumped into premature middle age. Her hair, unbrushed, was tied back from a face sullen with despair. Looking at her face, so like his own and yet so mysteriously different, he saw her unhappiness in the dark shadowed eyes which seemed focused on her own wretchedness. She dumped herself in an armchair.

He said, 'What would you like? Wine, coffee, tea?'

'Wine will do. Anything you've got opened.'

'White or red?'

'Oh, for God's sake, Dad! What does it matter? All right, red.'

He took the nearest bottle from the wine cupboard and brought it in with two glasses. 'What about food? Have you eaten? I'm just about to heat up some supper.'

'I'm not hungry. I've come because there are things we have to settle. First of all, you may as well know, Simon has walked out.'

So that was it. He wasn't surprised. He had only met her live-in lover once and had known then, with a rush of confused pity and irritation, that it was another mistake. It was the recurring pattern of her life. Her loves had always been consuming, impulsive and intense, and now that she was nearing thirty-four, her need of a loving commitment was fuelled by increasing desperation. He knew that there was nothing he could say which would give her comfort and that anything he said would be resented. His job had deprived her in adolescence of his interest and concern and the divorce had afforded her a new opportunity for grievance. All she ever demanded of him now was practical help.

He said, 'When did this happen?'

'Three days ago.'

'And it's final?'

'Of course it's final, it's been final for the last month but I didn't see it. And now I've got to get away, really away. I want to go abroad.'

'What about the job, the school?'

'I've chucked that.'

'You mean you've given a term's notice?'

'I haven't given any notice. I've walked out. I wasn't going back to that bloody bear garden to have the kids sniggering about my sex life.'

'But would they? How could they know?'

'For God's sake, Dad, live in the real world! Of course they know. They make it their business to know. It's bad enough being told that I wouldn't be a teacher if I was fit for anything else without having sexual failure flung in my face.'

'But you teach middle school. They're children.'

'These kids know more about sex at eleven than I did at twenty. And I was trained to teach, not to spend half my time filling in forms and the rest trying to keep order among twenty-five disruptive, foul-mouthed, aggressive kids with absolutely no interest in learning. I've been wasting my life. No more.'

'They can't all be like that.'

'Of course they're not, but there are enough of them to make a class unteachable. I've got two boys who've been diagnosed as needing psychiatric in-patient treatment. They've been assessed but there's no place for them. So what happens? They're thrown back at us. You're a psychiatrist. They're your responsibility, not mine.'

'But walking out! That isn't like you. It's hard on the rest of the staff.'

'The Head can cope with that. I've had precious little support from him these last few terms. Anyway, I've left.'

'And the flat?' They had, he knew, bought it jointly. He had loaned her the capital for the deposit and he supposed that it was her salary that had paid the mortgage.

She said, 'We'll sell it of course. But there's no hope now of dividing the profit. There won't be any profit. That hostel they're putting up opposite for homeless juvenile offenders has put a stop to that. Our solicitor should have found out about it, but it's no good suing him for negligence. We need to get the place sold for what we can get. I'm leaving that to Simon. He'll get on with it efficiently because he knows he's legally liable with me for the mortgage. I'm getting out. The thing is, Dad, I need money.'

He asked, 'How much?'

'Enough to live comfortably abroad for a year. I'm not asking you for it – at least not directly. I want my share of the profits from the museum. I want it closed. Then I can take a decent loan from you – about twenty thousand – and pay you back when the place has shut down. We're all entitled to something, aren't we, I mean, the trustees and the grandchildren?'

He said, 'I don't know how much. Under the trust deed all the valuable objects, including the pictures, will be offered to other museums. We get a share of what's left once it's sold. It could be as much as twenty thousand each, I suppose. I haven't calculated.'

'It'll be enough. There's a trustees' meeting tomorrow, isn't there? I phoned Aunt Caroline to enquire. You don't want it to go on, do you? I mean, you've always known that Grandad cared more for it than he did for you or any of his family. It was always a private indulgence. It isn't doing any good anyway. Uncle Marcus may think he can make a go of it, but he can't. He'll just keep spending money until he'll have to let it go. I want you to promise not to sign the new lease. That way I can borrow from you with a clear conscience. I'm not taking money from you otherwise, money I can't hope to pay back. I'm sick of being indebted, of having to be grateful.'

'Sarah, you don't have to be grateful.'

'Don't I? I'm not stupid, Dad. I know handing out cash is easier for you than loving me, I've always accepted that. I knew when I was a kid that love is what you gave to your patients, not to Mummy or me.'

It was an old complaint and he had heard it many times before, both from his wife and from Sarah. He knew there was some truth in it, but not as much as she and her mother had actually believed. The grievance had been too obvious, too simplistic and too convenient. The relationship between them had been subtler and far more complex than this easy psychological theorizing could explain. He didn't argue, but waited.

She said, 'You want the museum closed, don't you? You've always known what it did to you and Granny. It's the past, Dad. It's about dead people and dead years. You've always said that we're too obsessed with our past, with hoarding and collecting for the sake of it. For God's sake, can't you stand up for once to your brother and sister?'

The bottle of wine had remained unopened. Now, with his back to her, steadying his hand by an act of will, he uncorked the Margaux and poured two glasses. He said, 'I think the museum should be closed and I have it in mind to say so at tomorrow's meeting. I don't expect the others to agree. It's bound to be a battle of wills.'

'What do you mean, have it in mind? You sound like Uncle Marcus. You must know by now what you want to happen. And you don't have to do anything, do you? You don't even have to convince them. I know you'd rather do anything than face a family quarrel. All you've got to do is to refuse to sign the new lease by the due date and keep out of their way. They can't force you.'

Taking the wine over to her, he said, 'How soon do you need the money?'

'I want it within days. I'm thinking of flying to New

117

Zealand. Betty Carter is there. I don't suppose you remember her, but we trained together. She married a New Zealander and she's always been keen for me to take a holiday with them. I thought of starting in the South Island and then maybe moving on to Australia and then California. I want to be able to live for a year without having to work. After that I can decide what I want to do next. It won't be teaching.'

'You can't do anything in a hurry. There may be visa requirements, plane seats to be booked. It isn't a good time to leave England. The world couldn't be more unsettled, more dangerous.'

'You could argue that's a case for getting out and going as far as you can. I'm not worried about terrorism here or anywhere else. I've got to leave. I've been a failure at everything I've touched. I think I'll go mad if I have to stay another month in this bloody country.'

He could have said, *But you'll be taking yourself with you.* He didn't. He knew what scorn – and it would be justifiable scorn – she would pour on that platitude. Any agony aunt in any woman's magazine could have done as much for her as he was doing. But there was the money. He said, 'I could let you have a cheque tonight if you want it. And I'll stand firm on closing the museum. It's the right thing to do.'

He sat opposite her. They didn't look at each other, but at least they were sipping wine together. He was swept with a sudden yearning towards her so strong that, had they been standing, he might impulsively have moved to take her into his arms. Was this love? But he knew that it was something less iconoclastic and disturbing, something with which he could deal. It was that mixture of pity and guilt which he had felt for the Gearings. But he had made a promise and it was one he knew he would have to keep. He knew, too, and the realization came in a wave of self-disgust, that he was glad she would be moving. His over-burdened life would be easier with his only child at the other end of the world.

12

The time of the trustees' meeting on Wednesday 30 October – three o'clock – was arranged, so Neville understood, to suit Caroline, who had morning and evening commitments. It didn't suit him. He was never at his liveliest after lunch and it had meant rearranging his afternoon domiciliary visits. They were to meet in the library on the first floor as they usually did on these rare occasions when, as trustees, they had business to transact. With the room's rectangular central table, the three fixed lights under parchment shades, it was the obvious place, but it was not the one he would have chosen. He had too many memories of entering it as a child summoned by his father, his hands clammy and his heart thudding. His father had never struck him; his verbal cruelty and undisguised contempt for his middle child had been a more sophisticated abuse and had left invisible but lasting scars. He had never discussed their father with Marcus and Caroline except in the most general terms. They apparently had suffered less or not at all. Marcus had always been a self-contained, solitary and uncommunicative child, later brilliant at school and at university, and armed against the tensions of family life by an unimaginative self-sufficiency. Caroline, as the youngest and only daughter, had always been their father's favourite in so far as he was capable of demonstrating affection. The museum had been his life, and his wife, unable to compete and finding small consolation in her children, had opted out of the competition by dying before she was forty.

He arrived on time but Marcus and Caroline were there before him. He wondered if this was by prior arrangement. Had they discussed their strategy in advance? But of course they had; every manoeuvre in this battle would have been planned in advance. As he entered they were standing together at the far end of the room and now came towards him, Marcus carrying a black briefcase.

Caroline looked dressed for battle. She was wearing black trousers with an open-necked grey and white striped shirt in fine wool, a red silk scarf knotted at her throat, the ends flowing like a flag of defiance. Marcus, as if to emphasize the official importance of the meeting, was formally dressed for the office, the stereotype of an immaculate civil servant. Beside him Neville felt that his own shabby raincoat, the well-worn grey suit, inadequately brushed, made him look like a supplicant poor relation. He was, after all, a consultant; now without even the obligation of alimony, he wasn't poor. A new suit could well have been afforded if he hadn't lacked the time and energy to buy it. Now for the first time when meeting his siblings, he felt himself at a sartorial disadvantage; that the feeling was both irrational and demeaning made it the more irritating. He had only rarely seen Marcus in his non-working holiday clothes, the khaki shorts, the striped T-shirt or thick round-necked jersey he wore on vacations. So far from transforming him, the careful casualness had emphasized his essential conformity. Informally dressed he always looked to Neville's eyes a little ridiculous, like an over-grown boy scout. Only in his well-tailored formal suits did he appear at ease. He was very much at ease now.

Neville pulled off his raincoat, tossed it on a chair and moved across to the central table. Three chairs had been pulled out between the lights. At each place were a manila document folder and a glass tumbler. A carafe of water was set on a salver between two of the lights. Because it was the nearest, Neville moved to the single chair, then realized as he sat that he would be physically and psychologically disadvantaged from the start. But having sat he couldn't bring himself to change.

Marcus and Caroline took their places. Only by a swift glance did Marcus betray that the single chair had been intended for him. He put down the briefcase at his side. To Neville the table looked prepared for a viva voce examination. There could be no doubt which of them was the examiner; no doubt either who was expected to fail. The ceiling-high filled shelves with their locked glass seemed to bear down on him, bringing back his childish imagining that they were inadequately constructed and would break away from the wall, at first in slow motion, then in a thunder of falling leather, to bury him under the killing weight of the books. The dark recesses of the jutting piers at his back induced the same remembered terror of lurking peril. The Murder Room, which might have been expected to exert a more powerful if less personal terror, had evoked only pity and curiosity. As an adolescent he had stood looking in silent contemplation at those unreadable faces, as if the intensity of his gaze could somehow wrest from them some insight into their dreadful secrets. He would stare at Rouse's bland and stupid face. Here was a man who had offered a tramp a lift with the intention of burning him alive. Neville could imagine the gratitude with which the weary traveller had climbed into the car and to his death. At least Rouse had had the mercy to club or throttle him unconscious before setting him alight, but surely that had been expedience rather than pity. The tramp had been unacknowledged, unnamed, unwanted, still unidentified. Only in his terrible death had he gained a fleeting notoriety. Society, which had cared so little for him in life, had avenged him with the full panoply of the law.

He waited while Marcus, unhurried, opened his briefcase, took out his papers and adjusted his spectacles. He said, 'Thank you for coming. I've prepared three folders with the documents we need. I haven't included copies of the trust deed – the terms, after all, are well known to the three of us – although I have it in my briefcase if either of you wish to refer to it. The relevant paragraph for the present discussion is clause three. This provides that all major decisions regarding the museum, including the negotiation of a new lease, the appointment of senior staff and all acquisitions with a value of over £500 are to be agreed by the signature of all trustees. The present lease expires on fifteenth November of this year and its renewal accordingly requires our three signatures. In the event of the museum being sold or closed the trust provides that all pictures valued at more than £500 and all first editions shall be offered to named museums. The Tate has first refusal of the pictures and the British Library of the books and manuscripts. All remaining items are to be sold and the proceeds shared between the trustees then in office and all direct descendants of our father. That means the proceeds will be divided between we three, my son and his two children, and Neville's daughter. The clear intention of our father in establishing the family trust is, therefore, that the museum should continue in being.'

Caroline said, 'Of course it must continue in being. As a matter purely of interest, how much would we receive if it doesn't?'

'If we don't have our three signatures on the lease? I haven't commissioned a valuation so the figures are entirely my own estimate. Most of the exhibits left after the gifts are of considerable historic or sociological interest but probably not valuable on the open market. My estimate is that we would receive about £25,000 each.'

'Oh well, a useful sum, but hardly worth selling one's birthright for.'

Marcus turned a page in his dossier. 'I have provided a copy of the new lease as Appendix B. The terms except for the annual rent are unchanged in any significant respect. The term is for thirty years, the rent to be renegotiated every five. You'll see that the cost is still reasonable, indeed highly advantageous and far more favourable than we could hope to obtain for such a property on the open market. This, as you know, is because the landlord is prohibited from granting the lease except to an organization concerned with literature or the arts.'

Neville said, 'We know all this.'

'I realize that. I thought it would be helpful to reiterate the facts before we begin decision-making.'

Neville fixed his eyes on the works of H.G. Wells on the shelf opposite. Did anyone, he wondered, read them now? He said, 'What we have to decide is how we deal with closure. I ought to say now that I have no intention of signing a new lease. It's time for the Dupayne Museum to close. I thought it right to make my position clear at the outset.'

There was a few seconds' silence. Neville willed himself to look into their faces. Neither Marcus nor Caroline was giving anything away, neither showing any surprise. This salvo was the beginning of a battle they had expected and were prepared for. They had little doubt of the outcome, only of the most effective strategy.

Marcus's voice, when it came, was calm. 'I think that decision is premature. None of us can reasonably decide on the future of the museum until we have considered whether, financially, we can continue. How, for example, the cost of the new lease can be met and what changes are necessary to bring this museum into the twenty-first century.'

Neville said, 'As long as you realize that further discussion is a waste of time I'm not acting impulsively. I've been thinking this over since Father died. It's time for the museum to close and the exhibits to be distributed elsewhere.'

Neither Marcus nor Caroline replied. Neville made

no further protest. Reiteration would only weaken his case. Better let them talk and then simply and quickly restate his decision.

As if Neville hadn't spoken, Marcus went on, 'Appendix C sets out my proposals for the reorganizing and more effective funding of the museum. I have provided the accounts for last year, the figures for attendances and projected costing. You will see that I have proposed financing a new lease by the selling of a single picture, perhaps a Nash. This will be within the terms of the trust if the proceeds are totally committed to the more effective running of the museum. We can let one picture go without too great harm. After all, the Dupayne is not primarily a picture gallery. As long as we have a representative work of the major artists of the period, we can justify the gallery. We need then to look at staffing. James Calder-Hale is doing an efficient and useful job and may as well continue for the present, but I suggest that we shall eventually need a qualified curator if the museum is to develop. At present our staffing consists of James, Muriel Godby the secretary–receptionist, Tallulah Clutton in the cottage who does all except the heavy cleaning, and the boy Ryan Archer, part-time gardener and handyman. Then there are the two volunteers, Mrs Faraday who gives advice on the garden and grounds, and Mrs Strickland the calligrapher. Both are giving useful services.'

Caroline said, 'You might reasonably have included me on the list. I'm here at least twice a week. I'm virtually running the place since Father died. If there's any overall control it comes from me.'

Marcus said evenly, 'There's no effective overall control, that's the problem. I'm not underestimating what you do, Caroline, but the whole setup is essentially amateur. We have to start thinking professionally if we're going to make the fundamental changes we need to survive.'

Caroline frowned. 'We don't need fundamental changes. What we've got is unique. All right, it's small. It's never going to attract the public like a more comprehensive museum, but it was set up for a purpose and it fulfils it. From the figures you've produced here it looks as if you're hoping to attract official funds. Forget it. The Lottery won't give us a pound, why should it? And if it did we would have to supplement the grant, which would be impossible. The local authority is already hard pressed – all LAs are – and central government can't fund adequately even the great national museums, the V&A and the British Museum. I agree we've got to increase our income, but not by selling our independence.'

Marcus said, 'We're not going for public money. Not to the Government, not to the local authority, not to the Lottery. We wouldn't get it anyway. And we'd regret it if we did. Think of the British Museum: some five million in the red. The Government insists on a free admissions policy, funds them inadequately, they get into trouble and have to go back to the Government cap in hand. Why don't they sell off their immense surplus stock, charge reasonable admission fees for all except vulnerable groups and make themselves properly independent?'

Caroline said, 'They can't legally dispose of charitable gifts and they can't exist without support. I agree that we can. And I don't see why museums and galleries have to be free. Other cultural provision isn't – classical concerts, the theatre, dance, the BBC – assuming you think the Beeb still produces culture. And don't think of letting the flat, by the way. That's been mine since Father died and I need it. I can't live in a bed-sit at Swathling's.'

Marcus said calmly, 'I wasn't thinking of depriving you of the flat. It's unsuitable for exhibits and the access by one lift or through the Murder Room would be inconvenient. We're not short of space.'

'And don't think, either, of getting rid of Muriel or Tally. They both more than earn their inadequate salaries.'

'I wasn't thinking of getting rid of them. Godby in particular is too efficient to lose. I'm giving thought to some extended responsibilities for her – without, of course, interfering with what she does for you. But we need someone more sympathetic and welcoming on the front desk. I thought of recruiting a graduate as secretary–receptionist. One with the necessary skills, naturally.'

'Oh, come off it, Marcus! What sort of graduate? One from a basket-weaving university? You'd better be sure she's literate. Muriel deals with the computer, the internet and the accounts. Find a graduate who can do all that on her wages and you'll be bloody lucky.'

Neville had said nothing during this exchange. The adversaries might be turning on each other but essentially they had the same aim: to keep the museum going. He would wait his chance. He was surprised, not for the first time, how little he knew his siblings. He had never believed that being a psychiatrist gave him a passkey to the human mind, but no two minds were more closely barred to him than the two which shared with him the spurious intimacy of consanguinity. Marcus was surely more complicated than his carefully controlled bureaucratic exterior would suggest. He played the violin to near professional standard; that must mean something. And then there was his embroidery. Those pale, carefully-tended hands had peculiar skills. Watching his brother's hands, Neville could picture the long manicured fingers in a moving montage of activity: penning elegant minutes on official files, stopping the violin strings, threading his needles with silk, or moving as they did now over the methodically prepared papers. Brother Marcus with his boring conventional suburban house, his ultra-respectable wife who had probably never given him an hour's anxiety, his successful surgeon son now carving out a lucrative career in Australia. And Caroline. When, he wondered, had he ever begun to know what lay at the core of her life? He had never visited the school. He despised what he thought it stood for – a privileged preparation for a life of indulgence and idleness. Her life there was a mystery to him. He suspected that her marriage had disappointed her, but for eleven years it had endured. What now was her sexual life? It was difficult to believe that she was celibate as well as solitary. He was aware of weariness. His legs began a spasmodic juddering of tiredness and it was difficult to keep his eyes open. He willed himself into wakefulness and heard Marcus's even and unhurried voice.

'The investigations I have carried out during the last month led me to one inescapable conclusion. If it is to survive, the Dupayne museum must change, and change fundamentally. We can no longer continue as a small specialized repository of the past for a few scholars, researchers or historians. We have to be open to the public and see ourselves as educators and facilitators, not merely guardians of the long-dead decades. Above all, we must become inclusive. The policy has been set out by the government, in May 2000, in its publication *Centres for Social Change: Museums, Galleries and Archives for All*. It sees mainstreaming social improvement as a priority and states that museums should – and here I quote – *identify the people who are socially excluded . . . engage them and establish their needs . . . develop projects which aim to improve the lives of people at risk of social exclusion*. We have to be seen as an agent of social change.'

And now Caroline's laughter was both sardonic and genuinely full-throated. 'My God, Marcus, I'm astonished you never became head of a major Department of State! You've got all it takes. You've swallowed the whole contemporary jargon in one glorious gulp. What are we supposed to do? Go down to Highgate and Hampstead and find out what groups of people are not flattering us with their attendance? Conclude that we have too few unmarried mothers with two children, gays, lesbians, small shopkeepers, ethnic minorities? And then what do we do? Entice them in with a roundabout on the lawn for the kids, free cups of tea and a balloon to take away? If a museum does its job properly the people who are interested will come, and they won't only be one class. I was at the British Museum last week with a group from school. At five-thirty people of every possible kind were pouring out – young, old, prosperous-looking, shabby, black, white. They visit because the museum is free and it's magnificent. We can't be either, but we can go on doing what we have been doing well since Father founded us. For God's sake let's continue to do just that. It will be difficult enough.'

Neville said, 'If the pictures go to other galleries, nothing will be lost. They'll still be on public display. People will still be able to see them, probably far more people.'

Caroline was dismissive. 'Not necessarily. Highly unlikely, I should think. The Tate has thousands of pictures they haven't the space to show. I doubt whether either the National Gallery or the Tate will be much interested in what we have to offer. It may be different for the smaller provincial galleries but there's no guarantee they'll want them. The pictures belong here. They're part of a planned and coherent history of the inter-war decades.'

Marcus closed his dossier and rested his clasped hands on the cover. 'There are two points I want to make before Neville has his say. The first is this. The terms of the trust are intended to ensure that the Dupayne Museum continues in being. We can take that as agreed. A majority of us wish it to continue. This means, Neville, that we don't have to convince you of our case. The onus is on you to convince us. The second point is this. Are you sure of your own motives? Shouldn't you face the possibility that what is behind this disagreement has nothing to do with rational doubts about whether the museum is financially viable or fulfils a useful purpose? Isn't it possible that you're motivated by revenge – revenge against Father – paying him back because the museum meant more to him than his family, more to him than you? If I'm right, then isn't that rather childish, some might think ignoble?'

The words, delivered across the table in Marcus's unemphatic monotone, apparently without rancour, a reasonable man propounding a reasonable theory, struck Neville with the force of a physical blow. He felt that he recoiled in his chair. He knew that his face must betray the strength and confusion of his reaction, an uncontrolled upsurge of shock, anger and surprise that could only confirm Marcus's allegation. He had expected a fight, but not that his brother would venture on this perilous battleground. He was aware that Caroline was leaning forward, her eyes intently on his face. They waited for him to reply. He was tempted to say that one psychiatrist in the family was enough, but desisted; it wasn't a moment for cheap irony. Instead, after a silence which seemed to last for half a minute, he found his voice and was able to speak calmly.

'Even if that were true – and it is no more true of me than of any other member of the family – it would make no difference to my decision. There is no point in continuing this discussion, particularly if it's going to degenerate into psychological profiling. I have no intention of signing the new lease. And now I need to get back to my patients.'

It was at that moment that his mobile phone rang. He had meant to turn it off for the duration of the meeting but had forgotten. Now he went over to his raincoat and delved in the pocket. He heard his secretary's voice. She had no need to speak her name.

'The police have been in touch. They wanted to ring you but I said I'd break the news. Mrs Gearing has tried to kill herself and her husband. An overdose of soluble aspirin and plastic bags over their heads.'

'Are they all right?'

'The paramedics pulled Albert through. He'll make it. She's dead.'

He said through lips which felt swollen and as hard as muscle, 'Thank you for telling me. I'll speak later.'

He replaced the phone and walked back stiffly to his chair, surprised that his legs could carry him. He was aware of Caroline's incurious gaze. He said, 'Sorry. That was to say that the wife of one of my patients has killed herself.'

Marcus looked up from his papers. 'Not your patient? His wife?'

'Not my patient.'

'As it wasn't your patient it seems unnecessary, surely, for anyone to have troubled you.'

Neville didn't reply. He sat with his hands clasped in his lap afraid that his siblings might see their trembling. He was possessed by a terrifying anger so physical that it welled up like vomit. He needed to spew it out as if in one foul-smelling stream he could rid himself of the pain

133

and the guilt. He remembered Ada Gearing's last words to him. *I don't think I can go on.* She had meant it. Stoical and uncomplaining, she had realized her limit. She had told him and he hadn't heard. It was extraordinary that neither Marcus nor Caroline should apparently be aware of this devastating tumult of self-disgust. He stared across at Marcus. His brother was frowning with concentration but was apparently little worried, beginning already to formulate argument and devise strategy. Caroline's face was more easily read: she was white with anger.

Frozen for a few seconds in their tableau of confrontation, none of them had heard the door open. Now a movement caught their attention. Muriel Godby was standing in the doorway carrying a laden tray. She said, 'Miss Caroline asked me to bring up the tea at four o'clock. Shall I pour it now?'

Caroline nodded and began pushing the papers aside to make room on the table. Suddenly Neville could stand no more. He got up and, grabbing his raincoat, faced them for the last time.

'I've finished. There's nothing more to be said. We're all wasting our time. You may as well start planning for closure. I'll never sign that lease. Never! And you can't make me.'

Fleetingly he saw in their faces a spasm of contemptuous disgust. He knew how they must see him, a rebellious child wreaking his impotent anger on the grown-ups. But he wasn't impotent. He had power, and they knew it.

He made blindly for the door. He wasn't sure how it happened, whether his arm caught the edge of the tray or whether Muriel Godby had moved in an instinctive protest to block his way. The tray spun out of her hands. He brushed past her, aware only of her horrified cry, an arc of steaming tea and the crash of falling china. Without looking back he ran down the stairs, past Mrs Strickland's astonished eyes as she glanced up from the reception desk, and out of the museum.

13

Wednesday 30 October, the day of the trustees' meeting, began for Tally like any other. She made her way before daylight to the museum and spent an hour on her normal routine. Muriel arrived early. She was carrying a basket and Tally guessed that she had, as usual, baked biscuits for the trustees' tea. Remembering her schooldays, Tally thought, *She's sucking up to teacher*, and felt a spasm of sympathy for Muriel which she recognized as a reprehensible mixture of pity and slight contempt.

Returning from the small kitchen at the rear of the hall, Muriel explained the day's programme. The museum would be open in the afternoon except for the library. Mrs Strickland was due to arrive but had been told to work in the picture gallery. She could provide relief on the reception desk when Muriel was serving the tea. There would be no need to call on Tally. Mrs Faraday had phoned to say that she had a cold and wouldn't be coming in. Perhaps Tally would keep an eye on Ryan when he condescended to arrive to ensure that he didn't take advantage of her absence.

Back at the cottage Tally was restless. Her usual walk on the Heath, which she took despite the drizzle, served only to leave her unusually tired without calming her mind or body. By midday she found that she wasn't hungry and decided to postpone her lunch of soup and scrambled eggs until Ryan had had his. Today he had brought half a small loaf of sliced brown bread and a tin of sardines. The key of the tin snapped when he tried to unfurl the lid and he had to fetch a can opener from the kitchen. It proved too much for the tin and, uncharacteristically, he bungled the task, spurting oil on to the table cloth. The smell of fish rose strongly, filling the cottage. Tally moved to open the door and a window, but the wind was rising now, spattering thin shafts of rain against the glass. Returning to the table, she watched as Ryan smeared the mangled fish onto the bread using the butter knife instead of the one she had set out for him. It seemed petty to protest, but suddenly she wished he would go. The scrambled egg had lost its appeal and instead she went into the kitchen and opened a carton of bean and tomato soup. Carrying the large mug and soup spoon back into the sitting-room, she joined Ryan at the table.

He said through a mouth half-stuffed with bread, 'Is it true that the museum is going to close and we'll all be chucked out?'

Tally managed to keep the note of concern from her voice. 'Who told you that, Ryan?'

'No one. It's something I overheard.'

'Ought you to have been listening?'

'I wasn't trying to. I was vacuuming the hall on Monday and Miss Caroline was at the desk speaking to Miss Godby. She said, "If we can't convince him on Wednesday, the museum will close, it's as simple as that. But I think he'll see sense." Then Miss Godby said something I couldn't hear. I only heard a few more words before Miss Caroline left. She said, "Keep it to yourself." '

'Then shouldn't you be keeping it to yourself?'

He fixed on Tally his wide innocent stare. 'Well, Miss Caroline wasn't speaking to me, was she? It's Wednesday today. That's why the three of them are coming this afternoon.'

Tally wrapped her hands round the mug of soup, but had not begun to drink it. She was afraid that the action of lifting the spoon to her lips would be difficult without betraying the shaking of her hands. She said, 'I'm surprised you could hear so much, Ryan. They must have been speaking very quietly.'

'Yeah, they were. Talking as if it was secret. I only heard the last words. But they never notice me when I'm cleaning. It's like I'm not there. If they did notice me, I expect they thought I wouldn't hear above the noise of the vacuum. Perhaps they didn't care whether I heard or not because it wouldn't matter. I'm not important.'

He spoke with no trace of resentment, but his eyes were on her face and she knew that she was expected to respond. There was a single crust of bread left on his plate and, still looking at her, he began crumbling it, then rolling the crumbs into small balls which he arranged round the rim.

She said, 'Of course you're important, Ryan, and so is the job you do here. You mustn't get ideas that you're not valued. That would be silly.'

'I don't care whether I'm valued. Not by the others, anyway. I get paid, don't I? If I didn't like the job I'd leave. Seems like I'll have to.'

For the moment, concern for him overcame her personal anxieties. 'Where will you go, Ryan? What sort of job will you be looking for? Have you any plans?'

'I expect the Major will have plans for me. He's a great one for plans. What'll you do, Mrs Tally?'

'Don't worry about me, Ryan. There are plenty of jobs these days for housekeepers. The advertisement pages of *The Lady* are full of them. Or I may retire.'

'But where will you live?'

The question was unwelcome. It suggested that somehow he knew of her great unspoken anxiety. Had someone been talking? Was this also something he had overheard? Snatches of imagined conversation came into her mind. *Tally's going to be a problem. We can't just chuck her out. She's got nowhere to go as far as I know.*

She said evenly, 'That will depend on the job, won't it? I expect I'll stay in London. But there's no point in deciding until we're certain what will happen here.'

He looked into her eyes and she could almost believe that he was sincere. 'You could come to the squat if you don't mind sharing. Evie's twins make a lot of noise and they smell a bit. It's not too bad – I mean, it suits me all right – but I'm not sure you'd like it.'

Of course she wouldn't like it. How could he seriously have imagined that she would? Was he trying, however inappropriately, to be genuinely helpful, or was he playing some kind of game with her? The thought was uncomfortable. She managed to keep her voice kindly, even a little amused. 'I don't think it will come to that, thank you, Ryan. Squatting is for the young. And don't you think you'd better get back to work? It gets dark

139

early and haven't you some dead ivy to cut down on the west wall?'

It was the first time she had ever suggested he should go, but he got up at once without apparent resentment. He scraped a few crumbs from the table-cloth, then he took his plate, knife and glass of water into the kitchen and came back with a damp tea-cloth with which he began scrubbing at the stains of fish oil.

She said, trying to keep the note of irritation from her voice, 'Leave that, Ryan. I'll need to wash the cloth.'

Dropping it on the table, he left. She sighed with relief when the door closed behind him.

The afternoon wore on. She busied herself with small tasks about the cottage, too restless to sit and read. Suddenly it was intolerable not to know what was happening, or, if she couldn't know, intolerable to be stuck here apart as if she could be ignored. It wouldn't be difficult to find an excuse for going to the museum to speak to Muriel. Mrs Faraday had mentioned that she could do with more bulbs to plant in the fringes of the drive. Could Muriel meet this from petty cash?

She reached for her raincoat and tied a plastic hood over her head. Outside the rain was still falling, a thin soundless drizzle, shining the leaves of the laurels and coldly pricking against her face. As she reached the door, Marcus Dupayne came out. He walked swiftly, his face set, and seemed not to see her although they passed within feet. She saw that he hadn't even closed the front door. It was a little ajar and, pushing it, she went into the hall. It was lit only by two lamps on the reception desk where Caroline Dupayne and Muriel were standing together, both putting on their coats. Behind them the hall was an unfamiliar and mysterious place of dark shadows and cavernous corners, with the central staircase leading up to a black nothingness. Nothing was familiar or simple or comforting. For a moment she had a vision of faces from the Murder Room, victims and killers alike descending in a slow and silent procession down from the darkness. She was aware that the two women had turned and were regarding her. Then the tableau broke up.

Caroline Dupayne said briskly, 'All right then, Muriel, I'll leave you to lock up and set the alarm.'

With a brief good-night directed at neither Muriel nor Tally, she strode to the door and was gone.

Muriel opened the key cupboard and took out the front door and security keys. She said, 'Miss Caroline and I have checked the rooms so you needn't stay. I had an accident with the tea tray, but I've cleared up the mess.' She paused, then added, 'I think you'd better start looking for a new job.'

'You mean just me?'

'All of us. Miss Caroline has said that she'll look after me. I think she has something in mind that I might be willing to consider. But yes, all of us.'

'What's happened? Have the trustees come to a decision?'

'Not officially, not yet. They've had a very difficult meeting.' She paused, then said with the hint of relish of one giving bad news, 'Dr Neville wants to close the museum.'

'Can he?'

'He can stop it being kept open. It's the same thing. Don't let anyone know I've told you. As I've said, it's not official yet but, after all, you've worked here for eight years. I think you have a right to be warned.'

Tally managed to keep her voice steady. 'Thank you for telling me, Muriel. No, I won't say anything. When do you think it will be definite?'

'It's as good as definite now. The new lease has to be signed by the fifteenth of November. That gives Mr Marcus and Miss Caroline just over two weeks to persuade their brother to change his mind. He's not going to change it.'

Two weeks. Tally murmured her thanks and made for the door. Walking back to the cottage she felt that her ankles were shackled, her shoulders bending under the physical weight. Surely they couldn't throw her out in two weeks? Reason quickly took hold. It wouldn't be like that, it couldn't be. There would surely be weeks, probably months, even a year, before the new tenants moved in. All the exhibits and the furniture, their destination settled, would have to be moved out first, and that couldn't be done in a hurry. She told herself that there would be plenty of time to decide what to do next. She didn't deceive herself that any new tenants would be happy for her to stay in the cottage. They would need it for their own staff, of course they would. Nor did she deceive herself that her capital sum would buy her even a one-bedroom flat in London. She had invested it carefully but, with the recession, it was no longer increasing. It would be sufficient for a down payment but how could she, over sixty and with no assured income, qualify for or manage to afford a mortgage? But others had survived worse catastrophes; somehow she would too.

14

Nothing significant happened on Thursday and nothing was officially said about the future. None of the Dupaynes appeared and there was only a thin stream of visitors who seemed to Tally's eyes a dispirited and isolated group who wandered around as if wondering what they were doing in the place. On Friday morning Tally opened the museum at eight o'clock as usual, silenced the alarm system and reset it, then switched on all the lights and began her inspection. As there had been few visitors the previous day, none of the first-floor rooms needed cleaning. The ground floor, which had the heaviest wear, was Ryan's job. Now there were only finger-marks on some of the display cabinets to be eradicated, particularly in the Murder Room, and table-tops and chairs to be polished.

Muriel arrived as usual promptly at nine o'clock and the museum day began. A group of six academics from Harvard were due to come by appointment. The visit had been arranged by Mr Calder-Hale who would show them round, but he had little interest in the Murder Room and it was usual for Muriel to be with a group for this part of the tour. Although he accepted that murder could indeed be both symbolic and representative of the age in which it was committed, he argued that this point could be made without dedicating the whole room to killers and their crimes. Tally knew that he refused to explain or elaborate on the exhibits to visitors and was adamant that the trunk should not be opened merely so that the supposed bloodstains could be examined by visitors avid for an additional shiver of horror.

Muriel had been at her most repressive. At ten o'clock she came to find Tally, who was behind the garage discussing with Ryan what shrubs ought to be cut back and whether Mrs Faraday, still away, should be phoned for advice. Muriel had said, 'I've got to leave the desk temporarily. I'm wanted in the Murder Room. If you'd only agree to have a mobile phone I could be sure of reaching you when you're not in the cottage.'

Tally's refusal to have a mobile phone was a long-standing grievance but she had stood firm. She abominated mobiles, not least because people had a habit of leaving them turned on in galleries and museums, and shouting meaningless chatter into them while she was on the bus sitting peacefully in her favourite seat at the front of the upper deck looking down on the passing show. She knew that her hatred of mobile phones went beyond these inconveniences. Irrationally but inescapably their ringing had replaced the insistent sound which had dominated her childhood and adult life, the jangling of the shop doorbell.

Sitting at the desk and issuing the small stick-on tickets that were Muriel's way of keeping a toll of numbers, and hearing the subdued buzz of voices from the picture gallery, Tally's heart lightened. The day reflected her mood. On Thursday the sky had pressed down on the city, impervious as a grey carpet, seeming to absorb its life and energy. Even on the edge of the Heath the air had tasted sour as soot. But by Friday morning the weather had changed. The air was still cold, but livelier. By midday a fresh wind was shaking the thin tops of the trees, moving among the bushes and scenting the air with the earthy smell of late autumn.

While she was at the desk, Mrs Strickland, one of the volunteer helpers, arrived. She was an amateur calligrapher and came to the Dupayne on Wednesday and Friday to sit in the library and write any new notices required, fulfilling a triple purpose since she was competent to answer most of the visitors' questions about the books and manuscripts as well as keeping a discreet eye on their comings and goings. At one-thirty Tally was called again to take over the desk while Muriel had her lunch in the office. Although the stream of visitors had thinned by then, the museum seemed livelier than it had for weeks. At two there had been a small queue. As she smiled a welcome and handed out change, Tally's optimism grew. Perhaps after all a way of saving the museum would be found. But still nothing had been said.

Shortly before five o'clock all the visitors had gone and Tally returned for the last time to join Muriel on their tour of inspection. In old Mr Dupayne's time this had been her sole responsibility, but a week after Muriel's arrival she had taken it on herself to join Tally, and Tally, instinctively knowing that it was in her interests not to antagonize Miss Caroline's protégée, had not objected. Together as usual they went from room to room, locking the doors of the picture gallery and library, looking down into the basement archives room, which was always kept brightly lit because the iron staircase could be dangerous. All was well. No personal possessions had been left by the visitors. The leather covers over the glass exhibit cases had been conscientiously replaced. The few periodicals set out on the library table in their plastic covers required only to be put together in a tidier display. They turned the lights out after them.

Back in the main hall and gazing up at the blackness above the stairs, Tally wondered as she often did at the peculiar nature of the silent emptiness. For her the museum after five became mysterious and unfamiliar, as public places often do when everyone human has departed and silence, like an ominous and alien spirit, steals in to take possession of the night hours. Mr Calder Hale had left in late morning with his group of visitors, Miss Caroline had left by four and shortly afterwards Ryan had collected his day's wages and set off on foot for Hampstead Underground station. Now only Tally, Muriel and Mrs Strickland remained. Muriel had offered to give Mrs Strickland a lift to the station and by five-fifteen, a little earlier than usual, she and her passenger had left. Tally watched as the car disappeared down the drive, then set off to walk through the darkness to her cottage.

The wind was rising now in erratic gusts stripping her mind of the optimism of the daylight hours. Battling against it down the east end of the house, she wished she had left the lights on in the cottage. Since Muriel's arrival she had taught herself to be economical, but the heating and lighting of the cottage were on a separate circuit from the museum and, although no complaint

147

had been made, Tally knew that the bills were scrutinized. And Muriel was, of course, right. Now more than ever it was important to save money. But approaching the dark mass she wished that the sitting-room light was shining out through the curtains to reassure her that this was still her home. At the door she paused to look out over the expanse of the Heath to the distant glitter of London. Even when darkness fell and the Heath was a black emptiness under the night sky, it was still her beloved and familiar place.

There was a rustle in the bushes and Tomcat appeared. Without any demonstration of affection, or indeed acknowledgement of her presence, he ambled up the path and sat waiting for her to open the door.

Tomcat was a stray. Even Tally had to admit that no one would be likely to acquire him by choice. He was the largest cat she had ever seen, a particularly rich ginger with a flat square face in which one eye was set a little lower than the other, huge paws on squat legs and a tail which he seemed doubtfully aware was his since he seldom used it to demonstrate any emotion other than displeasure. He had emerged from the Heath the previous winter and had sat outside the door for two days until, probably unwisely, Tally had put out a saucer of cat food. This he had eaten in hungry gulps and had then stalked through the open door into the sitting-room and taken possession of a fireside chair. Ryan, who had been working that day, had eyed him warily from the door.

'Come in, Ryan. He's not going to attack you. He's only a cat. He can't help his looks.'

'But he's so big. What are you going to call him?'

'I haven't thought. Ginger and Marmalade are too obvious. Anyway, he'll probably go away.'

'He doesn't look as if he means to go away. Aren't ginger cats all toms? You could call him Tomcat.'

Tomcat he remained.

The reaction of the Dupaynes and the museum staff, voiced as they encountered him over the next few weeks, had been unenthusiastic. Disapproval had spoken plainly in Marcus Dupayne's voice: 'No collar, which suggests he wasn't particularly valued. I suppose you could advertise for the owner but they'll probably be glad to have seen the last of him. If you keep him, Tally, try to ensure that he doesn't get into the museum.'

Mrs Faraday had viewed him with the disapproval of a gardener, merely saying that she supposed it would be impossible to keep him off the lawn, such as it was. Mrs Strickland had said, 'What an ugly cat, poor creature! Wouldn't it be kinder to put it down? I don't think you should encourage it, Tally. It might have fleas. You won't let it near the library, will you? I'm allergic to fur.'

Tally hadn't expected Muriel to be sympathetic, and nor was she. 'You'd better see that he doesn't get into the museum. Miss Caroline would strongly dislike it and I've enough to do without having to keep an eye on him. And I hope you're not thinking of installing a cat-flap in the cottage. The next occupant probably won't want it.'

Only Neville Dupayne seemed not to notice him.

Tomcat quickly established a routine. Tally would feed him when she first got up and he would then disappear, rarely to be seen again until the late afternoon, when he would sit outside the door waiting to be admitted for his second meal. After that he would again absent himself until nine o'clock, when he would demand to be let in, occasionally condescending to sit briefly on Tally's lap, and would then occupy his usual chair until Tally was ready for bed and would put him out for the night.

Opening the tin of pilchards, his favourite food, she found herself unexpectedly glad to see him. Feeding him was part of her daily routine and now, with the future uncertain, routine was a comforting assurance of normality and a small defence against upheaval. So, too, would her evening be. Shortly she would set off for her weekly evening class on the Georgian architecture of London. It was held at six o'clock each Friday at a local school. Every week, promptly at five-thirty, she would set out to cycle there, arriving early enough for a cup of coffee and a sandwich in the noisy anonymity of the canteen.

At half-past five, in happy ignorance of the horrors ahead, she put out the lights, locked the cottage door and, wheeling her bicycle from the garden shed, she switched on and adjusted its single light and set off cycling energetically down the drive.

BOOK TWO

The First Victim

Friday 1 November–Tuesday 5 November

I

The neat handwritten notice on the door of Room Five confirmed what Tally had already suspected from the absence of people in the corridor: the class had been cancelled. Mrs Maybrook had been taken ill but hoped to be there next Friday. Tonight Mr Pollard would be happy to include students in his class on Ruskin and Venice at six o'clock in Room Seven. Tally felt disinclined to cope even for an hour with a new subject, a different lecturer and unfamiliar faces. This was the final and minor disappointment in a day which had begun so promisingly with intermittent sunshine reflecting a growing hope that all might yet be well, but which had changed with the onset of darkness. A strengthening erratic wind and an almost starless sky had induced an oppressive sense that nothing would come to good. And now there was this fruitless journey. She returned to the deserted bicycle shed and unlocked the padlock on the wheel of her machine. It was time to get back to the familiar comfort of the cottage, to a book or a video, back to Tomcat's undemanding if self-serving companionship.

Never before had she found the ride home so tiring. It wasn't only that the gusting wind caught her unawares. Her legs had become leaden, the bicycle a heavy encumbrance which it took all her strength to push forward. It was with relief that, after waiting for a short procession of cars to pass along Spaniards Road, she crossed and began pedalling down the drive. Tonight it seemed endless. The darkness beyond the smudge of the lights was almost palpable, choking her breath. She bent low over the handlebars, watching the circle of light from her bicycle lamp sway over the tarmac like a will-o'-the-wisp. Never before had she found the darkness frightening. It had become something of an evening routine to walk through her small garden to the edge of the Heath, to savour the earthy smell of soil and plants intensified by the darkness and watch the distant shivering lights of London, more harshly bright than the myriad of pinpoints in the arc of the sky. But tonight she would not go out again.

Turning the final bend which brought the house into view, she braked to a sudden stop in a confusion of horror – sight, smell and sound, combining to make her heart leap and begin thudding as if it would explode and tear her apart. Something to the left of the museum was burning. Either the garage or the garden shed was on fire. And then for a few seconds the world disintegrated. A large car was driving fast towards her, the headlights blinding her eyes. It was upon her before she had time to move, even to think. Instinctively she clutched the handlebars and felt the shock of the impact. The bicycle spun from her grasp and she was being lifted in a confusion of light and sound and tangled metal to be flung on the grass verge under the bicycle's spinning wheels. She lay for a few seconds temporarily stunned and too confused to move. Even thought was paralysed. Then her mind took hold and she tried to shift the machine. She found to her surprise that she could, that arms and legs had power. She was bruised but not seriously hurt.

She got with difficulty to her feet, clutching the bicycle. The car had stopped. She was aware of a man's figure, of a voice that said, 'I'm so sorry. Are you all right?'

Even in that moment of stress his voice made its impact, a distinctive voice which in other circumstances she would have found reassuring. The face bending down to hers was distinctive too. Under the dim lights of the drive she saw him clearly for a few seconds, fair-haired, handsome, the eyes alight with a desperate appeal.

She said, 'I'm perfectly all right, thank you I wasn't actually riding and I fell on the grass.' She reiterated, 'I'm all right.'

He had spoken with passionate concern but now she couldn't miss his frantic need to get away. He barely waited to hear her speak before he was gone, running back to the car. At the car door he turned. Gazing back at the flames which were leaping higher, he called back to her, 'It looks as if someone's lit a bonfire.' And then, in a rush of sound, the car was gone.

In the confusion of the moment and her desperate anxiety to get to the blaze, to call the Fire Brigade, she didn't ask herself who he could be and why, with the museum shut, he was there at all. But his last words had a dreadful resonance. Speech and image fused in a moment of appalled recognition. They were the words of the murderer Alfred Arthur Rouse, walking calmly away from the blazing car in which his victim was burning to death.

Trying to mount, Tally found that the bicycle was useless. The front wheel had buckled. She flung the machine back on to the grass verge and began running towards the blaze, her thudding heart a drumbeat accompaniment to her pounding feet. She saw even before she reached the garage that here was the seat of the fire. The roof was still burning and the tallest flames came from the small group of silver birch trees to the right of the garage. Her ears were full of sound, the gushing wind, the hiss and crackle of the fire, the small explosions like pistol shots as the top branches cast off burning twigs like fireworks to flame for a moment against the dark sky before falling spent around her feet.

At the open door of the garage she stood rooted in terror. She cried aloud, 'Oh no! Dear God no!' The anguished cry was tossed aside by a renewed gust of wind. She could gaze only for a few seconds before closing her eyes, but the horror of the scene could not be blotted out. It was imprinted now on her mind and she knew it would be there forever. She had no impulse to dash in and try to save; there was no one there to save. The arm, stuck out of the open car door as stiff as the arm of a scarecrow, had once been flesh, muscle and veins and warm pulsing blood, but was so no longer. The blackened ball seen through the shattered windscreen, the fixed snarl of teeth gleaming whitely against the charred flesh, had once been a human head. It was human no more.

There came into her mind a sudden vivid picture, a drawing once seen in her books about London, of the heads of executed traitors stuck on poles above London Bridge. The memory brought a second of disorientation, a belief that this moment was not here and now but a hallucination coming out of the centuries in a jumble of real and imagined horror. The moment passed and she took hold of reality. She must telephone for the Fire Brigade, and quickly. Her body seemed a dead weight clamped to the earth, her muscles rigid as iron. But that too passed.

Later she had no memory of reaching the cottage door. She pulled off and dropped her gloves, found the cold metal of her bunch of keys in the inner pocket of her handbag and tried to cope with the two locks. As she manoeuvred the security key she told herself aloud, 'Be calm, be calm.' And now she was calmer. Her hands were still shaking but the dreadful pounding of her heart had quietened and she was able to open the door.

Once inside the cottage her mind became more lucid with every second. She still couldn't control the shaking in her hands but her thoughts at last were clear. First the Fire Brigade.

The 999 call was answered within seconds but the wait seemed interminable. Asked by a woman's voice what service she required, she said, 'Fire, and it's very urgent please. There's a body in a burning car.' When the second, male, voice came on the line she gave the necessary details calmly in response to his questions, then sighed with relief as she replaced the handset.

Nothing could be done for that charred body however speedily the fire engine arrived. But help would soon be here – officials, experts, the people whose job it was to cope. A terrible weight of responsibility and impotence would be lifted from her shoulders.

And now she must ring Marcus Dupayne. Underneath the telephone which stood on her small oak desk, she kept a card enclosed in a plastic cover with the names and numbers of people she might need to call in an emergency. Until a week ago Caroline Dupayne's name had headed the list, but it had been Miss Caroline herself who had instructed her that, now Marcus Dupayne had retired, he should be informed first of any emergency. She had rewritten the card in her clear and careful print and now she tapped out the number.

Almost immediately a woman's voice answered. Tally said, 'Mrs Dupayne? This is Tally Clutton from the Museum. Is Mr Dupayne there, please? I'm afraid there's been a terrible accident.'

The voice was sharp. 'What kind of accident?'

'The garage is on fire. I've rung the Fire Brigade. I'm waiting for them now. Can Mr Dupayne come urgently, please?'

'He's not here. He's gone to see Neville at his Kensington flat.' And now the voice was sharp. 'Is Dr Dupayne's Jaguar there?'

'In the garage. I'm afraid it looks as if there's a body in it.'

There was a silence. The phone could have been dead. Tally was unable even to detect Mrs Dupayne's breathing. She wanted the woman to get off the line so that she could phone Caroline Dupayne. This wasn't the way she had intended to break the news.

Then Mrs Dupayne spoke. Her tone was urgent, commanding, brooking no argument. 'See if my husband's car is there. It's a blue BMW. At once. I'll hang on.'

It was quicker to obey than to argue. Tally ran round the back of the house to the car-park behind its shield of shrubs and laurels. There was only one car parked, Dr Neville's Rover. Back at the cottage she snatched up the receiver. 'There's no blue BMW there, Mrs Dupayne.'

Again a silence, but this time she could detect a small intake of breath, like a sigh of relief. The voice was calmer now. 'I'll tell my husband as soon as he returns. We have people coming to dinner so he won't be long, I can't reach him on his mobile because he switches it off when he's driving. In the mean time, ring Caroline.' Then she rang off.

Tally hadn't needed telling. Miss Caroline must be told. Here she was luckier. The telephone at the college produced the answerphone and Tally waited only for the first words of Caroline's recorded message before replacing the receiver and trying the mobile. The response to her call was prompt. Tally was surprised at how calmly and succinctly she was able to give her message.

'It's Tally, Miss Caroline. I'm afraid there's been a terrible accident. Dr Neville's car and the garage are on fire and it's spreading to the trees. I called the Fire Brigade and I've tried to get Mr Marcus, but he's out.' She paused and then blurted out the almost unsayable: 'I'm afraid there's a body in the car!'

159

It was extraordinary that Miss Caroline's voice could sound so ordinary, so controlled. She said, 'Are you saying that someone's been burned to death in my brother's car?'

'I'm afraid so, Miss Caroline.'

And now the voice was urgent. 'Who is it? Is it my brother?'

'I don't know, Miss Caroline. I don't know.' Even to Tally's ears her voice was rising to a despairing wail. The receiver was slipping through her clammy hands. She transferred it to her left ear.

Caroline's voice was impatient. 'Are you there, Tally? What about the museum?'

'It's all right. It's just the garage and the surrounding trees. I've called the Fire Brigade.'

Suddenly Tally's control broke and she felt hot tears smarting her eyes and her voice dying. Up to now it had all been horror and fear. Now for the first time she felt a terrible grief. It wasn't that she had liked or even really known Dr Neville. The tears sprang from a deeper well than regret that a man was dead and had died horribly. They were, she knew, only partly a reaction to shock and terror. Blinking her eyes and willing herself to calmness, she thought, it's always the same when someone we know dies. We weep a little for ourselves; but this moment of profound sorrow was more than the sad acceptance of her own mortality, it was part of a universal grieving for the beauty, the terror and the cruelty of the world.

And now Caroline's voice had become firm, authoritative and strangely comforting. 'All right, Tally. You've done well. I'll be there. It'll take about thirty minutes but I'm on my way.'

Replacing the receiver, Tally stood for a moment without moving. Ought she to ring Muriel? If Miss Caroline had wanted her to be there, wouldn't she have said so? But Muriel would be hurt and angry if she wasn't called. Tally felt she couldn't face the prospect of Muriel's displeasure and she was, after all, the person who effectively ran the museum. The fire might well become local news over the weekend. Well, of course it would. News like that always spread. Muriel had a right to be told now.

She rang the number but got the engaged signal. Replacing the receiver, she tried again. If Muriel was already on the telephone, she would be unlikely to answer her mobile, but it was worth trying. After about four rings, she heard Muriel's voice. Tally only had time to say who was calling when Muriel said, 'Why are you ringing my mobile? I'm at home.'

'But you've been on the phone.'

'No I haven't.' There was a pause, then she said, 'Hang on, will you.' Then another pause, but briefer. Muriel said, 'The bedside phone wasn't properly replaced. What's the matter? Where are you?'

She sounded cross. Tally thought, she hates admitting even to a slight carelessness. She said, 'At the museum. My evening class was cancelled. I'm afraid I've terrible news. There's been a fire in the garage and Dr Neville's car was in it. And there's a body. Someone's been burnt to death. I'm afraid it's Dr Neville. I've called the Fire Brigade and I've told Miss Caroline.'

This time the silence was longer. Tally said, 'Muriel, are you there? Did you hear?'

Muriel said, 'Yes, I heard. It's appalling. Are you sure he's dead? Couldn't you pull him out?'

The question was ludicrous. Tally said, 'No one could have saved him.'

'I suppose it is Dr Neville?'

Tally said, 'Who else could it be in his car? But I'm not certain. I don't know who it is. I only know he's dead. Do you want to come? I thought you'd like to know.'

'Of course I'll come. I was the last one at the museum. I ought to be there. I'll be as quick as I can. And don't tell Miss Caroline that it's Dr Neville until we know for certain. It could be anyone. Who else have you told?'

'I rang Mr Marcus but he isn't home yet. His wife will tell him. Ought I to ring Mr Calder-Hale?'

Muriel's voice was impatient. 'No. Leave that to Miss Caroline when she arrives. I don't see what help he can be anyway. Just stay where you are. Oh, and Tally . . .'

'Yes, Muriel?'

'I'm sorry I was sharp with you. After the Fire Brigade arrives, stay in your cottage. I'll be as quick as I can.'

Tally replaced the handset and went to the door of the cottage. Above the crackling of the fire and the hissing of the wind she could hear the sound of approaching wheels. She ran to the front of the house and gave a cry of relief. The great engine, its headlights bright as searchlights, advanced like some gigantic fabled monster, illuminating house and lawn, shattering the fragile calm with its clamour. She ran frantically towards it, waving unnecessarily toward the leaping flames of the fire. A great weight of anxiety fell from Tally's shoulders. Help had at last arrived.

2

Assistant Commissioner Geoffrey Harkness liked to have the wide windows of his sixth-floor office uncurtained. So too did Adam Dalgliesh, a floor below. A year earlier had seen a reorganization of accommodation at New Scotland Yard and now Dalgliesh's windows faced the gentler, more rural scene of St James's Park, at this distance more a promise than a view. For him the seasons were marked by changes in the park; the spring budding of the trees, their luxuriant summer heaviness, the crisping yellow and gold of autumn, brisk walkers high-collared against the winter cold. In early summer the municipal deck-chairs would suddenly appear in an outbreak of coloured canvas, and half-clad Londoners would sit on the tailored grass like a scene from Seurat. On summer evenings, walking home through the park, he would occasionally hear the brass crescendo of an Army band, and see the guests for the Queen's garden parties, self-conscious in their unaccustomed finery.

Harkness's view provided none of this seasonal variety. After dark, whatever the season, the whole wall was a panorama of London, outlined and celebrated in light. Towers, bridges, houses and streets were hung with jewels, clusters and necklaces of diamonds and rubies, which made more mysterious the dark thread of the river. The view was so spectacular that it diminished

Harkness's office, making the official furniture, appropriate to his rank, look like a shabby compromise and his personal mementoes, the commendations and the ranked shields from foreign police forces, as naïvely pretentious as the trophies of childhood.

The summons, in the form of a request, had come from the Assistant Commissioner but Dalgliesh knew within a second of entering that this wasn't routine Met business. Maynard Scobie from Special Branch was there with a colleague unknown to Dalgliesh but whom no one troubled to introduce. More significantly, Bruno Denholm from MI5 was standing looking out of the window. And now he turned and took his place beside Harkness. The faces of the two men were explicit. The Assistant Commissioner looked irritated, Denholm had the wary but determined look of a man who was about to be outnumbered but who holds the heavier weapon.

Without preliminaries, Harkness said, 'The Dupayne Museum, a private museum of the inter-war years. In Hampstead on the borders of the Heath. Do you know it, by any chance?'

'I've been there once, a week ago.'

'That's helpful, I suppose. I've never heard of the place.'

'Not many people have. They don't advertise themselves, although that may change. They're under new management. Marcus Dupayne has taken over.'

Harkness moved to his conference table. 'We'd better sit. This may take some time. There's been a murder – more accurately a suspicious death which the Fire Investigation Officer thinks is murder. Neville Dupayne has been burnt to death in his Jag in a lock-up garage at the museum. It's his habit, apparently, to collect the car at six p.m. on Fridays and drive off for the weekend. This Friday someone may have lain in wait for him, thrown petrol over his head and set him alight. That seems to be the possibility. We'd like you to take on the case.'

Dalgliesh looked at Denholm. 'As you're here, I take it you have an interest.'

'Only marginally, but we would like the case cleared up as soon as possible. We only know the barest facts but it looks fairly straightforward.'

'Then why me?'

Denholm said, 'It's a question of getting it cleared up with the minimum of fuss. Murder always attracts publicity but we don't want the press getting too inquisitive. We have a contact there, James Calder-Hale, who acts as a kind of curator. He's ex-FCO and an expert on the Middle East. Speaks Arabic and one or two dialects. He retired on health grounds four years ago but he keeps in touch with friends. More importantly, they keep in touch with him. We get useful pieces of jigsaw from time to time and we would like this to continue.'

Dalgliesh said, 'Is he on the payroll?'

'Not exactly. Certain payments have occasionally to be made. Essentially he's a freelance, but a useful one.'

Harkness said, 'MI5 isn't happy about passing on this information but we insisted, on a need-to-know basis. It stays with you, of course.'

Dalgliesh said, 'If I'm to conduct a murder investigation, my two DIs have to be told. I take it you have no objection to my arresting Calder-Hale if he killed Neville Dupayne?'

Denholm smiled. 'I think you'll find he's in the clear. He's got an alibi.'

Has he indeed, thought Dalgliesh. MI5 had been quick on the job. Their first reaction to hearing of the murder had been to contact Calder-Hale. If the alibi stood up, then he could be eliminated and everyone would be happy. But the MI5 involvement remained a complication. Officially they might think it expedient to keep clear; unofficially they would be watching his every move.

He said, 'And how do you propose to sell this to the local Division? On the face of it, it's just another case. A suspicious death hardly justifies calling in the Special Investigation Squad. They might want to know why.'

Harkness dismissed the problem. 'That can be dealt with. We'll probably suggest that one of Dupayne's patients somewhere in the past was an important personage and we want his murderer found without embarrassment. No one is going to be explicit. The important thing is to get the case solved. The Fire Investigation Officer is still at the scene and so are Marcus Dupayne and his sister. There's nothing to stop you from starting now, I suppose.'

And now he had to telephone Emma. Back in his own office, he was swept by a desolation as keen as the half-remembered disappointments of childhood and bringing with it the same superstitious conviction that a malignant fate had turned against him, judging him unworthy of happiness. He had booked a corner table at

The Ivy for nine o'clock. They would have a late dinner and plan the weekend together. He had judged the timing meticulously. His meeting at the Yard might well last until seven o'clock; to book an earlier meal would have been to invite disaster. The arrangement was that he would call for Emma at her friend Clara's flat in Putney by eight-fifteen. By now he should be on his way.

His PA could cancel the restaurant booking but he had never used her to convey even the most routine message to Emma and wouldn't now; it was too close to betraying that part of his very private life which he was keeping inviolate. As he punched out the numbers on his mobile, he wondered if this call would be the last time he would hear her voice. The thought appalled him. If she decided that this latest frustration was the end, he was determined on one thing; their last meeting would be face to face.

It was Clara who answered his call. As soon as he asked for Emma, she said, 'I suppose this is a chuck.'

'I'd like to speak to Emma. Is she there?'

'She's having her hair done. She'll be back any minute. But don't bother to ring again. I'll tell her.'

'I'd rather tell her myself. Tell her I'll ring later.'

She said, 'I shouldn't bother. No doubt there's an insalubrious corpse somewhere awaiting your attention.' She paused, then said conversationally, 'You're a bastard, Adam Dalgliesh.'

He tried to keep the surge of anger out of his voice, but knew that it must have come across to her, sharp as a whiplash. 'Possibly, but I'd rather hear it from Emma herself. She's her own person. She doesn't need a keeper.'

She said, 'Goodbye, Commander. I'll let Emma know,' and put down the receiver.

And now anger at himself and not Clara was added to his disappointment. He had mishandled the call, had been unreasonably offensive to a woman, and that woman Emma's friend. He decided to wait a little before ringing back. It would give them and himself time to consider what best to say.

But when he did ring it was again Clara who answered. She said, 'Emma decided to go back to Cambridge. She left five minutes ago. I gave her your message.'

The call was over. Moving over to his cupboard to take out his murder bag, he seemed to hear Clara's voice. *I suppose there's an insalubrious corpse somewhere awaiting your attention.*

But first he must write to Emma. They phoned each other as seldom as possible and he knew that it was he who had tacitly established this reluctance to speak when apart. He found it both too frustrating and anxiety-inducing to hear her voice without seeing her face. There was always the worry that the timing of his call might be inconvenient, that he might fall into banalities. Written words had a greater permanence and, therefore, a greater chance of remembered infelicities, but at least he could control the written word. Now he wrote briefly, expressed his regret and disappointment simply, and left it to her to say if and when she would like to see him. He could go to Cambridge, if that would be more convenient. He signed it simply, *Adam*. Until now they had always met in London. It was she who had had the inconvenience of a journey and he had decided that she felt less committed in London, that there was an emotional safety in seeing him on what for her was mutual ground. He wrote the address with care, affixed a first class stamp and put the envelope in his pocket. He would slip it in the box at the post office opposite New Scotland Yard. Already he was calculating how long it would be before he could hope for a reply.

3

It was seven fifty five and Detective Inspector Kate Miskin and Detective Inspector Piers Tarrant were drinking together in a riverside pub between Southwark Bridge and London Bridge. This part of the riverside close to Southwark Cathedral was, as always, busy at the end of a working day. The full-sized model of Drake's *Golden Hinde* moored between the cathedral and the public house had long closed to visitors for the night but there was still a small group slowly circling its black oak sides and gazing up at the fo'c'sle as if wondering, as Kate herself often did, how so small a craft could have weathered that sixteenth-century journey round the world across tumultuous seas.

Both Kate and Piers had had a hectic and frustrating day. When the Special Investigation Squad was temporarily not in operation they were assigned to other divisions. There neither felt at home and both were aware of the unspoken resentment of colleagues who saw Commander Dalgliesh's special murder squad as uniquely privileged and who found subtle and occasionally more aggressive ways of making them feel excluded. By seven-thirty the noise of the pub had become raucous and they had quickly finished their fish and chips and, with no more than a nod at each other, had moved with their glasses out on to the almost deserted decking. They had stood here together often before but tonight Kate felt that there was something valedictory about this evening's silent moving out of the frenetic bar into the quiet autumn night. The jangle of voices behind them was muted. The strong river smell drove out the fumes of the beer and they stood together gazing out over the Thames, its dark pulsating skin slashed and shivered with a myriad lights. It was low water and a turgid and muddy tide spent itself in a thin edging of dirty foam over the gritty shingle. To the north-west and over the towers of Cannon Street railway bridge the dome of St Paul's hung above the city like a mirage. Gulls were strutting about the shingle and suddenly three of them rose in a tumult of wings and swooped shrieking over Kate's head before settling on the wooden rail of the decking, white-chested against the darkness of the river.

Would this be the last time they drank together, Kate wondered? Piers had only three more weeks to serve before knowing whether his transfer to Special Branch had been approved. It was what he wanted and had schemed for, but she knew that she would miss him. When he had first arrived five years earlier to join the Squad she had thought him one of the most sexually attractive officers with whom she had served. The realization was surprising and unwelcome. It certainly wasn't that she thought him handsome; he was half an inch shorter than she with simian-like arms and a streetwise toughness about the broad shoulders and strong face. His well-shaped mouth was sensitive and seemed always about to curl into a private joke, and there was, too, a faint suggestion of the comedian in the slightly podgy face with its slanting eyebrows. But she had come to respect him as a colleague and a man and the prospect of adjusting to someone else wasn't welcome. His sexuality no longer disturbed her. She valued her job and her place in the squad too highly to jeopardize it for the temporary satisfaction of a covert affair. Nothing remained secret in the Met for long, and she had seen too many careers and lives messed up to be tempted down that seductively easy path. No affairs were more foredoomed than those founded on lust, boredom or a craving for excitement. It hadn't been difficult to keep her distance in all but professional matters.

Piers guarded his emotions and his privacy as rigorously as she did hers. After working with him for five years she knew little more about his life outside the Met than she had when he arrived. She knew that he had a flat above a shop in one of the narrow streets in the City and that exploring the Square Mile's secret alleyways, its clustered churches and mysterious history-laden river was a passion. But she had never been invited to his flat, nor had she invited him to hers, north of the river within half a mile of where they stood. If you were forced to face the worst that men and women can do to each other, if the smell of death seemed sometimes to permeate your clothes, there had to be a place where you could physically as well as psychologically shut the door on everything but yourself. She suspected that AD in his high flat on the river at Queenhithe felt the same. She didn't know whether to envy or pity the woman who thought she had the power to invade that privacy.

Three more weeks and Piers would probably be gone.

Sergeant Robbins had already left, his overdue promotion to Inspector having at last come through. It seemed to Kate that their companionable group, held together by such a delicate balance of personalities and shared loyalties, was falling apart.

She said, 'I'll miss Robbins.'

'I won't. That oppressive rectitude had me worried. I could never forget that he's a lay preacher. I felt under judgement. Robbins is too good to be true.'

'Oh well, the Met isn't exactly hampered by an excess of rectitude.'

'Come off it, Kate! How many rogue officers do you know? We deal with them. Odd how the public always expect the police to be notably more virtuous than the society from which they're recruited.'

Kate was silent for a moment, then said, 'Why Special Branch? It's not going to be easy for them to assimilate you at your grade. I'd have thought you'd have tried for MI5. Isn't this your chance to join the public-school toffs, not the plodding plebs?'

'I'm a police officer. If I ever chuck it, it won't be for MI5. I could be tempted by MI6.' He was silent for a moment, then said, 'Actually I tried for the Secret Service after I left Oxford. My tutor thought it might suit and he set up the usual discreet interviews. The assessment board thought otherwise.'

Coming from Piers it was an extraordinary admission and Kate knew from his overcasual voice what it had cost him to make it. Without looking at him, she said, 'Their loss, the Met's gain. And now we get Francis Benton-Smith. D'you know him?'

Piers said, 'Vaguely. You're welcome to him. Too good looking – Dad's English, Mum's Indian, hence the glamour. Mum's a paediatrician, Dad teaches at a comprehensive. He's ambitious. Clever, but a bit too obviously on the make. He'll call you Ma'am at every opportunity. I know the type. They come into the service because they think they're educationally over-qualified and will shine among the plodders. You know the theory: take a job where you'll be cleverer than the others from the start and with luck you'll climb up on their necks.'

Kate said, 'That's unfair. You can't possibly know. Anyway, you're describing yourself. Isn't that why you joined? You were educationally over-qualified. What about that Oxford degree in theology?'

'I've explained that. It was the easiest way to get into Oxbridge. Now, of course, I would just transfer to a deprived inner-city state school and with luck the government would make Oxbridge take me. Anyway, you're not likely to suffer Benton for long. Robbins's promotion wasn't the only one overdue. Rumour has it you'll make Chief Inspector within months.'

She had heard the rumour herself, and wasn't this what she too had wanted and worked for? Wasn't it ambition that had lifted her from that barricaded seventh-floor flat in an inner-city block to a flat which had once seemed the height of achievement? The Met she served in today wasn't the Force that she had joined. It had changed, but so had England, so had the world. And she too had changed. After the Macpherson Report she had become less idealistic, more cynical about the machinations of the political world, more guarded in what she said. The young Detective Constable Miskin had been naïvely innocent, but something more valuable than innocence had been lost. But the Met still held her allegiance and Adam Dalgliesh her passionate loyalty. She told herself that nothing could stay the same. The two of them would probably soon be the only original members of the Special Investigation Squad, and how long might he stay?

She said, 'Is anything wrong with AD?'

'How do you mean, wrong?'

'It's just that in the last months I've thought he was under more stress than usual.'

'Do you wonder? He's a kind of ADC to the Commissioner. His finger's in every pie. What with anti-terrorism, the committee on detective training, constant criticism of the Met's inadequacies, the Burrell case, the relationship with MI5 and everlasting meetings with the great and the good – you name it, he's under strain. We all are. He's used to it. He probably needs it.'

'I wondered whether that woman was playing him up, the one from Cambridge. The girl we met on the St Anselm's case.'

She had kept her voice casual, her eyes on the river, but she could imagine Piers's long amused glance. He would know that she might be reluctant to speak the name – and, for God's sake, why? – but that she hadn't forgotten it.

'Our beautiful Emma? What do you mean by "playing up"?'

'Oh don't try to be clever, Piers! You know damn well what I mean.'

'No I don't, you could mean anything from criticizing his poetry to refusing to go to bed with him.'

'Do you think they are – going to bed?'

'For God's sake, Kate! How do I know? And have you thought that you might have got it the wrong way round? AD might be playing her up. I don't know about bed, but she doesn't refuse to dine with him, if that's of any interest to you. I saw them a couple of weeks ago at The Ivy.'

'How on earth did you get a table at The Ivy?'

'It wasn't so much me as the girl I was with. I was sinning above my station – and, regrettably, above my income. Anyway, there they were at a corner table.'

'An odd coincidence.'

'Not really. That's London. Sooner or later you meet everyone you know. That's what makes one's sex life so complicated.'

'Did they see you?'

'AD did, but I was too tactful and too well brought-up to intrude without an invitation – which I didn't get. She had her eyes on AD. I'd say that at least one of them was in love, if that gives you any comfort.'

It didn't, but before Kate could reply, her mobile phone rang. She listened carefully and in silence for half a minute, said, 'Yes, sir. Piers is with me. I understand. We're on our way,' and slipped the phone back in her pocket.

'I take it that was the boss.'

'Suspected murder. A man burned to death in his car at the Dupayne Museum off Spaniards Road. We're to take the case. AD is at the Yard and he'll meet us at the Museum. He'll bring our murder bags.'

'Thank God we've eaten. And why us? What's special about this death?'

'AD didn't say. Your car or mine?'

'Mine is faster but yours is here. Anyway, with London traffic practically grid-locked and the mayor mucking about with the traffic lights, we'd be quicker on bicycles.'

She waited while he took their empty glasses back into the pub. How odd it was, she thought. A single man had died and the Squad would spend days, weeks, maybe longer deciding the how and why and who. This was murder, the unique crime. The cost of the investigation wouldn't be counted. Even if they made no arrest, the file wouldn't be closed. And yet at any minute terrorists might rain death on thousands. She didn't say this to Piers when he returned. She knew what his reply would be. *Coping with terrorists isn't our job. This is.* She gave a last glance across the river and followed him to the car.

4

It was a very different arrival from his first visit. As Dalgliesh turned the Jaguar into the drive even the approach seemed disconcertingly unfamiliar. The smudgy illumination from the row of lampposts intensified the surrounding darkness and the curdle of bushes seemed denser and taller, closing in on a drive narrower than he remembered. Behind their impenetrable darkness frail tree trunks thrust their half-denuded branches into the blue-black night sky. As he made the final turn the house came into sight, mysterious as a mirage. The front door was closed and the windows were black rectangles except for a single light in the left ground-floor room. Further progress was barred by tape and there was a uniformed police officer on duty. Dalgliesh was obviously expected: the officer needed only to glance briefly at the warrant card proffered through the window before saluting and moving the posts aside.

He needed no directions to the site of the fire. Although no flare lit up the darkness, small clouds of acrid smoke still wafted to the left of the house and there was an unmistakable fumy stench of burnt metal, stronger even than the autumnal bonfire smell of the scorched wood. But first he turned right and drove to the car-park behind its concealing hedge of laurels. The drive to Hampstead had been slow and tedious and he wasn't surprised to see that Kate, Piers and Benton-Smith had arrived before him. He saw too that other cars were parked, a BMW saloon, a Mercedes 190, a Rover and a Ford Fiesta. It looked as if the Dupaynes and at least one member of the staff had arrived.

Kate reported as Dalgliesh took the murder bags and the four sets of protective clothing from the car. She said, 'We got here about five minutes ago, sir. The lab's Fire Investigation Officer is at the scene. The photographers were leaving as we arrived.'

'And the family?'

'Mr Marcus Dupayne and his sister, Miss Caroline Dupayne, are in the museum. The fire was discovered by the housekeeper, Mrs Tallulah Clutton. She's in her cottage at the rear of the house with Miss Muriel Godby, the secretary–receptionist. We haven't spoken to them yet, except to say that you're on your way.'

Dalgliesh turned to Piers. 'Tell them, will you, that I'll be with them as soon as possible. Mrs Clutton first, then the Dupaynes. In the mean time you and Benton-Smith had better make a quick search of the grounds. It's probably a fruitless exercise and we can't search properly until morning, but it had better be done. Then join me at the scene.'

He and Kate walked together to the site of the fire. Twin arc-lights blazed on what was left of the garage and, moving closer, he saw the scene as garishly lit and staged as if it were being filmed. But this was how a murder scene, once lit, always looked to him; essentially artificial as if the murderer, in destroying his victim, had robbed even the surrounding commonplace objects of any semblance of reality. The fire service with their vehicles had gone, the engines leaving deep ruts in a grass verge flattened by the heavy coils of the hoses.

The Fire Investigation Officer had heard their approach. He was over six feet tall, with a pale craggy face and a thick bush of red hair. He was wearing a blue overall and Wellington boots and had a face mask slung round his neck. With his blaze of hair which even the arc-lights couldn't eclipse, and the strong bony face, he stood for a moment as rigidly hieratical as some mythical guardian of the gateway to Hell, needing only a gleaming sword to complete the illusion. Then it faded as he came forward with vigorous strides and wrenched Dalgliesh's hand.

'Commander Dalgliesh? Douglas Anderson, Fire Investigation Officer. This is Sam Roberts, my assistant.' Sam proved to be a girl, slight and with a look of almost childish intentness under a cap of dark hair.

Three figures, booted, white-overalled but with the hoods flung back, were standing a little apart. Anderson said, 'I think you know Brian Clark and the other SOCOs.'

Clark raised an arm in acknowledgement but didn't move. Dalgliesh had never known him to shake hands even when the gesture would have been appropriate. It was as if he feared that any human contact would transfer trace elements. Dalgliesh wondered whether guests to dinner with Clark were at risk of having their coffee cups labelled as exhibits or dusted for prints. Clark knew that a murder scene should be left undisturbed until the investigating officer had seen it and the photographers had recorded it, but he was making no attempt to conceal his impatience to get on with his job. His two colleagues, more relaxed, stood a little behind him like garbed attendants waiting to play their part in some esoteric rite.

Dalgliesh and Kate, white-coated and gloved, moved towards the garage. What remained of it stood some twenty yards from the wall of the museum. The roof had almost completely gone but the three walls were still standing and the open doors bore no marks of fire. It had once been backed by a belt of saplings and slim trees, but now nothing remained of them but jagged spurs of blackened wood. Within eight yards of the garage was a smaller shed with a water tap to the right of the door. Surprisingly the shed was only singed by the fire.

With Kate standing silently at his side, Dalgliesh stood for a moment at the garage entrance and let his eyes move slowly over the carnage. The scene was shadow-less, objects hard-edged, the colours drained in the power of the arc-lights, except for the front of the car's long bonnet which, untouched by the flames, shone as richly red as if newly painted. The flames had flared upwards to catch the corrugated plastic roof and he could see through the smoke-blackened edges the night sky and a sprinkling of stars. To his left and some four feet from the driver's seat of the Jaguar was a square window, the glass blackened and cracked. The garage was small, obviously a converted wooden shed, and low-roofed with only about four feet of space each side of the car and no more than a foot between the front of the bonnet and the double doors. The door to Dalgliesh's right had been pulled wide open; the left, on the driver's side of the car, looked as though someone had started to close it. There were bolts to the top and bottom of the left-hand door and the right was fitted with a Yale lock. Dalgliesh saw that the key was in place. To his left was a light switch and he saw that the bulb had been taken out of its socket. In the angle of the half-closed door and the wall was a five-litre petrol can lying on its side and untouched by the fire. The screw top was missing.

Douglas Anderson was standing a little behind the half-opened door of the car, watchful and silent as a chauffeur inviting them to take their seats. With Kate, Dalgliesh moved over to the body. It was slumped back in the driver's seat and turned slightly to the right, the remains of the left arm close to the side but the right flung out and fixed in a parody of protest. Through the half-closed door he could see the ulna, and a few burnt fragments of cloth adhered to a thread of muscle. All that could burn on the head had been destroyed and the fire had extended to just above the knees. The charred face, the features obliterated, was turned towards him and the whole head, black as a spent match, looked unnaturally small. The mouth gaped in a grimace, seeming to mock the head's grotesquerie. Only the teeth, gleaming white against the charred flesh, and a small patch of cracked skull proclaimed the corpse's humanity. From the car came the smell of burnt flesh and charred cloth and, less persuasive but unmistakable, the smell of petrol.

Dalgliesh glanced at Kate. Her face was greenish in

the glare of the lights and fixed in a mask of endurance. He remembered that she had once confided a fear of fire. He couldn't remember when or why, but this fact had lodged in his mind as had all her rare confidences. The affection he felt for her had deep roots in his complex personality and in their joint experience. There was respect for her qualities as a police officer and for the courageous determination which had got her where she now was, a half-paternal wish for her safety and success, and the attraction she held for him as a woman. This had never become overtly sexual. He didn't fall in love easily and the inhibition against a sexual relationship with a colleague was for him – and, he guessed, for Kate also – absolute. Glancing at her rigid features he felt a surge of protective affection. For a second he considered finding an excuse to release her and sending for Piers, but he didn't speak. Kate was too intelligent not to see through the ruse and so was Piers; he had no wish to humiliate her, particularly not in front of a male colleague. Instinctively he moved a little closer to her and her shoulder briefly touched his arm. He felt her body straighten. Kate would be all right.

Dalgliesh asked, 'When did the fire service arrive?'

'They were here by six forty-five. Seeing there was a body in the car they rang the Police Homicide Adviser. You may know him, sir, Charlie Unsworth. He used to be a SOCO with the Met. He made the preliminary inspection and didn't take much time concluding it was a suspicious death so he rang the FIU at the Met. As you know, we're on twenty-four-hour call and I got here at seven twenty-eight. We decided to start the investigation at once. The undertakers will collect the body as soon as you've finished. I've alerted the mortuary. We've made a preliminary inspection of the car but we'll get it moved to Lambeth. There may be prints.'

Dalgliesh's thoughts moved to his last case, at St Anselm's College. Father Sebastian, standing where he stood now, would have made the sign of the cross. His own father, a middle-of-the-road Anglican priest, would have bent his head in prayer, and the words would be there, hallowed by centuries of use. Both, he thought, were fortunate in being able to call on instinctive responses which could bestow on these awful charred remains the recognition that here had been a human being. There was a need to dignify death, to affirm that these remains, soon to become a police exhibit to be labelled, transported, dissected and assessed, still had an importance beyond the scorched carcass of the Jaguar or the stumps of the dead trees.

Dalgliesh at first left the talking to Anderson. It was the first time they had met but he knew that the FIO was a man with over twenty years' experience of death by fire. It was he, not Dalgliesh, who was the expert here. He said, 'What can you tell us?'

"There's no doubt about the seat of the fire, sir, the head and upper part of the body. The fire was mostly confined, as you can see, to the middle part of the car. The flames caught the soft top which was up, and then rose to set alight the corrugated plastic of the garage roof. The panes of the window probably cracked with the heat giving an inrush of air and an outrush of fire. That's why the flames spread to the trees. If they hadn't, the fire might have burned out before anyone noticed, anyone on the Heath or on Spaniards Road, I mean. Of course, Mrs Clutton would have known at once when she returned, flames or no flames.'

'And the cause of the fire?'

'Almost certainly petrol. Of course we'll be able to check that fairly quickly. We're taking samples from the clothing and the driver's seat and we'll get an immediate indication from the Sniffer – the TVA One Thousand – whether there are hydrocarbons present. But, of course, the Sniffer's not specific. We'll need gas chromatography for confirmation and that, as you know, will take about a week. But it's hardly necessary. I got the smell of petrol from his trousers and from part of the burnt seat as soon as I came into the garage.'

Dalgliesh said, 'And that, presumably, is the can. But where's the cap?'

'Here, sir. We haven't touched it.' Anderson led them to the back of the garage. Lying in the far corner was the cap.

Dalgliesh said, 'Accident, suicide or murder? Have you had time to reach a provisional view?'

'It wasn't an accident, you can rule that one out. And I don't think it was suicide. In my experience suicides who kill themselves with petrol don't hurl the can away. You usually find it in the foot-well of the car. But if he had doused himself and chucked the can away, why isn't the cap close to it, or dropped on the floor of the car? It looks to me as if the cap was removed by someone standing in the far left-hand corner. It couldn't have rolled into the back of the garage. The concrete's fairly even but the floor slopes from the back wall to the door. The slant's no more than four inches, I reckon, but that cap, if it rolled at all, would have been found near the can.'

Kate said, 'And the murderer – if there was one – would be standing in the dark. There's no bulb in the light.'

Anderson said, 'If the bulb had failed you'd expect it to be in place. Someone removed it. Of course, it could have been done perfectly innocently, maybe by Mrs Clutton or Dupayne himself. But if a bulb fails, you usually leave it in the socket until you've brought a new bulb to replace it. And then there's the seatbelt. The belt's burnt away but the clip's in place. He'd fastened the seatbelt. I've not known that before in a case of suicide.'

Kate said, 'If he was afraid of changing his mind at the last minute he might have strapped himself in.'

'Hardly likely though. With a head doused with petrol and a struck match, what chance of changing your mind?'

Dalgliesh said, 'So, the picture as we see it at present is this. The murderer takes out the bulb, stands in the dark of the garage, unscrews the cap on the can of petrol and waits, matches either in hand or ready in a pocket. With the can and the matches to cope with he probably found it convenient to drop the cap. He certainly wouldn't risk putting it in his pocket. He'd have known that the whole thing would have to be very quick if he'd to get out himself without being caught by the fire. The victim – we're assuming it's Neville Dupayne – opens the garage doors with the Yale. He knows where to find the light switch. He either sees or feels that the bulb is missing when the light fails to come on. He doesn't need it because he has only a few steps to walk to the car. He gets in and fastens his seatbelt. That's a bit odd. He was only going to drive out of the garage before getting out and shutting the doors. Belting himself in could have been instinctive. Then the assailant moves out of the shadows. I think it was someone he knew, someone he wouldn't fear. He opens the door to speak and is immediately doused in petrol. The assailant has the matches handy, strikes one, throws it at Dupayne and makes a quick exit. He wouldn't want to run round the back of the car; speed is everything. As it is, he was lucky to get out unscathed. So he pushes the car door half closed to give himself room to get past. We may find prints, but it's unlikely. This killer – if he exists – would have worn gloves. The left-hand garage door is half closed. Presumably he had a mind to close both doors on the blaze, then decided not to waste time. He had to make a getaway.'

Kate said, 'The doors look heavy. A woman might find it difficult even to half close them quickly.'

Dalgliesh asked, 'Was Mrs Clutton alone when she discovered the fire?'

'Yes sir, on her way home from an evening class. I'm not sure what she does here exactly but I think she looks after the exhibits, dusts them and so on. She lives in the cottage to the south of the house, facing the Heath. She rang the Fire Brigade from her cottage at once and then got in touch with Marcus Dupayne and his sister Caroline Dupayne. She also rang the secretary–receptionist here, a Miss Muriel Godby. She lives close by and got here first. Miss Dupayne arrived next and her brother soon after. We kept all of them well away from the garage. The Dupaynes are anxious to see you and they're adamant that they won't leave until their brother's body has been removed. That's assuming it is his body.'

'Any evidence to suggest it isn't?'

'None. We found keys in the trouser pocket. There's a weekend bag in the boot, but nothing to confirm identification. There are his trousers, of course. The knees aren't burnt. But I could hardly . . .'

'Of course not. A positive ID can wait for the autopsy, but there can't be any serious doubt.'

Piers and Benton-Smith came out of the darkness beyond the glare of the lights. Piers said, 'No one in the grounds. No vehicles unaccounted for. In the garden shed there's a lawn-mower, a bicycle and the usual garden paraphernalia. No can of petrol. The Dupaynes appeared about five minutes ago. They're getting impatient.'

That was understandable, thought Dalgliesh. Neville Dupayne had, after all, been their brother. He said, 'Explain that I need to see Mrs Clutton first. I'll be with them as soon as possible. Then you and Benton-Smith liaise here. Kate and I will be in the cottage.'

5

As soon as the Fire Brigade arrived an officer had suggested to Tally that she should wait in her cottage, but it had been a command rather than a request. She knew that they wanted her out of the way and she had no wish to be anywhere near the garage. But she found herself too restless to be confined between walls and instead walked round the back of the house past the parking lot and into the drive, pacing up and down, listening for the first sound of an approaching car.

Muriel was the first to arrive. It had taken her longer than Tally had expected. When she had parked her Fiesta, Tally poured out her story. Muriel listened in silence, then said firmly, 'There's no point in waiting outside, Tally. The Fire Brigade won't want us getting in the way. Mr Marcus and Miss Caroline will be as quick as they can. We'd better wait in the cottage.'

Tally said, 'That's what the fire officer said, but I needed to be outside.'

Muriel looked closely at her in the car-park light. 'I'm here now. You'll be better in the cottage. Mr Marcus and Miss Caroline will know where to find us.'

So they returned to the cottage together. Tally settled in her usual chair with Muriel opposite and they sat in a silence which both seemed to need. Tally had no idea how long it lasted. It was broken by the sound of footsteps on the path. Muriel got up the more quickly and was at the front door. Tally heard the murmur of voices and then Muriel returned, followed by Mr Marcus. For a few seconds Tally stared at him in disbelief. She thought, *He's become an old man*. His face was ashen, the small cluster of broken veins over the high cheekbones standing out like angry scratches. Beneath his pallor the muscles round the mouth and jaw were taut so that his face looked half paralysed. When he spoke she was surprised that his voice was almost unchanged. He waved aside her offer of a chair and stood very still while she told her story once again. He listened in silence to the end. Wishing to find some way, however inadequate, of showing sympathy, she offered him coffee. He refused so curtly that she wondered whether he had heard.

Then he said, 'I understand an officer from New Scotland Yard is on his way. I'll wait for him in the museum. My sister is already there. She'll be coming to see you later.'

It wasn't until he was at the door that he turned and said, 'Are you all right, Tally?'

'Yes thank you, Mr Marcus. I'm all right.' Her voice broke and she said, 'I'm so sorry, so sorry.'

He nodded and seemed about to say something, then went out. Within minutes of his departure the doorbell rang. Muriel was quick to respond. She returned alone to say that a police officer had called to check that they were all right and to let them know that Commander Dalgliesh would be with them as soon as possible.

And now, alone with Muriel, Tally was settled again in her fireside chair. With the porch door and the front door closed there was only a trace of acrid burning in the hall and, sitting by the fire in the sitting-room, she could almost imagine that nothing outside had changed. The curtains with their Morris pattern of green leaves were closed against the night. Muriel had turned the gas fire up high, and even Tomcat had mysteriously returned and was stretched out on the rug. Tally knew that outside there would be male voices, booted feet clumping on sodden grass, the blaze of arc-lights, but here at the back of the house all was quiet. She found she was grateful for Muriel's presence, for her calm authoritative control, for her silences which were non-censorious and almost companionable.

Now, rousing herself, Muriel said, 'You haven't had supper and nor have I. We need food. You sit there and I'll see to it. Have you any eggs?'

Tally had said, 'There's a new carton in the fridge. They're free-range but I'm afraid they're not organic.'

'Free-range will do. No, don't move. I expect I'll find what I want.'

How odd it was, thought Tally, to be feeling relieved at such a time that her kitchen was immaculate, that she had put out a clean dishcloth that morning and that the eggs were fresh. She was overcome with an immense weariness of the spirit that had nothing to do with tiredness. Leaning back in the fireside chair she let her eyes range over the sitting-room, mentally noting each item as if to reassure herself that nothing had changed, that the world was still a familiar place. The comfort of the small noises from the kitchen was almost sensually pleasurable and she closed her eyes and listened. Muriel seemed to be gone a long time, and then she appeared with the first of two trays and the sitting-room was filled with a smell of egg and buttered toast. They sat at the table opposite each other. The scrambled egg was perfect, creamy and warm and slightly peppery. There was a sprig of parsley on each plate. Tally wondered where it had come from before remembering that she had placed a bundle of the herb in a mug only the day before.

Muriel had made tea. She had said, 'I think tea goes better than coffee with scrambled eggs but I can make coffee if you'd prefer it.'

Tally said, 'No thank you, Muriel. This is perfect. You're very kind.'

And she was being kind. Tally hadn't realized that she was hungry until she began eating. The scrambled eggs and hot tea revived her. She felt a comforting reassurance that she was part of the museum, not just the house-keeper who cleaned and cared for it and was grateful for the refuge of her cottage, but a member of the small dedicated group to whom the Dupayne was their shared life. But how little she knew of them. Who would have supposed that she would find Muriel's company such a comfort? She had expected Muriel to be efficient and calm, but the kindness surprised her. Admittedly Muriel's first words on arriving had been to complain that the shed with the petrol should have been locked; she had said so to Ryan more than once. But she had almost immediately put that grumble aside and had devoted herself to hearing Tally's story and taking control.

Now she said, 'You won't want to be here alone

tonight. Have you any relations or friends you can go to?'

Until now Tally had given no thought to being alone after everyone had left, but now it burdened her with a new anxiety. If she rang Basingstoke, Jennifer and Roger would be glad enough to drive to London to collect her. After all, this wouldn't be an ordinary visit. Tally's presence, this time at least, would prove a lively source of excitement and conjecture for the whole crescent. Of course she would have to telephone Jennifer and Roger, and sooner rather than later. It wouldn't do for them to read about the death in the newspapers. But that could wait until tomorrow. She was too tired now to cope with their questions and concern. Only one thing was certain: she didn't want to leave the cottage. She had a half superstitious fear that, once abandoned, it would never receive her back.

She said, 'I'll be all right here, Muriel. I'm used to being alone. I've always felt safe here.'

'I dare say, but tonight is different. You've had a terrible shock. Miss Caroline wouldn't hear of you staying here without someone with you. She'll probably suggest you go back with her to the college.'

And that, thought Tally, was almost as unwelcome as the prospect of Basingstoke. Unspoken objections swarmed at once into her mind. Her night-dress and dressing-gown were perfectly clean and respectable, but old; how would they look in Miss Caroline's flat at Swathling's? And what about breakfast? Would that be in Miss Caroline's flat or in the school dining-room? The first would be embarrassing. What on earth would they say to each other? And she felt she couldn't cope with the noisy curiosity of a room full of adolescents. These worries seemed puerile and demeaning in the face of the horror outside, but she couldn't banish them.

There was a silence, then Muriel said, 'I could stay here tonight if you like. It won't take long to drive back for my night things and toothbrush. I'd invite you home but I think you'd prefer to be here.'

Tally's senses seemed to have sharpened. She thought, *And you'd prefer to be here than have me in your house.* The offer was meant to impress Miss Caroline as well as to help Tally. All the same, she was grateful. She said, 'If it's not putting you out too much, Muriel, I'd be glad of company just for tonight.'

Thank God, she thought, *the spare bed is always freshly made up, even though no one is ever expected. I'll put in a hot-water bottle while Muriel's away, and I could move up one of the African violets and put some books on the bedside table. I can make her comfortable. Tomorrow the body will be removed and I shall be all right.*

They carried on eating in silence, then Muriel said, 'We need to keep up our strength for when the police arrive. We have to prepare for their questions. I think we should be careful when talking to the police. We don't want them to get the wrong impression.'

'How do you mean careful, Muriel? We just tell them the truth.'

'Of course we tell them the truth. I mean that we shouldn't tell them things that aren't really our concern, things about the family, that conversation we had after the trustees' meeting, for example. We shouldn't tell

195

them that Dr Neville wanted to close the museum. If they need to know that, Mr Marcus can tell them. It isn't really our concern.'

Troubled, Tally said, 'I wasn't going to tell them.'

'Nor shall I. It's important they don't get the wrong idea.'

Tally was appalled. 'But Muriel, it was an accident, it has to be. You're not saying that the police will think the family had anything to do with it? They couldn't believe that. It's ridiculous. It's wicked!'

'Of course it is, but it's the kind of thing the police may seize on. I'm just saying that we ought to be careful. And they'll ask you about the motorist, of course. You'll be able to show them the damaged bicycle. That'll be evidence.'

'Evidence of what, Muriel? Are you saying that they'll think I might be lying, that none of it happened?'

'They might not go as far as that but they'll need some proof. The police believe nothing. That's the way they're trained to think. Tally, are you absolutely sure you didn't recognize him?'

Tally was confused. She didn't want to talk about the incident, not now and not to Muriel. She said, 'I didn't recognize him, but thinking about it now, I have a feeling I must have seen him before. I can't remember when or where, except that it wasn't at the museum. I'd have remembered if he came here regularly. Perhaps I saw his picture somewhere, in the newspapers or on TV. Or perhaps he resembles somebody well known. It's just a feeling I have. But it doesn't really help.'

'Well, if you don't know, you don't know. But they'll

have to try to trace him. It's a pity you didn't get the number of the car.'

'It was so quick, Muriel. He'd gone almost as soon as I got to my feet. I didn't think about taking the number, but I wouldn't anyway, would I? It was just an accident, I wasn't hurt. I didn't know then about Dr Neville.'

They heard a knock on the front door. Before Tally could get up Muriel had moved. She came back with two people following her, a tall dark-haired man with the woman police officer who had talked to them earlier.

Muriel said, 'This is Commander Dalgliesh, and Detective Inspector Miskin is back.' Then she turned to the Commander. 'Would you and the Inspector care for some coffee? Or there's tea if you'd like it. It won't take long.'

She had begun piling up plates and cups on the table.

Commander Dalgliesh said, 'Coffee would be very welcome.'

Muriel nodded, and without another word carried out the laden tray. Tally thought, *She's regretting the offer. She'd rather stay in here and listen to what I say.* She wondered whether the Commander had only accepted the coffee because he preferred to speak to her alone. He sat down at the table on the chair opposite while Miss Miskin seated herself by the fire. Astonishingly Tomcat took a sudden leap and settled himself on her lap. It was something he rarely did, but invariably to visitors who disliked cats. Miss Miskin was taking no liberties from Tomcat. Gently but firmly she rolled him off on to the mat.

Tally looked across at the Commander. She thought

of faces as being either softly moulded or carved. His was carved. It was a handsome authoritative face and the dark eyes that looked into hers were kindly. He had an attractive voice, and voices had always been important to her. And then she remembered Muriel's words. *The police believe nothing, that's the way they're trained to think.*

He said, 'This has been an appalling shock for you, Mrs Clutton. Do you feel able to answer a few questions now? It's always helpful to get the facts as soon as possible, but if you'd rather wait we can return early tomorrow.'

'No, please. I'd rather tell you now. I'm all right. I don't want to wait overnight.'

'Can you please tell us exactly what happened from the time the museum was closed this evening until now? Take your time. Try to remember every detail, even if it seems unimportant.'

Tally told her story. Under his gaze she knew that she was telling it well and clearly. She had an irrational need of his approval. Miss Miskin had taken out a notebook and was unobtrusively making notes, but when Tally glanced at her, she saw the Inspector's eyes fixed on her face. Neither of them interrupted her while Tally was speaking.

At the end, Commander Dalgliesh said, 'This fleeing car driver who knocked you down, you said you thought his face was vaguely familiar. Do you think that you might remember who he is or where you've seen him?'

'I don't think so. If I'd actually seen him before I'd probably have remembered at once. Not perhaps his name, but where I'd seen him. It wasn't like that. It was much less certain. It's just that I have an impression that he's quite well known, that I may have seen his photograph somewhere. But of course it might just be that he resembles someone I've seen, an actor on TV, a sportsman or a writer, someone like that. I'm sorry I can't be more helpful.'

'You have been helpful, Mrs Clutton, very helpful. We'll ask you to come to the Yard sometime tomorrow when it's convenient for you to look at some photographs of faces and perhaps speak to one of our artists. Together you might be able to produce a likeness. Obviously we have to trace this driver if we can.'

And now Muriel came in with the coffee. She had made it from fresh beans and the aroma filled the cottage. Miss Miskin came over to the table and they drank it together. Then, at Commander Dalgliesh's invitation, Muriel told her story.

She had left the museum at five-fifteen. The museum closed at five and she usually sat finishing her work until five-thirty except on a Friday when she tried to leave a little earlier. She and Mrs Clutton had checked that all visitors had left. She had given Mrs Strickland, a volunteer, a lift to Hampstead tube station and had then driven home to South Finchley, arriving there at about five forty-five. She didn't notice the precise time of Tally's call to her mobile but she thought it was about six-forty. She had come back to the museum at once.

Inspector Miskin broke in here. She said, 'It seems possible that the fire was caused by igniting petrol. Was petrol kept on the premises, and if so, where?'

Muriel glanced at Tally. She said, 'The petrol was brought for the lawn-mower. The garden isn't my responsibility but I knew the petrol was there. I think everyone must have known. I did tell Ryan Archer, the gardening boy, that the shed should be locked. Garden equipment and tools are expensive.'

'But as far as either of you know, the shed never was locked?'

'No,' said Tally. 'There isn't a lock on the door.'

'Can either of you remember when you last saw the can?'

Again they looked at each other. Muriel said, 'I haven't been to the shed for some time. I can't remember when I last had occasion to.'

'But you did speak to the gardener about keeping it locked? When was that?'

'Soon after the petrol was delivered. Mrs Faraday, the volunteer who works in the garden, brought it. I think it was in mid-September, but she will be able to give you the date.'

'Thank you. I'll need the names and addresses of everyone who works in the museum, including the volunteers. Is that one of your responsibilities, Miss Godby?'

Muriel coloured slightly. She said, 'Certainly. I could let you have the names tonight. If you're going to the museum to speak to Mr and Miss Dupayne, I could go with you.'

The Commander said, 'That won't be necessary. I'll get the names from Mr Dupayne. Do either of you know the name of the garage where Dr Dupayne's Jaguar was serviced?'

It was Tally who replied. 'It was looked after by Mr Stan Carter at Duncan's Garage in Highgate. I used to see him sometimes when he returned the car after servicing, and we'd have a chat.'

That was the final question. The two police officers got up. Dalgliesh held out his hand to Tally. He said, 'Thank you, Mrs Clutton. You've been very helpful. One of my officers will be in touch with you tomorrow. Will you be here? I don't expect it will be pleasant to stay in the cottage tonight.'

It was Muriel who spoke. She said stiffly, 'I've agreed to spend the night with Mrs Clutton. Naturally Miss Dupayne wouldn't dream of letting her stay here alone. I shall be at work as usual at nine on Monday, although I imagine Mr and Miss Dupayne will wish to close the museum, at least until after the funeral. If you need me tomorrow, I could of course come in.'

Commander Dalgliesh said, 'I don't think that will be necessary. We shall require the museum and the grounds to be closed to the public, at least for the next three or four days. Police constables will be here to guard the scene until the body and the car have been removed. I had hoped that this could be tonight but it seems that it may not happen until first light tomorrow. This motorist seen by Mrs Clutton, does her description of him mean anything to you?'

Muriel said, 'Nothing. He sounds like a typical museum visitor but no one I specifically recognize. It's unfortunate that Tally didn't get the car number. What is so odd is what he said. I don't know whether you visited the Murder Room, Commander, when you were here with Mr Ackroyd, but one of the cases featured is a death by fire.'

'Yes, I know the Rouse case. And I remember what Rouse said.'

He seemed to be waiting for one of them to comment further. Tally looked from him to Inspector Miskin. Neither was giving anything away. She burst out, 'But it's not the same! It can't be. This was an accident.'

Still neither of them spoke. Then Muriel said, 'The Rouse case wasn't an accident, was it?'

No one replied. Muriel, red faced, looked from the Commander to Inspector Miskin as if desperately seeking reassuring.

Dalgliesh said quietly, 'It's too early to say with certainty why Dr Dupayne died. All we know at present is how. I see, Mrs Clutton, that you have security locks on the front door, and window bolts. I don't think you're in any danger here but it would be sensible to make sure that you lock up carefully before you go to bed. And don't answer the door after dark.'

Tally said, 'I never do. No one I know would arrive after the museum is closed without telephoning first. But I never feel frightened here. I shall be all right after tonight.'

A minute later, with renewed thanks for the coffee, the police rose to go. Before leaving, Inspector Miskin handed both a card with a telephone number. If anything further occurred to either of them, they should telephone at once. Muriel, proprietorial as ever, went with them to the door.

Sitting alone at the table, Tally stared intently at the

two empty coffee mugs as if these commonplace objects had power to reassure her that her world hadn't broken apart.

6

Dalgliesh took Piers with him to interview the two Dupaynes, leaving Kate and Benton-Smith to liaise with the Fire Investigation Officer and, if necessary, have some final words with Tally Clutton and Muriel Godby. Moving to the front of the house he saw with surprise that the door was now ajar. A shaft of light streamed from the hall, its thin band illuminating the bed of shrubs in front of the house, bestowing on them an illusion of spring. On the gravel path small pellets of gravel glittered like jewels. Dalgliesh pressed the bell before he and Piers entered. The half-open door could be construed as a cautious invitation, but he had no doubt that limits would be set on what could be presumed. They entered the wide hall. Empty and utterly silent, it looked like a vast stage set for some contemporary drama. He could almost imagine the characters moving on cue through the ground floor doors and ascending the central staircase to take up their positions with practised authority.

As soon as their footsteps rang on the marble, Marcus and Caroline Dupayne appeared at the door of the picture gallery. Standing aside, Caroline Dupayne motioned them in. During the few seconds it took to make the introductions, Dalgliesh was aware that he and Piers were as much under scrutiny as were the Dupaynes. The impression that Caroline Dupayne made on him was immediate and striking. She was as tall as her brother – both slightly under six feet – wide-shouldered and long-limbed. She was wearing trousers and a matching jacket in fine tweed with a high-necked jumper. The words pretty or beautiful were inappropriate but the bone structure on which beauty is moulded revealed itself in the high cheekbones and the well-defined but delicate line of the chin. Her dark hair, faintly streaked with silver, was cut short and brushed back from her face in strong waves, a style which looked casual but which Dalgliesh suspected was achieved by expensive cutting. Her dark eyes met and held his for five seconds in a gaze speculative and challenging. It was not overtly hostile but he knew that, here, he had a potential adversary.

Her brother's only resemblance to her was in the darkness of the hair, his more liberally streaked with grey, and the jutting cheekbones. His face was smooth and the dark eyes had the inward look of a man whose preoccupations were cerebral and highly controlled. His mistakes would be mistakes of judgement, not of impulsiveness or carelessness. For such a man there was a procedure for everything in life, and a procedure, too, for death. Metaphorically he would even now be sending for the file, looking for the precedent, mentally considering the right response. He showed none of his sister's covert antagonism but the eyes, deeper set than hers, were wary. They were also troubled. Perhaps after all this was an emergency for which precedent offered no help. For nearly forty years he would have been protecting his Minister, his Secretary of State. Who, Dalgliesh wondered, would he be concerned to protect now?

He saw that they had been sitting in the two upright armchairs each side of the fireplace at the end of the room. Between the chairs was a low table holding a tray with a cafetière, a jug of milk and two mugs. There were also two tumblers, two wine glasses, a bottle of wine and one of whisky. Only the wine glasses had been used. The only other seating was the flat leather-buttoned bench in the centre of the room. It was hardly appropriate for a session of questions and answers, and no one moved towards it.

Marcus Dupayne looked round the gallery as if suddenly aware of its deficiencies. He said, 'There are some folding chairs in the office. I'll fetch them.' He turned to Piers. 'Perhaps you'd help me.' It was a command, not a request.

They waited in silence during which Caroline Dupayne moved over to the Nash painting and seemed to be studying it. Her brother and Piers appeared with the chairs within a few seconds and Marcus took control, placing them with care in front of the two armchairs in which he and his sister reseated themselves. The contrast between the deep comfort of the leather and the uncompromising slats of the folding chairs made its own comment.

Marcus Dupayne said, 'This isn't your first visit to the museum, is it? Weren't you here about a week ago? James Calder-Hale mentioned it.'

Dalgliesh said, 'Yes, I was here last Friday with Conrad Ackroyd.'

'A happier visit than this. Forgive me for introducing this inappropriate social note into what for you must be essentially an official visit. For us too, of course.'

Dalgliesh spoke the customary words of condolence. However carefully phrased they always sounded to him banal and vaguely impertinent, as if he were claiming some emotional involvement in the victim's death. Caroline Dupayne frowned. Perhaps she resented these preliminary courtesies as both insincere and a waste of time. Dalgliesh didn't blame her.

She said, 'I realize you've had things to do, Commander, but we've been waiting for over an hour.'

Dalgliesh replied, 'I'm afraid it's likely to be the first of many inconveniences. I needed to speak to Mrs Clutton. She was the first person at the fire. Do you both feel able to answer questions now? If not, we could return tomorrow.'

It was Caroline who replied, 'No doubt you'll be back tomorrow anyway, but for God's sake let's get the preliminaries over. I thought you might be in the cottage. How is Tally Clutton?'

'Shocked and distressed, as we would expect, but she's coping. Miss Godby is with her.'

'Making tea no doubt. The English specific against all disasters. We, as you see, have been indulging in something stronger. I won't offer you anything, Commander. We know the form. I suppose there can't be any doubt it is our brother's body in the car?'

Dalgliesh said, 'There will have to be a formal identification, of course, and if necessary the dental records and DNA will prove it. But I don't think there's room for doubt. I'm sorry.' He paused, then said, 'Is there a next of kin or close relative other than yourselves?'

It was Marcus Dupayne who replied. His voice was as controlled as if he were addressing his secretary. 'There's an unmarried daughter. Sarah. She lives in Kilburn. I don't know the exact address but my wife does. She has it on our Christmas card list. I telephoned my wife after I arrived here and she's driving over to Kilburn to break the news. I'm expecting her to ring back when she's had an opportunity to see Sarah.'

Dalgliesh said, 'I shall need Miss Dupayne's full name and address. Obviously we won't be troubling her tonight. I expect your wife will be giving her help and support.'

There was the trace of a frown on Marcus Dupayne's face but he replied evenly. 'We've never been close, but naturally we shall do everything we can. I imagine my wife will offer to stay the night if that's what Sarah wishes, or she may, of course, prefer to come to us. In either case, my sister and I will see her early tomorrow.'

Caroline Dupayne stirred impatiently and said curtly, 'There's not much we can tell her, is there? There's nothing we know for certain ourselves. What she'll want to know, of course, is how her father died. That's what we're waiting to hear.'

Marcus Dupayne's brief glance at his sister could have conveyed a warning. He said, 'I suppose it's too early for definite answers, but is there anything you can tell us?

How the fire started for example, whether it was an accident?'

'The fire started in the car. Petrol was thrown over the occupant's head and set alight. There is no way it could have been an accident.'

There was a silence which lasted for a quarter of a minute, then Caroline Dupayne said, 'So we can be clear about this. You're saying that the fire could have been deliberate.'

'Yes, we're treating this as a suspicious death.'

Again there was a silence. Murder, that ponderous uncompromising word, seemed to resonate unspoken on the quiet air. The next question had to be asked and even so it was likely to be at best unwelcome and at worst cause pain. Some investigating officers might have thought it more acceptable to defer all questioning until the next day; that was not Dalgliesh's practice. The first hours after a suspicious death were crucial. But his earlier words – 'Do you feel able to answer some questions?' – hadn't been merely a matter of form. At this stage – and he found the fact interesting – it was the Dupaynes who could control the interview.

Now he said, 'This is a difficult question both to ask and to answer. Was there anything in your brother's life which might cause him to wish to end it?'

They would be ready for the question; after all, they had been alone together for an hour. But their reaction surprised him. Again there was a silence, a little too long to be wholly natural, and he gained an impression of controlled wariness, of the two Dupaynes deliberately not meeting each other's eyes. He suspected that they had not only agreed what they would say, but who would speak first. It was Marcus.

'My brother wasn't a man to share his problems, perhaps least with members of the family. But he has never given me any reason to fear that he was or might be suicidal. If you had asked me that question a week ago I might have been more definite in saying that the suggestion was absurd. I can't be so certain now. When we last met at the trustees' meeting on Wednesday, he seemed more stressed than usual. He was worried – as we all are – about the future of the museum. He wasn't convinced that we had the resources successfully to keep it going and his own instinct was strongly for closure. But he seemed unable to listen to arguments or to take a rational part in discussions. During our meeting someone phoned from the hospital with news that the wife of one of his patients had killed herself. He was obviously deeply affected and soon afterwards walked out of the meeting. I'd never seen him like that before. I'm not suggesting that he was suicidal; the idea still seems preposterous. I'm only saying that he was under considerable stress and there may have been worries about which we knew nothing.'

Dalgliesh looked at Caroline Dupayne. She said, 'I hadn't seen him for some weeks prior to the trustees' meeting. He certainly seemed distracted and under stress then, but I doubt whether it was about the museum. He took absolutely no interest in it and my brother and I weren't expecting him to. The meeting we held was our first and we only discussed preliminaries. The trust deed is unambiguous but complicated and there's a great deal to sort out. I've no doubt Neville would have come round in the end. He had his share of family pride. If he was seriously under stress – and I think he was – you can put it down to his job. He cared too much and too deeply, and he's been overworked for years. I didn't know much about his life but I did know that. We both did.'

Before Marcus could speak, Caroline said quickly, 'Can't we continue this some other time? We're both shocked, tired and not thinking very clearly. We stayed because we wanted to see Neville's body moved, but I take it that that won't happen tonight.'

Dalgliesh said, 'It will happen as early as possible tomorrow morning. I'm afraid it can't be tonight.'

Caroline Dupayne seemed to have forgotten her wish for the interview to end. She said impatiently, 'If this is murder, then you have a prime suspect immediately. Tally Clutton must have told you about the motorist driving so quickly down the drive that he knocked her over. Surely finding him is more urgent than question-ing us.'

Dalgliesh said, 'He has to be found if possible. Mrs Clutton said that she thought she had seen him before, but she couldn't remember when or where. I expect she told you how much she saw of him in that brief encoun-ter. A tall fair-haired man, good looking and with a particularly agreeable voice. He was driving a large black car. Does that brief description bring anyone to mind?'

Caroline said, 'I suppose it's typical of some hundred thousand men throughout Great Britain. Are we seri-ously expected to name him?'

Dalgliesh kept his temper. 'I thought it possible that you might know someone, a friend or a regular visitor to the museum, who came to mind when you heard Mrs Clutton's description.'

Caroline Dupayne didn't reply. Her brother said, 'Forgive my sister if she seems unhelpful. We both want to co-operate. It's as much our wish as our duty. Our brother died horribly and we want his murderer – if there is a murderer – brought to justice. Perhaps further questioning could wait until tomorrow. In the mean time, I'll give some thought to this mysterious motorist, but I don't think I'll be able to help. He may be a regular visitor to the museum, but not one I recognize. Isn't it more likely that he was parking here illegally and took fright when he saw the fire?'

'That,' said Dalgliesh 'is a perfectly possible explanation. We can certainly leave any further discussion until tomorrow but there's one thing I'd like to get clear. When did you last see your brother?'

Brother and sister looked at each other. It was Marcus Dupayne who replied. 'I saw him this evening. I wanted to discuss the future of the museum with him. The meeting on Wednesday was unsatisfactory and inconclusive. I felt it would be helpful if the two of us could discuss the matter quietly together. I knew he was due here at six to take the car and drive off as he invariably did on Friday evenings, so I arrived at his flat at about five o'clock. It's in Kensington High Street and parking there is impossible, so I'd left the car in one of the spaces in Holland Park and walked through the park. It wasn't a good time to call. Neville was still distressed and angry and in no mood to discuss the museum. I realized that I'd do no good by staying and I left him within ten minutes. I felt the need to walk off my frustration but was worried that the park might have closed for the night. So I went back to the car by way of Kensington Church Street and Holland Park Avenue. Traffic in the Avenue was heavy — this was, after all, Friday night. When Tally Clutton phoned my house about the fire, my wife couldn't reach me on my mobile, so I didn't get the news until I arrived home. That was within minutes of Tally's call, and I came here immediately. My sister had already arrived.'

'So you were the last known person to see your brother alive. Did you feel when you left him that he was dangerously depressed?'

'No. If I had then, obviously, I wouldn't have left him.'

Dalgliesh turned to Caroline Dupayne. She said, 'I last saw Neville at the trustees' meeting on Wednesday. I haven't been in touch with him since either to discuss the future of the museum or for any other purpose. Frankly I didn't think I would be able to do much good. I thought he behaved oddly at the meeting and we'd do better to leave him alone for a time. I suppose you want to know my movements tonight. I left the museum shortly after four and drove to Oxford Street. I usually go to M&S and Selfridges Food Hall on a Friday to buy food for the weekend, whether I spend it in my flat at Swathling's or in my flat here. It wasn't easy finding a parking space, but I was lucky to get a meter. I always turn off my mobile when I'm shopping and I didn't switch it on again until I was back in the car. I suppose that was just after six as I'd just missed the beginning of the news on the radio. Tally phoned about half an hour later when I was still in Knightsbridge. I came back at once.'

It was time to finish the interview. Dalgliesh had no problem in dealing with Caroline Dupayne's barely concealed antagonism but he could see that both she and her brother were tired. Marcus, indeed, looked close to exhaustion. He kept them for only a few more minutes. Both confirmed that they knew their brother collected his Jaguar at six o'clock on Fridays but had no idea where he went and had never enquired. Caroline made it plain that she thought the question unreasonable. She wouldn't expect Neville to question her about what she did with her weekends, why should she question him? If he had another life, good luck to him. She admitted readily that she had known there was a can of petrol in the shed as she had been in the museum when Miss Godby paid Mrs Faraday for it. Marcus Dupayne said that until recently he had been seldom in the museum. Since, however, he did know that they had a motor-mower, he would have presumed that petrol was stored for it somewhere. Both were adamant that they knew of no one who wished their brother ill. They accepted without demur that the grounds of the museum, and therefore the house itself, would need to be closed to the public while the police continued the investigations on the site. Marcus said that in any case they had decided to shut the museum for a week, or until after their brother's private cremation.

Brother and sister saw Dalgliesh and Piers out of the

front door as punctiliously as if they had been invited guests. They stepped out into the night. To the east of the house Dalgliesh could see the glow from the arc-lights where two police constables would be guarding the scene behind the tape barring access to the garage. There was no sign of Kate and Benton-Smith; presumably they were already in the car park. The wind had dropped but, standing for a moment in the silence, he could hear a soft susurration as if its last breath still stirred the bushes and gently shook the sparse leaves of the saplings. The night sky was like a child's painting, an uneven wash of indigo with splurges of grubby clouds. He wondered what the sky was like over Cambridge. Emma would be home by now. Would she be looking out over Trinity Great Court or, as he might have done, be pacing the Court in a tumult of indecision? Or was it worse? Had it only taken that hour-long journey to Cambridge to convince her that enough was enough, that she wouldn't attempt to see him again?

Forcing his mind back to the matter in hand, he said, 'Caroline Dupayne is anxious to keep open the possibility of suicide and her brother is going along with that, but with some reluctance. From their point of view it's understandable enough. But why should Dupayne kill himself? He wanted the museum closed. Now that he's dead the two living trustees can ensure that it stays open.'

Suddenly he needed to be alone. He said, 'I want to have a last look at the scene. Kate's driving you, isn't she? Tell her and Benton that we'll meet in my room in an hour.'

7

It was eleven-twenty when Dalgliesh and the team met in his office to review progress. Seating himself in one of the chairs at the oblong conference table before the window, Piers was grateful that AD hadn't chosen his own office for the meeting. It was, as usual, in a state of half-organized clutter. He could invariably put his hand on whatever file was needed, but no one seeing the room would believe that possible. AD, he knew, wouldn't have commented; the Chief was methodically tidy himself but required of his subordinates only integrity, dedication and efficiency. If they could achieve this in the midst of a muddle, he saw no reason to interfere. But Piers was glad that Benton-Smith's dark judgemental eyes wouldn't range over the accumulated paper on his desk. In contrast to this disorder, he kept his flat in the city almost obsessively tidy as if this were one additional way of keeping separate his working and his private life.

They were to drink decaffeinated coffee. Kate, as he knew, couldn't take caffeine after seven o'clock without risking a sleepless night and it had seemed pointless and time-wasting to make two brews. Dalgliesh's PA had long since gone home and Benton-Smith had gone out to make the coffee. Piers awaited it without enthusiasm. Decaffeinated coffee seemed a contradiction in terms, but at least getting it and washing up the mugs afterwards would put Benton-Smith in his place. He wondered why he found the man so irritating; dislike was too strong a word. It wasn't that he resented Benton-Smith's spectacular good looks buttressed as they were by a healthy self-regard; he had never much cared if a colleague were more handsome than he, only if he were more intelligent or more successful. A little surprised at his own perception, he thought: *It's because, like me, he's ambitious and ambitious in the same way. Superficially we couldn't be more different. The truth is, I resent him because we're too alike.*

Dalgliesh and Kate settled into their seats and sat in silence. Piers's eyes, which had been fixed on the panorama of lights stretched out beneath the fifth-floor window, ranged round the room. It was familiar to him, but now he had a disconcerting impression that he was seeing it for the first time. He amused himself mentally assessing the occupant's character from the few clues it provided. Except to the keenest eye it was essentially the office of a senior officer, equipped to comply with regulations governing the furnishings considered appropriate to a Commander. Unlike some of his colleagues, AD had seen no need to decorate his walls with framed citations, photographs or the shields of foreign police forces. And there was no framed photograph on his desk. It would have surprised Piers had there been any such evidence of a private life. There were only two unusual features. One wall was completely covered with bookshelves but these, as Piers knew, bore little evidence of personal taste. Instead the shelves held a professional library: Acts of Parliament, official reports, White Papers, reference books, volumes of history,

Archbold on criminal pleading, volumes on criminology, forensic medicine and the history of the police, and the criminal statistics for the past five years. The only other unusual feature was the lithographs of London. Piers supposed that his Chief disliked a totally bare expanse of wall but even the choice of pictures had a certain impersonality. He wouldn't have chosen oils, of course; oils would have been inappropriate and pretentious. His colleagues, if they noticed the lithographs, probably regarded them as indicative of an eccentric but inoffensive taste. They could, thought Piers, offend no one and intrigue only those who had some idea what they must have cost.

Benton-Smith and the coffee arrived. Occasionally at these late-night sessions Dalgliesh would go to his cupboard and bring out glasses and a bottle of red wine. Not tonight, apparently. Deciding to reject the coffee, Piers drew the water carafe towards him and poured a glass.

Dalgliesh said, 'What do we call this putative murderer?'

It was his custom to let the team discuss the case before intervening, but first they would decide on a name for their unseen and as yet unknowable quarry. Dalgliesh disliked the usual police soubriquets.

It was Benton-Smith who replied. He said, 'What about Vulcan, the god of fire?'

Trust him to get in first, thought Piers. He said, 'Well, it's at least shorter than Prometheus.'

Their notebooks were open before them. Dalgliesh said, 'Right, Kate, will you start?'

Kate took a gulp of her coffee, apparently decided it

was too hot, and pushed the mug a little aside. Dalgliesh didn't invariably ask the most senior of his team to speak first, but tonight he did. Kate would already have given thought as to how best to present her arguments. She said, 'We began by treating Dr Dupayne's death as murder, and what we have learned so far confirms that view. Accident is out. He must have been soused with the petrol and, however that happened, it was deliberate. The evidence against suicide is the fact that he was wearing his seatbelt, the light bulb to the left of the door had been removed and the curious position of the petrol can and the screw-top. The top was found in the far corner and the can itself some seven feet from the car door. There's no problem about the time of death. We know that Dr Dupayne garaged his Jag at the museum and collected it every Friday at six o'clock. We also have Tallulah Clutton's evidence confirming the time of death as six o'clock or shortly afterwards. So we are looking for someone who knew Dr Dupayne's movements, had a key to the garage and knew that there was a can of petrol in the unlocked shed. I was going to add that the killer must have known Mrs Clutton's movements, that she regularly attended an evening class on Fridays. But I'm not sure that's relevant. Vulcan could have done a preliminary reconnaissance. He could have known what time the museum closed and that Mrs Clutton would be in her cottage after dark. This was a quick murder. He could expect to be away before Mrs Clutton even heard or smelt the fire.'

Kate paused. Dalgliesh asked, 'Any comments on Kate's summary?'

It was Piers who decided to come in first. 'This wasn't an impulsive murder, it was carefully planned. There's no question of manslaughter. On the face of it the suspects are the Dupayne family and the staff of the museum. All have the necessary knowledge, all have a motive. The Dupaynes wanted the museum kept open, so presumably did Muriel Godby and Tallulah Clutton. Godby would lose a good job, Clutton would lose her job and her home.'

Kate said, 'You don't kill a man in a particularly horrible way just to keep your job. Muriel Godby is obviously a capable and experienced secretary. She's not going to be out of work for long. The same goes for Tallulah Clutton. No good housekeeper needs to be out of work. Even if she can't find a job quickly, surely she's got a family? I can't see either of them as serious suspects.'

Dalgliesh said, 'Until we know more, it's premature to talk about motives. We know nothing yet about Neville Dupayne's private life, the people he worked with, where he went when he collected his Jaguar every Friday. And then there's the problem of the mysterious motorist who knocked down Mrs Clutton.'

Piers said, 'If he exists. We've only her bruised arm and the twisted bike wheel to suggest that he does. She could have contrived the fall and faked the evidence. You don't need much strength to bend a bike wheel. She could have crashed it against a wall.'

Benton-Smith had been silent. Now he said, 'I don't believe she had anything to do with it. I wasn't in the cottage for long but I thought she was an honest witness. I liked her.'

Piers leant back in his chair and slowly ran his finger round the rim of his glass. He said, with controlled calmness, 'And what the hell has that got to do with it? We look at the evidence. Liking or not liking doesn't come into it.'

Benton-Smith said, 'It does with me. The impression a witness makes is part of the evidence. It is for juries, why not for the police? I can't see Tallulah Clutton committing this murder, or any murder for that matter.'

Piers said, 'I suppose you'd make Muriel Godby your prime suspect rather than either of the Dupaynes because she's less attractive than Caroline Dupayne and Marcus has to be out because no senior civil servant could be capable of murder.'

Benton-Smith said quietly, 'No. I'd make her my prime suspect because this murder – if it is murder was committed by someone who is clever, but not as clever as he or she thinks they are. That points to Godby rather than to either of the Dupaynes.'

Piers said, 'Clever, but not as clever as they think they are? You should be able to recognize that phenomenon.'

Kate glanced at Dalgliesh. He knew the keen edge that rivalry could give to an investigation; he had never wanted a team of comfortable mutually admiring conformists. But surely Piers had gone too far. Even so, AD wouldn't reprimand him in front of a junior officer.

Nor did he. Instead, ignoring Piers, Dalgliesh turned to Benton-Smith. 'Your reasoning is valid, Sergeant, but it's dangerous to take it too far. Even an intelligent murderer can have gaps of knowledge and experience. Vulcan may have expected the car to explode and the corpse, garage and car to have been completely destroyed, particularly as he may not have expected Mrs Clutton to be on the scene so early. A devastating fire could have destroyed most of the clues. But let's leave the psychological profiling and concentrate on what needs to be done.'

Kate turned to Dalgliesh. 'D'you buy Mrs Clutton's story, sir? The accident, the fleeing motorist?'

'Yes I do. We'll put out the usual optimistic call asking him to get in touch but if he doesn't, tracing him won't be easy. All we have is her momentary impression, but that was remarkably vivid, wasn't it? The face bending over her with what she described as a look of mingled horror and compassion. Does that sound like our murderer? A man who has deliberately thrown petrol over his victim and burned him alive? He'd want to get away as quickly as possible. Would he be likely to stop because he'd knocked an elderly woman off her bicycle? If he did, would he show that degree of concern?'

Kate said, 'That comment he made about the bonfire, echoing the Rouse case. It obviously impressed Mrs Clutton and Miss Godby. Neither of them struck me as compulsive or irrational, but I could see that it worried them. Surely we aren't dealing with a copycat murder. The only fact the two crimes have in common is a dead man in a burning car.'

Piers said, 'It's probably a coincidence, the kind of throwaway remark anyone might make in the circumstances. He was trying to justify ignoring a fire. So was Rouse.'

Dalgliesh said, 'What worried the women was the

realization that the two deaths might have more in common than a few words. It may have been the first time that they mentally acknowledged that Dupayne could have been murdered. But it's a complication. If he isn't found, and we bring a suspect to trial, Mrs Clutton's evidence will be a gift to the defence. Any other comments on Kate's summary?'

Benton-Smith had been sitting very still and in silence. Now he spoke. 'I think you could make a case for suicide.'

Irritated, Piers said, 'Go on then, make it.'

'I'm not saying it was suicide, I'm saying that the evidence for murder isn't as strong as we're claiming. The Dupaynes have told us that the wife of one of his patients has killed herself. Perhaps we should find out why. Neville Dupayne may have been more distressed about the death than his siblings realized.' He turned to Kate. 'And taking your points, ma'am. Dupayne was wearing his seat belt. I suggest he wanted to make sure that he was strapped down and immobile. Wasn't there always the risk that, once alight, he'd change his mind, make a dash for it, try to get into the tall grass and roll over? He wanted to die, and to die in the Jag. Then there's the position of the can and the screw-top. Why on earth should he place the can close to the car? Wasn't it more natural to throw the top away first, and then the can? Why should he care where they landed?'

Piers said, 'And the missing light bulb?'

'We have no evidence to show how long it was missing. We haven't been able to contact Ryan Archer yet. He could have removed it, anyone could have –

Dupayne himself for one. You can't build a murder case on a missing light bulb.'

Kate said, 'But we've found no suicide note. People who kill themselves usually want to explain why. And what a way to choose! I mean, this man was a doctor, he had access to drugs. He could have taken them in the car and died in the Jag if that's what he wanted. Why should he set himself alight and die in agony?'

Benton-Smith said, 'It was probably very quick.'

Piers was impatient. 'Like hell it was! Not quick enough. I don't buy your theory, Benton. I suppose you'll go on to say that Dupayne himself removed the light bulb and placed the can where we found it so that his suicide could look like murder. A nice goodbye present for the family. It's the action of a petulant child or a madman.'

Benton-Smith said quietly, 'It's a possibility.'

Piers said angrily, 'Oh, anything's possible! It's possible that Tallulah Clutton did it because she'd been having an affair with Dupayne and he was dumping her for Muriel Godby! For God's sake, let's stay in the real world.'

Dalgliesh said, 'There's one fact which could suggest suicide rather than murder. It would be difficult for Vulcan to douse Dupayne's head with petrol using the can. It would come out too slowly. If Vulcan needed to incapacitate his victim, even for a few seconds, he would have to decant the petrol into something like a bucket. Either that, or knock him out first. We'll continue search-ing the grounds at first light, but even if a bucket had been used, I doubt whether we'll find it.'

Piers said, 'There wasn't a bucket in the garden shed, but Vulcan would have brought it with him. He would have poured in the petrol in the garage, not in the shed, before removing the light bulb. Then he'd kick the can into the corner. He'd want to minimize touching it, even wearing gloves, but it would be important to leave the can in the garage if he wanted the death to look like an accident or suicide.'

Kate broke in, controlling her excitement. 'Then, after the murder, Vulcan could dump all his protective clothing in the bucket. It would be easy enough later to get rid of the evidence. The bucket was probably the ordinary plastic type. He could stamp it out of shape and throw it into a skip, a handy rubbish bin or a ditch.'

Dalgliesh said, 'At present that's all conjecture. We're in danger of theorizing in advance of the facts. Let's move on, shall we? We need to settle the tasks for tomorrow. I've made an appointment to see Sarah Dupayne at ten o'clock with Kate. We may get some clue about what her father did at weekends. He could have had another life and, if so, we need to know where it was, whom he saw, the people he met. We're assuming that the killer got to the museum first, made his preparations and waited in the darkness of the garage, but it's possible that Dupayne wasn't alone when he arrived. He could have brought Vulcan with him, or he could have met him there by arrangement. Piers, you and Benton-Smith had better interview the mechanic at Duncan's Garage, a Stanley Carter. Dupayne may have confided in him. In any case he could have some idea of the mileage covered each weekend. And we need to interview Marcus and Caroline Dupayne again and, of course, Tallulah Clutton and Muriel Godby. After a night's sleep they may remember something they haven't told us. Then there are the voluntary workers, Mrs Faraday who does the garden and Mrs Strickland the calligrapher. I met Mrs Strickland in the library when I visited the museum on the twenty-fifth of October. And, of course, there's Ryan Archer. It's odd that this Major he's supposed to be staying with hasn't replied to the phone calls. Ryan should be coming to work by ten on Monday but we need to speak to him before then. And there's one piece of evidence we can hope to test. Mrs Clutton said that when she phoned Muriel Godby on the landline it was engaged and she had to ring her mobile. We know Godby's story, that the receiver hadn't been properly replaced. It would be interesting to know whether she was at home when she took that call. You're something of an expert here, aren't you, Sergeant?'

'Not an expert, sir, but I've had some experience. With a mobile, the base station used is recorded at the beginning and end of every call, whether outbound or inbound, including calls to retrieve voicemail. The system also records the base station used by the other person if they are part of the network. The data is held for several months and passed on when obliged by law. I've been on cases where we have been able to get it, but it's not always useful. Typically in cities you are unlikely to get a more accurate fix than a couple of hundred metres, maybe less. There's a very heavy call on the service. We may have to wait.'

Dalgliesh said, 'That's something we need to put in

hand. And we should interview Marcus Dupayne's wife. She can probably confirm her husband's story that he intended to call on his brother that evening.'

Piers said, 'Being his wife she probably will. They've had time enough to agree on their story. But that doesn't mean that the rest of it's true. He could easily have walked to his car, driven to the museum, killed his brother and then gone home. We need to look more closely at the timing but I reckon it's possible.'

It was then that Piers's phone rang. He answered it and listened, then said, 'I think, Sergeant, you had better speak to Commander Dalgliesh,' and handed the instrument over.

Dalgliesh listened in silence, then said, 'Thank you, Sergeant. We've got a suspicious death at the Dupayne Museum and Archer may be a material witness. We need to find him. I'll make an appointment for two of my officers to see Major Arkwright as soon as he's fit enough and back home.' Handing the phone back to Piers, he said, 'That was Sergeant Mason from the Paddington station. He's just returned to Major Arkwright's flat in Maida Vale after visiting him in St Mary's Hospital. When the Major returned home this evening at about seven, Ryan Archer attacked him with a poker. The woman in the flat below heard the crash when he fell and rang for an ambulance and the police. The Major isn't badly hurt. It's a glancing head wound but they're keeping him in for the night. He gave Sergeant Mason his keys so that the police could return to the flat and check that the windows were secure. Ryan Archer isn't there. He ran off after the attack and so far there's no news of him. I think it's unlikely that we shall see him returning for work on Monday morning. A call is being put out for him and we'll leave the search to those who've got the manpower.'

Dalgliesh went on, 'Priorities for tomorrow. Kate and I will see Sarah Dupayne in the morning and then go on to Neville Dupayne's flat. Piers, after you and Benton have been to the garage, make an appointment to see Major Arkwright with Kate. Then later we need to interview both the volunteers, Mrs Faraday and Mrs Strickland. I rang James Calder-Hale. He took the news of the murder as calmly as I'd have expected and will condescend to see us at ten o'clock on Sunday morning when he'll be in the museum doing some private work. We should know by nine tomorrow the time and place of the post-mortem. I'd like you to be there, Kate, with Benton. And you, Benton, had better make arrangements for Mrs Clutton to have a look at the Rogues' Gallery. It's unlikely she'll recognize anyone but the artist's impression following her description might prove useful. Some of this may spill over into Sunday or Monday. When the news breaks there'll be a fair amount of press publicity. Luckily there's enough happening at present to ensure we don't make the front page. Will you liaise with Public Relations, Kate? And see Accommodation and arrange for an office here to be set up as an incident room. There's no point in disturbing them at Hampstead, they're short enough of space as it is. Any further questions? Keep in touch tomorrow as I may need to vary the programme.'

8

It was eleven-thirty. Tally, corded in her woollen dressing gown, took the key from its hook and unlocked the bolt on her bedroom window. It was Miss Caroline who had insisted on the cottage being made secure as soon as she had taken over responsibility for the museum from her father, but Tally never liked to sleep with her window closed. Now she opened it wide and the cold air washed over her, bringing with it the peace and silence of the night. This was the moment at the end of the day which she always cherished. She knew that the peace stretching beneath her was illusory. Out there in the dark, predators were closing in on their prey, the unending war of survival was being waged and the air was alive with millions of small scufflings and creepings inaudible to her ears. And tonight there was that other image: white teeth gleaming like a snarl in a blackened head. She knew that she would never be able to banish it entirely from her mind. Its power could only be lessened by accepting it as a terrible reality with which she would have to live, as millions of others in a war-torn world had to live with their horrors. But now at last there was no lingering smell of fire and she gazed over the silent acres to where the lights of London were flung like a casket of jewels over a waste of darkness which seemed neither earth nor sky.

She wondered if Muriel, in that small spare room beside hers, was already asleep. She had returned to the cottage later than Tally expected and had explained that she had taken a shower at home; she preferred a shower to a bath. She had arrived with an additional pint of milk, the cereal she preferred for breakfast and a jar of Horlicks. She had heated the milk and made a drink for them both, and they had sat together watching *Newsnight*, since to let the moving images pass before their unheeding eyes at least gave an illusion of normality. As soon as the programme was over they had said good-night. Tally had been grateful for Muriel's company, but was glad that tomorrow she would be gone. She was grateful, too, to Miss Caroline. She and Mr Marcus had come to the cottage after Commander Dalgliesh and his team had finally left. It was Miss Caroline who had spoken for them both.

'We're so very sorry, Tally. It's been terrible for you. We want to thank you for being so brave and acting so promptly. No one could have done better.'

To Tally's great relief there had been no questions and they hadn't lingered. It was strange, she thought, that it had taken this tragedy to make her realize that she liked Miss Caroline. She was a woman who people tended either to like greatly or not at all. Recognizing Miss Caroline's power, Tally accepted that the basis of her liking was slightly reprehensible. It was simply that Miss Caroline could have made life at the Dupayne difficult for her and had chosen not to.

The cottage enclosed her as it always did. It was the place to which, after all the long-dead years of drudgery and self-denial, she had opened her arms to life as she had at the moment when huge but gentle hands had lifted her out of the rubble into the light.

Always she gazed into the darkness without fear. Soon after she had arrived at the Dupayne, an old gardener, now retired, had taken some pleasure in telling her of a Victorian murder which had taken place in the then private house. He had relished the description of the body, a dead servant girl, her throat cut, sprawled at the foot of an oak tree on the edge of the Heath. The girl had been pregnant and there had been talk that one of the family members, her employer or one of his two sons, had been responsible for the girl's death. There were those who claimed that her ghost, unappeased, still walked on the Heath by night. It had never walked for Tally, whose fears and anxieties took more tangible forms. Only once had she felt a *frisson*, less of fear than of interest, when she had seen movement under the oak, two dark figures forming themselves out of greater darkness, coming together, speaking, walking separately away. She had recognized one of them as Mr Calder-Hale. It was not the only time she was to see him walking with a companion by night. She had never spoken of these sightings to him or to anyone. She could understand the attraction of walking in the darkness. It was none of her business.

Partly closing the window, she went at last to bed. But sleep eluded her. Lying there in the darkness, the events of the day crowded in on her mind, each moment more vivid, more sharply etched than in reality. And there was something beyond the reach of memory, something fugitive and untold, but which lay at the back of her mind as a vague unfocused worry. Perhaps this unease arose only from guilt that she hadn't done enough, that she was in some way partly responsible, that if she hadn't gone to her evening class Dr Neville might still be alive. She knew that the guilt was irrational and resolutely she tried to put it out of mind. And now, with her eyes fixed on the pale blur of the half-open window, a memory came back from those childhood years of sitting alone in the half-light of a gaunt Victorian church in that Leeds suburb, listening to Evensong. It was a prayer she had not heard for nearly sixty years, but now the words came as freshly to her mind as if she were hearing them for the first time. *Lighten our darkness, we beseech thee, O Lord; and by thy great mercy defend us from all perils and dangers of this night; for the love of thy only Son, our Saviour Jesus Christ.* She held the image of that charred head in her mind and spoke the prayer aloud and was comforted.

9

Sarah Dupayne lived on the third floor of a period house in an undistinguished road of nineteenth-century terraced houses on the borders of Kilburn, which local estate agents no doubt preferred to advertise as West Hampstead. Opposite number sixteen was a small patch of rough grass and distorted shrubs which could be dignified as a park but was little more than a green oasis. The two half-demolished houses beside it were now a building site and were apparently being converted into a single dwelling. There was a high number of house agents' boards fixed to the small front gardens, one outside number sixteen. A few houses proclaimed by their gleaming doors and repointed brickwork that the aspiring young professional class had begun to colonize the street but, despite its nearness to Kilburn station and the attractions of Hampstead, it still had the unkempt, slightly desolate look of a street of transients. For a Saturday morning it was unusually calm, and there was no sign of life behind the drawn curtains.

There were three bells to the right of the door of number sixteen. Dalgliesh pressed the one with DUPAYNE written on a card above it. The name beneath had been strongly inked out and was no longer decipherable. A woman's voice answered the ring and Dalgliesh announced himself. The voice said, 'It's no good me pressing the buzzer to let you in. The bloody thing's broken. I'll come down.'

Less than a minute later the front door opened. They saw a woman, solidly built with strong features and heavy dark hair tugged back from a broad forehead and tightly tied with a scarf at the nape of the neck. When worn loose its luxuriance would have given her a gypsy-like raffishness, but now her face, devoid of make-up except for a slash of bright lipstick and drained of anima-tion, looked nakedly vulnerable. Dalgliesh thought that she was probably in her late thirties but the small ravages of time were already laid bare, the lines across the fore-head, the small creases of discontent at the corners of the wide mouth. She was wearing black trousers and a low-necked collarless top with a loose overshirt of purple wool. She wore no bra and her heavy breasts swung as she moved.

Standing aside to let them in, she said, 'I'm Sarah Dupayne. I'm afraid there's no lift. Come up, will you?' When she spoke there was a faint smell of whisky on her breath.

As she preceded them, firm-footed, up the stairs, Dalgliesh thought that she was younger than she had at first appeared. The strain of the last twelve hours had robbed her of any semblance of youth. He was surprised to find her alone. Surely, at such a time, someone could have come to be with her.

The flat into which they were shown looked out over the small green opposite and was filled with light. There were two windows and a door to the left which stood open and obviously led to the kitchen. It was an unsettling room. Dalgliesh had the impression that it had been furnished with some care and expense, but that the occupants had now lost interest and had, emotionally if not physically, moved out. There were grubby lines on the painted walls suggesting that pictures had been removed and the mantelshelf above the Victorian grate held only a small Doulton vase with two sprays of white chrysanthemums. The flowers were dead. The sofa, which dominated the room, was made of leather and modern. The only other large piece of furniture was a long bookcase covering one of the walls. It was half empty, the books tumbling against each other in disorder.

Sarah Dupayne invited them to sit and settled herself on the square leather pouf beside the fireplace. She said, 'Would you like some coffee? You're not supposed to have alcohol, are you? I think I've got enough milk in the fridge. I've been drinking myself, as you've probably noticed, but not much. I'm quite able to answer questions, if that's what you're worried about. D'you mind if I smoke?'

Without waiting for a reply she dug in her shirt pocket and pulled out a packet of cigarettes and a lighter. They waited while she lit up and began vigorously inhaling as if the nicotine were a life-saving drug.

Dalgliesh said, 'I'm sorry we have to bother you with questions so soon after the shock of your father's death. But in the case of a suspicious death, the first days of the investigation are usually the most important. We need to get essential information as quickly as possible.'

'A suspicious death? Are you sure? That means murder. Aunt Caroline thought it could be suicide.'

235

'Did she give any reason for thinking that?'

'Not really. She said you were satisfied that it couldn't be an accident. I suppose she thought that suicide was the only probable option. Anything is more likely than murder. I mean, who would want to murder my father? He was a psychiatrist. He wasn't a drug dealer or anything like that. As far as I know he hadn't any enemies.'

Dalgliesh said, 'He must have had at least one.'

'Well, it's no one I know about.'

Kate asked, 'Did he talk to you about anyone who might wish him ill?'

'Wish him ill? Is that police talk? Chucking petrol over him and burning him to death is certainly wishing him ill. God, you can say that again! No, I don't know anyone who wished him ill.' She emphasized each word, her voice heavy with sarcasm.

Kate said, 'His relationship with his siblings was good? They got on well?'

'You aren't very subtle, are you? No, I should think they occasionally loathed each other's guts. Families do, or haven't you noticed? The Dupaynes aren't close but that's not so unusual. I mean, you can be a dysfunctional family without wanting to burn each other to death.'

Dalgliesh asked, 'What was his attitude to the signing of the new lease?'

'He said he wouldn't do it. I went to see him on Tuesday, the evening before they were due to have a trustees' meeting. I told him I thought he should hold out and not sign. I wanted my share of the money, to be honest. He had other considerations.'

'How much would each trustee expect to get?'

236

'You'll have to ask my uncle. About twenty-five thousand, I think. Not a fortune by today's standards but enough to give me a year or two off work. Dad wanted the museum to close for more laudable reasons. He thought we cared too much about the past, a kind of national nostalgia, and that it stopped us from coping with the problems of the present.'

Dalgliesh asked, 'Those weekends away, it seems to have been a regular practice, collecting the car every Friday at six. Do you know where he went?'

'No. He never told me and I never asked. I know he was out of London at weekends but I didn't realize it happened every Friday. I suppose that's why he worked so late on the other four weekdays, to leave the Saturday and Sunday free. Perhaps he had another life. I hope he did. I'd like to think he had some happiness before he died.'

Kate persisted. 'But he never mentioned where he went, whether there was someone he was seeing? He didn't talk to you about it?'

'We didn't talk. I don't mean that we weren't on good terms. He was my father. I loved him. It's just that we didn't communicate much. He was overworked, I was overworked, we lived in different worlds. What was there to talk about? I mean, at the end of the day he was probably like me, collapsed exhausted in front of the box. He worked most evenings anyway. Why should he travel up to Kilburn just to tell me what a bloody day he'd had? He had a woman though, you could try asking her.'

'Do you know who she is?'

237

'No, but I expect you'll find out. That's your job, isn't it, hunting people down.'

'How do you know he had a woman?'

'I asked if I could use the flat one weekend while I was moving here from Balham. He'd been pretty careful, but I knew. I snooped round a bit – a woman always does. I won't tell you how I knew, I'll spare your blushes. It wasn't any business of mine anyway. I thought, good luck to him. I called him Dad, by the way. On my fourteenth birthday he suggested that I might like to call him Neville. I suppose he thought that's what I'd like, making him more a friend, less a father. Trendy. Well, he was wrong. What I wanted was to call him Daddy and to climb on his lap. Ridiculous, isn't it? But I can tell you one thing. Whatever the rest of the family tell you, Dad wouldn't have killed himself. He'd never do that to me.'

Kate saw that she was close to tears. She had stopped drawing on the cigarette and threw it, half smoked, into the empty grate. Her hands were trembling.

Dalgliesh said, 'This isn't a good time to be alone. Have you a friend who could be with you?'

'No one I can think of. And I don't want Uncle Marcus spouting platitudinous condolences, or Aunt Caroline looking at me sardonically and daring me to show any emotion, wanting me to be a hypocrite.'

Dalgliesh said, 'We could come back later if you'd rather stop now.'

'I'm all right. You go on. I don't suppose you'll be here much longer anyway. I mean, there's not much more I can tell you.'

'Who is your father's heir? Did he ever discuss his will?'

'No, but I suppose I am. Who else is there? I haven't got siblings and my mother died last year. She wouldn't have got anything anyway. They divorced when I was ten. She lived in Spain and I never saw her. She didn't remarry because she wanted the alimony, but that didn't exactly impoverish him. And I don't suppose he's left anything to Marcus or Caroline. I'll go to the Kensington flat later today and find out the name of Dad's solicitor. The flat'll be worth something, of course. He bought sensibly. I suppose you'll want to go there too.'

Dalgliesh said, 'Yes, we'll need to look at his papers. Perhaps we can be there at the same time. Have you a key?'

'No, he didn't want me walking in and out of his life. I usually brought trouble with me and I suppose he liked to be warned. Didn't you find his keys on the – in his pocket?'

'Yes, we have a set. I'd prefer to have borrowed yours.'

'I suppose Dad's have been collected as part of the evidence. The porter can let us in. You go when you like, I'd rather be there alone. I'm planning to spend a year abroad as soon as things are settled. Will I have to wait until the case is solved? I mean, can I leave after the inquest and the funeral?'

Dalgliesh asked gently, 'Will you want to?'

'I suppose not. Dad would warn me that you can't escape. You carry yourself with you. Trite but true. I'll be carrying a hell of a lot more baggage now, won't I?'

Dalgliesh and Kate got to their feet. Dalgliesh held out his hand. He said, 'Yes. I'm sorry.'

239

They didn't speak until they were outside and walking to the car. Kate was thoughtful. 'She's interested in the money, isn't she? It's important to her.'

'Important enough to commit patricide? She expected the museum to close. She could be certain eventually of getting her twenty-five thousand.'

'Perhaps she wanted it sooner rather than later. She's feeling guilty about something.'

Dalgliesh said, 'Because she didn't love him, or didn't love him enough. Guilt is inseparable from grieving. But there's more on her mind than her father's murder, horrible though that was. We need to know what he did at weekends. Piers and Benton-Smith might get something from the garage mechanic but I think our best bet could be Dupayne's PA. There's very little a secretary doesn't know about her boss. Find out who she is, will you, Kate, and make an appointment – for today if possible. Dupayne was a consultant psychiatrist at St Oswald's. I should try there first.'

Kate busied herself with directory inquiries, then phoned the hospital. There was a delay of some minutes in getting through to the extension she needed. The conversation lasted only a minute with Kate doing most of the listening.

Holding her hand over the mouthpiece, she said to Dalgliesh, 'Dr Dupayne's PA is a Mrs Angela Faraday. She works on Saturday mornings but the clinic will be over by quarter past one. She'll be working alone in her office between then and two o'clock. She can see you any time then. Apparently she doesn't take a lunch-break except for sandwiches in her office.'

'Thank her, Kate, and say I'll be there at half-past one.'

The appointment made and the call ended, Kate said, 'It's an interesting coincidence her having the same name as the volunteer gardener at the museum. That is, if it is a coincidence. Faraday's not a common name.'

Dalgliesh said, 'If it isn't a coincidence and they are related, it opens up a number of interesting possibilities. In the mean time, let's see what the Kensington flat has to tell us.'

Within half an hour they were parked and at the door. All the bell pushes were numbered but not named, except for flat number thirteen, which bore the label 'PORTER. He arrived within half a minute of Kate's pressing the bell, still putting on his uniform jacket. They saw a stockily-built sad-eyed man with a heavy moustache who reminded Kate of a walrus. He gave a surname which was long, intricate and which sounded Polish. Although taciturn, he was not disobliging and answered their questions slowly but readily enough. He must, surely, have heard of Neville Dupayne's death but he made no mention of it and nor did Dalgliesh. Kate thought that this careful joint reticence gave the conversation a somewhat surreal quality. He said, in answer to their questions, that Dr Dupayne was a very quiet gentleman. He rarely saw him and couldn't remember when they had last spoken. If Dr Dupayne had any visitors he had never seen them. He kept two keys to each of the flats in his office. On request, he handed over the keys to number eleven without demur, merely requesting a receipt.

But their examination was unrewarding. The flat,

which faced Kensington High Street, had the impersonal over-tidiness of an apartment made ready for prospective tenants to view. The air smelt a little stale; even at this height Dupayne had taken the precaution of closing or locking all the windows before leaving for the weekend. Making a preliminary tour of the sitting-room and two bedrooms, Dalgliesh thought he had never seen a victim's house so outwardly unrevealing of a private life. The windows were fitted with wooden slatted blinds as if the owner feared that even to choose curtains would be to risk betraying a personal choice. There were no pictures on the painted white walls. The bookcase held about a dozen medical tomes, but otherwise Dupayne's reading was chiefly confined to biographies, autobiographies and history. His main leisure interest was, apparently, listening to music. The equipment was modern and the cabinet of CDs showed a preference for the classics and New Orleans jazz.

Leaving Kate to examine the bedrooms, Dalgliesh settled himself at the desk. Here, as he had expected, all the papers were in meticulous order. He saw that regularly recurring bills were paid by standing order, the easiest and most trouble-free method. His garage bill was sent to him quarterly and paid within days. His portfolio showed a capital of just over £200,000 prudently invested. The bank statements, filed in a leather folder, showed no large payments in or significant withdrawals. He gave regularly and generously to charities, mainly ones concerned with mental health. The only entries of interest were those on his credit-card statements where, every week, a bill was paid to a country inn or hotel.

The locations were widely different and the amounts not large. It would, of course, be perfectly possible to find out whether the expenditure had been for Dupayne alone or for two people, but Dalgliesh was inclined to wait. It was still possible that the truth could be discovered in other ways.

Kate came back from the bedroom. She said, 'The spare room bed is made up, but there's no evidence anyone has recently stayed here. I think Sarah Dupayne was right, sir. He has had a woman in the flat. In the bottom drawer there's a folded linen bathrobe and three pairs of pants. They're washed but not ironed. In the bathroom cabinet there's a deodorant of a kind used mostly by women, and a glass with a spare toothbrush.'

Dalgliesh said, 'They could have belonged to his daughter.'

Kate had worked too long with him to be easily embarrassed, but now she coloured and there was a trace of it in her voice. She said, 'I don't think the pants belonged to his daughter. Why pants but no night-dress or bedroom slippers? I think if a lover was coming here and she liked being undressed by him, she'd probably bring clean pants with her. The bathrobe in the bottom drawer is too small for a man and his own is hanging on the bathroom door.'

Dalgliesh said, 'If a lover was his fellow traveller every Friday, I wonder where they met, whether he called for her or she came to the Dupayne and waited for him there? It seems unlikely. There would be the risk of someone working late and seeing her. At present it's all conjecture. Let's see what his PA can tell us. I'll drop you at the Dupayne, Kate. I'd like to see Angela Faraday on my own.'

Piers knew why Dalgliesh had chosen him and Benton-Smith to interview Stan Carter at the garage. Dalgliesh's attitude to a car was that it was a vehicle designed to transport him from one place to another. He required it to be reliable, fast, comfortable and agreeable to the eye. His present Jaguar fulfilled these criteria. Beyond that he saw no reason for discussion of its merits or cogitation about what new models might be worth a test drive. Car talk bored him. Piers, who seldom drove in town and liked to walk from his City flat to New Scotland Yard, shared his boss's attitude but combined it with a lively interest in models and performance. If car chat would encourage Stan Carter to be forthcoming, then Piers could supply it.

Duncan's Garage occupied the corner of a side road where Highgate merges into Islington. A high wall of grey London brick, smudged where largely ineffectual efforts had been made to remove graffiti, was broken by a double gate fitted with a padlock. Both gates were open. Inside to the right was a small office. A young woman with improbably yellow hair caught up with a large plastic clasp like a cockscomb was seated at the computer, a thickset man in a black leather jacket bending over her to study the screen. He straightened up at Piers's knock and opened the door.

Flipping open his wallet, Piers said, 'Police. Are you the manager?'

'So the boss tells me.'

'We'd like to speak to Mr Stanley Carter. Is he here?'

Without bothering to look at the identification, the man jerked his head towards the rear of the garage. 'Back there. He's working.'

Piers said, 'So are we. We won't keep him long.'

The manager went back to the computer screen, shutting the door. Piers and Benton-Smith skirted a BMW and a VW Golf, presumably belonging to the staff since both were recent models. Beyond them the space opened up into a large workshop with walls of white-painted brick and a high pitched roof. At the back a wooden platform had been erected to provide an upper storey, with a ladder to the right giving access. The front of the platform was decorated with a row of gleaming radiators like the captured trophies of battle. The left-hand wall was fitted with steel racks and everywhere – sometimes hung on hooks and labelled but more often in a jumble which gave the impression of organized chaos – were the tools of the trade. The room gave the impression familiar to Piers from visits to similar workplaces, of every item being hoarded in case it should later be found to be of use, a place where Carter could no doubt lay his hands on anything wanted. Ranged on the floor were oxy-acetylene gas cylinders, tins of paint and paint thinner, crumpled petrol cans and a heavy press, while above the racks hung spanners, jumpleads, fanbelts, welding masks and rows of paint guns. The garage was lit by two long fluorescent tubes. The air, which was cold, smelt of paint and faintly of oil. It was empty and silent, except for a low tapping from under a 1940s grey Alvis on the ramp. Piers crouched down and called, 'Mr Carter?'

The tapping stopped. Two legs slid out and then a body, clad in dirty overalls and a thick high-necked jumper. Stan Carter got to his feet, took a rag from his centre pocket, then slowly rubbed his hands, paying attention to each finger, meanwhile regarding the officers with a steady untroubled gaze. Satisfied with the redistribution of oil on his fingers, he shook hands firmly first with Piers, then with Benton-Smith, then rubbed his palms on his trouser legs as if to rid them of contamination. They were facing a small wiry man with a tonsured head, a thick fringe of grey hair cut very short in a regular line above a high forehead. His nose was long and sharp and there was a pallor over the cheekbones typical of a man whose working life was spent indoors. He could have been taken for a monk, but there was nothing contemplative about those keen and watchful eyes. Despite his height he held himself very upright.

Piers thought, ex-Army. He made the introductions, then said, 'We're here to ask you about Dr Neville Dupayne. You know he's dead?'

'I know. Murdered, I'm thinking. You wouldn't be here otherwise.'

'We know you serviced his E-type. Could you tell us how long you've been doing that, what the procedure is?'

'Twelve years come April. He drives it, I look after it. Always the same routine. He collects it at six every Friday evening from his lock-up at the museum and comes back late Sunday or by seven-thirty Monday morning.'

'And leaves it here?'

'He usually drives it straight back to the lock-up. That's as far as I know. Most weeks I go there on the Monday or Tuesday and bring it here for servicing, clean and polish, check the oil and water, fill her up with petrol, do anything necessary. He liked that car to be spotless.'

'What happened when he brought it straight here?'

'Nothing happened. He'd leave it for servicing. He knows I'm here by seven-thirty so if there was anything he wanted to tell me about the car he'd come here first then take a cab to the museum.'

'If Dr Dupayne drove the car back here, did you talk about his weekend, where he'd been, for example?'

'He wasn't one for talking except about the car. Might say a word or two, discussing the weather he'd had, maybe.'

Benton-Smith said, 'When did you last see him?'

'Two weeks ago on Monday. He brought the car here just after seven-thirty.'

'How did he seem? Depressed?'

'No more depressed than anyone else on a wet Monday morning.'

Benton-Smith asked, 'Drove fast, did he?'

'I wasn't there to see. Fast enough I reckon. No point in driving an E-type if you want to hang around.'

Benton-Smith said, 'I was wondering how far he got. It would give us an idea where he went. He didn't say, I suppose?'

'No. Not my business where he went. You asked me that before.'

Piers said, 'But you must have noted the mileage.'

'I might do that. She'd be due for her full service every three thousand miles. Not much to do usually. Balancing the carburettors took a bit of time, but she was a good car. Running very sweetly the whole time I had charge of her.'

Piers said, 'Launched in 1961, wasn't it? I don't think Jaguar made a more beautiful car.'

Carter said, 'She wasn't perfect. Some drivers found her heavy and not everyone liked her body, but Dr Dupayne did. He was powerfully fond of that car. If he had to go I reckon he'd be glad enough that the Jag and he went together.'

Ignoring this surprising outburst of sentimentality, Piers asked, 'What about the mileage?'

'Seldom under a hundred miles in a weekend. More often a hundred and fifty to two hundred. Sometimes a good bit more. That would be when he returned on the Monday, more than likely.'

Piers said, 'And he was alone?'

'How should I know? I never saw anyone with him.'

Benton-Smith said impatiently, 'Come off it, Mr Carter, you must have had some idea whether he had a companion. Week after week, servicing the car, cleaning it. There's always some evidence left sooner or later. A different smell even.'

Carter regarded him steadily. 'What kind of smell? Chicken vindaloo and chips? Usually he drove with the roof down, all weathers except rain.' He added with a

249

trace of sullenness, 'I never saw anyone and I never smelt anything out of the usual. What business of mine is it who he drove with?'

Piers said, 'What about the keys? If you collected the car from the museum on Mondays or Tuesdays you must have had keys both to the Jag and to the lock-up garage.'

'That's right. Kept in the office in the key cupboard.'

'Is the key cupboard locked?'

'Mostly, with the key in the desk drawer. Might be kept in the lock, likely as not if Sharon or Mr Morgan was in the office.'

Benton-Smith said, 'So other people could get their hands on it?'

'Don't see how. There's always someone here and the gates are padlocked at seven o'clock. If I'm working after that I get in by the door round the corner with my own key. There's a doorbell. Dr Dupayne knew where to find me. Anyway, the car keys aren't named. We know which is which, but I don't see how anyone else can.'

He turned and looked towards the Alvis in a clear indication that he was a busy man who had said all that was necessary. Piers thanked him and gave him his card, asking him to get in touch if he later remembered anything relevant he hadn't mentioned.

In the office Bill Morgan confirmed the information about the keys more obligingly than Piers had expected, showed them the key cupboard and, taking the key from the right-hand drawer to his desk, locked and unlocked it several times as if to demonstrate the ease with which it worked. They saw the usual row of hooks, none of them labelled.

Walking to the car, which by some miracle wasn't adorned with a parking ticket, Benton-Smith said, 'We didn't get much out of him.'

'Probably all there was to get. And what was the point in asking him if Dupayne was depressed? He hadn't seen him for a couple of weeks. Anyway, we know this isn't suicide. And you needn't have been so sharp with him about the possible passenger. That type doesn't respond to bullying.'

Benton-Smith said stiffly, 'I didn't think I was bullying, sir.'

'No, but you were getting close to it. Move over, Sergeant. I'll drive.'

II

It was not the first time that Dalgliesh had visited St Oswald's. He could recall two past occasions when, as a detective sergeant, he had gone there to interview victims of attempted murder. The hospital was in a square in North West London and when he reached the open iron gates he saw that outwardly little had changed. The nineteenth-century building of ochre-coloured brick was massive and with its square towers, great rounded arches and narrow pointed windows, looked more like a Victorian educational establishment or a gloomy conglomeration of churches than it did a hospital.

He found a space for his Jaguar without difficulty in the visitors' parking lot and passed under a ponderous porch and through doors that opened automatically at his approach. Inside there had been changes. There was now a large and modern reception desk with two clerks on duty and, to the right of the entrance, an open door leading into a waiting-room furnished with leather armchairs and a low table holding magazines.

He didn't report at the desk; experience had taught him that few people entering a hospital with assurance were challenged. Among a multitude of signs was one with an arrow pointing the way to Psychiatric Outpatients and he followed it along the vinyl-floored corridor. The shabbiness he remembered had vanished. The walls were freshly painted and were hung with a succession of framed sepia photographs of the hospital's history. The children's ward of 1870 showed rail cots, children with bandaged heads and frail unsmiling faces, Victorian lady visitors in their bustles and immense hats, and nurses with their ankle-length uniforms and high goffered caps. There were pictures of the bomb-damaged hospital during the V2 bombardment, and others showing the hospital tennis and football teams, the open days, the occasional visit by royalty.

The Psychiatric Outpatients department was in the basement and he followed the arrow down the stairs into a waiting-room which was now almost deserted. There was another reception desk with an attractive Asian girl sitting at a computer. Dalgliesh said that he had an appointment with Mrs Angela Faraday and, smiling, she pointed the way to a far door and said that Mrs Faraday's office was on the left. He knocked and the voice he had heard on the phone immediately answered.

The room was small and overcrowded with filing cabinets. There was hardly room for the one desk, the desk chair and a single armchair. The window gave a view of a back wall in the same ochre brick. Beneath it was a narrow flower-bed, in which a large hydrangea, now leafless and dry-stemmed, showed its clumps of dried flowers, the petals delicately coloured and thin as paper. Beside it in the gritty earth was an unpruned rose-bush, its leaves brown and shrivelled and with one cankered pink bud.

The woman who held out her hand to him was, he guessed, in her early thirties. He saw a pale, fine-featured, intelligent face. The mouth was small but full-lipped. The dark hair fell like feathers over the high forehead and the cheeks. Her eyes were huge under the high curved brows and he thought he had never seen such pain in any human eyes. She held her thin body tautly as if only containing by an act of will a grief which threatened to shake it into a flood of tears.

She said, 'Won't you sit down?', and pointed to the upright armchair set beside the desk.

Dalgliesh hesitated for a moment, thinking that this must be Neville Dupayne's chair, but there was no other and he told himself that the instinctive initial reluctance had been a folly.

She left him to begin and he said, 'It's good of you to see me. Dr Dupayne's death must have been a terrible shock for people who knew him and worked with him. When did you hear?'

'On the local radio news early this morning. They didn't give any details, just that a man had been burnt to death in a car at the Dupayne Museum. I knew then that it was Neville.'

She didn't look at him but the hands lying in her lap clenched and unclenched. She said, 'Please tell me, I have to know. Was he murdered?'

'We can't be absolutely sure at present. I think it likely that he was. In any case we have to treat his death as suspicious. If this proves to be murder, then we need to know as much as possible about the victim. That's why I'm here. His daughter said that you'd worked for her father for ten years. One gets to know a person well in ten years. I'm hoping you can help me to know him better.'

She looked at him and their eyes held. Hers was a gaze of extraordinary intensity. He felt himself to be under judgement. But there was something more; an appeal for some unspoken assurance that she could talk freely and be understood.

He waited. Then she said simply, 'I loved him. For six years we've been lovers. That stopped three months ago. The sex stopped, the loving didn't. I think Neville was relieved. He worried about the constant need for secrecy, the deceit. He was finding it difficult enough to cope without that. It was one anxiety less when I went back to Selwyn. Well, I'd never really left him. I think one of the reasons I married Selwyn was because I knew in my heart that Neville wouldn't want me for ever.'

Dalgliesh asked gently, 'Did the affair end by your wish or by his?'

'By both, but mine chiefly. My husband is a good and kind man and I love him. Not perhaps the way I love Neville, but we were happy – we are happy. And then there's Selwyn's mother. You'll probably meet her. She's a volunteer at the Dupayne. She's not an easy woman but she adores him and she's been good to us, buying us a house, the car, being happy for him. I began to realize how much hurt I would cause. Selwyn is one of those people who love absolutely. He's not very clever but he knows about love. He would never be suspicious, never even imagine that I could deceive him. I began to feel that what Neville and I had was wrong. I don't think he felt the same, he hadn't a wife to worry about, and he and his daughter aren't close. But he wasn't really distressed when the affair ended. You see, I was always more in love with him than he was with me. His life was so over-busy, so full of stress that it was probably a relief to him not to have to worry any more – worry about my happiness, about being found out.'

'And were you? Found out?'

'Not as far as I know. Hospitals are great places for gossip – I suppose most institutions are – but we were very careful. I don't think anyone knew. And now he's dead and there's no one I can talk to about him. It's odd, isn't it, that it's a relief just speaking of him to you. He was a good man, Commander, and a good psychiatrist. He didn't think he was. He never quite managed to be as detached as he needed to be for his own peace of mind. He cared too much and he cared terribly about the state of the psychiatric service. Here we are, one of the richest countries in the world, and we can't look after the old, the mentally sick, those who've spent a lifetime working, contributing, coping with hardship and poverty. And now, when they're old and disturbed and need loving care, perhaps a hospital bed, we offer them so little. He cared, too, about his schizophrenic patients, the ones who won't take their medication. He thought there ought to be refuges, places where they could be admitted until the crisis was over, somewhere they might even be relieved to go to. And then there are the Alzheimer's cases. Some of their carers are coping with appalling problems. He couldn't detach himself from their suffering.'

Dalgliesh said, 'Given that he was chronically over-worked, perhaps it isn't surprising that he didn't want to devote more time to the museum than he was already.'

'He didn't devote any time to it. He went to the quarterly trustees' meeting, he more or less had to. Otherwise he kept away and left the place to his sister to manage.'

'Not interested?'

'Stronger than that. He hated the place. He said it had robbed him of enough of his life already.'

'Did he explain what he meant by that?'

'He was thinking of his childhood. He didn't talk about it much, but it wasn't happy. There wasn't enough love. His father gave all his energy to the museum. Money too, although he must have spent a bit on their education – prep schools, public schools, universities. Neville did talk sometimes about his mother, but I gained the impression that she wasn't a strong woman, psychologically or physically. She was too afraid of his father to protect the children.'

Dalgliesh thought, *There wasn't enough love – but then is there ever? And protect against what? Violence, abuse, neglect?*

She went on, 'Neville thought we were too obsessed with the past history, tradition, the things we collect. He said we clutter ourselves with dead lives, dead ideas, instead of coping with the problems of the present. But he was obsessed with his own past. You can't write it out, can you? It's over but it's still with us. It's the same whether it's a country or a person. It happened. It made us what we are, we have to understand it.'

Dalgliesh thought, *Neville Dupayne was a psychiatrist. He must have understood better than most how these strong indestructible tentacles can quiver into life and fasten round the mind.*

Now that she had begun talking he could see that she couldn't stop. 'I'm not explaining this very well. It's just something I feel. And we didn't talk about it often, his childhood, his failed marriage, the museum. There wasn't time. When we did manage an evening together all he wanted really was to eat, make love, sleep. He didn't want to remember, he wanted relief. At least I could give him that. Sometimes, after we'd made love, I used to think that any woman could have done the same for him. Lying there I felt more apart from him than I did in the clinic taking dictation, discussing his week's appointments. When you love someone you long to meet your lover's every need, but you can't, can you? No one can. We can only give what the other person is willing to take. I'm sorry, I don't know why I'm telling you all this.'

Dalgliesh thought, *Hasn't it always been like this? People tell me things. I don't need to probe or question, they tell.* It had begun when he was a young detective sergeant and then it had surprised and intrigued him, feeding his poetry, bringing the half-shameful realization that for a detective it would be a useful gift. The pity was there. He had known from childhood the heartbreak of life and that, too, had fed the poetry. He thought, *I have taken people's confidences and used them to fasten gyves round their wrists.*

He said, 'Do you think the pressures of his work, the unhappiness he shared, made him unwilling to go on living?'

'To kill himself? To commit suicide? Never!' Now her voice was emphatic. 'Never, never. Suicide was

258

something we talked about occasionally. He was strongly against it. I'm not thinking of the suicide of the very old or the terminally ill; we can all understand that. I'm talking of the young. Neville said suicide was often an act of aggression and left terrible guilt for family and friends. He wouldn't leave his daughter a legacy like that.'

Dalgliesh said quietly, 'Thank you. That's very helpful. There's one other thing. We know that Dr Dupayne kept his Jaguar in a garage at the museum and drove it away shortly after six o'clock every Friday evening, returning late on Sunday, or early on Monday morning. Obviously we need to know where he went on those weekends, whether there was someone he regularly visited.'

'You mean whether he had another life, a secret life apart from me?'

'Whether those weekends had anything to do with his death. His daughter has no idea where he went and seems not to have enquired.'

Mrs Faraday got up suddenly from her chair and walked over to the window. There was a moment's silence, then she said, 'No, she wouldn't. I don't suppose any of the family asked or cared. They led separate lives, rather like royalty. I've often wondered whether this is because of their father. Neville sometimes spoke of him. I don't know why he bothered to have children. His passion was the museum, acquiring exhibits, spending money on it. Neville loved his daughter but felt guilty about her. You see, he was afraid that he'd behaved in exactly the same way, that he'd given to his job the care

259

and attention he should have given to Sarah. I think that's why he wanted the museum closed. That, and perhaps because he needed some money.'

Dalgliesh said, 'For himself?'

'No, for her.'

She had returned to her desk. He said, 'And did he ever tell you where he went on those weekends?'

'Not where he went, but what he did. The weekends were his liberation. He loved that car. He wasn't mechanical and he couldn't repair it or service it, but he loved driving it. Every Friday he drove into the country and walked. He walked for the whole of Saturday and Sunday. He would stay at small inns, country hotels, sometimes in a bed and breakfast. He liked good food and comfort so he chose carefully. But he didn't repeat his visits too regularly. He didn't want people to be curious about him or to ask questions. He would walk in the Wye Valley, along the Dorset coast, sometimes by the sea in Norfolk or Suffolk. It was those solitary walks away from people, away from the phone, away from the city, which kept him sane.'

She had been looking down at her hands clasped before her on the desk. But now she raised her eyes and gazed at Dalgliesh and he saw again, with a stab of pity, the dark wells of inconsolable pain. Her voice was close to a cry. 'He went alone, always alone. That's what he needed and that's what hurt. He didn't even want me. After I married it wouldn't have been easy to get away, but I could have managed it. We had so little time together, just snatched hours in his flat. But never the weekends. Never those long hours together, walking,

260

talking, spending the whole night in the same bed. Never, never.'

Dalgliesh said gently, 'Did you ever ask him why not?'

'No. I was too afraid that he might tell me the truth, that his solitude was more necessary to him than I was.' She paused, and then said, 'But there's something I did do. He'll never know and it doesn't matter now. I arranged to be free next weekend. It meant lying to my husband and mother-in-law, but I did it. I was going to ask Neville to take me with him, just for once. It would only have been for once, I would have promised him that. If I could have been with him for just that one weekend I think I would have been willing to let go.'

They sat in silence. Outside the office the life of the hospital went on, the births and the deaths, the pain and the hope, ordinary people doing extraordinary jobs; none of it reached them. It was difficult for Dalgliesh to see such grief without seeking for words of comfort. There were none that he could give. His job was to discover her lover's murderer. He had no right to deceive her into thinking that he came as a friend.

He waited until she was calmer, then said, 'There's one last question. Had he any enemies, any patients who might wish him harm?'

'If anyone hated him enough to wish him dead I think I'd have known. He wasn't greatly loved, he was too solitary for that, but he was respected and liked. Of course there is always a risk, isn't there? Psychiatrists accept that and I don't suppose they're more at risk than the staff in Accident and Emergency, especially on Saturday nights when half the patients come in drunk or on drugs. Being a nurse or doctor on A and E is a dangerous occupation. That's the kind of world we've produced. Of course there are patients who can be aggressive, but they couldn't plan a murder. Anyway, how could they know about his car and his regular visit to collect it every Friday?'

Dalgliesh said, 'His patients will miss him.'

'Some of them, and for a time. Mostly they'll be thinking of themselves. "Who'll look after me now? Who shall I see at next Wednesday's clinic?" And I shall have to go on seeing his handwriting in the patients' records. I wonder how long it will be before I can't even remember his voice.'

She had had herself under control, but now, suddenly, her voice changed. 'What's so awful is that I can't grieve, not openly. There's no one I can talk to about Neville. People hear gossip about his death and speculate. They're shocked of course, and seem genuinely distressed. But they're also excited. Violent death is horrible but it's also intriguing. They're interested. I can see it in their eyes. Murder corrupts, doesn't it? It takes so much away, not just a life.'

Dalgliesh said, 'Yes, it's a contaminating crime.'

Suddenly she was openly crying. He moved towards her and she clung to him, her hands clawing at his jacket. He saw that there was a key in the door, perhaps a necessary safeguard, and half carrying her across the room he turned it. She gasped, 'I'm sorry, I'm sorry,' but the weeping didn't stop. He saw that there was a second door on the left wall and, placing her gently in her chair, he opened it carefully. To his relief it was as he hoped.

It led to a small corridor with a unisex lavatory to the right. He went back to Mrs Faraday who was a little calmer now and helped her towards the door, then closed it after her. He thought he could hear the rush of running water. No one knocked or tried the handle of the other door. She was not away long. Within three minutes she was back, outwardly calm, her hair combed in place and with no trace of the passionate weeping except for a puffiness of the eyes.

She said, 'I'm sorry, that was embarrassing for you.'

'There's no need to apologize. I'm only sorry that I have no comfort to offer.'

She went on formally as if there had been nothing between them but a brief official encounter 'If there's anything else you need to know, anything I can help with, please don't hesitate to ring. Would you like my home number?'

Dalgliesh said, 'It would be helpful,' and she scribbled the digits on her notepad, tore out the page and handed it over.

He said, 'I'd be grateful if you could look through the patients' records and see if there is anything there that could help with the inquiry. A patient who felt resentful or tried to sue him, a dissatisfied relation, anything that might suggest he had an enemy among those he treated.'

'I can't believe that's possible. If he had I think I would know. Anyway, the patients' records are confidential. The hospital wouldn't agree to anything being passed on without the right authority.'

'I know that. If necessary the authority would have to be obtained.'

She said, 'You're a strange policeman, aren't you? But you are a policeman. It would never be wise for me to forget that.'

She held out her hand and he took it briefly. It was very cold.

Walking down the corridor towards the waiting-room and the front door, he had the sudden need of coffee. It coincided with seeing a sign pointing to the cafeteria. Here, at the start of his career, when he had visited the hospital he had snatched a quick meal or a cup of tea. He recalled that it had been run by the League of Friends and wondered whether it still looked the same. It was certainly in the same place, a room some twenty feet by ten with windows looking out on a small paved garden. The grey brick opposite the high arched windows reinforced the impression that he was in a church. The tables he remembered with their red checked cloths had been replaced by sturdier Formica-topped tables, but the serving counter to the left of the door with its hissing urns and glass display shelves looked much the same. The menu too was little different: baked potatoes with various fillings, beans and egg on toast, bacon rolls, tomato and vegetable soup and a variety of cakes and biscuits. It was a quiet time, the people wanting lunch had left and there was a high pile of dirty plates on a side table below a notice requesting people to clear their own tables. The only people there were two large workmen in their overalls at a far table and a young woman with a baby in a buggy. She seemed unaware of a toddler who, finger in mouth, swung herself round on the leg of a chair, singing unmelodiously, then stood stock-still, regarding Dalgliesh with wide curious eyes. The mother was sitting with a cup of tea in front of her, gazing out into the garden while perpetually rocking the buggy with her left hand. It was impossible to see whether her look of tragic unawareness was caused by tiredness or grief. Dalgliesh reflected that a hospital was an extraordinary world in which human beings encountered each other briefly, bearing an individual weight of hope, anguish or despair, and yet was a world curiously familiar and accommodating, paradoxically both frightening and reassuring.

The coffee, served at the counter by an elderly woman, was cheap but good and he drank quickly, suddenly anxious to be away. This brief respite had been an indulgence in the over busy day. The prospect of interviewing the senior Mrs Faraday had assumed greater interest and importance. Had she known of her daughter-in-law's infidelity? If so, how much had she cared?

When he regained the main corridor he saw Angela Faraday immediately in front of him and paused to study one of the sepia photographs to give her time to avoid him. When she reached the waiting-room a young man appeared, as promptly as if he had recognized the sound of her footsteps. Dalgliesh saw a face of remarkable beauty, sensitive, fine-boned and with wide luminous eyes. The young man didn't see Dalgliesh. His eyes were on his wife as he stretched out his hand to grasp hers and then joined her, his face suddenly irradiated with trust and an almost childlike joy.

Dalgliesh waited until they had left the hospital. For some reason which he was unable to explain it was an encounter that he wished he had not seen.

12

Major Arkwright lived in the first-floor flat of a converted period house in Maida Vale. It was meticulously maintained behind iron railings that looked newly painted. The brass plate bearing the names of the four tenants was polished to a silvery whiteness and there were two tubs, each containing a bay tree, one on either side of the door. A male voice responded quickly when Piers pressed the bell. There was no lift.

At the top of the carpeted stairs Major Arkwright awaited them at the open door. He was a dapper little man wearing a tailored suit with matching waistcoat and what could have been a regimental tie. His moustache, a thin pencil line in contrast to the bushiness of his eyebrows, was a fading ginger, but little could be seen of his hair. His whole head, looking unusually small, was enclosed in a close-fitting cap of muslin beneath which the pad of white gauze was visible above the left ear. Piers thought that the cap made him look like an elderly, out-of-work but undiscouraged Pierrot. Two eyes of remarkable blue gave Piers and Kate a keen appraising look but it was not unfriendly. He glanced at their warrant cards with no evident concern, merely nodding them in as if in approval that they had arrived so precisely on time.

It was at once apparent that the Major collected

antiques, particularly Staffordshire commemorative figures. The narrow hall was so crowded that Kate and Piers entered it gingerly, as if venturing into an over-stocked antiques market. A narrow shelf ran the whole length of the wall on which were arrayed an impressive collection: the Duke of Clarence, Edward the Seventh's ill-fated son, and his fiancée, Princess May; Queen Victoria in state robes; a mounted Garibaldi; Shakespeare leaning on a pillar topped with books, resting his head on his right arm; notable Victorian preachers fulmin-ating from their pulpits. On the opposite wall there was a miscellaneous collection chiefly of Victoriana, silhouettes in their oval frames, a framed sampler dated 1852, small oil paintings of nineteenth-century rural scenes in which country labourers and their families, looking unconvincingly well-fed and clean, gambolled or sat peacefully outside their picturesque cottages. Piers's practised eyes took in the details at a glance, with some surprise that nothing seen so far reflected the Major's military career.

They were led through a sitting-room, comfortable if over-furnished with a display cabinet crammed with similar Staffordshire figures, then down a short passage and into a conservatory built out over the garden. It was furnished with four cane armchairs and a table with a glass top. Shelves round the base of the wall held a remarkable selection of plants, most of them evergreens and all of them flourishing.

The Major seated himself and waved Piers and Kate to the other chairs. He seemed as cheerfully unconcerned as if they were old friends. Before Piers or Kate could speak, he said in a gruff staccato voice, 'Found the boy yet?'

'Not yet, sir.'

'You will. I don't think he'll have thrown himself in the river. Not that kind. He'll surface as soon as he realizes I'm not dead. You needn't bother about the fracas we had – but then you aren't bothered, are you? More important concerns. I wouldn't have called the ambulance or the police if Mrs Perrifield – she lives downstairs – hadn't heard me fall and come up. A well-meaning woman, but inclined to interfere. Ryan bumped into her as he dashed out of the house. He'd left the door open. She called the ambulance and the police before I could stop her. I was a bit dazed – well, unconscious really. Surprised she didn't call the fire brigade, the army, and anyone else she could think of. Anyway, I'm not pressing charges.'

Piers was anxious to get a quick answer to the one vital question. He said, 'We're not concerned with that, sir, not primarily. Can you tell us at what time Ryan Archer arrived home yesterday evening?'

''Fraid not. I was in South Ken at a sale of Staffordshire pottery. One or two pieces I fancied. Outbid on all of them. Used to be able to pick up a commemorative piece for about £30. Not now.'

'And you got back when, sir?'

'About seven o'clock, near enough. Met a friend outside the auction room and we went to a local pub for a quick drink. Ryan was here when I got back.'

'Doing what, sir?'

'Watching television in his room. I hired a separate

set. The boy watches different programmes from me and I like some privacy in the evenings. Works all right on the whole.'

Kate said, 'How did he seem when you got in?'

'How d'you mean?'

'Was he agitated, distressed, different from his usual self?'

'I didn't see him for about fifteen minutes. Just called out and he answered. Can't remember what we said. Then he came in and the row developed. My fault really.'

'Can you tell us exactly what happened?'

'It began when we started talking about Christmas. I'd arranged to take him to Rome, hotel booked, flights fixed. He said he'd changed his mind, that he'd been invited to spend Christmas with someone else, a woman.'

Choosing her words carefully, Kate said, 'Did this upset you? Did you feel disappointed, jealous?'

'Not jealous, bloody angry. I'd bought the air tickets.'

'Did you believe him?'

'Not really, not about the woman.'

'What then?'

'It was obvious he didn't want to come to Rome. I thought he could have told me before I booked. And I'd sent for some information about possible further education. The boy's bright enough, but he's virtually uneducated. Truanted most of the time. I left him the brochures to look through so we could discuss the possibilities. He'd done nothing. There was an argument about the whole idea. I thought he was keen, but apparently not. He said he was sick of my interference, something like that. Don't blame the boy. As I said, the whole thing was my fault. I used the wrong words.'

'Which were?'

'I said, "You'll never amount to anything in life." Was going on to say, "Unless you get some education or training." Never got the chance to complete the sentence. Ryan went berserk. Those must have been the words he heard from his stepfather. Well, not the stepfather, the man who moved in with his mother. It's the usual story, you must have heard it a dozen times. Father moves out, mother takes a succession of lovers and eventually one of them moves in. Son and lover detest each other and one of them has to go. No prize for guessing which. The man was obviously a brute. Funny, some women seem to like that kind of thing. Anyway, he more or less turned Ryan out. Surprising Ryan didn't lay him out with a poker.'

Kate said, 'He told the housekeeper at the museum that he'd been in care since childhood.'

'Lot of rot! He lived at home until he was fifteen. His dad died eighteen months before then. Ryan hints that it was a particularly tragic death but he never explained. Probably another fantasy. No, he was never in care. The boy's a mess, but not as big a mess as he'd be if the care authorities had got their hands on him.'

'Had he ever been violent to you before?'

'Never. Not a violent boy. As I said, it was my fault. Wrong words, wrong time.'

'And he didn't say anything about the day, what he'd been doing at work, what time he left, when he got home?'

'Nothing. Wouldn't expect it though, would you? We didn't have much time to chat before he lost his temper, picked up the poker and went for me. Caught me a blow on the right shoulder. Knocked me over and I cracked my head on the edge of the TV set. Whole bloody thing went over.'

Piers asked, 'Can you tell us something about his life here, how long you've been together, how you met?'

'Picked him up in Leicester Square nine months ago. Could have been ten. Difficult to estimate time. Late January or early February. He was different from the other boys. He spoke first and I could see he was heading for trouble. It's a terrible life, prostitution. Go down that road and you may as well be dead. He hadn't started on it, but I thought he might. He was sleeping rough at the time so I brought him back here.'

Kate said frankly, 'And lived with him. I mean, you were lovers.'

'He's gay, of course, but that wasn't why I brought him home. I have someone else, have done for years. He's doing a six-month consultancy job in the Far East but he's due back early January. I'm rather hoping to get Ryan settled by then. This flat's too small for the three of us. Ryan came to my room that first night, seemed to think he had to pay in kind for his lodging. I soon put him right on that. I never mix sex and commerce. Never have. And I'm not much attracted to the young. Makes me odd, I dare say, but that's how it is. I liked the boy and was sorry for him, but that's all there was to it. He came and went, you know. Sometimes he told me he'd be off, sometimes not. Usually he came back within a week or two, wanted a bath, clean clothes, a comfortable bed. He was in a succession of squats but none of them lasted long.'

'Did you know he was working at the Dupayne Museum as a gardener?'

'I gave him a reference. He told me he worked there Mondays, Wednesdays and Fridays. He usually went off early on those days and came back at about six. I assume he was where he said he was, at the Dupayne.'

Kate said, 'How did he get there?'

'By tube and walking. He had an old bicycle but that disappeared.'

'Isn't five rather late to be working in winter? The light's gone much earlier.'

'He said there were always a few odd jobs. He helped in the house as well as the garden. I didn't ask questions. Too much like his stepfather. Ryan can't tolerate inter-ference. Don't blame him. Feel the same myself. Look, would you care for something to drink? Tea or coffee? Forgot to ask.'

Kate thanked him and said that they needed to be on their way. The Major nodded, and said, 'Hope you find him. If you do, tell him I'm all right. The bed's here if he cares to come back. For the present anyway. And he didn't murder that doctor – what's his name, Dupayne?'

'Dr Neville Dupayne.'

'You can put that out of your minds. The boy's not a killer.'

Piers said, 'If he'd struck you harder and in a different place, he could have been.'

'Well he didn't, did he? Watch that watering-can as

you go out. Sorry I can't be more helpful. You'll let me know when you find him?'

Surprisingly at the door he held out his hand. He gripped Kate's so hard that she almost winced. She said, 'Yes sir, we'll be sure to let you know.'

After the door had closed, Kate said, 'We could try Mrs Perrifield. She might know when Ryan got home. She sounds the kind of woman who keeps an eye on what's happening with her neighbours.'

On the ground floor they rang the bell. It was opened by a stout elderly woman, somewhat over-enthusiastically made up and rigidly coiffured. She was wearing a patterned suit with four pockets on the jacket, all adorned with large brass buttons. She had opened the door, keeping the chain on, and had gazed at them through the aperture with suspicious eyes. But when Kate had shown her warrant card and explained that they were enquiring about Ryan Archer, she immediately unchained the door and invited them in. Kate suspected that they might have difficulty in getting away, so explained that they hoped not to keep Mrs Perrifield long. Could she tell them what time Ryan had arrived home yesterday evening?

Mrs Perrifield was vehement in her protestations that she would like to help but, alas, she couldn't. Friday afternoon was her bridge afternoon. Yesterday she had been playing with friends in South Kensington and after tea had stayed on for sherry. She had arrived home only some fifteen minutes before the appalling attack. Piers and Kate had to hear every detail of how Mrs Perrifield had fortuitously been able to save the Major's life by her

273

prompt action. She hoped that he would now realize that you can be too trusting, too compassionate. Ryan Archer was not the kind of tenant they wanted in a respectable house. She reiterated how very sorry she was not to be able to help, and Kate believed her. She had no doubt Mrs Perrifield would have been delighted had she been able to tell them that Ryan returned home smelling strongly of petrol, hot-foot from the scene of the crime.

Walking back to the car, Kate said, 'So Ryan hasn't an alibi, at least as far as we know. But I find it difficult to believe . . .'

Piers broke in. 'Oh for God's sake, Kate, not you too! None of them is a likely murderer. He's a suspect like the rest of them. And the longer he stays away, the worse it looks for him.'

13

Mrs Faraday's house was the eighth in a mid-nineteenth-century terrace on the south side of an Islington square. The houses, no doubt built originally for the superior working class, must have gone through the usual trans-mogrification of rising rents, neglect, war damage and multi-occupancy, but had long been taken over by those of the middle class who valued proximity to the City, the nearness of good restaurants and the Almeida Theatre, and the satisfaction of proclaiming that they lived in an interesting, socially and ethnically diverse community. From the number of window grilles and burglar alarm systems, it was apparent that the occupants had protected themselves against any unwelcome mani-festation of this rich diversity. The terrace had an attrac-tive architectural unity. The identical façades of cream stucco and black iron balconies were broken up by the shining paint of different coloured doors and the varied brass knockers. In spring this architectural conformity would be enlivened by the blooms of cherry trees, their trunks protected by railings, but now the autumn sun shone on a patterned avenue of bare branches, touching the trunks with gold. An occasional window box was bright with trailing ivy and the yellow of winter pansies.

Kate pressed the bell in its brass surround and it was quickly answered. They were courteously received by an elderly man with carefully brushed-back white hair, and a resolutely non-committal face. His clothes struck a note of eccentric ambiguity; striped black trousers, a brown linen jacket which looked newly pressed and a spotted bow tie. He said, 'Commander Dalgliesh and Inspector Miskin? Mrs Faraday is expecting you. She's in the garden but perhaps you won't mind going through.' He added, 'My name is Perkins,' as if this somehow explained his presence.

It was neither the house nor the reception that Kate had expected. There were now very few houses where the door was opened by a butler, nor did the man they were following look like one. In demeanour and assurance he seemed like an old retainer, or was he perhaps a relation of the family who had decided, for his perverse amusement, to play a part?

The hall was narrow and made more so by the slender mahogany grandfather clock to the right of the door. The walls were covered with water-colours so closely hung that little of the patterned dark green paper was visible. A door to the left gave Kate a glimpse of book-covered walls, an elegant fireplace and a portrait in oils above it. This wasn't a house where you would expect to find prints of wild horses galloping out of the sea or a green-faced oriental woman. An elegantly-carved mahogany banister led upstairs. At the end of the corridor Perkins opened a white-painted door which led into a conservatory stretching the width of the house. It was a room of casual intimacy; coats slung over low wicker chairs, magazines on the wicker table, a profusion of green plants obscuring the glass and giving the light a greenish tinge as if they were under water. A small flight of steps gave access to the garden. A path of York stone set in the lawn led down to the greenhouse. Through the glass they could see the figure of a woman stooping and rising in a rhythmic sequence with the precision of a formal dance. The movements didn't stop even when Dalgliesh and Kate reached the door and saw that she was washing and disinfecting flowerpots. There was a bowl of soapy water on the ledge and she was taking the scrubbed pots one by one, stooping to dip them in a pail of disinfectant, then placing them on a high shelf in order of their size. After a few seconds she chose to see her visitors and opened the door. They were met by a strong smell of Jeyes Fluid.

She was tall, almost six feet, and was wearing grubby corduroy trousers, a dark blue Guernsey jumper, rubber boots and red rubber gloves. Her grey hair, combed back from a high forehead, was bundled beneath a trilby hat which sat rakishly above her strong-boned, intelligent face. Her eyes were dark and keen under heavy lids. Although the skin over the nose and cheekbones was a little weather-coarsened, her face was almost unlined, but when she drew off the gloves Kate saw from the blue cords of the veins and the delicate crumpled skin of her hands that she was older than she had expected; she must surely have been over forty when her son was born. Kate glanced at Dalgliesh. His face told her nothing but she knew that he must be sharing her thoughts. They were facing a formidable woman.

Dalgliesh said, 'Mrs Faraday?'

Her voice was authoritative and carefully articulated.

'Of course, who else? This is my address, this is my garden, this is my greenhouse, and it was my man who showed you in.' Her tone, thought Kate, was deliberately light, intended to rob the words of any offence. She went on, 'And you, of course, are Commander Dalgliesh. Don't bother to show me your warrant card or whatever it is you have to carry. I was expecting you, of course, but I don't know why I thought you would come alone. This, after all, is hardly a social visit.'

The look she gave Kate, although not unfriendly, was as swiftly appraising as if she were assessing the virtue and merits of a new parlour maid. Dalgliesh made the introductions. Mrs Faraday somewhat surprisingly shook hands with them both, then put her gloves back on.

She said, 'Please excuse me if I continue with this task. It isn't my favourite chore and, once started, I like to get it finished. That wicker chair is reasonably clean, Miss Miskin, but I'm afraid I have nothing to offer you, Mr Dalgliesh, but this upturned box. I think you'll find it's safe enough.'

After a second Kate sat, but Dalgliesh remained standing. Before he could speak, Mrs Faraday went on, 'You've come about Dr Dupayne's death, of course. I take it your presence here means that you don't think it was an accident.'

Dalgliesh had decided to be blunt. 'Neither an accident nor suicide. I'm afraid this is a murder investigation, Mrs Faraday.'

'So I suspected, but isn't it attracting a somewhat unusual level of expertise? Forgive me, but does Dr Dupayne's death, however lamentable, deserve the

278

attention of a commander as well as a detective inspector?' Receiving no reply, she went on, 'Please ask your questions. If I can help, obviously I would wish to do so. I know some of the details, of course. News like this gets round very quickly. It was a terrible death.'

She went on with her task. Watching the scrubbed pots being lifted from the suds, dipped and shelved, Dalgliesh had a vivid childhood memory of the potting shed in the rectory garden. This had been one of his childhood tasks, helping the gardener with the annual flowerpot cleaning. He could remember the warm woody smell of the potting shed and old Sampson's stories about his exploits in the First World War. Most of them, he later recognized, were fictitious, but at the time they had enthralled a ten-year-old, turning the task into a looked for treat. The old man had been an inventive fantasist. He suspected that he was now facing a woman whose lies, if she told them, would be more convincing.

He said, 'Can you tell us about your own involvement with the museum? We understand that you're one of the volunteers. How long have you been there and what do you do? I know this may not seem relevant, but at the moment we need to know as much as possible about Dr Dupayne's life, both professionally and at the museum.'

'Then you'll need to see the members of his family and the people who worked with Dr Dupayne at the hospital. One of them, as I expect you know, is my daughter-in-law. My own involvement with the family goes back twelve years. My husband was a friend of Max

Dupayne who founded the museum, and we've always been supporters. When Max was alive they had an elderly and not very competent gardener and Max asked whether I could help by coming in once a week, or at least with some regularity, to give advice. At present, as I expect you know, the garden is looked after by Ryan Archer, who also acts as part-time cleaner and handyman. The boy is ignorant but willing, and my visits have continued. After Max Dupayne's death James Calder-Hale, the archivist, asked me to carry on. He took over the job of vetting the voluntary helpers.'

Kate asked, 'Did they need vetting?'

'A reasonable question. Apparently Mr Calder-Hale took the view that there were too many of them and most were more trouble than they were worth. Museums do tend to attract enthusiasts who have little practical skill to contribute. He cut down the numbers to three – myself, Miss Babbington who assisted Muriel Godby on the reception desk, and Mrs Strickland who works in the library. Miss Babbington had to give up about a year ago because of increasing arthritis. There are now just the two of us. We could do with more.'

Dalgliesh said, 'Mrs Clutton told us that it was you who provided the can of petrol for the lawn-mower. When was that?'

'In September, about the time of the last grass-cutting. Ryan had run out of petrol and I said I'd bring in a can to save the cost of delivery. It was never used. The machine had been malfunctioning for some time and the boy had absolutely no skill in maintaining it, let alone repairing it. I came to the conclusion it had to be replaced. In the mean time Ryan used the manual lawn-mower. The can of petrol was left in the shed.'

'Who knew it was there?'

'Ryan obviously. Mrs Clutton, who keeps her bicycle in the shed, and probably Miss Godby. I certainly told her that the old mower would have to be replaced. She was worried about the cost, but obviously there was no great hurry; the grass probably wouldn't need another cutting until the spring. Come to think of it, I must have told her about the petrol because she paid me the cost of it and I signed a chitty. The Dupaynes and Mr Calder-Hale may have known. You'll have to ask them.'

Kate asked, 'Didn't it occur to you that, since it was no longer needed, you could take the can home?'

Mrs Faraday gave her a look which suggested that the question was hardly one which would occur to an intelligent enquirer. She replied, 'No, it didn't. Should it have? I'd been paid for it.'

Kate, refusing to be intimidated, tried another tack. 'You have been visiting the museum for twelve years. Would you describe it as a happy place? I mean, the people who work there.'

Mrs Faraday took up the next pot, examined it critically, dipped it in disinfectant and up-ended it on the bench. She said, 'I've really no way of knowing. None of the staff complained to me of unhappiness and had they done so I wouldn't have listened.'

As if fearing that her reply had been minatory, she added, 'After the death of Max Dupayne there was a certain lack of overall control. Caroline Dupayne has been nominally in charge, but she has her own responsibilities at the school. As I said, Mr Calder-Hale takes an interest in the voluntary workers and the boy does the garden – or at least makes some attempt at keeping it in shape. After Muriel Godby came, things improved. She's a capable woman and seems to relish responsibility.'

Dalgliesh wondered how he could introduce the complication of her daughter-in-law's relationship with Neville Dupayne. He needed to know if the affair was as secret as Angela Faraday had said; in particular he needed to know how much Mrs Faraday might have guessed or been told.

He said, 'We have already spoken to your daughter-in-law as Dr Dupayne's personal secretary, and I understand she had general responsibility for his outpatient clinics. She's obviously a person whose opinion of his state of mind on that Friday is important.'

'And does his state of mind have any relevance to the fact that he was murdered? I take it you are not now suggesting that this could have been suicide?'

Dalgliesh said, 'I have to decide what is relevant, Mrs Faraday.'

'And was my daughter-in-law's relationship with Neville Dupayne relevant? She told you, of course? Well, naturally she would. Love, the satisfaction of being wanted, is always something of a triumph. Very few people mind confessing that they have been desirable. Where sexual mores today are concerned, it isn't adultery that's contemptible.'

Dalgliesh said, 'I think she found the affair more

distressing than fulfilling, the need for secrecy, the worry that your son might find out and be hurt.'

'Yes,' she said with bitterness. 'Angela's not without a conscience.'

It was Kate who asked the question. 'Did he find out, Mrs Faraday?'

There was a silence. Mrs Faraday was too intelligent to miss the significance. It was a question, thought Kate, that she must have been expecting. In one sense she had invited it. It was she who had first mentioned her daughter-in-law's affair. Was this because she was convinced that the truth would eventually come out and that her silence would then need some explaining? She turned the scrubbed pot in her hands, scrutinizing it carefully, then bent and dipped it in the disinfectant. Dalgliesh and Kate waited. It wasn't until Mrs Faraday had straightened up that she replied.

'No, he doesn't know, and it's my business to ensure that he never does. I hope I can rely on your co-operation, Commander. I take it that neither of you is in the business of deliberately inflicting pain.'

Dalgliesh heard Kate's quick intake of breath, as quickly disciplined. He said, 'I'm in the business of investigating a murder, Mrs Faraday. I can't give guarantees except to say that facts which aren't relevant won't unnecessarily be made public. I'm afraid a murder investigation always causes pain. I wish it were only to the guilty.' He paused, then added, 'How did you come to know?'

'By seeing them together. It was three months ago when a minor Royal came to the hospital to open the new

283

theatre complex. Neville Dupayne and Angela weren't officially together, nothing like that. He was on the list of consultants to be presented. She was helping with the arrangements, directing visitors, escorting VIPs, that kind of thing. But they met fortuitously and stood together for a couple of minutes. I saw her face, their hands quickly clasp and as quickly part. It was enough. You can't hide love, not if you're caught unawares.'

Kate said, 'But if you saw it, why shouldn't others?'

'Perhaps some people who worked closely with them did. But Angela and Neville Dupayne kept their private lives separate. I doubt whether anyone would pass on the news to me or to my son even if they did suspect. It might be a cause of gossip among the hospital staff but not a reason for interference or making mischief. I saw them in an unguarded moment. I have no doubt they had learned how to dissemble.'

Dalgliesh said, 'Your daughter-in-law told me that the affair was at an end. They had decided that the potential harm didn't justify its continuing.'

'And you believed her?'

'I saw no reason not to.'

'Well, she lied. They were planning on going away together next weekend. My son phoned to suggest that we spend the weekend together because Angela was visiting an old school friend in Norwich. She has never spoken of her school or of her friends. They were going away together for the first time.'

Kate said, 'You can't be sure of that, Mrs Faraday.'

'I can be sure.'

Again there was a silence. Mrs Faraday continued with

her task. Kate asked, 'Were you happy about your son's marriage?'

'Very happy. I had to face it that it wouldn't be easy for him to find a wife. Plenty of women would be happy to sleep with him, but not to spend the rest of their lives with him. Angela seemed genuinely fond of him. I think she still is. They met at the museum, incidentally. It was one afternoon three years ago. Selwyn had a free afternoon and had come to help me with the garden. There was a meeting of the trustees after lunch and Neville Dupayne had forgotten his agenda and papers. He phoned the hospital and Angela brought them to him. Afterwards she came to see what we were planting and we spent some time chatting. That's when she and Selwyn met. I was happy and relieved when they began seeing each other and eventually got engaged. She seemed exactly the right wife for him, kind, sensible and maternal. Of course their joint incomes aren't great but I was able to buy them a small house and provide a car. It was obvious how much she meant to him – still means to him.'

Dalgliesh said, 'I saw your son. He was in the waiting-room at St Oswald's when I left after seeing your daughter-in-law.'

'And what impression did you gain, Commander?'

'I thought he had a remarkable face. He could be called beautiful.'

'So was my husband, but not egregiously so. Good-looking would perhaps be a more accurate description.' She seemed to be pondering for a moment, then her face broke into a reminiscent, transforming smile.

'Very good-looking. Beautiful is an odd word to apply to a man.'

'It seems appropriate.'

The last of the pots had been inspected and doused. Now they were ranged in neat lines according to size. Regarding them with the satisfaction of completing a job well done, she said, 'I think I had better explain to you about Selwyn. He is not intelligent. I would say that he has always had learning difficulties but that phrase diagnostically has become meaningless. He can survive in our remorseless society but he can't compete. He was educated with so-called normal children but didn't achieve any examination results, didn't indeed try for them except in two non-academic subjects. University was obviously out of the question, even one at the bottom of the league tables where they're so desperate to keep up the numbers that I'm told they'll take people who are barely literate. They wouldn't have taken Selwyn. His father was highly intelligent and Selwyn is our only child. Naturally his limitations as they became apparent were a disappointment to him – perhaps grief wouldn't be too strong a word. But he loved his son, as do I. What we have both wanted is for Selwyn to be happy and to find a job within his capabilities which would be useful to others and satisfying for him. The happiness was no problem. He was born with a capacity for joy. He works as a hospital porter at St Agatha's. He likes the work and is good at it. One or two of the older porters take an interest in him, so he's not without friends. He also has a wife he loves. I intend that he shall continue to have a wife he loves.'

Dalgliesh asked quietly, 'What were you doing, Mrs Faraday, between the hours of half-past five and half-past six yesterday?'

The question was brutally stark, but it was one she must have been expecting. She had handed him a motive almost without prompting. Now would she be providing an alibi?

She said, 'I realized when I heard that Neville Dupayne had died that you would be looking into his private life, that the relationship with my daughter-in-law would come to light sooner or later. Colleagues at the hospital wouldn't betray suspicions of the affair to me or her husband. Why should they? They'll take a very different attitude when it comes to murder. I realize too, of course, that I could be a suspect. Yesterday I planned to drive to the museum and to be there when Neville Dupayne arrived. I knew, of course, that he came every Friday to collect his Jaguar. I imagine everyone at the museum knew that. It seemed the best chance of seeing him in absolute privacy. There wouldn't have been any sense in making an appointment at the hospital. He would always be able to make excuses on the grounds that he hadn't time. And then there was the complication of Angela being there. I wanted to see him alone to try to persuade him to end the affair.'

Kate said, 'Had you any idea how you could do that I mean, what arguments you could use other than the harm he was doing to your son?'

'No. I didn't have anything specific to threaten him with, if that's what you mean. Selwyn wasn't his patient, I don't think the General Medical Council would be

287

interested. My only weapon, if one chooses to use that term, would be an appeal to his decency. After all, there was a chance he might be regretting the affair, wanting to get out. I left home at five o'clock precisely. I planned to be at the museum at half-past five or soon after in case he arrived early. It closes at five so the staff would be gone. Mrs Clutton might see me but I thought it unlikely as her cottage is at the back of the house. In any case I had a right to be there.'

'And did you see Dr Dupayne?'

'No, I gave up the attempt. The traffic was very heavy – it usually is on a Friday – and there were plenty of times when I wasn't moving apart from stops at traffic lights. I had time to think. It struck me that the enterprise was ill-conceived. Neville Dupayne would be looking forward to his weekend, anxious to get away. It would be the worst time to accost him. And I'd only have the one chance. If this failed I would be helpless. I told myself I'd have a better chance if I tackled Angela first. After all, I'd never spoken to her about the affair. She had no idea that I knew. The fact that I did might change everything for her. She's fond of my son. She's not a ruthless predator. I would probably have a better chance of succeeding with her than I would with Dupayne. My son would like a child. I have taken medical advice and there's no reason why his children shouldn't be normal. I rather think that my daughter-in-law would like a baby. She could hardly expect to have one with Dupayne. Of course, they would need some financial help. When I got as far as Hampstead Pond I decided to drive home. I didn't note the time, why should I? But I can tell you that I was back here by six-twenty and Perkins will confirm it.'

'And no one saw you? No one who could recognize you or the car?'

'Not as far as I know. And now, unless you have any other questions, I think I'll return to the house. Incidentally, Commander, I'll be grateful if you would not speak directly to my son. He was on duty at St Agatha's when Dupayne was murdered. The hospital will be able to confirm that without the need to talk to Selwyn.'

The interview was over. And they had, thought Kate, got more than she had expected.

Mrs Faraday didn't go with them to the front door but left Perkins, hovering in the conservatory, to let them out. At the door, Dalgliesh turned to him. 'Could you let us know, please, the time at which Mrs Faraday returned home yesterday evening?'

'It was six twenty-two, Commander. I happened to glance at the clock.'

He held open the door wide. It seemed less an invitation to leave than a command.

They were both silent on their way back to the car. Once strapped in her seat, Kate's irritation burst out. 'Thank God she's not my mother-in-law! There's only one person she cares for and that's her precious son. You bet he wouldn't have married Angela if Mummy hadn't approved. It's Mummy who buys the house, provides the car. So he'd like to have a baby, would he? She'd buy that for him too. And if that means Angela giving up her job, then Mummy will subsidize the family. No suggestion that Angela might have a point of view, might not want a child – or not yet – might actually enjoy working at the hospital, might value her independence. That woman's utterly ruthless.'

She was surprised by the strength of her anger – against Mrs Faraday for her arrogance, her effortless superiority, and against herself for giving way to an emotion so unprofessional. Anger at the scene of crime was natural and could be a laudable spur to action. A detective who had become so blasé, so case-hardened that pity and anger could find no place in his or her response to the pain and waste of murder would be wise to look for another job. But anger against a suspect was an indulgence which could dangerously pervert judgement. And tangled with this anger she was trying to control was an emotion equally reprehensible. Essentially honest, she recognized it with some shame: it was class-resentment.

She had always seen the class war as the resort of people who were unsuccessful, insecure or envious. She was none of these things. So why was she feeling such anger? She had spent years and energy putting the past behind her: her illegitimacy, the acceptance that she would now never know the name of her father, that life in the city tower block with her disgruntled grand-mother, the smell, the noise, the all-pervading hopeless-ness. But in escaping to a job which had got her away more effectively from Ellison Fairweather Buildings than could any other, had she left something of herself behind, a vestigial loyalty to the dispossessed and the poor? She had changed her lifestyle, her friends – even, by imperceptible stages, the way she spoke. She had become middle-class. But when the chips were down, wasn't she still on the side of those almost forgotten neighbours? And wasn't it the Mrs Faradays, the prosperous, educated, liberal middle-class who in the end controlled their lives? She thought, *They criticize us for illiberal responses which they never need experience. They don't have to live in a local authority tower block slum with a vandalized lift and constant incipient violence. They don't send their children to schools where the classrooms are battlefields and eighty per cent of the children can't speak English. If their kids are delinquent they get sent to a psychiatrist, not a Youth Court. If they need urgent medical treatment they can always go private. No wonder they can afford to be so bloody liberal.*

She sat in silence, watching AD's long fingers on the wheel. Surely the air in the car must be throbbing with the turbulence of her feelings.

Dalgliesh said, 'It isn't as simple as that, Kate.'

Kate thought, *No, nothing ever is. But it's simple enough for me.* She said suddenly, 'Do you think she was telling the truth – about the affair still carrying on, I mean? We've only her word for it. Did you think Angela was lying, sir, when she spoke to you?'

'No. I think most of what she said was the truth. And now Dupayne's dead she may have convinced herself that the affair had effectively ended, that one weekend away with him would mark the end. Grief can play odd tricks with people's perception of the truth. But as far as Mrs Faraday is concerned, it doesn't matter whether the lovers were or weren't proposing to have that weekend. If she believes they were, the motive's there.'

Kate said, 'And she had means and opportunity. She knew the petrol was there, she supplied it. She knew Neville Dupayne would be at the garage at six o'clock but that the staff of the museum would have left. She handed it to us, didn't she? All of it.'

Dalgliesh said, 'She was remarkably frank, surprisingly so. But where the love-affair is concerned she only told us what she knew we'd find out. I can't see her asking her servant to lie. And if she did actually plan to murder Dupayne, she would take care to do it when she knew her son couldn't be suspected. We'll check on Selwyn Faraday's alibi. But if his mother says he was on duty at the hospital, I think we'll find that he was.'

Kate said, 'About the affair, does he need to know?'

'Not unless his mother is charged.' He added, 'It was an act of horrible cruelty.'

Kate didn't reply. He couldn't mean, surely, that Mrs Faraday was a woman incapable of such a murder. But then he came from the same background. He would have felt at home in that house, in her company. It was a world he understood. But this was ridiculous. He knew even better than did she that you could never predict, any more than you could completely understand, what human beings were capable of. Before an overwhelming temptation everything went down, all the moral and legal sanctions, the privileged education, even religious belief. The act of murder could surprise even the murderer. She had seen, in the faces of men and women, astonishment at what they had done.

Dalgliesh was speaking. 'It's always easier if you don't have to watch the actual dying. The sadist may enjoy the cruelty. Most murderers prefer to convince themselves that they didn't do it, or that they didn't cause much suffering, that the death was quick or easy, or even not unwelcome to the victim.'

Kate said, 'But none of that is true of this murder.'

'No,' said Dalgliesh. 'Not of this murder.'

14

James Calder-Hale's office was on the first floor at the back of the house, situated between the Murder Room and the gallery devoted to Industry and Employment. On his first visit, Dalgliesh had noticed the discouraging words on a bronze plaque to the left of the door: CURATOR. STRICTLY PRIVATE. But now he was awaited. The door was opened by Calder-Hale at the moment of his knock.

Dalgliesh was surprised at the size of the room. The Dupayne suffered less than more pretentious or famous museums from lack of space, limited as it was in scope and ambition to the inter-war years. Even so, it was surprising that Calder-Hale was privileged to occupy a room considerably larger than the ground-floor office.

He had made himself very comfortable. A large desk with a superstructure was at right angles to the single window and gave a view of a tall beech hedge, now at the height of its autumnal gold, and behind it the roof of Mrs Clutton's cottage and the trees of the Heath. A fireplace, clearly an original Victorian but less ostentatious than those in the galleries, was fitted with a gas fire simulating coals. This was lit, the spurting blue and red flames giving the room a welcoming domestic ambience, enhanced by two high-backed armchairs, one each side of the fireplace. Above it hung the only picture in the room, a water-colour of a village street which looked like an Edward Bawden. Fitted bookshelves covered all the walls except above the fireplace and to the left of the door. Here was a white-painted cupboard with a vinyl worktop holding a microwave, an electric kettle and a cafetière. Beside the cupboard was a small refrigerator with a wall cupboard above it. To the right of the room a half-open door gave a glimpse of what was obviously a bathroom. Dalgliesh could see the edge of a shower cubicle and a wash-basin. He reflected that, if he wished, Calder-Hale need never emerge from his office.

Everywhere there were papers – plastic folders of press cuttings, some brown with age; box files ranged on the lower shelves; heaped pages of manuscript overflowing the compartments of the desk's high superstructure; parcels of typescript tied with tape piled on the floor. This superabundance might, of course, represent the administrative accumulation of decades, although most of the manuscript pages looked recent. But surely being curator of the Dupayne hardly involved this volume of paperwork. Calder-Hale was presumably engaged in some serious writing of his own, or he was one of those dilettantes who are happiest when engaged on an academic exercise which they have no intention – and indeed may be psychologically incapable – of completing. Calder-Hale seemed an unlikely candidate for this group, but then he might well prove as personally mysterious and complex as were some of his activities. And however valuable those exploits might be, he was as much a suspect as anyone intimately involved with the Dupayne Museum. Like them, he had means and opportunity. Whether he had motive remained to be seen. But it was possible that, more than all the others, he had the necessary ruthlessness.

There was a couple of inches of coffee in the cafetière. Calder-Hale motioned a hand towards it. 'Would you care for coffee? A fresh brew is easily made.' Then, after Dalgliesh and Piers had declined, he seated himself in the swivel armchair at his desk and regarded them.

'You'd better make yourselves comfortable in the armchairs, although I take it that this won't be prolonged.'

Dalgliesh was tempted to say that it would take as long as necessary. The room was uncomfortably hot, the gas fire an auxiliary to the central heating. Dalgliesh asked for it to be turned down. Taking his time, Calder-Hale walked over and turned off the tap. For the first time Dalgliesh was struck that the man looked ill. On their first encounter, flushed with indignation, real or assumed, Calder-Hale had given the impression of a man in vigorous health. Now Dalgliesh noticed the pallor under the eyes, the stretch of the skin over the cheek-bones and a momentary tremor of the hands as he turned the tap.

Before taking his seat, Calder-Hale went to the window and jerked the cords of the wooden slatted blind. It came rattling down, just missing the pot of African violets. He said, 'I hate this half-light. Let's shut it out.' Then he placed the plant on his desk and said, as if some apology or explanation were needed, 'Tally Clutton gave me this on the third of October. Someone had told her it was my fifty-fifth birthday. It's my least favourite flower, but shows an irritating reluctance to die.'

He settled himself in his chair and swivelled it to regard the two detectives with some complacency. He had, after all, the physically dominant position.

Dalgliesh said, 'Dr Dupayne's death is being treated as murder. Accident is out of the question and there are contra-indications to suicide. We're looking for your co-operation. If there is anything you know or suspect which could help, we need it now.'

Calder-Hale took up a pencil and began doodling on his blotter. He said, 'It would help if you told us more. All I know, all any of us knows, is what we have learned from each other. Someone threw petrol over Neville from a tin in the garden shed and set it alight. So you're confident that it wasn't suicide?'

'The physical evidence is against it.'

'What about the psychological evidence? When I saw Neville last Friday week when you were here with Conrad Ackroyd, I could see he was under stress. I don't know what his problems were, apart from overwork which we can take for granted. And he was in the wrong job. If you want to take on the more intractable of human ills it's as well to make sure that you've got the mental resistance and the essential detachment. Suicide is understandable; murder incomprehensible. And such an appalling murder! He had no enemies as far as I know, but then how should I know? We hardly ever met. He's garaged his car here ever since his father died, and he's been arriving each Friday at six and making off in it. Occasionally I would be leaving as he arrived. He never explained where he was going and I never asked. I've been curator here for four years now and I don't think I've seen Neville in the museum more than a dozen times.'

'Why was he here last Friday?'

Calder-Hale appeared to have given up interest in his doodle. Now he was attempting to balance his pencil on the desk. 'He wanted to find out what my views were about the future of the museum. As the Dupaynes have probably told you, the new lease has to be signed by the fifteenth of this month. I gather he was in some doubt whether he wanted the place to continue. I pointed out that it was no use asking for my support: I'm not a trustee and I wouldn't be at the meeting. Anyway, he knew my views. Museums honour the past in an age which worships modernity almost as much as it does money and celebrity. It's hardly surprising that museums are in difficulties. The Dupayne will be a loss if it closes, but only to people who value what it offers. Do the Dupaynes? If they haven't the will to save this place, no one else will.'

Dalgliesh said, 'Presumably now it will be safe. How much would it have mattered to you if the lease hadn't been signed?'

'It would have been inconvenient, to me and to certain people who are interested in what I do here. I've settled in comfortably in the last few years as you can see. But I do have a flat of my own and a life beyond this place. I doubt whether Neville would have stuck it out when it came to the crunch. He's a Dupayne, after all. I think he'd have gone along with his siblings.'

Piers spoke for the first time. He said uncompromisingly, 'Where were you, Mr Calder-Hale, between, say, five o'clock and seven o'clock on Friday evening?'

'An alibi? Isn't that stretching it rather? Surely the time you're interested in is six o'clock? But let's be meticulous by all means. At a quarter to five I left my flat in Bedford Square and went by motorcycle to my dentist in Weymouth Street. He had to complete some work on a crown. I usually leave the machine in Marylebone Street but all the places were taken, so I went to Marylebone Lane at Cross Keys Close and parked there. I left Weymouth Street at about five twenty-five, but I expect the dental nurse and the receptionist will be able to confirm the time. I found that my motorcycle had been taken. I walked home, cutting through the streets north of Oxford Street and taking my time, but I suppose I got there at about six o'clock. I then rang the local police station and no doubt they'll have recorded the call. They seemed remarkably unconcerned about the theft and I've heard nothing from them since. With the present level of gun crime and the terrorism threat, a stolen motorcycle is hardly a high priority. I'll give it a couple of days and then write it off and claim the insurance. It'll be dumped in a ditch somewhere. It's a Norton – they're not made now – and I was fond of it, but not as obsessively fond as poor Neville was of his E-type.'

Piers had made a note of the times. Dalgliesh said, 'And there's nothing else you can tell us?'

'Nothing. I'm sorry I haven't been more helpful. But as I said, I hardly knew Neville.'

'You'll have heard about Mrs Clutton's encounter with the mysterious motorist?'

'I've heard as much about Neville's death as I imagine you have. Marcus and Caroline have told me about your interview with them on Friday and I've spoken to Tally Clutton. She's an honest woman, by the way. You can rely on what she says.'

Asked whether Mrs Clutton's description struck a chord, Calder-Hale said, 'He sounds like a fairly average visitor to the Dupayne. I doubt whether he's significant. A fleeing murderer, particularly one who burns his victim alive, is hardly likely to stop to comfort an elderly lady. Anyway, why risk her taking his number?'

Piers said, 'We're putting out a call for him. He may come forward.'

'I shouldn't rely on it. He may be one of those sensible people who don't regard innocence as a protection against the more casuistical machinations of the police.'

Dalgliesh said, 'Mr Calder-Hale, I think it's possible you may know why Dupayne died. If so, it would save my time and some inconvenience to both of us if you would say so now.'

'I don't know. I wish I did. If I knew I'd tell you. I can accept the occasional necessity for murder, but not this murder and not this method. I may have my suspicions. I could give you four names and in order of probability, but I imagine you've got the same list and in the same order.'

It looked as if there was nothing more to be learned at present. Dalgliesh was about to get up when Calder-Hale said, 'Have you seen Marie Strickland yet?'

'Not officially. We met briefly when I came to the museum a week ago last Friday. At least I assume it was Mrs Strickland. She was working in the library.'

'She's an amazing woman. Have you checked up on her?'

'Should I?'

'I was wondering whether you had interested yourself in her past. In the war she was one of the women agents of the Special Operations Executive who were parachuted into France on the eve of D-Day. The project was to rebuild a network in the northern occupied zone which had been broken up after a great betrayal the previous year. Her group suffered the same fate. The group had a traitor who is rumoured to have been Strickland's lover. They were the only two members who weren't rounded up, tortured and killed.'

Dalgliesh asked, 'How do you know this?'

'My father worked with Maurice Buckmaster at SOE headquarters in Baker Street. He had his share of responsibility for the débâcle. He and Buckmaster were warned but refused to believe that the radio messages they were receiving were coming from the Gestapo. Of course I wasn't born at the time, but my father told me something of it before he died. In his last weeks before the morphine took over he made up for twenty-five years of non-communication. Most of what he told me is no secret. With the release of official papers, it's coming into the public domain anyway.'

'Have you and Mrs Strickland ever spoken about this?'

'I don't think she suspects that I know. She must realize that I'm Henry Calder-Hale's son, or at least related, but that wouldn't be a reason for getting together for a cosy chat about the past. Not that past and not with my name. Still, I thought you'd be interested to know. I always feel a little uneasy when I'm with Marie Strickland, though not uncomfortable enough to wish she weren't here. It's just that her kind of bravery is incomprehensible to me: it leaves me feeling inadequate. Charging into battle is one thing; risking betrayal, torture, a lonely death is another. She must have been extraordinary when young, a combination of delicate English beauty and ruthlessness. She was caught once on an earlier mission but managed to talk herself out of trouble. I imagine that the Germans couldn't believe she was other than she seemed. And now she sits in the library, hour after hour, an old woman with arthritic hands and faded eyes, writing out elegant notices which would be just as effective if Muriel Godby typed them on her computer.'

They sat in silence. Calder-Hale's last bitterly ironic comment seemed to have exhausted him. His eyes were straying towards a heap of papers on his desk but less with eagerness than with a kind of weary resignation. There would be no more to be learned at present; it was time to leave.

On the way to the car, neither spoke of Mrs Strickland. Piers said, 'It's not much of an alibi, is it? Motorbike parked in a busy street. Who'd be able to say what time it was left or taken away? He'd have been wearing a helmet, a pretty effective disguise. If it's dumped anywhere, it's probably in the bushes on Hampstead Heath.'

Dalgliesh said, 'We've got the time he left the dentist.

That can probably be confirmed accurately. The receptionist would keep an eye on the appointment times. If he did leave at five twenty-five, could he get to the Dupayne before six? Presumably, if he was lucky with the traffic flow and the lights. He'd need some time in hand. Benton-Smith had better time the journey, preferably with a Norton. The garage might be able to help there.'

'We'll need a couple of Nortons, sir. I fancy making a race of it.'

'One Norton will do. There are enough fools racing on the roads. Benton-Smith can do the journey several times. You'd better discuss alternate routes. Calder-Hale would have done some trial runs. And Benton needn't go mad – Calder-Hale wouldn't have risked shooting the lights.'

'You don't want me at the PM, sir?'

'No. Kate can take Benton. It'll be experience for him. The cause of death was always obvious but it will be interesting to know his general state of health and the blood alcohol level.'

Piers said, 'You think he could have been drunk, sir?'

'Not incapable, but if he had been drinking heavily it could give credence to the suicide theory.'

'I thought we had discounted suicide.'

'We have. I'm thinking of the defence. A jury could find it reasonable. The family are anxious for the body to be released for the cremation. Apparently they've got a slot for Thursday.'

Piers said, 'That's quick. They must have reserved a slot soon after their brother died. A bit insensitive. It looks as if they couldn't wait to complete the job that somebody had already started. At least they didn't reserve it before he was killed.'

Dalgliesh didn't reply, and it was in silence that they buckled themselves into the Jaguar.

15

Marcus Dupayne had summoned a meeting of the staff
for ten o'clock on Monday the fourth of November. This
had been done by a note as formally phrased as if he
were summoning an official body instead of just four
people.

Tally went to the museum to do her usual morning
chores as she had over the weekend, although the
museum was closed and her routine dusting hardly
necessary. But there was reassurance in carrying on with
her normal routine.

Back in the cottage she took off her working overall, washed, and after some thought, put on a clean
blouse, and returned to the museum just before ten.
They were to meet in the library and Muriel was already
there, setting out cups for the coffee. Tally saw that she
had, as usual, baked biscuits. This morning they looked
like plain oatmeal; perhaps, thought Tally, Muriel had
considered florentines inappropriately festive for the
occasion.

Both the Dupaynes arrived promptly and Mr Calder-
Hale strode in a few minutes later. They spent a few
minutes drinking coffee at the small table in front of the
northern window, as if anxious to separate a minor social
occasion from the serious business in hand, then moved
to their places at the middle table.

Marcus Dupayne said, 'I've asked you here for three reasons. The first is to thank you, James, Muriel and Tally, for your expressions of sympathy on the death of our brother. At a time like this, grief is subsumed in shock and shock in horror. We shall have time – too little time, perhaps – to mourn Neville and to realize what we and his patients have lost. The second reason is to let you know what my sister and I have decided about the future of the Dupayne Museum. The third is to discuss our response to the police investigation of what they have now decided, and we have to accept, is murder, and how we deal with the publicity which has, of course, already started. I left the meeting until this morning because I felt that we were all too shocked at the weekend to think clearly.'

James Calder-Hale said, 'I take it, then, that the new lease will be signed and the Dupayne will continue?'

Marcus said, 'The lease has already been signed. Caroline and I went to Lincoln's Inn by appointment at half-past eight this morning.'

James said, 'Before Neville has been cremated? Do I detect the smell of funeral baked meats?'

Caroline's voice was cold. 'All the preliminaries had been completed. Nothing was necessary except the signature of the two surviving trustees. It would have been premature to have had this meeting without being able to assure you that the museum would continue.'

'Wouldn't it have been seemly to have waited a few days?'

Marcus was unmoved. 'Why precisely? Are you

developing sensitivity to public opinion, or is there some ethical or theological objection that I've overlooked?'

James's face creased briefly into a wry smile that was half a grimace, but he didn't reply.

Marcus went on, 'The inquest will be opened and adjourned tomorrow morning and if the body is released for burial the cremation will take place on Thursday. My brother was not religious so it will be secular and private. Only close family will attend. It seems that the hospital will want later to arrange a memorial service in the chapel and we shall, of course, be there. I imagine that anyone else who wishes to attend will be welcome. I have only had a brief telephone call with the administrator. Nothing is yet settled.

'Now for the future of the museum. I shall take over as general administrator and Caroline will continue to work part-time and will be responsible for what we might describe as the front of house: tickets, administration, finance, housekeeping. You, Muriel, will continue to be responsible to her. I know you have some private arrangement concerning the care of her flat and that will continue. We would like you, James, to carry on as curator with responsibility for accessions, the preservation and display of exhibits, relationships with researchers and the recruitment of volunteers. You, Tally, will continue as you are, living in the cottage and being responsible to my sister for the general cleaning and to Muriel when she requires help on the desk. I shall be writing to our two existing volunteers, Mrs Faraday and Mrs Strickland, to ask them to continue if they are willing. If the museum expands, as I hope it will, we may need additional paid staff and we could certainly make use of more volunteers. James will continue to vet them. The boy Ryan may as well continue if he condescends to turn up.'

Tally spoke for the first time. She said, 'I'm worried about Ryan.'

Marcus was dismissive. 'I don't think the police are going to suspect Ryan Archer. What possible motive had the boy, even if he had the wit to plan this murder?'

James said gently, 'I don't think you need worry, Tally. Commander Dalgliesh has told us what happened. The boy made off because he'd attacked Major Arkwright and probably thought he'd killed him. He'll turn up when he realizes he hasn't. Anyway, the police are looking for him. There's nothing we can do.'

Marcus said, 'Obviously they need to talk to him. We can't hope that he'll be discreet in what he tells them.'

Caroline said, 'But what can he tell them?'

There was a silence which was broken by Marcus. 'Perhaps it's time now that we moved on to the investigation. What I find rather surprising is the level of police commitment. Why Commander Dalgliesh? I thought his squad was set up to investigate murder cases of particular difficulty or sensitivity. I can't see that Neville's death qualifies.'

James rocked back precariously in his chair. 'I can give you a number of suggestions. Neville was a psychiatrist. Perhaps he was treating someone powerful whose reputation needs more than the usual protection. It wouldn't be good, for example, if it became known that a Minister at the Treasury was a kleptomaniac, a bishop a serial bigamist, or a pop star had a predilection for under-age girls. Then the police could suspect that the museum is being used for a criminal purpose, receiving stolen goods and concealing them among the exhibits, or organizing a spy-ring for international terrorists.'

Marcus frowned. 'I find humour a little inappropriate at a time like this, James. But it could well be something to do with Neville's job. He must have known a number of dangerous secrets. His work brought him into contact with a wide variety of people, most of them psychologi-cally disturbed. We know nothing of his private life. We don't know where he went on Fridays or whom he met. We don't know whether he brought someone with him or met someone here. It was he who had the keys cut for the garage. We have no way of knowing how many he had cut or who had access to them. That one spare key in the cupboard downstairs was probably not the only spare.'

Muriel said, 'Inspector Miskin asked me about it when she and the Sergeant saw Tally and me last thing on Friday after Commander Dalgliesh left. They were sug-gesting that someone could have taken the garage key and replaced it with another Yale, then returned the proper key later. I pointed out that I wouldn't have noticed the difference if they had. One Yale looks very like another unless you examine it closely.'

Caroline said, 'And then there's the mysterious motor-ist. Obviously he's the prime suspect at present. Let's hope the police manage to trace him.'

James was executing a doodle of remarkable complexity. Still working on it, he said, 'If they don't, they'll find it difficult to pin the crime on anyone else. Someone may be hoping that he remains a fugitive in more senses than one.'

Muriel broke in. 'And then there's those extraordinary words he said to Tally. *It looks as if someone's lit a bonfire.* That's exactly what Rouse said. Couldn't this be a copycat murder?'

Marcus frowned. 'I don't think we should indulge in fantasy. It was probably coincidence. Still, the motorist has to be found and in the mean time we have a duty to give the police every assistance. That doesn't mean volunteering information for which they haven't asked. It's extremely unwise to speculate either among ourselves or to other people. I suggest that no one speaks to the press and no press calls should be returned. If anyone is persistent, refer them to the Metropolitan Police public relations branch or to Commander Dalgliesh. You'll have seen that a barrier has been erected across the drive. I've got keys here for you all. Only those with a car will, of course, need them. I think, Tally, you will be able to wheel your bicycle round the edge or take it underneath the barrier. The museum will be closed for this week but I hope to re-open next Monday. There's one exception. Conrad Ackroyd has a small group of Canadian academics arriving on Wednesday and I'm letting him know that we shall open especially for that visit. We must expect that the murder will bring in additional visitors and this may not be easy to cope with at first. I shall spend as much time as possible at the museum and I'm hoping to take on escort duties, but I shan't be able to be here on Wednesday. I have to confer with the bank. Has anyone any questions?'

He looked round the table but no one spoke. Then Muriel said, 'I think we would all like to say how delighted we are that the Dupayne Museum will stay open. You and Miss Caroline will have our full support in making it a success.'

There was no murmur of assent. Perhaps, Tally thought, Mr Calder-Hale shared her view that both the words and the timing were inappropriate.

It was then that the telephone rang. It had been switched through to the library and Muriel moved quickly to take the call. She listened, turned and said, 'It's Commander Dalgliesh. He's trying to identify one of the visitors to the museum. He's hoping I can help.'

Caroline Dupayne said shortly, 'Then you'd better take the call in the office. My brother and I will be using this room for some time now.'

Muriel took her hand from the mouthpiece. She said, 'Will you hold on please, Commander. I'll just go down to the office.'

Tally followed her down the stairs and went out of the front door. In the office Muriel picked up the receiver.

Dalgliesh said, 'When I came with Mr Ackroyd two Fridays ago, there was a young man in the picture gallery. He was interested in the Nash. He was alone, thin faced, wearing blue jeans worn at the knees, a thick anorak, a woollen hat pulled down over his ears and blue and white trainers. He told me he'd visited the museum before. I'm wondering if by any chance you recall him.'

'Yes, I think I do. He wasn't our usual type of visitor so I noticed him particularly. He wasn't alone the first time he came. Then he had a young woman with him. She was carrying a baby in one of those slings parents have – you know, the baby is held to the chest with its legs dangling. I remember thinking that it looked like a monkey clinging to its mother. They didn't stay long. I think they only visited the picture gallery.'

'Did anyone escort them?'

'It didn't seem necessary. The girl had a bag, I remember, flowered cotton with a drawstring. I expect it was for nappies and the baby's bottle. Anyway, she checked it in at the cloakroom. I can't think of anything portable they would be interested in stealing, and Mrs Strickland was working in the library so they couldn't get their hands on any of the books.'

'Did you have reason to suppose they might want to?'

'No, but many of the volumes are valuable first editions. We can't be too careful. But as I said, Mrs Strickland was there. She's the volunteer who writes our labels. She may remember them if they went into the library.'

'You have a remarkably good memory, Miss Godby.'

'Well, as I said, Commander, they weren't our usual kind of visitor.'

'Who is?'

'Well, they tend to be more middle-aged. Some are very old, I suppose they're the ones who actually remember the inter-war years. But then there are the researchers, writers and historians. Mr Calder-Hale's visitors are usually serious students. I believe he shows some of them around by special appointment after our normal hours. Naturally they don't sign in.'

'You didn't by any chance take the young man's name? Did he sign in?'

'No. Only Friends of the museum who don't pay sign in.' Then her voice changed. She said with a note of satisfaction, 'I've just remembered. I believe I am able to help you, Commander. Three months ago – I can give you the exact date if you need it – we planned a lecture with slides on painting and print-making in the 1920s to be given in the picture gallery by a distinguished friend of Mr Ackroyd. There was a £10 admission charge. We hoped that it would be the first of a series. The programmes weren't yet ready. Some lecturers had promised, but I had problems fixing convenient dates. I set out a book and asked visitors who might be interested in attending to leave their names and addresses.'

'And he gave you his?'

'His wife did. It was that time when they came together. At least, I'm assuming she was his wife; she was wearing a wedding ring, I noticed. The visitor leaving just before them had signed, so it seemed natural to invite the couple to do so. It would look invidious otherwise. So she wrote it down. After they left the desk and were walking to the door I saw him talking to her. I think he was remonstrating with her, telling her that she shouldn't have done it. Of course neither of them came to the lecture. At £10 a head I didn't expect them to.'

'Could you look up the entry, please? I'll hang on.'

There was a silence. After less than a minute she spoke again. 'I think I've found the young man you want. The girl has written them down as a married couple. Mr David Wilkins and Mrs Michelle Wilkins, 15A Goldthorpe Road, Ladbroke Grove.'

16

After Muriel's return from dealing with Commander Dalgliesh's telephone call, Marcus brought the meeting to a close. The time was ten forty-five.

Tally's telephone rang just as she was entering the cottage. It was Jennifer. She said, 'Is that you, Mother? Look, I can't talk for long, I'm ringing from work. I tried to get you early this morning. Are you all right?'

'Perfectly all right thank you, Jennifer. Don't worry.'

'Are you sure you don't want to come to us for a time? Are you sure you're safe in that cottage? Roger could come to collect you.'

Tally reflected that, now that the news of the murder was in the papers, Jennifer's workmates must have been talking. Perhaps they had hinted that Tally ought to be rescued from this as yet unknown murderer and taken to stay in Basingstoke until the case was solved. Tally felt a spasm of guilt. Perhaps she was being unreasonably judgemental. Perhaps Jennifer really was worried; she had been telephoning daily since the news broke. But somehow Roger must be stopped from coming. She used the one argument which she knew might prevail.

'Please don't worry, dear. It really isn't necessary. I don't want to leave the cottage. I don't want to risk the Dupaynes putting someone else in, however temporarily. I've got locks on the doors and all the windows and I feel perfectly safe. I'll let you know if I start feeling nervous, but I'm sure I shan't.'

She could almost hear the relief in Jennifer's voice. 'But what's happening? What are the police doing? Are they bothering you? Are you being worried by the press?'

'The police are being very polite. Of course we've all been questioned and I expect we shall be again.'

'But they can't possibly think . . .'

Tally cut her short. 'Oh no, I'm sure no one at the museum is really under suspicion. But they're trying to find out as much as they can about Dr Neville. The press aren't worrying us. This number is ex-directory and we've got a barrier across the drive so cars can't get in. The police are being very helpful about that and about press conferences. The museum is closed for the moment, but we hope to open again next week. Dr Neville's funeral has been arranged for Thursday.'

'I suppose you'll be attending that, Mother.'

Tally wondered if she was about to be given advice on what to wear. She said hurriedly, 'Oh no, it's going to be a very quiet cremation with just the family there.'

'Well, if you really are all right . . .'

'Perfectly all right thank you, Jennifer. It's good of you to phone. Give my love to Roger and the children.'

She rang off more promptly than Jennifer would have thought polite. Almost immediately the telephone rang again. Picking up the receiver, she heard Ryan's voice. He was speaking very quietly against a confused clatter of background noise. 'Mrs Tally, it's Ryan.'

She breathed a sigh of relief and quickly transferred the receiver to her left ear where her hearing was keener.

'Oh Ryan, I'm glad you phoned. We've been worried about you. Are you all right? Where are you?'

'Oxford Circus Underground. Mrs Tally, I've got no money. Can you ring back?'

He sounded desperate. She said, keeping her voice very calm, 'Yes, of course. Give me the number. And speak clearly, Ryan. I can hardly hear you.'

Thank goodness, she thought, that she always kept a notepad and pen handy. She took down the digits and made him repeat them. She said, 'Stay where you are. I'll ring back immediately.'

He must have snatched up the receiver. He said, 'I've killed him, haven't I, the Major? He's dead.'

'No, he isn't dead, Ryan. He wasn't badly hurt and he's not pressing charges. But obviously the police want to interview you. You know that Dr Neville has been murdered?'

'It's in the papers. They'll think I did that too.' He sounded sulky rather than worried.

'Of course they won't, Ryan. Try to be sensible and think clearly. The worst thing you can do is run away. Where've you been sleeping?'

'I found a place near King's Cross, a boarded-up house with a front basement. I've been walking since dawn. I didn't like to go to the squat because I knew the police would be looking for me there. Are you sure the Major's all right? You wouldn't lie to me, would you, Mrs Tally?'

'No, I don't lie, Ryan. If you'd killed him it would be in the newspapers. But now you must come home. Have you any money at all?'

'No. And I can't use my mobile. It's run out.'

'I'll come and fetch you.' She thought quickly. Finding him at Oxford Circus wasn't going to be easy and it would take time to get there. The police were looking for him and might pick him up at any moment. It seemed important that she should get to him first. She said, 'There's a church, Ryan, All Saints, Margaret Street. It's close to where you are. Walk up Great Portland Street towards the BBC and Margaret Street is on the right. You can sit quietly in the church until I come. No one will worry or interfere with you. If anyone does speak to you, it's because they think you may need help. Say you're waiting for a friend. Or you can kneel. No one will speak to you then.'

'Like I'm praying? God'll strike me dead!'

'Of course He won't, Ryan. He doesn't do things like that.'

'He does! Terry – my mum's last bloke – he told me. It's in the Bible.'

'Well, He doesn't do things like that now.'

Oh dear, she thought, *I've made it sound as if He's learnt better. How did we get involved in this ridiculous theological argument?* She said firmly, 'Everything's going to be all right. Go to the church as I said. I'll come as quickly as I can. You remember the directions?'

She could detect the sullenness in his voice. 'Up towards the BBC, Margaret Street's on the right. That's what you said.'

'Good. I'll be there.'

She put down the receiver. It was going to be an expensive jaunt and it might take longer than she wished. She wasn't used to phoning for taxis and had to look up

the number in the telephone directory. She stressed that
the call was urgent and the girl who answered said they
would do their best to get a cab to her within fifteen
minutes, which was longer than she had hoped. Her
morning's work at the museum was finished but she
wondered whether she ought to go back and let Muriel
know that she would be absent for the next hour or so.
Mr Marcus and Miss Caroline were still there. Any of
them might want her and wonder where she was. After
a little thought she sat at the desk and wrote a note.
*Muriel, I've had to go to the West End for an hour or so but
should be back before one. I thought you might like to know
in case you wonder where I am. Everything is all right. Tally.*

She decided to put the note through the museum
door before she left. Muriel would think it an odd way
of communicating but she couldn't risk questions. And
what about the police? They ought to be told at once so
that the search could be called off. But Ryan would see
it as an act of betrayal if the police arrived first. But they
wouldn't if she didn't tell them where to find him. She
put on her hat and coat, checked that she had sufficient
money in her purse to get to Margaret Street and back,
then rang the number Inspector Miskin had given her.
A male voice answered at once.

She said, 'It's Tally Clutton here. Ryan Archer has just
rung me. He's perfectly all right and I'm going to fetch
him. I'll bring him back here.'

Then immediately she put down the receiver. The
phone rang again before she got to the door but she
ignored it and went quickly out, locking the cottage
behind her. After pushing her note through the letter-box

of the museum, she walked up the drive to wait for the cab on the other side of the barrier. The minutes seemed interminable and she couldn't resist perpetually looking at her watch. It was nearly twenty minutes before the cab came. She said, 'All Saints church, Margaret Street, please – and please be as quick as you can.'

The elderly driver didn't reply. Perhaps he was tired of passengers exhorting him to speed when speed wasn't possible.

The lights were against them and at Hampstead they joined a long queue of vans and taxis crawling southwards towards Baker Street and the West End. She sat bolt upright, clutching her handbag, willing herself to be calm and patient since agitation was useless. The driver was doing the best he could.

When they reached the Marylebone Road she leaned forward and said, 'If it's difficult to get to the church because of the one-way, you can leave me at the end of Margaret Street.'

All he replied was, 'I can get you to the church all right.'

Five minutes later he did. She said, 'I'm just collecting someone. Will you wait a moment please, or would you like me to pay now?'

'That's all right,' he said. 'I'll wait.'

She had been horrified at the sum showing on the meter. If it cost as much getting back, she would have to get to the bank next day.

She passed through the small unpromising courtyard and pushed open the door. She had first come to All Saints a year ago when Jennifer had sent her a book token for Christmas and she had bought Simon Jenkins's *England's Thousand Best Churches*. She had decided to visit all his London choices but, because of the distances, progress had been slow. But the quest had opened her eyes to a new dimension of London life and an architectural and historical heritage previously unvisited.

Even in this hour of concentrated anxiety with the taxi fare inexorably mounting and the possibility that Ryan wouldn't have waited, the gloriously adorned interior imposed its moment of astonished quietude. From floor to roof no part of it had been left undecorated. The walls gleamed with mosaics and murals and the great reredos with its row of painted saints drew the eye towards the glory of the high altar. On her first visit, her response to this ornate contrivance had been uncertain, amazement rather than reverence. It was only on a second visit that she had felt at home. She was used to seeing it during High Mass, the robed priests moving ceremoniously before the high altar, the soaring voices of the choir rising with the waves of pungent incense. Now, as the door closed grindingly behind her the quiet air and the serried rows of empty chairs imparted a more subtle mystery. Somewhere, she supposed, there must be a custodian but none was visible. Two nuns were seated in the front row before the statue of the Virgin and a few candles burned steadily, not flickering as she closed the door.

She saw Ryan almost immediately. He was seated at the back and came forward at once to join her. Her heart leapt with relief. She said, 'I've got a cab waiting. We'll go straight home.'

'But I'm hungry, Mrs Tally. I'm feeling faint. Can't we have burgers?' His tone had become infantile, a childish whine.

Oh dear, she thought, *those dreadful burgers!* Occasionally he would bring them for his lunch and heat them up under the grill. Their rich onion smell lingered for too long. But he did indeed look faint and the omelette she had planned to cook for him probably wasn't what he needed.

The prospect of a quick meal immediately revived him. Opening the cab door for her, he called to the driver with cocky assurance, 'The nearest burger bar will do us fine, mate. Make it quick.'

They were there within minutes and she paid off the cab, tipping an extra pound. Inside she gave Ryan a five-pound note so that he could stand in line and get what he wanted and a coffee for herself. He came back with a double cheeseburger and a large milk shake, and then returned for her coffee. They settled down at a seat as far as possible from the window. He seized the hamburger and began cramming it into his mouth.

She said, 'Were you all right in the church? Did you like it?'

He shrugged. 'It was OK. Weird. They've got the same joss-sticks we've got in the squat.'

'You mean the incense?'

'One of the girls in the squat, Mamie, used to light the joss-sticks and then we sat in the dark and she'd get in touch with the dead.'

'She couldn't do that, Ryan. We can't speak to the dead.'

'Well, she could. She spoke to my dad. She told me things she wouldn't have known if she hadn't spoken to Dad.'

'But she lived with you in the squat, Ryan. She must have known things about you and about your family. And some things she told you were probably lucky guesses.'

'No,' he said. 'She spoke to my dad. Can I go back for another shake?'

There was no problem in hailing a taxi for the return journey. It was only then that Ryan asked about the murder. She gave him the facts as simply as she could, not dwelling on the horror of the discovery and giving him none of the details.

She said, 'We have a team from New Scotland Yard investigating, Commander Dalgliesh and three assistants. They'll want to talk to you, Ryan. Obviously you must answer their questions honestly. We all need to get this terrible mystery cleared up.'

'And the Major? He's OK, you said?'

'Yes. He's fine. The head wound bled a lot but it really wasn't serious. But it could've been, Ryan. Why on earth did you lose your temper like that?'

'He gave me aggravation, didn't he?'

He turned to stare resolutely out of the window and Tally thought it prudent to say nothing more. She was surprised that he showed so little curiosity about Dr Neville's death. But the press accounts, so far, had been short and ambiguous. He was probably too concerned about his attack on the Major to care about Dr Neville.

She paid off the taxi, horrified at the total cost, and

again added an extra pound as tip. The driver seemed satisfied. She and Ryan ducked under the barrier and walked in silence to the house.

Inspector Tarrant and Sergeant Benton-Smith were coming out of the museum. The inspector said, 'So you found Ryan, Mrs Clutton. Jolly good. We've some questions for you, young man. The sergeant and I are off to the station. You better come with us. It won't take long.'

Tally said quickly, 'Couldn't you talk to Ryan in the cottage? I could leave you alone in the sitting-room.' She nearly committed the folly of offering him coffee as an inducement.

Ryan's eyes shifted from her to the inspector. 'Are you arresting me then?'

'No, just taking you to the station for a chat. We've got some things to clear up. You can call it helping the police with their inquiries.'

Ryan found some spirit. 'Oh yeah? I know what that means. I want a brief.'

'You're not a juvenile, are you?'

The Inspector's voice was suddenly sharp. Tally guessed that dealing with juveniles would be difficult and time-consuming. It wasn't a prospect the police would relish.

'No. I'm nearly eighteen.'

'That's a relief. You can have a brief if you want one. We've got 'em on call. Or you could phone a friend.'

'All right. I'll phone the Major.'

'That forgiving chap? OK, you can ring him from the station.'

Ryan departed with them willingly enough, even with a slight swagger. Tally suspected that he was prepared to enjoy his period of notoriety. She could understand why the police hadn't wanted to question him in the cottage. Even if she left them alone, she would be too close for comfort. She was involved in this mystery, possibly even a suspect. They wanted to talk to Ryan in complete privacy. With a sinking of the heart she had no doubt they would get from him what they wanted.

17

Kate wasn't surprised that Dalgliesh was to go with her to interview David Wilkins. It was after all necessary; only AD could identify him. Wilkins had been in the museum the week before the Dupayne murder and had admitted to a grievance against the museum. However unlikely a suspect, he had to be seen. And one never knew what part of an investigation AD might decide to take a personal hand in. He was, after all, a poet with a writer's interest in the fabric of other lives. His poetry was a mystery to her. The man who had produced *A Case to Answer and Other Poems* bore no relation to the senior detective she served under with a passionate commitment. She could recognize some of his moods, feared his occasional if quiet criticism, rejoiced to know that she was a valued member of his team, but she didn't know him. And she had long learned first to discipline and finally to put aside, any hope of his love. Someone else, she suspected, now had that. She, Kate, had always believed in limiting ambition to what was achievable. She told herself that if AD were to be lucky in love, she would be glad for him, but she was surprised and a little disturbed by the vehement resentment she felt against Emma Lavenham. Couldn't the woman see what she was doing to him?

They walked the last fifty yards in silence through

the thin drizzle. Goldthorpe Road was a terrace of late
Victorian stuccoed houses running off the north end of
Ladbroke Grove. No doubt these solid monuments to
nineteenth-century domestic aspirations would one day
be acquired, upgraded, converted into expensive flats
and priced out of reach of all but two salaried pro-
fessionals with an eye for a street on its way up. But now
decades of neglect had sunk the terrace into decrepitude.
The cracked walls were grimed with years of London
dirt, the stucco had fallen in lumps from the porticoes,
revealing the bricks beneath, and paint was flaking from
the front doors. It didn't need the racks of doorbells to
see that this was a street of multi-occupancy, but it was
strangely, even ominously, quiet as if the inhabitants,
aware of some impending contagion, had stolen away in
the night.

The Wilkins's flat, 15A, was in the basement. Thin
curtains, drooping in the middle, hung from the single
window. The latch on the iron gate was broken and the
gate kept shut by a wire clothes hanger twisted into a
loop. Dalgliesh raised this and he and Kate went down
the stone steps to the basement area. Some effort had
been made to sweep it but there was still a moist heap
of debris – cigarette packets, fragments of newspaper,
crumpled brown bags and a filthy handkerchief – blown
into the corner by the wind. The door was to the left
where the pavement arched over the area, making the
entry invisible from the road. The number 15A was
crudely painted in white on the wall and Kate saw that
there were two locks, a Yale and a security one below.
Beside the door was a green plastic pot containing a

geranium. The stem was woody, the few leaves were dry and brown and the single pink flower on its etiolated stem was as small as a daisy. How, Kate wondered, could anyone have expected it to flourish without sun?

Their arrival had been noticed. Glancing to her right, Kate saw the edge of the curtains twitch. She rang and they waited. Looking at Dalgliesh, Kate saw that he was gazing upwards at the railings, his face expressionless. The street lamp shining through the shafts of drizzle picked out the taut line of the jaw and planes of the face. *Oh God*, she thought, *he looks tired to death*.

There was still no reply, and after a minute she rang again. This time the door was cautiously opened. Above the chain a pair of frightened eyes met hers.

Kate said, 'Is Mr David Wilkins at home? We want to have a word with him. We're from the police.'

She had tried to sound unfrightening while realizing that the effort was futile. A visit from the police is seldom good news and in this street it was probably a harbinger of catastrophe.

The chain was still in place. The girl's voice said, 'Is it about the rent? Davie's seeing to it. He's not here now, he's at the chemist's picking up his prescription.'

Kate said, 'It's nothing to do with the rent. We're making enquiries about a case and we think Mr Wilkins may be able to help us with some information.'

And that was hardly more reassuring. Everyone knew what was meant by helping the police with their inquiries. The gap in the door widened until the chain was stretched to its full extent.

Dalgliesh turned and said, 'Are you Mrs Michelle

Wilkins?' She nodded and he went on, 'We won't keep your husband long. We're not even sure that he can help us but we have to try. If he's expected back soon, perhaps we could wait.'

Of course they could wait, thought Kate. Inside or outside, they could wait. But why this pussyfooting?

And now the chain was removed. They saw a thin young woman who looked little more than sixteen. The strands of light brown hair hung each side of a pale narrow face in which the anxious eyes looked into Kate's for a moment of mute appeal. She was wearing the ubiquitous blue jeans, grubby trainers and a man's pull-over. She didn't speak and they followed her down a narrow passage, easing their way past a folding pram. Ahead a door to the bathroom was open giving a view of an old-fashioned WC with a high cistern and hanging chain. At the base of the wash-basin there was a heap of towels and linen pushed against the wall.

Michelle Wilkins stood back and motioned them through to a door on the right. The narrow room ran the whole width of the house. There were two doors in the rear wall, both standing wide open. One led to a cluttered kitchen, the other to what was obviously the bedroom. A railed cot and a double divan took up almost the whole space under the single window. The bed was unmade, the pillows ruffled and the duvet slipping off to expose a rumpled undersheet.

The sitting-room was furnished only with a square table with four upright wooden chairs, a battered sofa covered with a throw in Indian cotton, a pine chest of drawers and a large television set beside the gas fire.

Kate, in her years with the Met, had been in grubbier, more depressing rooms. They seldom worried her, but now she felt what she so rarely did, a moment of discomfort, even of embarrassment. What would she feel if the police arrived unannounced, requesting or demanding admission to her flat? It would be immaculate, why shouldn't it be? There was no one there to make it untidy but herself. Even so, the intrusion would be insupportable. She and Dalgliesh needed to be here, but it was still an intrusion.

Michelle Wilkins closed the door to the bedroom then made a gesture which could have been an invitation towards the sofa. Dalgliesh sat, but Kate moved over to the table. Set in its centre was a Moses basket holding a plump pink-cheeked baby. Kate thought that it must be a girl. She was wearing a short frilled dress in pink cotton with an embroidered bib of daisies and a white knitted cardigan. In contrast to the rest of the room, everything about her was clean. Her head with its moss of milk-white hair rested on a pristine pillow; the blanket, now drawn aside, was spotless, and the dress looked as if it had been recently ironed. It seemed extraordinary that a girl so fragile could have produced this cheerfully robust baby. Two strong legs separated by a bunch of nappy were vigorously kicking. Then the child lay quietly, holding up hands like starfish and focusing on the moving fingers as if gradually realizing that they belonged to her. After a few aborted efforts she managed to insert a thumb into her mouth and quietly began sucking.

Michelle Wilkins moved over to the table, and Kate

and she looked down at the baby together. Kate asked, 'How old is she?'

'Four months. She's Rebecca, but Davie and I call her Becky.'

Kate said, 'I don't know much about babies but she looks very forward for her age.'

'Oh she is, she is. She can arch her back very strongly and she can sit up. If Davie and I hold her upright you can see her trying to stand.'

Kate's thoughts were in a mild emotional confusion. What was she expected to feel? Unhappy awareness of that much-discussed inexorable ticking away of the years, each one after thirty making it less likely that she would ever be a mother? Wasn't that the dilemma facing all successful professional women? So why didn't she feel it? And was this only a temporary reluctance? Would the time come when she would be overcome by a need, physical or psychological, to bear a child, to know that something of herself would survive her death, a craving which might become so imperative and overwhelming that she would be driven to some modern humiliating expedient to get her wish? The thought horrified her. Surely not. Illegitimate, brought up by an elderly grandmother, she had never known her mother. She thought, *I shouldn't know how to begin. I'd be hopeless. You can't give what you've never had.* But what were the responsibilities of her job, even at its most demanding, compared to this: to bring another human being into the world, to be responsible for her until she was eighteen, never to be free of caring and worrying until you died? And yet the girl beside her was happily coping. Kate thought, *There's a world of experience I know nothing about*. Suddenly and with sadness she felt herself diminished.

Dalgliesh said, 'Your husband visited the Dupayne Gallery fairly regularly, didn't he? We met while I was there ten days ago. We were both looking at the same painting. Did you often go with him?'

The girl bent suddenly over the cot and began fussing with the blanket. Her lank hair fell forward obscuring her face. She seemed not even to hear. Then she said, 'I did go once. That was about three months ago. Davie hadn't a job at the time so he was let in free, but the woman at the desk said I had to pay because I wasn't on jobseekers' allowance. It's £5, so we couldn't afford it. I told Davie to go in on his own, but he wouldn't. Then a man arrived and came over to the desk to ask what was wrong. The woman there called him Dr Dupayne so he must have been something to do with the museum. He told her she had to let me in. He said, "What do you expect this visitor to do, wait outside in the rain with her baby?" Then he told me to leave the pram where the coats are hung, just inside the door, and take Becky in with me.'

Kate said, 'I don't suppose that made the woman on the desk very happy.'

Michelle's face brightened. 'No it didn't. She went red and looked daggers after Dr Dupayne. We were glad to get away from her and look at the pictures.'

Dalgliesh said, 'One particular picture?'

'Yes. It's one that belonged to Davie's grandad. That's why Davie likes to go and see it.'

It was then that they heard the creak of the gate and

the clatter of feet on the steps. Michelle Wilkins vanished silently through the door. They could hear the low mutter of voices in the passage. David Wilkins came in and stood for a moment irresolute in the doorway as if it were he who was the visitor. His wife moved close to him and Kate saw their hands touch and then clasp.

Dalgliesh got up. He said, 'I'm Commander Dalgliesh and this is Inspector Miskin from the Metropolitan Police. We're sorry to come without warning. We won't keep you long. Hadn't we all better sit down?'

With their hands still clasped, husband and wife moved to the sofa. Dalgliesh and Kate sat at the table. The baby, who had been gently gurgling, now let out a sudden cry. Michelle rushed to the table and picked her up. Holding her against her shoulder, she moved back to the sofa. Husband and wife gave all their attention to Rebecca.

The boy said, 'Is she hungry?'

'You get the bottle, Davie.'

Kate saw that nothing more could be done until Rebecca had been fed. The bottle was produced with extraordinary speed. Michelle Wilkins cradled her child who began lustily munching on the teat. There was no sound but this vigorous feeding. The room had suddenly become domestic and very peaceful. It seemed ludicrous to talk about murder.

Dalgliesh said, 'You've probably guessed that we want to talk about the Dupayne Museum. I expect you know that Dr Neville Dupayne has been murdered.'

The boy nodded but didn't speak. He had huddled close to his wife and both kept their gaze on the child.

Dalgliesh said, 'We're talking to as many people as possible who either worked at the Dupayne or visited regularly. I'm sure you understand why. First I have to ask where you were and what you were doing last Friday between, say, five o'clock and seven.'

Michelle Wilkins looked up. She said, 'You were at the doctor's, Davie.' She turned to Dalgliesh. 'The evening surgery starts at quarter past five and Davie's appointment was for quarter to six. Not that he gets seen then, but he always gets there in good time, don't you, Davie?'

Kate asked, 'When were you seen?'

Davie said, 'About twenty past six. I didn't wait long really.'

'Is the surgery close to here?'

'It's in St Charles Square. Not far really.'

His wife said encouragingly, 'You've got your appointment card, haven't you, Davie? Show them the card.'

David fumbled in his trouser pocket, produced it and handed it to Kate. It was crumpled and bore a long list of appointments. Undoubtedly the boy was due at the surgery on the previous Friday evening. It would be a matter of minutes only to verify that he had actually attended. She noted the details and gave back the card.

Michelle said, 'Davie gets bad asthma and his heart isn't very strong. That's why he can't always work. Sometimes he's on sick pay and sometimes on job-seekers' allowance. He started a new job last Monday, didn't you, Davie? Now we've got this place everything should be better.'

Dalgliesh said, 'Tell me about the picture. You said

your grandfather owned it. How did it come to be in the Dupayne Museum?'

Kate wondered why Dalgliesh was going on with the interview. They had got what they wanted. She had never thought David Wilkins a likely suspect, but nor had Dalgliesh, so why not leave now? But so far from resenting the question, the boy seemed eager to talk.

'It belonged to my grandad. He had a little village shop in Cheddington, that's in Suffolk near Halesworth. He did all right until the supermarkets came and then the business fell off. But before that he bought the Nash picture. It was in the sale at a local house and he and my grandma went round to bid for a couple of easy chairs. Grandad took to the picture and got it. There wasn't much local interest because people thought it was so gloomy and there weren't any other paintings in the sale so I don't suppose people knew about it. But Max Dupayne knew about it, only he got there too late. He tried to persuade Grandad to sell it to him but Grandad wouldn't. He said, "If ever you want to sell I'll be interested, only you may not get the price I'm offering you now. It's not a valuable picture but I fancy it." But Grandad fancied it too. You see, his dad – that's my great-grandad – was killed in the 1914–18 war at Passchendaele, and I think he wanted this as a kind of memorial. It hung in their living-room until the shop finally failed and they moved into a house in Lowestoft. Then things got bad for them. Anyway Max Dupayne must have kept in touch, for he arrived one day to ask about the picture and said again that he wanted to buy it. Grandad had got into debt so he had to agree.'

Dalgliesh asked, 'Do you know what he paid?'

'He said he'd give Grandad what he'd paid for it, which was just over £300. Of course it was an awful lot to Grandad when he bought the picture. I think he and my gran had a row over it. But now he had to let it go.'

Kate said, 'Didn't it occur to him to get someone from one of the London or provincial auction houses to give him a valuation? Sotheby's, Christie's, someone like that?'

'No, I don't think so. He didn't know about auction houses. He said Mr Dupayne told him he'd never get the same amount selling it that way, that they took a big commission and the tax man would be after him. Something about paying capital gains tax.'

Kate said, 'Well, he wouldn't. He didn't make any capital gain anyway, did he?'

'I know, but I think Mr Dupayne muddled him up, and in the end he sold. After grandad died, Dad told me about it. When I found out where it was, I went to see it.'

Dalgliesh said, 'Did you hope somehow to get it back?'

There was a silence. In the last few minutes David had forgotten he was speaking to a police officer. Now he looked at his wife. She shifted the baby on her lap and said, 'Better tell him, Davie. Tell him about the masked man. You never did nothing wrong.'

Dalgliesh waited. He had always, thought Kate, known when to wait. After a minute the boy said, 'OK, I did think I might steal it. I knew I couldn't buy it back. I'd read about thefts from galleries, how the picture is cut out of its frame and rolled up and taken off. It wasn't

336

real, I just liked thinking about it. I knew there would be some kind of alarm on the door but I thought I might break in through the window and grab the picture before anyone came. I thought the police couldn't get there in under ten minutes if someone did ring them, and there wasn't anyone close enough to hear the alarm anyway. It was a stupid idea, I know that now, but I used to brood about it and think about it, how it might be done.'

His wife said, 'But you didn't do it, Davie. You only thought about it. You said yourself it wasn't real. You can't be had up for planning something you didn't do. That's the law.'

Well, not precisely, thought Kate. But Wilkins hadn't after all been in a conspiracy to cause an explosion.

Dalgliesh said, 'But in the end you didn't try?'

'I went there one night thinking I might. But then someone arrived. That was on February the fourteenth. I went by bike and hid it in the bushes along the drive and I'd taken a large black plastic bag, one of those big rubbish bags, to wrap the picture in. I don't know whether I'd actually have tried the robbery. When I got there I realized I hadn't anything strong enough to break the ground-floor window and that the window was higher from the ground than I'd thought. I hadn't really planned it properly. And then I heard a car. I hid in the bushes and watched. It was a powerful car and the driver drove into the car-park behind the laurels. I watched when he got out and then I crept off. I was scared. My bike was a bit further down the drive and I made my way to it through the bushes. I know he didn't see me.'

Kate said, 'But you saw him.'

'Not to recognize him again. I didn't see his face. When he got out of the car he was wearing a mask.'

Dalgliesh asked, 'What kind of a mask?'

'Not the kind you see in crime programmes on TV. Not the stocking pulled over the face. This just covered the eyes and the hair. The sort of thing you see in pictures of people at carnivals.'

Dalgliesh said, 'So you cycled home and gave up the idea of stealing the picture?'

'I don't think it was ever serious. I mean, I thought it was serious at the time, but it was more in my imagination. If it had been real I would have taken more trouble.'

Kate said, 'But if you had managed to get it you wouldn't have been able to sell it. It may not have been recognized as valuable when your grandad bought it, but it would be now.'

'I didn't want to sell it. I wanted to put it on the wall here. I wanted it in this room. I wanted it because Grandad had loved it and because it reminded him of Great-Grandad. I wanted it because of the past.'

Suddenly the pale face contorted and Kate saw two tears rolling down his cheeks. He put up a fist like a child and scrubbed them away. As if in a gesture of comfort, his wife handed him the baby. He cradled the child and nuzzled his lips in her hair.

Dalgliesh said, 'You did nothing wrong and we are grateful to you for helping us. Perhaps we'll see each other again when you come back to look at the picture. A lot of people enjoy it. I know I did. If it hadn't been for your grandfather it wouldn't be in the Dupayne

Museum and perhaps we wouldn't have a chance of seeing it.'

As if she too had forgotten that they were police officers and were thinking of them as guests, Michelle Wilkins said, 'Would you like some tea? I'm sorry I didn't think of offering. Or there's some Nescafé.'

Dalgliesh said, 'That's very kind but I think we'd better not wait. Thank you again, Mr Wilkins, for being so co-operative, and if there's anything else that occurs to you, you can reach us at New Scotland Yard. The number's on this card.'

It was Michelle Wilkins who showed them out. At the door she said, 'He won't get into trouble, will he? He didn't do anything wrong. He wouldn't steal anything really.'

'No,' said Dalgliesh. 'He won't get into trouble. He's done nothing wrong.'

Dalgliesh and Kate buckled themselves into their car. Neither spoke. Kate felt a mixture of depression and anger. She thought, *God, what a dump! They're a couple of children waiting to be exploited by anyone who thinks they're worth bothering with. The baby looked fine, though. I wonder what they have to pay for that hovel. Still, the fact that they've got it won't help them with the local authority housing waiting list. They'll be pensioners before they qualify. They'd have done better to sleep on the streets, then at least they'd get priority. Not necessarily for a decent place, though. Probably they'd end up in a bed and breakfast. God, this is a terrible country to be really poor in. That's if you're honest. The scroungers and cheats do well enough, but try to be independent and see what help you get.*

She said, 'That wasn't particularly useful, sir, was it? Wilkins saw the masked man in February. That's eight months before Dupayne's murder and I can't see Wilkins and his wife as serious suspects. He might have a grievance against the Dupayne family but why pick on Neville?'

'We'll check on that alibi but I think we'll find he was where he said he was last Friday evening, at the doctor's surgery. David Wilkins is just trying to connect.'

'To connect, sir?'

'With his father and grandfather. With the past. With life.'

Kate was silent. After a couple of minutes, Dalgliesh said, 'Ring the museum, will you Kate, and see if anyone's there. It'll be interesting to see what the Dupaynes have to say about their masked visitor.'

Muriel Godby answered the call. She asked Kate to hold on but spoke again within seconds. She said that both Caroline Dupayne and Mr Calder-Hale were in the museum. Miss Caroline was about to leave but would wait until Commander Dalgliesh arrived.

18

They found Caroline Dupayne studying a letter at the desk with Miss Godby and at once she led them into the office. Dalgliesh was interested that she was at the museum on a Monday and wondered how long she could absent herself from her job at the school. The family probably felt that if the police were going to infest the place, a Dupayne should be present to keep an eye on them. He sympathized. In times of complicated danger nothing is more impolitic than to distance oneself from the action.

He said, 'A young man who came to the museum on the night of February the fourteenth saw a man arriving by car. He was wearing a face mask. Have you any idea who it could have been?'

'None.' She took the question with what he thought was a careful assumption of only the mildest interest. She added, 'What an extraordinary question, Commander. Oh, I'm sorry, you wondered if he could have been visiting me. It was February the fourteenth – St Valentine's Day. No, I'm too old for that kind of frolicking. Actually I was too old for it at twenty-one. He probably was a reveller, though. It's a problem we have occasionally. Parking in Hampstead is pretty impossible and if people know this place, it's a temptation to drive in and leave their cars here. Luckily it seems to happen less often now, although we can't be sure. The place isn't really convenient and the walk along Spaniards Road is gloomy at night. Tally is here, of course, but I have told her that if she hears noises after dark not to leave the cottage. She can phone me if she's worried. The museum is isolated and we live in a dangerous world. You know that better than I do.'

Dalgliesh said, 'You haven't thought of putting up a gate?'

'We've thought of it, but it isn't really practical. Anyway, who would be the gatekeeper? The access to the museum has to be open.' She paused, then added, 'I don't see what this has to do with my brother's murder.'

'Nor do we at present. It shows again how easily people can get in unseen.'

'But we knew that already. Neville's murderer did just that. I'm more interested in the young man who saw the mysterious masked visitor. What was he doing here, illegally parking?'

'No, he didn't have a car. He was just curious. He did no harm, made no attempt to break in.'

'And the masked visitor?'

'Presumably he parked and left too. The young man found the encounter rather frightening and didn't wait to see.'

'Yes, it would be – frightening I mean. This place is eerie at night and there was a murder here before. Did you know?'

'I've not heard of it. Was it recent?'

'It was in 1897, two years after the house was built. A parlour maid, Ivy Grimshaw, was found stabbed to death on the edge of the Heath. She was pregnant. Suspicion fell on the house owner and on his two sons, but there was no real evidence linking any of the three to the crime. And they were, of course, prosperous, respectable local dignitaries. Perhaps more to the point, they owned a button factory and local people depended on the family for their living. The police found it convenient to believe that Ivy had gone out to meet her lover and that he disposed of her and the inconvenient child with one slash of the knife.'

'Was there evidence of any lover outside the household?'

'None came to light. The cook told the police that Ivy had confided to her that she had no intention of being thrown out onto the streets and could make things difficult for the family. But the cook later retracted. She went off for another job somewhere on the south coast with, I believe, a substantial farewell present from a grateful employer. The story of an outside lover was apparently accepted and the case died. It's a pity it didn't happen in the 1930s. We could have featured it in the Murder Room.'

Except, thought Dalgliesh, even in the 1930s it couldn't have happened in quite that way. The brutal murder of an immoral and friendless young woman had gone unavenged and respectable local people had kept their jobs. Ackroyd's thesis might be simplistic and his choice of examples conveniently selective, but it was founded on truth; murder frequently was a paradigm of its age.

Upstairs in his office, and breaking off reluctantly from his writing, Calder-Hale said, 'February the fourteenth?

343

Probably a Valentine's Day party guest. Strange that he was on his own, though. People usually party in pairs.'

Dalgliesh said, 'Stranger that he put on his mask here. Why not wait until he had arrived at the party?'

'Well, it wasn't being held here. Not unless Caroline was partying.'

'She says not.'

'No, it would be unlike her. I expect he was using the place as a handy illicit car-park. I turned away a car full of young revellers a couple of months ago. I tried to frighten them with the empty threat that I'd telephone the police. Anyway, they drove off quietly enough and even apologized. Probably didn't want to leave their Mercedes to my mercy.' He added, 'What about the young man? What did he say he was doing here?'

'A casual explorer. He left in some hurry after the masked man arrived. He was perfectly harmless.'

'No car?'

'No car.'

'Odd.' He turned again to his paper. 'Your masked visitor, if he ever existed, had nothing to do with me. I may play my little games, but face masks are altogether too histrionic.'

The interview was obviously at an end. Turning to go, Dalgliesh thought, *That's close to an admission of his secret activities, but why not? He's been told that I know. We're both playing the same game and let's hope on the same side. What he's doing, however apparently trivial and amateur, is part of a greater pattern. It's important and he has to be protected – protected against everything but an accusation of murder.*

He would check with Marcus Dupayne but expected much the same explanation: a knowledgeable local making use of the place for a few hours' free parking. It was reasonable enough. But one small thing intrigued him: faced with two mysterious visitors, both Caroline Dupayne and James Calder-Hale had been more concerned about the mysterious young man than about the masked driver. He wondered why.

Calder-Hale was still in the frame. Earlier that evening Benton-Smith had timed the motorcycle journey from Marylebone to the Dupayne. His second journey had been the quicker, beating the first by four minutes. He had said, 'I was lucky with the traffic lights. If Calder-Hale had equalled my best time it would have given him three-and-a-half minutes to set up the murder. He could have done it, sir, but only with luck. You can't base a murder plan on luck.'

Piers had said, 'On the other hand, he might have thought it was worth a try. That dental appointment gave him an alibi of a kind. He couldn't wait indefinitely if his motive was to keep the museum open. What puzzles me is why he should give a damn whether it closed or not. He's got a cosy little set-up but if he wants to do private work, there are other offices in London.'

But not, thought Dalgliesh, offices which offered so convenient a location for Calder-Hale's secret activities for MI5.

19

When Kate telephoned to make an appointment she reported that Mrs Strickland had asked to see Commander Dalgliesh on his own. The request was odd – their one encounter in the library on Dalgliesh's first visit had hardly made them acquaintances – but he was happy to agree. Mrs Strickland was not at present a serious suspect and, until and unless she became one, it would be foolish to jeopardize any useful information she might have by insisting on police protocol.

The address, given to him by Caroline Dupayne, was in the Barbican and proved to be a flat on the seventh floor. It was not an address he had expected. This intimidating concrete block of serried windows and pathways seemed more appropriate to young financiers from the City than to an elderly widow. But when Mrs Strickland opened the door and showed him into the sitting-room he could understand why she had chosen this flat. It looked out over the wide courtyard and beyond the lake to the church. Below, foreshortened figures of couples and small groups arriving for the evening's performances strolled in what seemed a deliberately changing pattern of colour. The noise of the city, always muted at the end of the working day, was a rhythmic hum more soothing than distracting. Mrs Strickland inhabited a peaceful City eyrie with a panorama of changing skies and constant human activity where she could feel part of the City's life and yet be lifted above its frenetic getting and spending. But she was a realist: he had noticed the two security locks on the outer door.

The interior of the flat was equally surprising. Dalgliesh would have expected the owner to be prosperous but young, as yet unburdened by the weight of the dead years, by family possessions, sentimental mementoes, by objects which, through long association, linked past to present and gave an illusion of permanence. If a landlord were furnishing a flat for a demanding tenant able to pay a high rent, it would look very like this. The sitting-room was furnished with well-designed modern pieces in pale wood. To the right of the window, which stretched almost the whole length of the wall, was her desk with a spotlight and a revolving typist's chair. It was apparent that occasionally she brought her work home. There was a round table in front of the window with two armchairs in grey leather. The single picture was an abstract relief in oil, he thought by Ben Nicholson. It could have been chosen to tell him nothing about her except that she had been able to afford it. He found it interesting that a woman who had so ruthlessly expunged the past should choose to work in a museum. The only furnishing which alleviated the flat's functional anonymity was the fitted bookcase which ran floor to ceiling along the right-hand wall. It was filled with leather-bound volumes so closely shelved that they looked gummed together. These she had found worth preserving. It was obviously a personal library. He wondered whose.

Mrs Strickland motioned him towards one of the chairs. She said, 'I usually have a glass of wine about this time. Perhaps you'll join me. Do you prefer red or white? I have claret or a Riesling.'

Dalgliesh accepted the claret. She walked a little stiffly out of the room and returned within minutes, pushing the door open with her shoulders. He rose at once to help her, carrying the tray with the bottle, a corkscrew and two glasses, and placing it on the table. They sat facing each other and she left him to uncork and pour the wine, watching him, he thought, with indulgent satisfaction. Even with changing public views on when the late middle years have made their inexorable slide into old age, Mrs Strickland was old, he guessed in her mid-eighties; given her history she could hardly be less. In youth, he thought, she must have had that admired blonde blue-eyed English prettiness which can be deceptive. Dalgliesh had seen enough photographs and newsreels of women at war, uniformed or in civilian clothes, to know that this feminine gentleness could be wedded to strength and purpose, occasionally even to ruthlessness. Hers had been a vulnerable beauty, particularly susceptible to the dilapidations of the years. Now the spongy skin was criss-crossed with fine lines and her lips looked almost bloodless. But there were still traces of gold in the thin grey hair, brushed back and twisted into a plait at the back of her head, and although the irises had faded into a pale milky blue, her eyes were still huge under the delicately curved brows and they met Dalgliesh's with a look both questioning and alert. Her hands reaching out for her glass were distorted with the excrescence of

348

arthritis and, watching them fasten on the wine glass, he wondered how she managed such fine calligraphy.

As if guessing his thought, she looked at her fingers and said, 'I can still write, but I can't be sure how long I'll be useful. It's odd that my fingers occasionally shake, but not when I'm doing calligraphy. I'm not trained. It's just something I've always enjoyed.'

The wine was excellent, the temperature right. Dalgliesh asked, 'How did you come to help at the Dupayne Museum?'

'Through my husband. He was a history professor at London University and knew Max Dupayne. After Christopher died, Max asked if I could help with the lettering. Then when Caroline Dupayne took over I continued. James Calder-Hale took charge of the volunteers and cut down the numbers considerably, some thought rather ruthlessly. He said there were too many people running about the museum like rabbits; lonely, most of them. We all had to have a useful job to stay on. Actually we could do with a few extras now, but Mr Calder-Hale seems reluctant to recruit them. Muriel Godby would welcome some help on the desk, provided we could find the right person. At present I relieve her occasionally when I'm in the museum.'

Dalgliesh said, 'She seems very efficient.'

'She is. She's made a great difference since she arrived two years ago. Caroline Dupayne has never taken a very active part in the day-to-day management. She can't, of course, with her duties at the school. Miss Godby does the accounts to the satisfaction of the auditor and everything runs much more smoothly now. But you're not

349

here to be bored with details of the office, are you? You want to talk about Neville's death.'

'How well did you know him?'

She paused, then sipped her wine and put down the glass. She said, 'I think I knew him better than anyone else at the museum. He wasn't an easy man to know and he came in seldom, but during the past year he'd occasionally arrive early on a Friday and come in to the library. It didn't happen often, about once every three weeks or so. He gave no explanation. Sometimes he would prowl around then settle down with an old *Blackwood's Magazine*. Sometimes he'd ask me to unlock a cabinet and he'd take down a book. Mostly he sat in silence. Sometimes he talked.'

'Would you describe him as a happy man?'

'No, I wouldn't. It isn't easy to judge another's happiness, is it? But he was overworked, worried that he was letting down his patients, that he hadn't enough time for them, and angry about the state of the psychiatric services. He thought that neither the government nor society generally cared enough about the mentally ill.'

Dalgliesh wondered whether Dupayne had confided where he went at the weekends or whether only Angela Faraday had been told. He asked and she said, 'No. He was reticent about his own affairs. We spoke only once about his personal life. I think he came because he found it restful to watch me working. I've been thinking about it and that seems the likeliest explanation. I would always go on with what I was doing and he liked to watch the letters forming. Perhaps he found it soothing.'

Dalgliesh said, 'We're treating his death as murder. It

seems highly unlikely to have been suicide. But would that surprise you, the thought that he might have wanted to end his life?'

And now the old voice, which had been tiring, regained its strength. It was with firmness that she said, 'It would amaze me. He wouldn't commit suicide. You can discount that possibility. There may be members of the family who find the idea convenient, but you can put it out of mind. Neville didn't kill himself.'

'Can you really be that sure?'

'I can be that sure. Part of the reason is a discussion we had two weeks before he died. That would be the Friday before you first came to the museum. He said that his car wasn't absolutely ready. A man at the garage – I think his name is Stanley Carter – had promised to deliver it by six-fifteen. I stayed on after the museum closed and we had a whole hour together. We were speaking about the future of the library and he said that we lived too much in the past. He was thinking of our own pasts, as well as of our history. I found that I was confiding in him. I find this difficult, Commander. Private confidences aren't natural to me. I would have thought it presumptuous and somehow demeaning to use him as my private unpaid psychiatrist, but it must have been something like that. But he used me too. We used each other. I said that in old age the past wasn't so easily shaken off. The old sins return, weighted by the years. And the nightmares, the faces of the dead who shouldn't have died come back and look, not with love, but with reproach. For some of us that small diurnal death can be a nightly descent into a very private hell. We spoke

351

about atonement and forgiveness. I'm the only child of a French devoutly Roman Catholic mother and an atheist father. I spent much of my childhood in France. I said that believers can deal with guilt by confession, but how could those of us without faith find our peace? I remembered some words I'd read written by a philosopher, I think Roger Scruton. "The consolation of imaginary things is not imaginary consolation." I told him I sometimes craved even imaginary consolation. Neville said we have to learn to absolve ourselves. The past can't be altered and we have to face it with honesty and without excuses, then put it aside; to be obsessed by guilt is a destructive indulgence. He said that to be human is to feel guilt: I am guilty therefore I am.'

She paused, but Dalgliesh didn't speak. He was waiting to know why she was so sure Dupayne hadn't committed suicide. She would come to it in her own time. He saw with compassion that the reciting of that remembered conversation was painful. She reached out a hand to the bottle of claret, but her fingers were shaking. He took the bottle and topped up both their glasses.

After a minute, she said, 'One would wish in old age to remember only the happiness of life. It doesn't work like that, except for the lucky ones. Just as polio can return in some form and strike again, so can the past mistakes, the failures, the sins. He said he understood. He said, "My worst failure comes back to me in flames of fire".'

The silence was longer now. This time Dalgliesh had to ask, 'Did he explain?'

'No. And I didn't ask. It wouldn't have been possible

to ask. But he did say one thing. Perhaps he thought that I imagined that this had something to do with not wanting the museum to continue. Anyway, he said it had nothing to do with anyone at the Dupayne.'

'You're quite sure about that, Mrs Strickland? What he was telling you, the failure that came back in flames of fire, had nothing to do with the museum?'

'Absolutely sure. Those were his words.'

'And suicide? You said you were confident he would never kill himself.'

'We spoke of that too. I think I said that in extreme old age one could be certain of relief before too long. I went on to say that I was content to wait for it, but even at the worst times of my life I had never thought of taking my own way out. It was then he said that he thought suicide was indefensible, except for the very old or those suffering continuous pain with no hope of relief. It left too great a burden on the bereaved. Apart from the loss, there was always guilt and a lurking horror that the impulse to self-destruction could be hereditary. I told him that I thought he was being a little hard on people who found life intolerable, that their final despair should evoke pity, not censure. After all, he was a psychiatrist, a member of the modern priesthood. Wasn't it his job to understand and absolve? He didn't resent what I said. He admitted that perhaps he had been over-emphatic. But one thing he was sure of: a person in his right mind who kills himself should always leave an explanation. The family and friends he leaves behind have a right to know why they are suffering such pain. Neville Dupayne would never have killed himself, Commander. Or perhaps it would be better to say that he would never have killed himself without leaving a letter of explanation.' She looked into Dalgliesh's eyes. 'My information is that he left no letter, no explanation.'

'None was found.'

'Which is not quite the same thing.'

This time it was she who reached for the bottle and held it out. Dalgliesh shook his head but she filled her own glass. Watching her, Dalgliesh was visited by a revelation so astonishing that he spoke it naturally and almost without thinking. 'Was Neville Dupayne adopted?'

Her eyes met his. 'Why do you ask that, Mr Dalgliesh?'

'I'm not sure. The question came into my mind. Forgive me.'

And now she smiled, and for a moment he could glimpse that bright loveliness which had disconcerted even the Gestapo. She said, 'Forgive you? For what? You're perfectly right, he was adopted. Neville was my son, mine and Max Dupayne's. I left London for five months before the birth and he was placed with Max and Madeleine within days and later adopted. Those things were arranged much more easily in those days.'

Dalgliesh asked, 'Is this generally known? Do Caroline and Marcus Dupayne know that Neville was their half brother?'

'They knew he was adopted. Marcus was only a three-year old and Caroline, of course, wasn't born when the adoption took place. All three children were told of it from an early age, but not that I was the mother and

Max the father. They grew up accepting the adoption as a more or less normal fact of life.'

Dalgliesh said, 'Neither of them mentioned it to me.'

'That doesn't in the least surprise me. Why should they? Neither is given to confiding private family matters and the fact that he was adopted isn't relevant to Neville's death.'

'And he never made use of the existing law to discover his parentage?'

'Never, as far as I know. This wasn't a matter I intended to discuss with you. I know I can rely on your discretion, that you won't divulge what I've told you to anyone else, not even to the members of your team.'

Dalgliesh paused. He said, 'I shall say nothing unless the adoption becomes relevant to my investigation.'

And now at last it was time to go. She saw him to the door and held out her hand. Clasping it, he felt that the gesture was more than an unexpectedly formal goodbye: it was a confirmation of his promise. She said, 'You have a talent for encouraging confidence, Mr Dalgliesh. It must be useful in a detective. People tell you things that you can then use against them. I suppose you would say that it's in the cause of justice.'

'I don't think I'd use so large a word. I might say in the cause of truth.'

'Is that such a small word? Pontius Pilate didn't find it so. But I don't think I've told you anything I'm likely to regret. Neville was a good man and I shall miss him. I had a great affection for him, but no maternal love. How could I have? And what right have I, who gave him up so easily, to claim him now as my son? I'm too old to grieve, but not too old to feel anger. You'll discover who killed him and he'll be in prison for ten years. I should like to see him dead.'

On the way back to the car his mind was preoccupied with what he had learned. Mrs Strickland had asked to see him alone to tell him two things: her absolute conviction that Neville Dupayne would not have killed himself, and his cryptic remark about seeing his failure through flames of fire. She had not intended to divulge the truth of his parentage and she was probably sincere in her belief that it wasn't relevant to her son's death. Dalgliesh was less sure. He pondered on the tangle of personal relationships focused on the museum: the traitor in the SOE who had betrayed his comrades and Henry Calder-Hale whose naïvety had contributed to that betrayal, the secret love and the secret birth, lives lived intensely under the threat of torture and death. The agonies were over, the dead would not come back except in dreams. It was difficult to see how any of this history could provide a motive for Neville Dupayne's murder. But he could think of a reason why the Dupaynes might have thought it prudent not to divulge that Neville had been adopted. To be frustrated in what you passionately wanted by a blood brother was difficult enough to bear; from an adopted brother it would be even less forgivable, and the remedy, perhaps, easier to contemplate.

BOOK THREE

The Second Victim

Wednesday 6 November–
Thursday 7 November

I

On Wednesday the sixth of November the day broke imperceptibly, the first light seeping through an early morning sky which lay furred as a blanket over the city and river. Kate made early morning tea and, as always, carried the beaker out on to the balcony. But today there was no freshness. Beneath her the Thames heaved as sluggish as treacle, seeming to absorb rather than to reflect the dancing lights across the river. The first barges of the day moved ponderously, leaving no wake. Usually this moment was one of deep satisfaction and occasionally even of joy born of physical well-being and the promise of the new day. This river view and the two-bedroom flat behind her represented an achievement which every morning brought a renewal of satisfaction and reassurance. She had achieved the job she wanted, the flat she wanted in the part of London she had chosen. She could look forward to a promotion which it was rumoured would come soon. She worked with people she liked and respected. She told herself this morning, as she did nearly every day, that to be a single woman with your own home, a secure job and money enough for your needs, was to enjoy more freedom than did any other human being on earth.

But this morning the gloom of the day infected her. The present case was still young but it was now entering the doldrums, that depressingly familiar part of a murder investigation when the initial excitement sinks into routine and the prospect of a quick solution lessens by the day. The Special Investigation Unit weren't used to failure, were indeed regarded as a guarantee against failure. Fingerprints had been taken for elimination purposes from everyone who could legitimately have handled the can or entered the garage, and no unexplained prints had been found. No one admitted removing the light bulb. It seemed that Vulcan, by cleverness, luck or a mixture of both, had left no incriminating evidence. It was ridiculously premature with the case so young to be worried about the outcome, but she couldn't shake off a half-superstitious fear that they might never have enough evidence to justify an arrest. And even if they did, would the CPS let the case go to court when that mysterious motorist who had run into Tally Clutton at the house was still unidentified? And did he exist? True, there was the evidence of the twisted bicycle wheel, the bruise on Tally's arm. Both could be easily fabricated, a deliberate fall, the ramming of the bicycle against a tree. The woman seemed honest and it was difficult to think of her as a ruthless murderer, particularly this murder; less difficult, perhaps, to imagine her as an accomplice. After all, she was over sixty; she obviously valued her job and the security of that cottage. It could be as important to her that the museum continued as it was to the two Dupaynes. The police knew nothing of her private life, her fears, her psychological needs, what resources she had to buttress herself against disaster. But if the mysterious motorist existed and was an innocent visitor, why hadn't he come forward? Or was she being naïve? Why should he? Why subject yourself to a police interrogation, the exposure of your private life, the dragging into light of possible secrets, when you could keep quiet and remain undetected? Even if innocent, he would know that the police would treat him as a suspect, probably their prime suspect. And if the case remained unsolved, he would be seen as a possible murderer all his life.

This morning the museum was to open at ten o'clock for Conrad Ackroyd's four Canadian guests to be shown round. Dalgliesh had instructed her to be there with Benton-Smith. He had given no explanation but she remembered his words from a previous case: 'With murder, always stay as close as you can to the suspects and the scene of the crime.' Even so, it was difficult to see what he hoped to gain. Dupayne hadn't died in the museum, and Vulcan, when he arrived last Friday, would have had no reason to enter the house. How, in fact, could he have done so without the keys? Both Miss Godby and Mrs Clutton had been adamant that the museum door had been locked when they left. Vulcan would have concealed himself among the trees or in the garden shed, or – most likely of all – in the corner of the unlit garage, waiting, petrol in hand, for the sound of the door being pulled open and the dark figure of his victim to stretch out his hand to the light switch. The house itself was uncontaminated by horror but for the first time she was reluctant to return. Already it too was becoming tainted with the sour smell of failure.

By the time she was ready to leave, the day had hardly

lightened but there was no rain except for a few heavy drops splodging the pavement. Rain must have fallen in the early hours as the roads were greasy, but it had brought no freshness to the air. Even when she had reached the higher ground of Hampstead and had opened the car windows there was little relief from the oppression of polluted air and a smothering cloud base. The lamps were still lit in the drive leading to the museum and when she turned the final corner she saw that every window blazed as if the place were preparing for a celebration. She glanced at her watch; five minutes to ten. The visiting group would be here already.

She parked as usual behind the laurel bushes, thinking again how convenient a shield it was for anyone wanting to park unseen. A row of cars was already neatly aligned. She recognized Muriel Godby's Fiesta and Caroline Dupayne's Mercedes. The other car was a people carrier. It must, she thought, have brought the Canadians. Perhaps they had hired it for their English tour. It was apparent that Benton-Smith had not yet arrived.

Despite the blaze of light, the door was locked and she had to ring. It was opened by Muriel Godby who greeted her with unsmiling formality which suggested that, although this particular visitor was neither distinguished nor welcome, it was prudent to show her proper respect. She said, 'Mr Ackroyd and his party have arrived and are having coffee in Mr Calder-Hale's office. There's a cup for you, Inspector, if you want it.'

'Right, I'll go up. Sergeant Benton-Smith should be arriving soon. Ask him to join us, will you please?'

The door to Calder-Hale's office was shut but she

could hear subdued voices. Knocking and entering, she saw two couples and Ackroyd seated on an assortment of chairs, most of them obviously brought in from one of the other rooms. Calder-Hale himself was perched on the side of his desk and Caroline Dupayne was seated in his swivel chair. They were all holding coffee cups. The men rose as Kate entered.

Ackroyd made the introductions. Professor Ballantyne and Mrs Ballantyne, Professor McIntyre and Dr McIntyre. All four were from universities in Toronto and were particularly interested in English social history between the wars. Ackroyd added, speaking directly to Kate, 'I've explained about Dr Dupayne's tragic death and that the museum is closed to the public at present while the police carry out an investigation. Well, shall we get started? That is, unless you'd like some coffee, Inspector.'

This casual reference to the tragedy was received without comment. Kate said she didn't need coffee; it had hardly been an invitation she was expected to accept. The four visitors seemed to take her presence for granted. If they were wondering why, as strangers to the museum, they needed to be accompanied by a senior police officer on what was after all a private visit, they were too well mannered to comment. Mrs Ballantyne, pleasant-faced and elderly, seemed not to realize that Kate was a police officer and even asked her as they left the office whether she was a regular visitor to the museum.

Calder-Hale said, 'I suggest that we start on the ground floor with the History Room, and then the Sports and

363

Entertainment Gallery, before coming up to the gallery floor and the Murder Room. We'll leave the Library to the last. I'll leave Conrad to describe the exhibits in the Murder Room. That's more in his line than mine.'

They were interrupted at this point by the sound of running feet on the stairs and Benton-Smith appeared. Kate introduced him somewhat perfunctorily and the little group set out on its tour. She was irritated by his belated arrival but, glancing at her watch, realized that she couldn't later complain. He had in fact arrived precisely on time.

They descended to the History Room. Here one wall with a range of display cabinets and shelves dealt with the main events of British history from November 1918 to July 1939. Opposite a similar collage showed what was happening in the wider world. The photographs were of remarkable quality and some, Kate guessed, were valuable and rare. The slowly moving group contemplated the arrival of world statesmen at the Peace Conference, the signing of the Versailles Treaty, the starvation and destitution of Germany compared with the celebrations of the victorious Allies. A procession of dethroned kings passed before them, their ordinary faces dignified – and sometimes made ridiculous – by lavishly decorated uniforms and ludicrous headgear. The new men of power favoured a more proletarian and utilitarian uniform; their jackboots were made to wade through blood. Many of the political pictures meant little to Kate, but she saw that Benton-Smith was engaging in an intense discussion with one of the Canadian professors about the significance for organized labour of the General

Strike of May 1926. Then she remembered that Piers had told her that Benton had a degree in history. Well, he would have. Sometimes Kate reflected wryly that she would soon be the only person under thirty-five without a degree. Perhaps that might in time confer its own prestige. The visitors seemed to take it for granted that she and Benton were as interested in the exhibits as were they and had as much right to express an opinion. Following them round, she told herself ironically that an investigation of murder was turning into something of a social occasion.

She followed the party into the gallery concerned with sports and entertainment. Here were the women tennis players in their bandeaux and encumbering long skirts, the men in their pressed white flannels; posters of hikers with their rucksacks and shorts, striding into an idealized English countryside; the Women's League of Health and Beauty in black satin knickers and white blouses, performing their mass rhythmic exercises. There were original railway posters of blue hills and yellow sands, bobbed-haired children flourishing buckets and spades, the parents in their discreet bathing costumes all apparently oblivious to the distant clangour of a Germany arming for war. And here, too, was the ever-present, unbridgeable gulf between the rich and the poor, the privileged and the underprivileged, emphasized by the clever grouping of the photographs, parents and friends at the 1928 Eton–Harrow cricket match compared with the bleak expressionless faces of ill-fed children photographed at their annual Sunday school outing.

And now they moved upstairs and into the Murder

Room. Although the lights were already on, the darkness of the day had intensified and there was a disagreeable mustiness about the air. Caroline Dupayne, who had been an almost silent member of the party, spoke for the first time. 'It smells stale in here. Can't we open a window, James? Let in some cold air on this stuffiness.'

Calder-Hale went to a window and, after a slight struggle, opened it about six inches at the top.

Ackroyd now took over. What an extraordinary little man he was, Kate thought, with his plump, carefully tailored body, restless with enthusiasm, his face as innocently excited as a child's above that ridiculous spotted bow tie. AD had told the team about his first visit to the Dupayne. Always over-busy, he had given up valuable time to drive Ackroyd to the museum. She wondered, not for the first time, at the singularity of male friendship founded apparently on no bedrock of personality, no shared view of the world, based often on a single common interest or mutual experience, uncritical, undemonstrative, undemanding. What on earth did AD and Conrad Ackroyd have in common? But Ackroyd was clearly enjoying himself. Certainly his knowledge of the murder cases displayed was exceptional and he spoke without notes. He dealt at some length with the Wallace case and the visitors dutifully examined the notice from the Central Chess Club showing that Wallace was due to play on the evening before the murder, and gazed in respectful silence at Wallace's chess set displayed under glass.

Ackroyd said, 'This iron bar in the display cabinet isn't

the weapon; a weapon was never found. But a similar bar used to scrape ashes from beneath the grate was missing from the house. These two blown-up police photographs of the body taken within minutes of each other are interesting. In the first you can see Wallace's crumpled mackintosh, heavily bloodstained, tucked against the victim's right shoulder. In the second photograph it has been pulled away.'

Mrs Ballantyne gazed at the photographs with a mixture of distaste and pity. Her husband and Professor McIntyre conferred together on the furniture and pictures in the cluttered sitting-room, that seldom-used sanctum of upper-working-class respectability which, as social historians, they obviously found more fascinating than blood and smashed brains.

Ackroyd concluded, 'It was a unique case in three ways. The Court of Appeal quashed the verdict on the grounds that it was "unsafe having regard to the evidence", in fact saying that the jury had been wrong. This must have been galling for Lord Chief Justice Hewart who heard the Appeal and whose philosophy was that the British jury system was virtually infallible. Secondly, Wallace's trade union financed the appeal, but only after calling the people concerned to the London office and in effect holding a mini trial. Thirdly, it was the only case for which the Church of England authorized a special prayer that the Appeal Court should be guided to a right decision. It's rather a splendid prayer – the Church knew how to write liturgy in those days – and you can see it printed in the order of service in the display case. I particularly like that last sentence. "And you shall pray for the learned counsels of our Sovereign Lord the King, that they may be faithful to the Christian injunction of the apostle Paul. Judge nothing until God brings to light hidden things of darkness and makes manifest the counsels of the heart." The Prosecuting Counsel, Edward Hemmerde, was furious about the prayer and probably more furious when it was effective.'

Professor Ballantyne, the elder of the two male visitors, said, 'The counsels of the heart.' He took out a notebook and the group waited patiently while, peering at the printed service, he wrote down the last sentence of the prayer.

Ackroyd had less to say about the Rouse case, concentrating on the technical evidence about the possible cause of the fire and saying nothing about Rouse's explanation of a bonfire. Kate wondered whether this was prudence or sensitivity. She hadn't expected Ackroyd to mention the similarity with the Dupayne murder and he managed to avoid it with some skill. Kate knew that no one outside those most concerned had been told of the mysterious motorist or of how his words to Tally Clutton had so uncannily echoed those of Rouse. She glanced at Caroline Dupayne and James Calder-Hale during Ackroyd's careful recital; neither betrayed a flicker of particular interest.

They moved on to the Brighton Trunk Murder. It was a case less interesting to Ackroyd and one which it was more difficult to justify as typical of its age. He concentrated on the trunk.

'This was precisely the kind of tin trunk used by the poor when they travelled. It would have held virtually everything the prostitute Violette Kaye owned, and in the end it was her coffin. Her lover, Tony Mancini, was tried at Lewes Assize Court in December 1934 and acquitted after a brilliant defence by Mr Norman Birkett. It was one of the few cases where the forensic pathologist, Sir Bernard Spilsbury, had his evidence successfully challenged. The case is an example of what is important in a trial for murder: the quality and reputation of the Defence Counsel. Norman Birkett – later Lord Birkett of Ulverston – had a remarkably beautiful and persuasive voice, a most potent weapon. Mancini owed his life to Norman Birkett and we trust that he was appropriately grateful. Before he died, Mancini confessed that he had killed Violette Kaye. Whether he intended murder is another matter.'

The little group surveyed the trunk, Kate thought, more from politeness than genuine interest. The sourness of the air seemed to have intensified. She wished that the party could move on. The Murder Room, and indeed the whole museum, had oppressed her from the moment of her first entry. There was something alien to her spirit about its careful reconstruction of the past. For years she had tried to throw off her own history and she resented and was half afraid of the clarity and the awful inevitability with which it was now returning month by month. The past was dead, finished with, unalterable. Nothing about it could be compensated for and surely nothing fully understood. These sepia photographs which surrounded her had no more life than the paper on which they were printed. Those long-dead men and women had suffered and caused suffering and were gone.

What extraordinary impulse had led the founder of the Dupayne to display them with so much care? Surely they had no more relevance to their age than had those photographs of old cars, the clothes, the kitchens, the artefacts of the past. Some of these people were buried in quicklime and some in churchyards, but they might just as well have been dumped together in a common grave for all that mattered now. She thought, *How can I live safely except in this present moment, the moment which, even as I measure it, becomes the past?* The uneasy conviction she had felt when leaving Mrs Faraday's house returned. She couldn't safely confront those early years or nullify their power by being a traitor to her past.

They were about to move on when the door opened and Muriel Godby appeared. Caroline Dupayne was standing close to the trunk and Muriel, a little flushed, moved up beside her. Ackroyd, about to introduce the next case, paused and they waited.

The deliberate silence and the circle of faces turned towards her disconcerted Muriel. She had obviously hoped to deliver her message discreetly. She said, 'Lady Swathling is on the telephone for you, Miss Dupayne. I told her you were engaged.'

'Then tell her I'm still engaged. I'll ring her back in half an hour.'

'She says it's urgent, Miss Dupayne.'

'Oh very well, I'll come.'

She turned to go, Muriel Godby at her side, and the group again turned their attention to Conrad Ackroyd. And at that moment it happened. A mobile phone began ringing, shattering the silence, as startling and ominous as a fire alarm. There was no doubt from where it came. All their eyes turned to the trunk. For Kate the few seconds before anyone moved or spoke seemed to stretch into minutes, a suspension of time in which she saw the group frozen into a tableau, every limb as fixed as if they were dummies. The tinny ringing continued.

Then Calder Hale spoke, his voice deliberately light. 'Someone seems to be playing tricks. Juvenile but surprisingly effective.'

It was Muriel Godby who acted. Scarlet-faced, she burst out with 'Stupid, stupid!' and, before anyone could move, dashed to the trunk, knelt and lifted the lid.

The stench rose into the room, overpowering as a gas. Kate, at the back of the group, had only a glimpse of a hunched torso and a spread of yellow hair before Muriel's hands fell from the lid and it dropped back with a low clang. Her legs were shaking, her feet scrabbling at the floor as if she were trying to rise, but the strength had gone out of her body. She lay across the trunk making stifled noises, shuddering groans and pitiful squeals like a distressed puppy. The ringing had stopped. Kate heard her muttering, 'Oh no! Oh no!' For a few seconds she too was rooted. Then quietly she came forward to take command and do her job.

She turned to the group, her voice studiously calm, and said, 'Stand back please.' Moving to the trunk she put her arms round Muriel's waist and tried to lift her. She herself was strong-limbed, but the woman was heavily built and a dead weight. Benton-Smith came to help and together they got Muriel to her feet and half carried her to one of the armchairs.

Kate turned to Caroline Dupayne. 'Is Mrs Clutton in her cottage?'

'I suppose so. She may be. I really don't know.'

'Then take Miss Godby to the ground-floor office here and look after her, will you? Someone will be with you as soon as possible.'

She turned to Benton-Smith. 'Get the key from Miss Dupayne and check that the front door is locked. See that it remains locked. No one is to leave at present. Then ring Commander Dalgliesh and come back here.'

Calder-Hale had been silent. He was standing a little apart, his eyes watchful. Turning to him, Kate said, 'Will you and Mr Ackroyd take your group back to your study, please? We'll be needing their names and their addresses in this country, but after that they'll be free to leave.'

The little group of visitors stood in stunned bewilderment. Scanning their faces, it seemed to Kate that only one of them, the elderly Professor Ballantyne, who had been standing with his wife nearest the trunk, had actually glimpsed the body. His skin looked like grey parchment and, putting out his arm, he drew his wife to him.

Mrs Ballantyne said nervously, 'What is it? Was there an animal trapped in there? Is it a dead cat?'

Her husband said, 'Come along dear,' and they joined the small group moving towards the door.

Muriel Godby was calm now. She got to her feet and said with some dignity, 'I'm sorry, I'm sorry. It was the shock. And it was so horrible. I know it's stupid, but for a second I thought it was Violette Kaye.' She looked piteously at Caroline Dupayne. 'Forgive me, forgive me. It was the shock.'

Ignoring her, Caroline Dupayne hesitated, then moved towards the trunk, but Kate barred the way. She said again, more firmly, 'Please take Miss Godby to the office. I suggest you make a hot drink, tea or coffee. We're phoning Commander Dalgliesh and he'll join you as soon as he can. It may be some time.'

There were a few seconds of silence in which Kate half-expected that Caroline would protest. Instead she merely nodded and turned to Benton-Smith. 'The front door keys are in the key cupboard. I'll let you have them if you come down with us.'

Kate was alone. The silence was absolute. She had kept on her jacket and now felt in the pocket for her gloves, then remembered that they were in the compartment of the car. But she did have a large clean handkerchief. There was no hurry, AD would be here soon with their murder bags, but she needed at least to open the trunk. But not at this moment. It might be important to have a witness; she would do nothing until Benton-Smith returned. She stood motionless looking down at the trunk. Benton-Smith could only have been absent for a couple of minutes but they stretched into a limbo of waiting in which nothing in the room seemed real except that battered receptacle of horror.

And now at last he was at her side. He said, 'Miss Dupayne wasn't too happy about being told where she was to wait. The front door was already locked and I've got the keys. What about the visitors, ma'am? Is there any point in holding them?'

'No. The sooner they're off the premises the better. Go to Calder-Hale's office, will you, take their names and addresses and say something reassuring – if you can think of anything. Don't admit that we've found a body, although I don't imagine they're in much doubt.'

Benton-Smith said, 'Should I make sure there's nothing useful they can tell us, nothing they've noticed?'

'It's unlikely. She's been dead some time and they've only been in the museum for an hour. Get rid of them with as much tact and as little fuss as possible. We'll question Mr Calder-Hale later. Mr Ackroyd should leave with them, but I doubt whether you'll shift Calder-Hale. Come back here as soon as you've seen them out.'

This time the wait was longer. Although the trunk was closed, it seemed to Kate that the smell intensified with every second. It brought back the other cases, other corpses, and yet was subtly different, as if the body were proclaiming its uniqueness even in death. Kate could hear subdued voices. Benton had closed the door of the Murder Room behind him, muffling all sound except a high explanatory voice which could have been Ackroyd's and, briefly, the sound of footsteps on the stairs. Again she waited, her eyes on the trunk. Was it, she wondered, actually the one that had held Violette Kaye's body? Up until now, whether or not it was genuine, it had held no particular interest for her. But now it stood, black and a little battered, seeming to challenge her with its ominous secrets. Above it the eyes of Tony Mancini stared defiantly into hers. It was a brutal face, the eyes darkly fierce, the large mouth obstinately set in a stubble of hair; but then, the photographer hadn't set out to make him look appealing. Tony Mancini had died in his bed because Norman Birkett had defended him, just as Alfred

Arthur Rouse had been hanged because Norman Birkett had appeared for the Crown.

Benton-Smith had returned. He said, 'Pleasant people. They made no trouble and they have nothing to tell except that they had noticed the stale smell in the room. God knows what stories they'll take back to Toronto. Mr Ackroyd went under protest. He's avid with curiosity. Not much hope of his keeping quiet, I should say. I couldn't shift Mr Calder-Hale. He insists there are things he needs to do in his office. Mr Dalgliesh was in a meeting but he's leaving now. He should be here in twenty minutes or so. Do you want to wait, ma'am?'

'No,' said Kate. 'I don't want to wait.'

She wondered why it was so important that it was she who opened the trunk. She squatted and, with her right hand swathed in the handkerchief, slowly lifted the lid and threw it back. Her arm seemed to have grown heavy but its upward movement was as graceful and formal as if this action were part of a ceremonial unveiling. The stink rose up so strongly that her breath caught in her throat. It brought with it, as always, confused emotions of which only shock, anger and a sad realization of mortality were recognizable. These were replaced by resolution. This was her job. This was what she had been trained for.

The girl was crammed into the trunk like an over-grown foetus, the knees drawn up together, her bent head almost touching them over folded arms. The impression was that she had been neatly packed like an object into the cramped space. Her face wasn't visible, but strands of bright yellow hair lay delicate as silk over her legs and shoulders. She was wearing a cream trouser suit and short boots in fine black leather. The right hand lay curved above her left upper arm. Despite the long nails lacquered in a vivid red and the heavy gold ring on the middle finger of the right hand, it looked as small and vulnerable as the hand of a child.

Benton-Smith said, 'No handbag and I can't see the mobile phone. It's probably in one of the pockets of her jacket. At least it will tell us who she is.'

Kate said, 'We won't touch anything else. We'll wait for Mr Dalgliesh.'

Benton-Smith bent lower. 'What are those dead flowers sprinkled over her hair, ma'am?'

The small flowerlets still held a trace of purple and Kate recognized the shape of the two leaves. She said, 'They are – or were – African violets.'

2

Dalgliesh was relieved that Miles Kynaston, when telephoned at his teaching hospital, had been found beginning a lecture and was able to postpone it and be immediately available. As one of the world's most eminent pathologists, he might well have been already crouched over some malodorous corpse in a distant field, or called to a case overseas. Other Home Office pathologists could be called, and all were perfectly competent, but Miles Kynaston had always been Dalgliesh's pathologist of choice. It was interesting, he thought, that two men who knew so little of the other's private life, had no common interest except in their work and who seldom saw each other except at the site of a dead and often putrefying body, should meet always with the comfortable assurance of instinctive understanding and respect. Fame and the notoriety of some highly publicized cases hadn't made Kynaston a prima donna. He came promptly when called, eschewed the graveside humour which some pathologists and detectives employed as an antidote to horror or disgust, produced autopsy reports which were a model of clarity and good prose, and in the witness-box was listened to with respect. He was indeed in danger of being regarded as infallible. The memory of the great Bernard Spilsbury was still green. It was never healthy for the criminal justice system when an expert witness had only to step into the witness-box to be believed.

Rumour said that Kynaston's ambition had been to train as a physician but that he had to change course at registrar level because of his reluctance ever to have to watch human suffering. Certainly as a forensic pathologist he was spared it. It wouldn't be he who would knock at unfamiliar doors, steeling himself to break the dreaded news to some waiting parent or partner. But Dalgliesh thought the rumour unfounded; an aversion to encountering pain would surely have been discovered before undertaking medical training. Perhaps what drove Kynaston was an obsession with death, its causes, its manifold manifestations, its universality and inevitability, its essential mystery. Without religious belief as far as Dalgliesh knew, he treated each cadaver as if dead nerves could still feel and the glazed eyes could still entreat his verdict of hope. Watching his stubby latex-clad hands moving over a body, Dalgliesh sometimes had the irrational thought that Kynaston was administering his own secular Last Rites.

For years he had seemed unchanged, but he had visibly aged since their last meeting, as if he had suddenly dropped to a lower level on the continuum of physical decline. His solid frame was more cumbersome; the hairline above the high speckled forehead had receded. But his eyes were still as keen and his hands as steady.

It was now three minutes after midday. The blinds had been earlier drawn down, seeming to disconnect time as well as shutting out the surly half-light of late morning. To Dalgliesh the Murder Room seemed crowded with people, yet there were only six present in addition to Kynaston, himself, Kate and Piers. The two photographers had finished their work and were beginning quietly to pack up, but there was still one high light shining down on the body. Two fingerprint experts were dusting the trunk and Nobby Clark and a second scene of crime officer were meticulously prowling over ground which, on the face of it, offered little hope of yielding physical clues. Clad in the garb of their trade, all moved with quiet confidence, their voices low but not unnaturally muted. They could, thought Dalgliesh, be engaged on some esoteric rite best hidden from public view. The photographs on the walls were ranged like a line of silent witnesses, infecting the room with the tragedies and miseries of the past: Rouse, sleek-haired with his complacent seducer's smile; Wallace in his high collar, mild eyed beneath the steel spectacles; Edith Thompson in a wide-brimmed hat, laughing beside her young lover under a summer sky.

The corpse had been lifted from the trunk and now lay beside it on a sheet of plastic. The merciless glare of the light shining directly on her drained away the last traces of humanity so that she looked as artificial as a doll laid out ready to be parcelled. The bright yellow hair showed brown at the roots. She must have been pretty in life with a fair kittenish sexuality, but there was no beauty or peace in this dead face. The slightly exophthalmic pale blue eyes were wide open; they looked as if pressure on the forehead would dislodge them and they would roll like glass balls over the pale cheeks. Her mouth was half open, the small perfect teeth resting in a snarl on the lower lip. A thin trickle of mucus had dried on the upper lip. There was a bruise on either side of the delicate neck where strong hands had crushed the life out of her.

Dalgliesh stood silently watching as, crouching, Kynaston moved slowly round the body, gently spread out the pale fingers and turned the head from left to right, the better to scrutinize the bruises. Then he reached in the old Gladstone bag he always carried for his rectal thermometer. Minutes later, the preliminary examination complete, he got to his feet.

'Cause of death obvious. She was strangled. The killer was wearing gloves and was right-handed. There are no fingernail impressions and no scratching, and no signs of the victim trying to loosen the grip. Unconsciousness may have supervened very quickly. The main grip was made by the right hand from the front. You can see a thumb impression high up under the lower jaw over the *cornu* of the thyroid. There are finger-marks on the left side of the neck from the pressure of the opposing fingers. As you can see, these are a little low down along the side of the thyroid cartilage.'

Dalgliesh asked, 'Could a woman have done it?'

'It would have needed strength, but not remarkable strength. The victim is slight and the neck fairly narrow. A woman could have done it, but not, for example, a frail woman or anyone with arthritic hands. Time of death? That's complicated by the fact that the trunk is practically airtight. I may be able to be more precise after the PM. My present estimate is that she's been dead at least four days, probably nearer five.'

Dalgliesh said, 'Dupayne died at about eighteen hundred hours last Friday. Is it possible that this death occurred at approximately the same time?'

'Perfectly possible. But even after the PM I couldn't pinpoint as accurately as that. I've a free slot tomorrow morning at eight thirty and I'll try to get a report to you by early afternoon.'

They had found the mobile, one of the most recent designs, in her jacket pocket. Moving to the far end of the room and with gloved hands, Piers pressed the buttons to discover the source of the call, then called the number.

A male voice answered. 'Mercer's Garage.'

'I think we just missed a call from you.'

'Yes sir. It's to say that Celia Mellock's car is ready. Does she want to collect it, or shall we deliver it?'

'She said she'd like it delivered. You have the address, presumably?'

'That's right, sir, 47 Manningtree Gardens, Earls Court Road.'

'On second thoughts, better leave it. You've just missed her and she might prefer to collect it. Anyway, I'll let her know it's ready. Thanks.'

Piers said, 'We've got the name and address, sir. And we know now why she didn't come by car to the museum. It was at the garage. Her name's Celia Mellock and the address is 47 Manningtree Gardens, Earls Court Road.'

The girl's hands had been mittened in plastic, the red nails shining through as if they had been dipped in blood. Dr Kynaston gently raised the hands and folded them on the girl's breast. The plastic sheet was folded over the body and the body bag zipped up. The photographer began dismantling his lamp and Dr Kynaston, gloveless now, was removing his overall and stuffing it back in his Gladstone bag. The mortuary van had been summoned and Piers had gone downstairs to await its arrival. It was then that the door opened and a woman came purposefully in.

Kate's voice was sharp. 'Mrs Strickland, what are you doing here?'

Mrs Strickland said calmly, 'It's Wednesday morning. I'm always here on Wednesdays from nine-thirty to one, and on Fridays from two to five. Those are the times I have set aside. I thought you knew that.'

'Who let you in?'

'Miss Godby, of course. She perfectly understood that we volunteers have to be meticulous about our obligations. She said that the museum was closed to visitors, but I'm not a visitor.'

She moved without apparent repugnance towards the body bag. 'You've a dead body in there, obviously. I detected the unmistakable smell the moment I opened the library door. My sense of smell is acute. I was wondering what had happened to Mr Ackroyd's group of visitors. I was told that they would visit the library and I put out some of the more interesting publications for them to see. I take it, now, that they won't be coming.'

Dalgliesh said, 'They've left, Mrs Strickland, and I'm afraid I have to ask you to leave.'

'I shall in ten minutes, my time will be up. But I need to put away the display I arranged. That was a waste of time, I'm afraid. I wish someone had told me what was going on. And what is going on? I assume this is a second suspicious death as you're here, Commander. No one from the museum, I hope.'

'No one from the museum, Mrs Strickland.' Dalgliesh, anxious to get rid of her but not to antagonize her, kept his patience.

She said, 'A man, I suppose. I see you haven't a handbag. No woman would be found without a handbag. And dead flowers? They look like African violets. They are violets, aren't they? Is it a woman?'

'It is a woman, but I must ask you to say nothing about this to anyone. We need to inform the next of kin. Someone must be missing her, worried where she is. Until the next of kin are told, any talk might hamper the investigation and cause distress. I'm sure you will understand that. I'm sorry we didn't know you were in the museum. It's fortunate you didn't come in earlier.'

Mrs Strickland said, 'Dead bodies don't cause me distress. Living ones do occasionally. I'll say nothing. I suppose the family know – the Dupaynes I mean?'

'Miss Dupayne was here when we made the discovery, as was Mr Calder-Hale. I've no doubt one or both of them will have telephoned Marcus Dupayne.'

Mrs Strickland was at last turning away. 'She was in the trunk, I suppose.'

'Yes,' said Dalgliesh, 'she was in the trunk.'

'With the violets? Was someone trying to make a connection with Violette Kaye?'

Their eyes met but there was no hint of recognition. It was as if that hour of confidence in the Barbican flat, the shared wine, the intimacy, had never been. He could have been talking to a stranger. Was this her way of distancing herself from someone to whom she had been dangerously confiding?

Dalgliesh said, 'Mrs Strickland, I must insist that you leave now so that we can get on with what we have to do.'

'Of course. I've no intention of obstructing the police in the execution of their duty.' Her voice had been ironic. Now she walked towards the door, then turned and said, 'She wasn't in the trunk at four o'clock last Friday, if that's any help.'

There was a silence. If Mrs Strickland had wanted to leave on a high dramatic note, she had succeeded.

Dalgliesh's voice was calm. 'How can you be sure of that, Mrs Strickland?'

'Because I was here when the trunk was opened by Ryan Archer. I suppose you want to know why.'

Dalgliesh had to resist the ridiculous impulse to say that he wouldn't dream of asking. Mrs Strickland went on: 'It was pure curiosity – perhaps impure curiosity would be more appropriate. I think the boy had always wanted to see inside the trunk. He had just finished vacuuming the corridor outside the library. It wasn't a convenient time, of course, it never is. I find it difficult to concentrate with that disagreeable background noise and if there are visitors he has to stop. Anyway, there he was. When he switched off the vacuum cleaner he came into the library. I don't know why. He may have fancied some company. I'd just finished writing some new labels for the Wallace exhibits and he came over to look at them. I mentioned that I was taking them to the Murder Room and he asked if he could come with me. I saw no reason why he shouldn't.'

'And you're sure about the time?'

'Perfectly sure. We came into this room just before four. We stayed about five minutes and then Ryan left to collect his wages. I left soon after five. Muriel Godby was on the desk and, as you know, she offered to give me a lift to Hampstead Underground station. I waited while she and Tally Clutton checked the museum. I suppose it was about five-twenty when we finally drove off.'

Kate asked, 'And the trunk was empty?'

Mrs Strickland looked at her. 'Ryan is not the most intelligent or reliable of boys, but if he had found a body in the trunk I think he would have mentioned the fact. Apart from that, there would have been other indications, that is if she'd been there any length of time.'

'Do you remember what was said between you? Anything significant?'

'I believe I told Ryan that he wasn't supposed to touch the exhibits. I didn't reprove him. His action seemed to me perfectly natural. I believe he did say that the trunk was empty and that he didn't see any bloodstains. He sounded disappointed.'

Dalgliesh turned to Kate. 'See if you can find Ryan Archer. It's Wednesday, he should be here. Did you see anything of him when you arrived?'

'Nothing, sir. He'll probably be somewhere in the garden.'

'See if you can find him and get confirmation. Don't

tell him why you're asking. He'll know soon enough, but the later the better. I doubt whether he could resist spreading the story. The priority now is to notify the next of kin.'

Mrs Strickland turned to go. She said, 'By all means get confirmation. I shouldn't frighten the boy though. He'll only deny it.'

And then she was gone. Running down the stairs, Kate saw her re-entering the library.

At the front door Benton-Smith was standing guard. He said, with a nod towards the office, 'They're getting impatient. Miss Dupayne has been out twice to ask when the Commander will be seeing them. Apparently she's needed at the college. They've got a prospective student and her parents coming to look over the place. That's why Lady Swathling phoned earlier.'

Kate said, 'Tell Miss Dupayne it won't be long now. Have you seen anything of Ryan Archer?'

'No ma'am. What's up?'

'Mrs Strickland says that she was in the Murder Room with Ryan at four o'clock last Friday and he opened the trunk.'

Benton was already unlocking the door. 'That's useful. Is she sure about the time?'

'She says so. I'm off to check with Ryan now. It's Wednesday. The boy should be here somewhere.'

Despite the gloom of the day it was good to be in the fresh air, good to be out of the museum. She ran to look up the drive but could see no trace of Ryan. The mortuary van was arriving and, as she watched, Benton-Smith came out of the Museum and walked quickly to unlock the barrier. She didn't wait. The body would be moved without her help. Her job was to find Ryan. Moving past the burnt-out garage to the back of the museum, she saw that he was working in Mrs Clutton's garden. He was wearing a stout duffle-coat over his grubby jeans and a woollen hat with a pom-pom, and was kneeling beside the bed in front of the window, plunging his dibber into the soil and planting bulbs. He looked up as she approached and she saw his look of mingled wariness and fear.

She said, 'You need to plant them deeper than that, Ryan. Didn't Mrs Faraday show you?'

'She doesn't know I'm working here. Not that she'd care. I can lend a hand in Mrs Tally's garden when I've got time. This is to surprise her next spring.'

'It'll surprise you too, Ryan, when they don't come up. You're planting them upside down.'

'Does that matter?' He looked down at the last shallow hole with some dismay.

Kate said, 'I expect they'll right themselves and come up eventually. I'm not an expert. Ryan, did you look in the trunk in the Murder Room? I'm talking about last Friday. Did you open the lid?'

He dug the dibber viciously deeper into the soil. 'No, I never. Why would I do that? I'm not allowed in the Murder Room.'

'But Mrs Strickland says that you were there with her. Are you saying she's lying?'

He paused, then said, 'Well, maybe I was. I forget. There's no harm anyway. It's only an empty trunk.'

'So that's all it was, empty?'

'Well, there wasn't any dead tart in it when I looked. There wasn't even any blood. Mrs Strickland was there, she'll tell you. Who's complaining anyway?'

'No one's complaining, Ryan. We just wanted to be sure of the facts. So you're telling the truth now? You were with Mrs Strickland just before you left the museum and you looked into the trunk?'

'I've said so, haven't I?' Then he looked up and she saw horror dawning in his eyes. 'Why are you asking? What's it to do with the police? You've found something, haven't you?'

It would be disastrous if he spread the story before the next of kin were informed, better indeed that it wasn't told at all. But that was hardly practicable; he would learn the truth soon enough. She said, 'We have found a body in the trunk but we don't know how it got there. Until we do, it's important you say nothing. We shall know if you do speak because no one else will. Do you understand what I'm saying, Ryan?'

He nodded. She watched while he picked up another bulb with his ungloved grubby hands and inserted it carefully into the hole. He looked incredibly young and vulnerable. Kate was filled with an uncomfortable and, she thought, irrational pity. She said again, 'You do promise to say nothing, Ryan?'

He said grumpily, 'What about Mrs Tally then? Can't I tell Mrs Tally? She'll be back here soon. She's had her bike fixed and she's gone into Hampstead to do some shopping.'

'We'll speak to Mrs Tally. Why don't you go home now?'

He said, 'This is my home. I'm staying here with Mrs Tally for a while. I'll be going when I'm ready.'

'When Mrs Tally comes home, will you tell her that the police are here and ask her to come to the museum. Mrs Tally, Ryan, not you.'

'OK, I'll tell her. I suppose I can say why?'

He looked up at her, his face innocently bland. She wasn't deceived. 'Tell her nothing, Ryan. Just do as I ask. We'll talk to you later.'

Without another word, Kate left. The mortuary van, sinister in its black anonymity, was still outside the entrance. She had reached the front of the museum when she caught the sound of wheels on the gravel and, turning, saw Mrs Clutton cycling down the drive. Her bicycle basket was piled with plastic bags. She dismounted and carefully wheeled her machine on to the grass verge round the post of the barrier. Kate went to meet her.

She said, 'I've just been speaking to Ryan. I'm afraid I have distressing news. We've found another body, a young woman, in the Murder Room.'

Mrs Clutton's hands tightened on the handlebars. She said, 'But I was in the Murder Room doing my dusting at nine o'clock this morning. She wasn't there then.'

There was no way of softening the brutal facts. 'She was in the trunk, Mrs Clutton.'

'How horrible! It's something I've sometimes dreaded, that a child would decide to get in and be trapped. It was never a rational fear. Children aren't allowed in the Murder Room and an adult wouldn't be trapped. The lid isn't self-locking and it can't be very heavy. How did it happen?'

They had begun walking together towards the house. Kate said, 'I'm afraid it wasn't an accident. The young woman has been strangled.'

And now Mrs Clutton faltered and for a moment Kate thought she would fall. She put out a supporting hand. Mrs Clutton was leaning against the bicycle, her eyes on the distant mortuary van. She had seen it before. She knew what it was. But she was under control.

She said, 'Another death, another murder. Does anyone know who she is?'

'We think she's called Celia Mellock. Does that name mean anything to you?'

'No, nothing. And how could she have got in? There was no one in the museum when Muriel and I checked last night.'

Kate said, 'Commander Dalgliesh is here and so are Mr and Miss Dupayne and Mr Calder-Hale. We'd be grateful if you'd join them.'

'And Ryan?'

'I don't think he'll be needed at present. We'll call him if we want him.'

They had reached the museum. Mrs Clutton said, 'I'll just put my bicycle in the shed and then join you.'

But Kate didn't leave her. They walked together to the shed and she waited while Mrs Clutton took her plastic bags from the supermarket into the cottage. There was no sign of Ryan although his trug and dibber were still on the flowerbed. Together they walked in silence back to the museum.

3

Kate returned to the Murder Room. Dr Kynaston had left.

Dalgliesh asked Kate, 'Where are they?'

'They've moved to the picture gallery, sir, including Calder-Hale. Tally Clutton has come back and she's with them. Do you want to see them together?'

'It would be a convenient way to check one story against another. We know the time she died fairly accurately. Taking Mrs Strickland's evidence and Dr Kynaston's preliminary assessment puts it at some time on Friday night, earlier rather than late. Common sense suggests that she died either shortly before or soon after the Dupayne murder. A double killing. I refuse to believe that we have two separate murderers at work at the same place on the same evening at approximately the same time.'

Leaving Benton-Smith in the Murder Room, Dalgliesh, Kate and Piers went down together through the empty hall and into the picture gallery. Six pairs of eyes turned to them, it seemed simultaneously. Mrs Strickland and Caroline Dupayne had taken the armchairs before the fire. Muriel Godby and Tally Clutton were seated on the padded bench in the middle of the room. Marcus Dupayne and James Calder-Hale stood together at one of the windows. Looking at Muriel Godby and Tally

Clutton, Kate was reminded of patients she had seen in an oncologist's waiting-room, keenly aware of each other but not speaking or meeting each other's eyes since each knew that she could safely bear only her own anxieties. But she sensed also an atmosphere of mingled excitement and apprehension to which only Mrs Strickland seemed immune.

Dalgliesh said, 'As you're all here, it seems a convenient time to confirm earlier information and discover what, if anything, you know about this latest death. The museum will have to remain closed so that the scene of crime officers can examine all the rooms. I shall need all the keys. How many sets are there and who has them?'

It was Caroline Dupayne who replied. 'My brother and I have sets, as do Mr Calder-Hale, Miss Godby, Mrs Clutton and the two volunteers. There is also one spare set kept in the office.'

Muriel Godby said, 'I've been having to let Mrs Strickland in. She told me ten days ago that she'd lost her keys. I said we'd better wait a week or so before issuing a duplicate set.'

Mrs Strickland made no comment.

Dalgliesh turned to Caroline. 'I shall also need to go with you later this afternoon to see the rooms in your flat.'

Caroline was composing herself with difficulty. 'Is that really necessary, Commander? The only access to the galleries from my apartment is kept bolted and only myself and Miss Godby have keys to the ground-floor entrance.'

'If it were not necessary, I should not have asked.'

Calder-Hale said, 'We can't quit the museum at a moment's notice. I have things I need to do in my room, papers to take away to work on tomorrow.'

Dalgliesh said, 'You're not being asked to leave immediately, but I should like the keys to be handed over by the end of the afternoon. In the mean time, the scene of crime officers and Sergeant Benton Smith will be here, and the Murder Room will, of course, be closed to you.'

The implication was as plain as it was unwelcome. While in the museum they would be under discreet but effective supervision.

Marcus Dupayne said, 'So this wasn't an accident? I thought the girl might have climbed into the trunk, perhaps out of curiosity or in response to some sort of dare, and got trapped when the lid fell on her. Isn't that a possibility? Death by suffocation?'

Dalgliesh said, 'Not in this case. But before we go on talking it would be convenient to leave the museum to the scene of crime officers. I'm wondering, Mrs Clutton, if you would mind our using your sitting-room.'

Tally Clutton and Mrs Strickland had both got to their feet. Now Tally, disconcerted, looked at Caroline Dupayne. The woman shrugged and said, 'It's your cottage while you're living there. If you can fit us in, why not?'

Tally said, 'I think there'll be room. I could bring extra chairs from the dining-room.'

Caroline Dupayne said, 'Then let's go and get it over.'

The little group left the gallery and paused outside while Dalgliesh relocked the door. They trailed round the corner of the house in silence like a dispirited group of mourners leaving the crematorium. Following Dalgliesh through the porch of the cottage, Kate almost expected to find ham sandwiches and a restorative bottle waiting on the sitting-room table.

Inside the room there was a slight commotion as extra chairs were brought in by Marcus Dupayne helped by Kate, and people arranged themselves round the centre table. Only Caroline Dupayne and Mrs Strickland seemed at ease. Both selected the chair they preferred, sat promptly down and waited, Caroline Dupayne in grim acquiescence and Mrs Strickland with a look of controlled expectation as if she were prepared to stay as long as she remained interested in the proceedings.

It was an incongruous room for such a meeting, its cheerful homeliness so at odds with the business in hand. The gas fire was already on but turned very low, probably, Kate thought, for the benefit of the large ginger cat which was curled in the more comfortable of the two fireside chairs. Piers, who wanted to hold a watching brief away from the group round the table, unceremoniously tipped him out and the cat, affronted, walked to the door, his tail thrashing, and then made a dash for the stairs. Tally Clutton cried, 'Oh dear, he'll get on the bed! Tomcat knows he's not allowed to do that. Excuse me.'

She rushed after him while the others waited with the awkwardness of guests who have arrived at an inconvenient moment. Tally appeared at the door with a docile Tomcat in her arms. She said, 'I'll put him out. He usually does go out until late afternoon but this morning he just took possession of the chair and fell asleep. I hadn't the heart to disturb him.'

They heard her admonishing the cat and then the sound of her closing the front door. Caroline Dupayne glanced at her brother, eyebrows raised, her mouth twisted into a brief sardonic smile. They were settled at last.

Dalgliesh stood beside the southern window. He said, 'The dead girl is Celia Mellock. Does anyone here know her?'

He didn't miss the quick glance which Muriel Godby cast at Caroline Dupayne. But she said nothing and it was Caroline who replied.

'Both Miss Godby and I know her – or rather, knew her. She was a student at Swathling's last year but left at the end of the spring term. That would be the spring of 2001. Miss Godby was working as a receptionist at the college the term before. I haven't seen Celia since she left. I didn't teach her but I did interview her and her mother before she was admitted. She only stayed for two terms and it wasn't a success.'

'Are her parents in England? We know Miss Mellock's address is 47 Manningtree Gardens, Earls Court Road. We've phoned, but there's no one there at the moment.'

Caroline Dupayne said, 'I imagine that's her address, not her parents'. I can tell you something of the family but not a great deal. Her mother married for the third time a month or so before Celia came to the college. I can't remember the new husband's name. He's some kind of industrialist, I believe. Rich, of course. Celia herself wasn't poor. Her father left a trust fund and she got access to the capital at eighteen. Too young, but that's how it was. I seem to remember her mother used to spend most of the winter abroad. If she isn't in London she'll probably be in Bermuda.'

Dalgliesh said, 'That's a useful feat of memory. Thank you.'

Caroline Dupayne shrugged. 'I don't usually make a bad choice. This time I did. Our failures are rare at Swathling's. I tend to remember them.'

It was Kate who took over. She said to Muriel Godby, 'How well did you know Miss Mellock while you were at the college?'

'Not at all. I had very little contact with the students. That which I did have wasn't pleasant. Some of them resented me, I can't think why. One or two were actually hostile and I remember them very clearly. She wasn't among them. I don't think that she was often in college. I doubt whether we ever spoke.'

'Did anyone else here know the girl?' No one replied, but they shook their heads. 'Has anyone any idea why she should have come to the museum?'

Again they shook their heads. Marcus Dupayne said, 'Presumably she came as a visitor, either alone or with her murderer. It seems unlikely that it was a chance encounter. Perhaps Miss Godby might remember her.'

All eyes turned to Muriel. She said, 'I doubt whether I'd have known her if I had seen her arriving. Perhaps she'd have recognized me and said something, but it's unlikely. I can't remember her so why should she remember me? She didn't come in while I was on the desk.'

Dalgliesh said, 'Presumably Swathling's have a name and address for Miss Mellock's mother. Would you telephone the college, please, and ask for it?'

It was obvious that the request was unwelcome. Caroline said, 'Won't that seem a little unusual? The girl left last year and after only two terms.'

'And the records are destroyed so quickly? Surely not. There's no need to speak to Lady Swathling. Ask one of the secretaries to look up the file. Aren't you the joint Principal? Why shouldn't you ask for any information you need?'

Still she hesitated. 'Can't you discover it another way? It's not as if the girl's death has anything to do with Swathling's.'

'We don't yet know what it has to do with. Celia Mellock was a student at Swathling's, you are the joint Principal, she's been found dead in your museum.'

'If you put it like that.'

'I do put it like that. We need to inform the next of kin. There are other ways of finding their address but this is the quickest.'

Caroline made no further objection. She lifted the telephone receiver.

'Miss Cosgrove? I need the address and telephone number of Celia Mellock's mother. The file is in the left-hand cabinet, the ex-student section.'

The wait lasted a full minute, then Caroline noted down the information and handed it to Dalgliesh. He said, 'Thank you,' and handed it to Kate. 'See if you can make an appointment as soon as possible.'

Kate needed no instruction to make the call outside

the cottage on her mobile. The door closed behind her.

The gloom of the early morning had lifted but there was no sun and the wind was chill. Kate decided to make the phone call from her car. The address was in Brook Street and the call was answered by the unctuous voice of someone who was obviously a member of the staff. Lady Holstead and her husband were at their house in Bermuda. He was not authorized to give the number.

Kate said, 'This is Detective Inspector Miskin of New Scotland Yard. If you wish to verify my identity, I can give you a number to ring. I would prefer that we don't waste time. I need urgently to speak to Sir Daniel.'

There was a pause. The voice said, 'Will you please hold on a minute, Inspector?'

Kate heard the sound of footsteps. Thirty seconds later the voice spoke again and gave the Bermudian number, repeating it carefully.

Kate rang off and thought for a moment before making the second call. But there was no option; the news would have to be quickly given by telephone. Bermuda was probably about four hours behind Greenwich Mean Time. The call might be inconveniently early, but surely not unreasonably so. She dialled and was answered almost immediately.

A man's voice came over, sharp and indignant. 'Yes? Who is it?'

'This is Detective Inspector Kate Miskin of New Scotland Yard. I need to speak to Sir Daniel Holstead.'

'Holstead speaking. And it's a particularly inconsiderate hour to ring. What is it? Not another attempted break-in at the London flat?'

'Are you alone, Sir Daniel?'

'I'm alone. I want to know what the hell this is about.'

'It's about your step-daughter, Sir Daniel.'

Before Kate could go on, he broke in. 'And what in God's name has she been up to now? Look, my wife isn't any longer responsible for her and I never was. The girl is nineteen, she leads her own life, she's got her own flat. She must cope with her own problems. She's been nothing but trouble to her mother from the day she could speak. What is it now?'

It was apparent that Sir Daniel was not at his sharpest in the early morning. That fact could have its uses.

Kate said, 'I'm afraid it's bad news, Sir Daniel. Celia Mellock has been murdered. Her body was found earlier this morning in the Dupayne Museum, Hampstead Heath.'

The silence was so complete that Kate wondered whether she had been heard. She was about to speak when Holstead said, 'Murdered? How murdered?'

'She was throttled, Sir Daniel.'

'You're telling me that Celia has been found throttled in a museum? This isn't some kind of sick joke?'

'I'm afraid not. You can verify the information by telephoning the Yard. We thought it best to speak to you first so that you can break the news to your wife. I'm sorry. This must be a terrible shock.'

'My God it is! We'll fly back today by the company jet. Not that there's anything useful we can tell you. Neither of us has seen Celia for the past six months. And she never phones. No reason why she should, I suppose. She's got her own life. She's always made it plain what she thought of any interference from her mother and me. I'll go now and break the news to Lady Holstead. I'll let you know when we arrive. You've no idea yet who did it, I suppose?'

'Not at present, Sir Daniel.'

'No suspect? No obvious boyfriend? Nothing?'

'Not at present.'

'Who's in charge? Do I know him?'

'Commander Adam Dalgliesh. He'll come to see you and your wife when you get back. We may have a little more information then.'

'Dalgliesh? The name's familiar. I'll ring the Commissioner when I've spoken to my wife. You could have broken the news with more consideration. Goodbye, Inspector.'

Before Kate could speak, the receiver had been banged down. He had a point, she thought. Had she broken the news of the murder immediately, she wouldn't have heard that small outburst of rancour. She knew rather more about Sir Daniel Holstead than he would have wished. The thought gave her a small glow of satisfaction; she wondered why it also made her a little ashamed.

4

Kate returned to the cottage and took her seat, nodding a confirmation to Dalgliesh that the message had been given. They could discuss the details later. She saw that Marcus Dupayne still sat at the head of the table, his hands clasped before him, his face a mask. Now he said to Dalgliesh, 'We are, of course, perfectly free to leave if that's what any of us want or need to do?'

'Perfectly free. I've asked you to come here because questioning you now is the quickest way to get the information I need. If any of you find that inconvenient, I can arrange to see you later.'

Marcus said, 'Thank you. I thought it as well to establish the legal position. My sister and I naturally wish to co-operate in any way we can. This death is a terrible shock. It's also a tragedy – for the girl, for her family and for the museum.'

Dalgliesh did not reply. He privately doubted whether the museum would suffer. Once reopened, the Murder Room would double in attraction. He had a vivid picture of Mrs Strickland sitting in the library, those careful arthritic hands writing a new label, the Dupaynes standing each side of her. *The original trunk in which the bodies of Violette Kaye and Celia Mellock were concealed is at present in the possession of the police. This trunk here is similar in age and type.* The fantasy was disagreeable.

He said, 'Can you, between you, go through last Friday. We know, of course, what you were doing after the museum closed. Now we need a detailed account of what happened during the day.'

Caroline Dupayne looked at Muriel Godby. It was she who began, but gradually all those present except Calder-Hale added to or confirmed what was said. A detailed picture of the day emerged, hour by hour, from the moment Tally Clutton arrived at eight o'clock for her regular cleaning until Muriel Godby finally locked the door and drove Mrs Strickland to Hampstead Underground station.

At the end Piers said, 'So there are two occasions on which Celia Mellock and her killer could have got in unseen, at ten o'clock in the morning and at one-thirty when Miss Godby left the desk and went over to the cottage to fetch Mrs Clutton.'

Muriel Godby said, 'The desk couldn't have been unattended for more than five minutes. If we had a proper telephone system, or if Mrs Clutton would agree to have a mobile, I wouldn't need to go over to the cottage. It's ridiculous trying to manage with an old-fashioned system without even an answerphone.'

Piers asked, 'Supposing Miss Mellock and her killer did get in undetected, are there any rooms in which they could have been concealed overnight? What are the arrangements for internal locking of the doors?'

It was Muriel Godby who replied. 'After the front door has been locked to visitors at five, I go round with Tally to check that no one is in the museum. Then I lock the only two doors to which there are keys, the picture gallery and the library. Those contain the most valuable exhibits. No other room is locked except Mr Calder-Hale's office, and that isn't my responsibility. He usually keeps it locked when he's not there. I didn't try his door.'

Calder-Hale spoke for the first time. 'If you had, you would have found it locked.'

Piers asked, 'What about the basement?'

'I opened the door and saw that the light was still on. I went to the top of the iron platform and looked down into the basement. No one was there so I turned off the light. There isn't a lock on that door. With Mrs Clutton I also checked that all the windows were locked. I left at five-fifteen with Mrs Strickland and dropped her at Hampstead tube station. Then I drove home. But you know all that, Inspector. We've been questioned before about last Friday.'

Piers ignored the protest. He said, 'So it would be possible for someone to be concealed down there in the archives between the sliding steel shelves? You didn't go down the steps to check?'

It was then that Caroline Dupayne broke in. She said, 'Inspector, we're running a museum, not a police station. We've had no break-in and no detectable theft for the last twenty years. Why on earth should Miss Godby search the archives room? Even if someone had been concealed when the museum was locked, how could he get out? The ground-floor windows are locked at night. Miss Godby, with Mrs Clutton, carried out their usual routine.'

Her brother had remained silent. Now he said, 'We are all suffering from shock. I don't need to say that we are as anxious as you to have this mystery solved and we intend to co-operate fully in the investigation. But there is no reason to suppose that any person who worked at the museum had anything to do with the girl's death. Miss Mellock and her killer may have come to the museum merely as visitors or for some purpose known only to themselves. We know how they could have got in and how they could have been concealed. There is no problem about an intruder leaving undetected. After my brother's death my sister and I waited for you in the picture gallery here. We left the front door ajar knowing that you were due to arrive. We waited for you for over an hour, plenty of time for the killer to make his escape unseen.'

Mrs Strickland said, 'He'd be taking a terrible risk, of course. You or Caroline might have come out of the picture gallery or Commander Dalgliesh might have come through the front door at any moment.'

Marcus Dupayne dealt with the comment with the controlled impatience with which he might have greeted a subordinate's intervention at a departmental meeting. 'He took a risk, of course. He had no option but to take a risk if he were to avoid being trapped in the museum all night. He had only to look briefly out of the basement door to see that the hall was empty and the front door was ajar. I'm not suggesting that the murder took place in the basement. The Murder Room seems the more likely. But the archives room offered the best – indeed the only – safe hiding place until he could get away. I'm not arguing that it must have happened this way, only that it could have.'

Dalgliesh said, 'But the door to the picture gallery was also ajar. Surely you or your sister would have heard someone passing through the hall?'

Marcus said, 'Since it's obvious that someone must have passed through the hall and we heard nothing, the answer is incontrovertible. We were, I remember, sitting with our drinks in front of the fireplace. We were nowhere near the door and we had no view of the hall.'

His sister looked straight at Dalgliesh. She said, 'I don't want to seem to be doing your job for you, Commander, but isn't there a possible reason why Celia came to the museum? She may have had a lover with her. Perhaps he was the kind who needs an element of risk to give sex that extra edge. Celia may have suggested the Dupayne as a possible venue. Knowing that I was a trustee here might have added a spice of danger to the sexual thrill. Then things got out of hand and she ended up dead.'

Kate had not spoken for some time. Now she asked Caroline, 'From your knowledge of Miss Mellock, is that the kind of behaviour you'd think likely?'

There was a pause. The question was unwelcome. 'As I said, I didn't teach her and I know nothing of her private life. But she was an unhappy, confused and difficult student. She was also easily led. Nothing she did would ever surprise me.'

Piers thought, *We should recruit this lot to the squad. Give them another half hour and they'll have both murders solved.* But that pompous ass Marcus Dupayne had a point. The scenario might be unlikely but it was possible.

It would be a gift to a defending counsel. But if it had happened that way, with luck Nobby Clark and his boys would find some evidence, perhaps in the basement archives room. But it hadn't happened that way. It was beyond credibility that two separate murderers were at the museum on the same night at roughly the same time killing such very different victims. Celia Mellock had died in the Murder Room, not in the basement, and he was beginning to think he knew why. He glanced across at his chief. Dalgliesh's look was serious and a little withdrawn, almost contemplative. Piers knew that look. He wondered whether their thoughts were running along the same lines.

Dalgliesh said, 'We already have your fingerprints which were taken after Dr Dupayne's murder. I'm sorry that the sealing of the Murder Room and the temporary closing of the museum will cause inconvenience to you all. I hope we shall be finished by Monday. In the mean time I think we have finished with everyone except Mrs Clutton and Mrs Strickland. We have, of course, all your addresses.'

Marcus Dupayne said, 'Aren't we to be allowed to know how the girl died? I imagine the news will be leaked to the press soon enough. Haven't we a reasonable right to be told first?'

Dalgliesh said, 'The news will not be leaked and nor will it be made public until the next of kin have been informed. I would be grateful if you would all keep silent to avoid unnecessary distress to family and friends. Once the murder does become public there will obviously be press interest. That will be dealt with by the Met public relations department. You may wish to take your own precautions against being pestered.'

Caroline asked, 'And the post-mortem? The inquest? What will be the timing there?'

Dalgliesh said, 'The autopsy will take place tomorrow morning and the inquest as soon as it can be arranged by the Coroner's office. Like the inquest on your brother, it will be opened and adjourned.'

The two Dupaynes and Calder-Hale got up to go. Piers thought that brother and sister resented being excluded from further discussion. Miss Godby apparently felt the same. She got up reluctantly and looked across at Tally Clutton with a mixture of curiosity and resentment.

After the door had closed, Dalgliesh seated himself at the table. He said, 'Thank you, Mrs Strickland, for not mentioning the violets.'

Mrs Strickland said evenly, 'You told me to say nothing and I said nothing.'

Tally Clutton half rose from her seat. Her face paled. She said, 'What violets?'

Kate said gently, 'There were four dead African violets on the body, Mrs Clutton.'

Eyes widening with horror, Tally glanced from face to face. She said in a whisper, 'Violette Kaye! So these are copy-cat murders.'

Kate moved to sit beside her. 'It's one of the possibilities we have to consider. What we need to know is how the murderer got access to the violets.'

Dalgliesh spoke to her carefully and slowly. 'We've seen small terracotta pots of these violets in two rooms, Mr Calder-Hale's and yours. I saw Mr Calder-Hale's plants on Sunday morning at about ten o'clock when I went to interview him. They were intact then, though I thought he was going to decapitate them when he yanked down the window blind. Inspector Miskin thinks there were no broken flowers when she was in Mr Calder-Hale's room with his visitors shortly before ten this morning, and Sergeant Benton-Smith noticed them when he went to the room shortly after the discovery of Celia Mellock's body. They were complete at about ten-thirty this morning. We've checked and they're complete now. One of the plants you have on your window-sill here has four stems broken off. So it looks as if the violets came from here and that means the person who put them on Celia Mellock's body must have had access to the cottage.'

Tally said simply, as if there could be no question that she would be disbelieved, 'But the ones in here are from Mr Calder-Hale's office! I changed his pot for one of mine on Sunday morning.'

Kate was practised in concealing her excitement. She said quietly, 'How did that happen?'

But it was to Dalgliesh that Tally turned, as if willing him to understand. 'I gave a pot of African violets to Mr Calder-Hale for his birthday. That was on 3rd October. I suppose it was a silly thing to do. One ought to check with people first. He never has plants in his room and perhaps he's too busy to want the bother of them. I knew he'd be in his room working on Sunday, he nearly always does come in on a Sunday, so I thought I'd water the violets and take off any dead flowers or leaves before he arrived. It was then that I saw four of the blooms were missing. I thought, like you, that they must have got broken off when he lowered the blind. He hadn't been watering the pot either and the leaves weren't looking very healthy. So I brought the pot back here to give it some care and substituted one of mine. I don't suppose he even noticed.'

Dalgliesh asked, 'When did you last see the African violets undamaged in Mr Calder-Hale's office?'

Tally Clutton thought. 'I think it was on Thursday, the day before Dr Dupayne's murder, when I cleaned his office. It's kept locked but there's a key in the key cabinet. I remember thinking then that they didn't look very healthy, but all the blooms were intact.'

'What time on Sunday did you substitute the pots?'

'I can't remember exactly but it was early, soon after I arrived. Perhaps between half-past eight and nine.'

Dalgliesh said, 'I have to ask you, Mrs Clutton. You didn't break off those flowers yourself?'

Still gazing into his eyes she answered, as docile as an obedient child, 'No, I didn't break off any of the flowers.'

'And you're quite certain of the facts you've told us? The African violets in Mr Calder-Hale's office were undamaged on Thursday 31st October and you found them damaged and replaced them on Sunday 3rd November? You have absolutely no doubt about this?'

'No, Mr Dalgliesh. I have no doubt at all.'

They thanked her for the use of the cottage and prepared to leave. It had been useful to have Mrs Strickland there as a witness to their questioning of Tally, and now she made it apparent that she had no intention of hurrying away. Tally seemed glad of her company and made a tentative suggestion that they might have some soup and an omelette before Ryan returned. There had been no sign of him since Kate had spoken to him, and he would have to be seen and questioned again, now more particularly about what he had done during the day last Friday.

On Monday, after Tally had brought him back, he had provided one useful piece of evidence, the bitterness between Neville Dupayne and his siblings about the future of the museum. He had said that after receiving his day's pay, he had gone back to a previous squat with a view to taking out his friends for a drink, but had found the house repossessed by its owners. He had then wandered round the Leicester Square area for a time before deciding to walk back to Maida Vale. He thought he had arrived home at about seven o'clock but couldn't be sure. None of this had been verifiable. His account of the assault had agreed with that of the Major, although he hadn't volunteered why he had found the Major's words so offensive. It was difficult to see Ryan Archer as a prime suspect, but that he was a suspect at all was a complication. Wherever he was now, Dalgliesh devoutly hoped that the boy was keeping his mouth shut.

Calder-Hale was still in his room and Kate and Dalgliesh saw him together. They couldn't claim that he was uncooperative, but he seemed to be sunk in apathy. He was slowly collecting papers together and stuffing them into a commodious and shabby briefcase. Told that four stalks of African violets had been found on the body, he showed as little interest as if this had been an unexciting detail which wasn't his concern. Casually glancing at the violets on his windowsill, he said that he hadn't noticed that the pots had been exchanged. It was kind of Tally to remember his birthday but he preferred not to mark these anniversaries. He disliked African violets. There was no particular reason, they were just plants which had no appeal. It would have been ungracious to tell Tally this and he hadn't done so. Usually he locked the door to his room when he left, but not invariably. After Dalgliesh and Piers had interviewed him on Sunday he had continued working until twelve-thirty and had then gone home; he couldn't remember whether he had locked his door on leaving. As the museum was closed to the public and was remaining closed until after Dupayne's funeral, he thought it probable that he hadn't bothered to lock his office.

During the questioning he had continued to collect his papers, tidy his desk and take a mug into his bathroom to rinse it out. Now he was ready to leave and showed every inclination to do so without enduring further questioning. Handing his keys to the museum to Dalgliesh, he said that he'd be glad to have them returned as soon as possible. It was highly inconvenient not to have the use of his room.

Last of all, Dalgliesh and Kate called Caroline Dupayne and Muriel Godby from the downstairs office. Miss Dupayne had apparently reconciled herself to the inspection of the flat. The door was to the rear of the house and on the west side, and was unobtrusive. Miss Dupayne unlocked it and they entered a small vestibule with a modern lift controlled by pushbuttons. Punching out the sequence, Caroline Dupayne said, 'The lift was installed by my father. He lived here in old age and was obsessive about security. So am I when I'm here alone. I also value my privacy. No doubt you do too, Commander. I find this inspection an intrusion.'

Dalgliesh didn't reply. If there were evidence that Celia Mellock had been here or could have entered the museum from the flat, then Miss Dupayne would be faced with a professional search which would indeed be intrusive. The tour of the flat, if it could be called that, was perfunctory, but he was unworried. Briefly she showed him the two spare bedrooms – both with adjoining bathroom and shower and neither showing any sign of recent use – the kitchen with a huge refrigerator, a small utility-room with its large washing machine and drier, and the sitting-room. It could not have been more different from Neville Dupayne's room. Here were comfortable chairs and a sofa in pale green linen. The low bookcase ran the length of three walls, and rugs covered almost the whole of the polished floor. Above the bookcases the walls were hung with small pictures, water-colours, lithographs and oils. Even on this dull day light poured in from the two windows with their view of the sky. This was a comfortable room which, in its airy silence, must provide a relief from the noise, the impersonality and lack of privacy of her apartment at Swathling's, and he could understand its importance for her.

Last of all, Caroline Dupayne showed them her bedroom. The room surprised Kate. It was not what she had expected. It was unfussy but comfortable, even luxurious, and, despite a hint of austerity, it was very feminine. Here, as in all the other rooms, the windows were fitted with blinds as well as curtains. They didn't go in but stood briefly at the door which Caroline had opened wide, standing back against it and gazing fixedly at Dalgliesh. Kate caught a look that was both challenging and lubricious. The look intrigued her. It went some way to explaining Caroline Dupayne's attitude to the investigation. And then, still in silence, Caroline closed the door.

But what interested Dalgliesh was the possible access to the museum. A white-painted door led to a short flight of carpeted steps and to a narrow hallway. The mahogany door facing them had bolts at top and bottom and a key hanging on a hook to the right. Caroline Dupayne stood silent and motionless. Taking his latex gloves from his pocket, Dalgliesh put them on and then drew back the bolts and unlocked the door. The key turned easily but the door was heavy and, once open, it needed his weight to prevent it from swinging back.

Before them was the Murder Room. Nobby Clark and one of the fingerprint officers looked at them with surprise. Dalgliesh said, 'I want the museum side of this door dusted for prints.' Then he closed and bolted it again.

In the last few minutes Caroline Dupayne hadn't spoken, and Miss Godby hadn't uttered a word since their arrival. Returning to the flat, Dalgliesh said, 'Will you confirm that only you two have keys to the ground-floor door?'

Caroline Dupayne said, 'I've already told you so. No other keys exist. No one can get into the flat from the

Murder Room. There's no handle on the door. That, of course, was deliberate on my father's part.'

'When were you, either of you, first in the flat following Dr Dupayne's murder?'

And now Muriel Godby spoke. 'I came in early on Saturday because I knew Miss Dupayne planned to be in the flat for the weekend. I did some dusting and checked that things were in order for her. The door to the museum was locked then.'

'Was it normal for you to check that door? Why should you?'

'Because it's part of my routine. When I come to the flat I check that everything is in order.'

Caroline Dupayne said, 'I arrived at about three o'clock and stayed here on Saturday night alone. I left by ten-thirty on Sunday. No one, to my knowledge, has been here since.'

And if they had, thought Dalgliesh, the conscientious Muriel Godby would have eliminated any trace. It was in silence that the four of them descended to the ground floor and in silence that Miss Dupayne and Miss Godby handed over their sets of the museum keys.

It was shortly after midnight before Dalgliesh was at last in his high riverside flat at the top of a converted nineteenth-century warehouse at Queenhithe. He had his own entrance and a secure lift. Here, except during the working week, he lived above silent and empty offices in the solitude he needed. By eight o'clock every evening even the cleaners had gone. Returning home he could picture below him the floors of deserted rooms with the computers shut down, the waste-paper baskets emptied, the telephone calls unanswered, and with only the occasional bleep of the fax machine to break the eerie silence. The building had originally been a spice warehouse and a pungent evocative aroma had permeated the wood-lined walls and was faintly detectable even above the strong sea smell of the Thames. As always he moved over to the window. The wind had dropped. A few frail shreds of cloud stained ruby by the glare of the city hung motionless in a deep purple sky spangled with stars. Fifty feet below his window the full tide heaved and sucked at the brick walls; T.S. Eliot's brown god had taken on his black nocturnal mystery.

He had received a letter from Emma in reply to his. Moving over to his desk, he read it again. It was brief but explicit. She could be in London on Friday evening and planned to catch the six-fifteen train, arriving at

King's Cross at three minutes past seven. Could he meet her at the barrier? She would need to set out by five-thirty, so could he phone her before then if he couldn't make it. It was signed simply *Emma*. He reread the few lines in her elegant upward strokes, trying to decide what might lie behind the words. Did this brevity convey the hint of an ultimatum? That wouldn't be Emma's way. But she had her pride and after his last cancellation might now be telling him that this was his last chance, their last chance.

He hardly dared hope that she loved him, but even if she were on the edge of love she might draw back. Her life was in Cambridge, his in London. He could, of course, resign from his job. He had inherited enough money from his aunt to make him comparatively rich. He was a respected poet. From boyhood he had known that poetry would be the mainspring of his life, but he had never wanted to be a professional poet. It had been important to him to find a job which would be socially useful – he was, after all, his father's son – a job in which he could be physically active and preferably occasionally in danger. He would set up his ladder, if not in W.B. Yeats's foul rag-and-bone shop of the heart, at least in a world far removed from the seductive peace of that Norfolk rectory, from the subsequent privileged years of public school and Oxford. Policing had provided all that he was looking for and more. His job had ensured his privacy, had protected him from the obligations of success, the interviews, the lectures, the overseas tours, the relentless publicity, above all from being part of the London literary establishment. And it had fuelled the best of his poetry. He couldn't give it up, and he knew Emma wouldn't ask that of him, any more than he would ask her to sacrifice her career. If by a miracle she loved him, somehow they would find a way to make a life together.

And he would be at King's Cross station on Friday to meet that train. Even if there were important developments by Friday afternoon, Kate and Piers were more than competent to cope with anything that happened over the weekend. Only an arrest would keep him in London, and none was imminent. Already he had Friday evening planned. He would go early to King's Cross and spend the half hour before the train was due to arrive in the British Library, then stroll the short distance to the station. If the skies fell, she would see him waiting at the barrier when she arrived.

His last act was to write a letter to Emma. He hardly knew why he needed now, in this moment of quietude, to find the words which might convince her of his love. Perhaps the time would come when she no longer wanted to hear his voice or, if she listened, might need time to think before she responded. If that moment ever came, the letter would be ready.

6

On Thursday 7th November, Mrs Pickering arrived to open the charity shop in Highgate promptly at nine-thirty as she always did. She saw with annoyance that there was a black plastic bag outside the door. The top was open revealing the usual jumble of wool and cotton. Unlocking the door, she dragged the bag in behind her with small clucks of irritation. It really was too bad. The notice pasted to the inside of the window stated plainly that donors shouldn't leave bags outside the door because of the risk of theft, but they still did it. She went through to the small office to hang up her coat and hat, dragging the bag with her. It would have to wait until Mrs Fraser arrived, shortly before ten. It was Mrs Fraser, nominally in charge of the charity shop and an acknowledged expert on pricing the items, who would go through the bag and decide what should be put on display and how much should be charged.

Mrs Pickering had no great expectations of her find. All the voluntary workers knew that people with clothes worth buying liked to bring them in themselves, not leave them outside to be pilfered. But she couldn't resist a preliminary inspection. Certainly there seemed nothing interesting in this bundle of faded jeans, woollen jumpers felted with washing, a very long hand-knitted cardigan which looked quite promising until she saw the moth-holes in the sleeves, and some half-dozen cracked and distorted pairs of shoes. Lifting the items one by one and thrusting her hands among them, she decided that Mrs Fraser would probably reject the lot. And then her hand encountered leather and a narrow metal chain. The chain had become entangled with the laces on a man's shoe but she pulled it through and found herself looking at an obviously expensive handbag.

Mrs Pickering's place in the charity shop's hierarchy was lowly, a fact she accepted without resentment. She was slow in giving change, completely confused when Euro notes or coins were proffered and inclined to waste time when the shop was busy, chatting with the customers and helping them to decide which item of clothing would best suit their size and colouring. She herself recognized these failings but was untroubled by them. Mrs Fraser had once said to a fellow worker, 'She's hopeless on the till, of course, and dreadfully chatty, but she's thoroughly reliable and good with the customers and we're lucky to have her.' Mrs Pickering had only caught the last part of this sentence but would probably not have been dismayed had she heard the whole. But although the assessing of quality and the pricing were privileges reserved for Mrs Fraser, she could recognize good leather when she saw it. This was certainly an expensive and unusual handbag. She smoothed her hands over it, feeling the suppleness of the leather, then placed it back on the top of the bundle.

The next half hour was spent as usual in dusting the shelves, rearranging the items in the order prescribed by Mrs Fraser, re-hanging the clothes which eager hands had dislodged from their hangers, and setting out the cups for the Nescafé which she would make as soon as Mrs Fraser arrived. That lady, as usual, was on time. Relocking the door behind her and casting a preliminary approving look over the shop interior, she went into the back room with Mrs Pickering.

'There's this bundle,' said Mrs Pickering. 'Left outside the door as usual. Really, people are very naughty, the notice is perfectly plain. It doesn't look very interesting, except for a handbag.'

Mrs Fraser, as her companion knew, could never resist a new sack of donations. While Mrs Pickering switched on the kettle and doled out the Nescafé, she went to the bag. There was a silence. Mrs Pickering watched while Mrs Fraser unclipped the bag, examined the fastener carefully, turned it over in her hands. Then she opened it. She said, 'It's a Gucci, and it looks as if it's hardly been used. Who on earth would have given us this? Did you see who left the sack?'

'No, it was here when I arrived. The handbag wasn't on the top, though. It was stuffed well down the side. I just felt around out of curiosity and found it.'

'It's very strange. It's a rich woman's bag. The rich don't give us their cast-offs. What they do is send their maids to sell them at those upmarket second-hand shops. That's how the rich stay rich. They know the value of what they've got. We've never had a bag of this quality before.'

There was a side pocket and she slipped her fingers into it, then drew out a business card. Coffee forgotten, Mrs Pickering came over and they looked at it together.

It was small and the lettering was elegant and plain. They read: CELIA MELLOCK, and at the bottom left-hand corner, POLLYANNE PROMOTIONS, THEATRICAL AGENTS, COVENT GARDEN, WC2.

Mrs Pickering said, 'I wonder if we ought to get in touch with the agency and try to trace the owner? We could return the bag. It might have been given to us by mistake.'

Mrs Fraser had no truck with such inconvenient sensitivities. 'If people give things by mistake, it's up to them to come in and ask for them back. We can't make that sort of judgement. After all, we have to remember the cause, the refuge for old and unwanted animals. If the goods are left outside, we're entitled to sell them.'

Mrs Pickering said, 'We might put it by for Mrs Roberts to have a look at. I think she'd give a very good price. Isn't she due in this afternoon?'

Mrs Roberts, an occasional and not particularly reliable volunteer, had an eye for a bargain, but as she always gave at least ten per cent more than Mrs Fraser would dare ask of ordinary customers, neither lady saw any moral difficulty in accommodating their colleague.

But Mrs Fraser didn't reply. She had become very quiet, so quiet indeed that she seemed for the moment incapable of movement. Then she said, 'I've remembered. I know this name. Celia Mellock. I heard it on this morning's local radio. It's the girl who was found dead in that museum – the Dupayne, wasn't it?'

Mrs Pickering said nothing. She was affected by her companion's obvious if repressed excitement, but couldn't for the life of her see the significance of the find.

Feeling at last that some comment was required, she said, 'So she must have decided to give the bag away before she was killed.'

'She could hardly decide to do so after she was killed, Grace! And look at the rest of these things. They can't have come from Celia Mellock. Obviously someone shoved this handbag among the other things as a way of getting rid of it.'

Mrs Pickering had always regarded Mrs Fraser's intellect with awe and, faced with this remarkable deductive power, struggled to find an adequate comment. At last she said, 'What do you think we should do?'

'The answer's perfectly plain. We keep the CLOSED notice showing on the door and we don't open it at ten o'clock. And now we phone the police.'

Mrs Pickering said, 'You mean ring Scotland Yard?'

'Precisely. They're the ones dealing with the Mellock murder and one should always go to the top.'

The next hour and three quarters were extremely gratifying to the two ladies. Mrs Fraser rang while her friend stood by admiring the clear way in which she gave the news of their find. At the end she heard Mrs Fraser say, 'Yes, we've already done that, and we'll stay in the back office so that people won't see us and start hammering on the door. There's an entrance at the rear, if you want to arrive discreetly.'

She put down the receiver and said, 'They're sending someone round. They told us not to open the shop and to wait for them in the office.'

The wait was not long. Two male officers arrived by car at the back entrance, one rather stocky who was obviously senior, and a tall dark one so handsome that Mrs Pickering could hardly take her eyes off him. The senior introduced himself as Detective Inspector Tarrant and his colleague as Detective Sergeant Benton-Smith. Mrs Fraser, shaking hands with him, gave him a look which suggested that she wasn't sure if police officers should be as good looking as this. Mrs Pickering told her story again while Mrs Fraser, exerting considerable self-control, stood by, prepared to correct any small inaccuracies and to save her colleague from police harassment.

Inspector Tarrant put on gloves before handling the bag and slipping it into a large plastic envelope which he then sealed, writing something on the flap. He said, 'We're grateful to you two ladies for letting us know about this. The bag may well be of interest. If it is, we need to know who's handled it. Do you think you could come with us now and have your fingerprints taken? They're needed, of course, for the purposes of elimination. They'll be destroyed if and when they're no longer required.'

Mrs Pickering had imagined herself driving in splendour to New Scotland Yard in Victoria Street. She had seen the revolving sign often enough on television. Instead, and somewhat to her disappointment, they were taken to the local police station where their fingerprints were taken with the minimum of fuss. As each of Mrs Pickering's fingers was gently taken and rolled on the pad, she felt all the excitement of a totally new experience and chattered happily about the process. Mrs Fraser, retaining her dignity, merely asked what procedure was followed to ensure the prints would be destroyed when appropriate. Within half an hour they were back in the shop and settling down to a fresh cup of coffee. After the excitement of the morning both felt they needed it.

Mrs Pickering said, 'They took it all very calmly, didn't they? They didn't tell us anything, not really. Do you think the handbag really is important?'

'Of course it is, Grace. They wouldn't have taken all that trouble and asked for our fingerprints if it isn't.' She was about to add, *all that apparent indifference is just their cunning*, but said instead, 'I thought it rather unnecessary of that senior officer, Inspector Tarrant, to hint that if this came out it would have to be we two who were responsible. After all, we did give him our assurance that we wouldn't tell anyone and we're obviously both responsible women. That should have been sufficient for him.'

'Oh Elinor, I don't think he was hinting that. It's a pity, though, isn't it? I always like to have something to tell John at the end of the day when I've been here. I think he enjoys hearing about the people I've met, particularly the customers. Some of them have such interesting stories once you get talking, haven't they? It seems a shame not to be able to share the most exciting thing that's ever happened.'

Privately Mrs Fraser agreed. Returning in the police car she had impressed on Mrs Pickering the need for silence but she was already contemplating perfidy. She had no intention of not telling her husband. After all, Cyril was a magistrate and knew the importance of keeping a secret. She said, 'I'm afraid your John will have to wait. It would be disastrous if this got round the golf course. And you have to remember, Grace, that it was you who actually found the handbag. You may be wanted as a witness.'

'Good gracious!' Mrs Pickering paused, coffee cup half-way to her lips, then replaced it in the saucer. 'You mean I'd have to go into the witness-box? I'd have to attend court?'

'Well, they'll hardly hold the trial in the public lavatory!'

Really, thought Mrs Pickering, for the daughter-in-law of a previous Lord Mayor, sometimes Elinor could be very crude.

7

The meeting with Sir Daniel Holstead had been arranged for half-past nine, a time suggested by Sir Daniel when he rang Dalgliesh an hour earlier. It would hardly give him and his wife a chance to recover from the flight but their anxiety to hear from the police first had been imperative. Dalgliesh doubted whether either of them had slept except in snatches since learning the news. He thought it prudent as well as considerate to see the couple himself, taking Kate with him. Their address, in a modern block in Brook Street, had a commissionaire at the reception desk who scrutinized their warrant cards and announced them by telephone, then showed them to a lift controlled by a security device. He punched out the numbers, then ushered them in and said, 'You just press the button there, sir. It's a private lift that goes straight to Sir Daniel's apartment.'

The lift was fitted with a low padded seat along one side and three of the walls were lined with mirrors. Dalgliesh saw himself and Kate reflected in an apparently unending line. Neither of them spoke. The upward journey was swift and the lift came gently to a stop. Almost at once the doors opened silently.

They found themselves in a wide corridor with a series of doors opening on either side. The wall facing them was hung with a double row of prints of exotic birds. As they stepped out of the lift, they saw two women coming towards them soundlessly on the soft carpet. One, in a black trouser suit and with a look of slightly intimidating self-confidence, had the brisk efficiency of a personal assistant. The other, fair-haired and younger, was wearing a white overall and carrying a folded massage table, the straps slung over one shoulder.

The older woman said, 'Until tomorrow then, Miss Murchison. If you can be through in an hour I can fit you in before the hair appointment and manicure. It will mean your arriving fifteen minutes early. I know Lady Holstead dislikes hurrying a massage.'

The masseuse stepped into the lift and the door closed. Then the woman turned to Dalgliesh. 'Commander Dalgliesh? Sir Daniel and Lady Holstead are expecting you. Will you come this way, please?'

She had taken no notice of Kate, nor did she introduce herself. They followed her down the corridor to a door which she opened with easy confidence and announced, 'Commander Dalgliesh and his colleague, Lady Holstead,' then closed the door behind her.

The room was low but large with four windows looking out over Mayfair. It was richly, indeed luxuriously, furnished in the style of an expensive hotel suite. Despite an arrangement of photographs in silver frames on a side-table beside the fireplace, there was little to indicate individual taste. The fireplace was ornate and in marble, and clearly hadn't originally been part of the room. There was a fitted carpet in silver grey and over it an assortment of large rugs, the colours a brighter version of the satin cushions, sofas and armchairs. Over the fireplace was a large portrait of a fair-haired woman in a scarlet ball-gown.

The subject of the portrait was sitting beside the fire, but as Dalgliesh and Kate entered, she rose in one elegant movement and came towards them, stretching out a tremulous hand. Her husband had been standing behind her chair but now he too came forward and put his hand under her forearm. The impression was of delicate feminine anguish supported by impressive masculine strength. Gently he led her back to the chair.

Sir Daniel was a large man, broad of shoulder, heavy featured and with strong iron-grey hair brushed back from a wide forehead. His eyes were rather small above the double pouches and the look they fixed on Dalgliesh gave nothing away. Looking at his bland unrevealing face sparked off for Dalgliesh a childhood memory. A multimillionaire, in an age when a million meant something, had been brought to dinner at the rectory by a local landowner who was one of his father's church-wardens. He too had been a big man, affable, an easy guest. The fourteen-year-old Adam had been disconcerted to discover during the dinner conversation that he was rather stupid. He had then learned that the ability to make a great deal of money in a particular way is a talent highly advantageous to its possessor and possibly beneficial to others, but implies no virtue, wisdom or intelligence beyond expertise in a lucrative field. Dalgliesh reflected that it was easy but dangerous to stereotype the very rich, but they did hold qualities in common, among them the self-confident exercise of power. Sir Daniel might possibly be impressed by a high court judge, but he could certainly take a commander of the Metropolitan Police and a detective inspector in his stride.

His wife said, 'Thank you for coming so quickly. Let's all sit down, shall we?' She looked at Kate. 'I'm sorry, I didn't realize you wouldn't be alone.'

Dalgliesh introduced Kate and the four of them moved to the two immense sofas set at right angles to the fire. Dalgliesh would have preferred almost any other seat in the room to this smothering opulence. He sat forward on the edge and looked across at the two Holsteads.

He said, 'I'm sorry we had to give you such terrible news, and by telephone. It's too early to give you very much information about how Miss Mellock died, but I'll do what I can.'

Lady Holstead leaned forward. 'Oh do, please do. One feels so utterly helpless. I don't think I've taken it in yet. I almost expected you to say that it's some terrible mistake. Please forgive me if I'm not more coherent. The flight . . .' She broke off.

Her husband said, 'You could have broken the news with more tact, Commander. The female officer who telephoned – I presume it was you, Inspector Miskin – was hardly considerate. I was given no indication that the call was particularly important.'

Dalgliesh said, 'We wouldn't have telephoned you and woken you at that hour if this had been a minor matter. I'm sorry if you feel that the news was insensitively broken. Obviously Inspector Miskin wanted to speak to you rather than Lady Holstead so that you could decide how best to tell her.'

Lady Holstead turned to him. 'And you were sweet, darling. You did your best, but you can't really break news like that gently, can you? Not really. Telling a mother her child has been murdered, there's no way of softening it. None.'

The distress, Dalgliesh thought, was genuine enough. How could it be otherwise? It was unfortunate that everything about Lady Holstead suggested a certain theatricality that was close to falseness. She was dressed to perfection in a black suit reminiscent of a military uniform, short-skirted and with a row of small brass buttons at the cuffs. The blonde hair looked as if it had been recently set and her makeup, the careful shading of rouge on the cheekbones and the meticulous outlining of the lips, could not have been achieved except with a steady hand. Her skirt was drawn up above her knees and she sat with her shapely thin legs stretched side by side, the bones sharp under the sheen of the fine nylon. You could see this perfection as the courage of a woman who preferred to face life's tragedies as well as its minor imperfections looking her best. He could see no resemblance to her daughter, but that was hardly surprising. Violent death erased more than the semblance of life.

Her husband, like Dalgliesh, was sitting well forward on the sofa, his arms dangling between his knees. His face was impassive and his eyes, fixed for most of the time on his wife's face, were watchful. He couldn't, thought Dalgliesh, be expected to feel a personal loss for a girl whom he had hardly known and who had probably been an irritant in his busy life. And now he was faced with this very public tragedy for which he would be expected to show appropriate feeling. He was probably no different from other men. He wanted domestic peace with a happy – or at least contented – wife, not a perpetually grieving mother. But all this would pass. She would forgive herself for being unloving, perhaps by persuading herself that she *had* loved her child, however unrewardingly, perhaps more rationally by accepting that one cannot love even a child by an act of will. She now seemed more confused than grief-stricken, holding out her arms to Dalgliesh in a gesture more histrionic than pathetic. Her nails were long and painted a bright red.

She said, 'I still can't believe it. Even with you here it doesn't make sense. Coming over in the jet I imagined that we'd touch down and she'd be there waiting, explaining that it was all a mistake. If I saw her I'd believe it, but I don't want to see her. I don't think I could bear that. I don't have to see her, do I? They can't make me do that.'

She turned imploring eyes on her husband. Sir Daniel was having difficulty in keeping the impatience out of his voice. 'Of course they can't. If it's necessary, I'll identify her.'

She turned her eyes to Dalgliesh. 'To have your child die before you, it's not natural, it's not meant to be.'

'No,' he said. 'It's not meant to be.'

His own child, a boy, had died with his mother soon after his birth. They were stealing into his mind more often now than they had for years, bringing back long-dormant memories: the dead young wife; that early impulsive marriage when giving her what she so desperately wanted – himself – had seemed so slight a

431

gift; the face of his stillborn son with its look of almost smug contentment, as if he who had known nothing, would never know anything, now knew it all. Grief for his lost son had been subsumed in the greater agony of his wife's death and in an overwhelming sense of participating in a universal sorrow, of becoming part of something not previously understood. But the long years had gradually laid down their merciful cicatrice. He still lit a candle for her on the anniversary of her death because that was what she would have wanted, but he could think of her now with nostalgic sadness and without pain. And now, if all went well, there might still be a child, his and Emma's. That such a thought, compounded of fear and an unfounded longing, should come into his mind at this moment unnerved him.

He was aware of the intensity of Lady Holstead's gaze. Something passed between them which she could believe was a moment of shared sympathy. She said, 'You do understand, don't you? I can see you do. And you will find out who killed her? Promise me that.'

He said, 'We shall do all we can, but we need your help. We know very little of your daughter's life, her friends, her interests. Do you know if there's anyone close to her, someone she might have gone to meet at the Dupayne Museum?'

She looked helplessly at her husband. He said, 'I don't think you've grasped the situation, Commander. I thought I'd made it clear that my stepdaughter lived as an independent woman. She came into her money on her eighteenth birthday, bought the London flat and virtually moved out of our lives.'

His wife turned to him. 'The young do, darling. They want to be independent. I understood that, we both did.'

Dalgliesh asked, 'Before she moved, did she live here with you?'

Again it was Sir Daniel who replied. 'Normally, yes. But she spent some time at our house in Berkshire. We keep the minimum staff there and occasionally she would turn up, sometimes with friends. They used the house for parties, usually to the inconvenience of the staff.'

Dalgliesh asked, 'Did you or Lady Holstead meet any of these friends?'

'No. I imagine they were temporary hangers-on rather than friends. She never spoke of them. Even when we were in England we rarely saw her.'

Lady Holstead said, 'I think she resented my divorce from her father. And then, when he was killed in that air crash, she blamed me. If we'd been together he wouldn't have been on that plane. She adored Rupert.'

Sir Daniel said, 'So I'm afraid there's very little we can tell you. I know she was trying to become a pop star at one time and spending a great deal of money on singing lessons. She actually had an agent, but it came to nothing. Before she came of age we managed to persuade her to go to a finishing school, Swathling's, for a year. Her education had been very neglected. There was one school after another. Swathling's has a good reputation. But of course she didn't stay.'

Kate said, 'I don't know whether you know that Miss Caroline Dupayne, one of the trustees of the museum, is the Joint Principal at Swathling's.'

'You mean that Celia went to the museum to meet her?'

'Miss Dupayne says not, and it seems unlikely. But she may have known of the museum through that connection.'

'But surely someone saw her arriving? Someone must have noticed whom she was with.'

Dalgliesh said, 'The museum is understaffed and it is possible that both she and her killer got into the museum unobserved. It is also possible that her killer may have left that Friday night without being seen. At present we don't know. The fact that Dr Neville Dupayne was also murdered on that Friday suggests there may be a connection. But at present nothing can be said with any certainty. The investigation is in its very early stages. We shall, of course, keep you informed of progress. The autopsy is being carried out this morning. The cause of death, strangulation, was self-evident.'

Lady Holstead said, 'Please tell me that it was quick. Please say that she didn't suffer.'

'I think it was quick, Lady Holstead.' What else could he say? Why burden her with her child's final moment of utter terror?

Sir Daniel asked, 'When will the body be released?'

'The inquest will be opened tomorrow and adjourned. I don't know when the coroner will release the body.'

Sir Daniel said, 'We'll arrange a quiet funeral, a cremation. We'll be grateful for any help you can give in keeping the gawpers away.'

'We'll do what we can. The best way of ensuring privacy is to keep the place and time secret, if that's possible.'

Lady Holstead turned to her husband. 'But darling,

we can't just put her away as if she was nobody! Her friends will want to say goodbye. There ought at least to be a memorial service, a nice church somewhere. London would be most convenient. Hymns, flowers, something beautiful to celebrate her life – a service people will remember.'

She looked at Dalgliesh as if he could be expected to conjure up the appropriate setting, priest, organist, choir, congregation and flowers.

It was her husband who spoke. 'Celia never went near a church in her life. If a murder is notorious or tragic enough you can fill a cathedral. I doubt whether that's the case here. I have no wish to provide a photo opportunity for the tabloid press.'

He could not have demonstrated his dominance more clearly. His wife looked at him, then her eyes fell and she said meekly, 'If that's what you think, darling.'

They left soon afterwards. Sir Daniel had asked, or rather demanded, to be kept in touch with the progress of the investigation and a guarded assurance had been repeated. There was nothing more to be learned and nothing more to be said. Sir Daniel saw them to the door of the lift, and then down to the ground floor. Dalgliesh wondered whether this courtesy was to give him an opportunity for a private word, but he said nothing.

In the car Kate was for a few minutes silent, then she said, 'I wonder how long it took her this morning to put on that make-up and paint her nails. Hardly the grieving mother, was she?'

Dalgliesh kept his eyes on the road ahead. He said, 'If it's important to her self-respect to face the day groomed and painted, if it's as normal a routine for her as a morning shower, do you expect her to neglect it just so that she can look appropriately distraught? The rich and the famous are as capable of murder as the rest of us; privilege doesn't confer immunity to the seven deadly sins. We should remember that they are also capable of other human emotions, including the confusing devastation of grief.'

He had been speaking quietly and to himself, but that is not how Kate heard him. Criticism came rarely from Dalgliesh but, when it did, she knew better than to attempt explanation or excuse. She sat red-faced and consumed with misery.

He went on, his voice gentler, as if the previous words had never been spoken. 'I'd like you and Piers to interview Lady Swathling. Find out if she's prepared to be more forthcoming about Celia Mellock than was Caroline Dupayne. They'll have consulted, of course. There's nothing we can do about that.'

It was then that Kate's mobile rang. Answering it she said, 'It's Benton-Smith, sir. He's just had a telephone call from a charity shop in Highgate. It looks as if they've found the handbag. Piers and Benton are on their way.'

8

Lady Swathling received Kate and Piers in what was obviously her office. Motioning them to a sofa with a gesture as contrived as a royal wave, she said, 'Please sit down. Can I offer you anything? Coffee? Tea? I know you're not supposed to drink on duty.'

To Kate's ears her tone managed to convey subtly that off duty they were commonly sunk in an alcoholic stupor. She said, before Piers could answer, 'No thank you. We won't need to interrupt you for long.'

The office had the discordant look of a dual-purpose room unsure of its primary function. The double desk before the south window, the computer, the fax machine, and the row of steel filing cabinets lining the wall to the left of the door constituted the office. The right side of the room had the comfortable domesticity of a sitting-room. In the elegant period fireplace, the simulated blue flames of a gas fire gave out a gentle heat supplementing the radiators. Above the mantelpiece with its row of small porcelain figurines was an oil painting. An eighteenth-century woman with pursed lips and protuberant eyes, in a low-necked dress of rich blue satin, was holding an orange in tapering fingers as delicately as if she expected it to explode. There was a cabinet against the farther wall containing a variety of porcelain cups and saucers in pink and green. To the right of the fire was a sofa and to the left a single armchair, their immaculate covers and cushions echoing the pale pinks and greens in the cabinet. The right-hand side of the room had been carefully contrived to produce a certain effect, of which Lady Swathling was part.

It was Lady Swathling who took the initiative. Before either Kate or Piers could speak, she said, 'You're here, of course, because of the tragedy at the Dupayne Museum, the death of Celia Mellock. Naturally I wish to help with your inquiries if I can, but it's difficult to see how you imagine that I can. Miss Dupayne surely told you that Celia left the school in the spring of last year after only two terms. I've absolutely no information about her subsequent life or activities.'

Kate said, 'In any case of homicide we need to know as much as possible about the victim. We're hoping you might be able to tell us something about Miss Mellock – her friends, perhaps, what she was like as a student, whether she was interested in visiting museums?'

'I'm afraid I can't. Surely these questions should be addressed to her family or to people who knew her. These two tragic deaths have nothing to do with Swathling's.'

Piers kept his eyes on Lady Swathling with a gaze that was half-admiring, half contemptuous. Kate recognized the look; he had taken against Lady Swathling. Now he said smoothly, 'But there is a connection, isn't there? Celia Mellock was a pupil here, Miss Dupayne is Joint Principal, Muriel Godby worked here and Celia died in the museum. I'm afraid in a case of homicide, Lady Swathling, questions have to be asked that are as inconvenient to the innocent as they are unwelcome to the guilty.'

Kate said to herself, *He thought that one out in advance. It's neat and he'll use it again.*

It had its effect on Lady Swathling. She said, 'Celia wasn't a satisfactory student, largely because she was an unhappy child and had absolutely no interest in what we have to offer. Miss Dupayne was reluctant to accept her but Lady Holstead, with whom I am acquainted, was very persuasive. The girl had been expelled from two of her previous schools and her mother and stepfather were anxious that she should get some education. Unfortunately Celia came under protest, which is never a helpful beginning. As I have told you, I know nothing about her recent life. I saw very little of her while she was at Swathling's and we never met after she had left.'

Kate asked, 'How well did you know Dr Neville Dupayne, Lady Swathling?'

The question was met with a mixture of distaste and incredulity. 'I've never met him. As far as I know, he's never visited the school. Mr Marcus Dupayne came to one of our students' concerts about two years ago, but not his brother. We've never even spoken by telephone and we've certainly never met.'

Kate asked, 'He was never called in to treat any of your students? Celia Mellock, for example?'

'Certainly not. Has anyone suggested such a thing?'

'No one, Lady Swathling. I just wondered.'

Piers intervened, 'What relationship was there between Celia and Muriel Godby?'

'Absolutely none. Why should there be? Miss Godby

was merely the receptionist. She wasn't popular with some of the girls, but as far as I can remember Celia Mellock made no complaint.' She paused, then said, 'And in case you were thinking of asking – which I must say I would greatly have resented – I was in college the whole of last Friday from three o'clock, when I returned from a luncheon date, for the rest of the day and evening. My afternoon engagements are listed in my desk diary and my visitors, including my lawyer who arrived at half-past four, will be able to confirm my movements. I'm sorry I can't be more helpful. If anything relevant should come to mind I shall, of course, get in touch.'

Kate said, 'And you are sure that you never saw Celia after she left Swathling's?'

'I have already said so, Inspector. And now, if there are no more questions, I have matters I need to attend to. I shall, of course, write a letter of sympathy to Lady Holstead.'

She rose from her chair in one swift movement and went to the door. Outside the uniformed porter who had let them in was already waiting. No doubt, thought Kate, he had been stationed there throughout the interview.

As they reached the car, Piers said, 'Artificial set-up, wasn't it? No prizes for guessing her priorities, self first and the school second. Did you see the difference in those two desks? One practically empty, the in and out trays on the other full of papers. No prizes, either, for guessing who sits where. Lady Swathling impresses the parents with her aristocratic elegance and Caroline Dupayne does all the work.'

'Why should she? What's she getting out of it?'

'Perhaps she hopes to take over. She wouldn't get the house, though, unless it's willed to her. Perhaps that's what she's hoping for. I can't see her affording it.'

Kate said, 'I imagine she's well paid for what she does. What I find interesting is not why Dupayne stays here, but why she's so keen on keeping the museum open.'

Piers said, 'Family pride. The flat is her home. She must want to get away from the school occasionally. You didn't take to Lady S, did you?'

'Or to the school. Nor did you. Kind of privileged place the bloody rich send their kids to in the hope of getting them out of their hair. Both parties know what the bargain is, what the parents are paying through the nose for. See she doesn't get pregnant, keep her off the drugs and booze and make sure she meets the right kind of men.'

'That's a bit harsh. I once dated a girl who'd been there. It didn't seem to have done her much harm. Not exactly Oxbridge entrance, but she knew how to cook. That wasn't her only talent.'

'And you, of course, were the right kind of man.'

'Her mama didn't think so. Do you want to drive?'

'You'd better, until I simmer down. So we report to AD that Lady S probably knows something but isn't talking?'

'You're suggesting she's a suspect?'

'No. She wouldn't have given us that alibi if she didn't know it would stand up. We'll check if we need to. At present it would be a waste of time. She's in the clear for both murders, but she could be an accomplice.'

Piers was dismissive. 'That's going a bit far. Look at the facts. At present we're assuming that the two deaths are connected. That means that if Lady S is mixed up with Celia's death, she's mixed up also with Neville Dupayne's. And if one thing she said struck me as true, it was her claim that she's never even met him. And why should she care if the museum closes? It might even suit her, keep Caroline Dupayne more closely tied to the school. No, she's in the clear. OK, there's something she either lied about or isn't telling, but what's new about that?'

9

It was three fifteen on Thursday 7 November and in
the incident room the team were discussing progress.
Benton-Smith had earlier brought in sandwiches and
Dalgliesh's PA had provided a large cafetière of strong
coffee. Now all evidence of the meal had been cleared
away and they settled down to their papers and
notebooks.

The discovery of the handbag had been interesting
but had got them no further. Any of the suspects could
have shoved it into the black bag whether the ploy
had been planned or decided on impulse. It was an idea
which might occur more readily to a woman than a
man, but that was hardly firm evidence. They were still
awaiting information from the mobile telecommunica-
tions service about the location of Muriel Godby's mobile
when she answered Tally Clutton's call. The demands
on the service were heavy and there were other priority
requests. Inquiries put in hand about Neville Dupayne's
professional life before he moved to London from the
Midlands in 1987 had resulted only in silence from the
local police force. None of this was particularly dis-
appointing; the case was still less than a week old.

Now Kate and Piers were to report on their visit to
Celia's flat. A little to Dalgliesh's surprise Kate was silent
and it was Piers who spoke. Within seconds it was

apparent that he was enjoying himself. In short staccato sentences the picture came alive.

'It's a ground-floor flat looking out on a central garden. Trees, flowerbeds, well-kept lawn, on the expensive side of the block. Grilles in the windows and two security locks on the door. Large sitting-room at the front, and three double bedrooms with bathrooms *en suite*. Probably bought as an investment on the advice of Daddy's lawyer and at present prices worth over a million, I'd say. Aggressively modern kitchen. No sign that anyone bothers to cook. The refrigerator's stinking with sour milk and out-of-date cartons of eggs and supermarket meals. She left the place in a mess. Clothes strewn all over her own bed and those in the other two rooms, cupboards stuffed, wardrobes crammed. About fifty pairs of shoes, twenty handbags, some hooker-chic dresses designed to show as much thigh and crotch as possible without risking arrest. Most of the rest of the stuff expensive designer gear. Not much luck from examining her desk. She didn't go in for paying the bills on demand or for answering official letters, even those from her lawyers. A City firm looks after her portfolio, the usual mixture of equities and government stock. She was getting through the money pretty quickly though.'

Dalgliesh asked, 'Any sign of a lover?'

Now it was Kate who took over. 'There are stains on a fitted bottom sheet stuffed into the clothes basket. They look like semen but they're not fresh. Nothing else. She was on the pill. We found the packet in the bathroom cupboard. No drugs but plenty to drink. She seems to have tried modelling, there's a portfolio of photographs. She'd also set her heart on being a pop star. We know that she was on the books of that agency and she was paying through the nose for singing lessons. I think she was being exploited. What's odd, sir, is that we found no invitations, no evidence she had friends. You'd think that with a three-bedroom flat she'd want to share, if only for company and to help with expenses. There's no evidence of anyone being there except herself, apart from that stained sheet. We had our murder bags with us so we put it in an exhibit pouch and brought it away. I've sent it to the lab.'

Dalgliesh asked, 'Books? Pictures?'

Kate said, 'Every woman's magazine on the market including fashion magazines. Paperbacks, mostly popular fiction. There are photographs of pop stars. Nothing else.' She added, 'We didn't find either a diary or an address book. She may've had them in her handbag, in which case her murderer has them if they haven't been destroyed. There was a message on her answerphone; the local garage rang to say that her car was ready for collection. If she didn't come with her killer it was probably by taxi – I can't see a girl like that taking a bus. We've been on to the public carriage office in the hope they can trace the driver. There were no other answerphone messages and no private letters. It was odd: all that clutter and no evidence of a social or personal life. I felt sorry for her. I think she was lonely.'

Piers was dismissive. 'I can't think why the hell she should be. We know the modern holy trinity is money, sex and celebrity. She had the first two and had hope of the third.'

Kate said, 'No realistic hope.'

'But she had money. We saw the bank statements and the investment portfolio. Daddy left her two and a half million. Not a vast fortune by modern standards but you could live on it. A girl with that kind of money and her own flat in London doesn't have to be lonely for long.'

Kate said, 'Not unless she's needy, the sort that falls in love, clings and won't let go. Money or no money, men may've seen her as bad luck.'

Piers said, 'One of them obviously did and took pretty effective action.' There was a silence, then he went on, 'Chaps would have to be pretty unfastidious to put up with that mess. There was a note pushed through the door from her cleaning woman, saying that she wouldn't be able to come on the Thursday because she had to take her kid to hospital. I hope she got well paid.'

Dalgliesh's quiet voice broke in. 'If you get yourself murdered, Piers, which is not entirely beyond the bounds of possibility, we must hope that the investigating officer who rummages among your intimate possessions won't be too censorious.'

Piers said gravely, 'It's a possibility I keep in mind, sir. At least he'll find them in good order.'

I deserved that, thought Dalgliesh. It had always been a part of his job which he found difficult, the total lack of privacy for the victim. Murder stripped away more than life itself. The body was parcelled, labelled, dissected; address books, diaries, confidential letters, every part of the victim's life was sought out and scrutinized. Alien hands moved among the clothes, picked up and examined the small possessions, recorded and labelled for public view the sad detritus of sometimes pathetic lives. This life too, outwardly privileged, had been pathetic. The picture they now had was of a rich but vulnerable and friendless girl, seeking entry into a world which even her money couldn't buy.

He said, 'Have you sealed the flat?'

'Yes sir. And we've interviewed the caretaker. He lives in a flat on the north side. He's only been in the post for six months and knows nothing about her.'

Dalgliesh said, 'That note through the door, it looks as if the cleaning woman isn't trusted with a key unless, of course, someone delivered the letter for her. We may need to trace her. What about Brian Clark and his team?'

'They'll be there first thing tomorrow, sir. The sheet's obviously important. We've got that. I doubt they'll find much else. She wasn't killed there, it isn't a murder scene.'

Dalgliesh said, 'But the SOCOs had better take a look. You and Benton-Smith could meet them there. Some of the near neighbours might have information about possible visitors.'

They turned to Dr Kynaston's post-mortem report which had been received an hour previously. Taking his copy, Piers said, 'Attending one of Doc Kynaston's PMs may be instructive, but it's hardly therapeutic. It isn't so much the remarkable thoroughness and precision of his butchery, it's his choice of music. I don't expect a chorus from *The Yeoman of the Guard*, but *Agnus Dei* from Fauré's *Requiem* is hard to take given the circumstances. I thought you were going to keel over, Sergeant.'

Glancing at Benton-Smith, Kate saw his face darken and the black eyes harden into polished coal. But he took the gibe without flinching and said calmly, 'So for a moment did I.' He paused, then looked at Dalgliesh. 'It was my first with a young woman victim, sir.'

Dalgliesh had his eyes on the PM report. He said, 'Yes, they're always the worst, young women and children. Anyone who can watch a PM on either without distress should ask himself whether he's in the right job. Let's see what Dr Kynaston has to tell us.'

The pathologist's report confirmed what he had found on his first examination. The main pressure had been from the right hand squeezing the voice box and fracturing the superior *cornu* of the thyroid at its base. There was a small bruise at the back of the head suggesting that the girl had been forced back against the wall during strangulation, but no evidence of physical contact between the assailant and the victim, and no evidence under the nails to suggest that the girl had fought off the attack with her hands. An interesting finding was that Celia Mellock had been two months pregnant.

Piers said, 'So here we have a possible additional motive. She could have arranged to meet her lover either to discuss what they should do, or to pressurize him into marriage. But why choose the Dupayne? She had a flat of her own.'

Kate said, 'And with this girl, rich and sexually experienced, pregnancy is an unlikely motive for murder, no more than a little difficulty which could be got rid of by an overnight stay in an expensive clinic. And how come she was pregnant, when she was apparently on

448

the pill? Either it was deliberate or she had stopped bothering with contraception. The packet we found was unopened.'

Dalgliesh said, 'I don't think she was murdered because she was pregnant; she was murdered because of where she was. We have a single killer and the original and intended victim was Neville Dupayne.'

The picture, although as yet no more than supposition, came into his mind with astonishing clarity; that androgynous figure, its sex as yet unknown, turning on the tap at the corner of the garden shed. A strong spurt of water washing away all traces of petrol from the rubber-gloved hands. The furnace roar of the fire. And then, half-heard, the sound of breaking glass and the first crackle of wood as the flames leapt to catch the nearest tree. And what had made Vulcan look up at the house, a premonition or a fear that the fire might be getting out of control? It would have been in that upward glance that he saw, staring down at him from the Murder Room window, a wide-eyed girl with her yellow hair framed with fire. Was it in that one moment and with that single glimpse that Celia Mellock was doomed to die?

He heard Kate speaking. 'But we're still left with the problem of how Celia got into the Murder Room. One way would be through the door of Caroline Dupayne's flat. But if so, how did she get into the flat and why did she go there? And how could we prove it when it's perfectly possible that she and her killer got into the museum while the reception desk was unattended?'

It was then that the phone rang. Kate picked up the receiver, listened and said, 'Right, I'll come down at once.' She spoke to Dalgliesh. 'Tally Clutton has turned up, sir. She wants to see you. She says it's important.'

Piers said, 'It must be, to bring her here personally. I suppose it's too much to hope that at last she may have recognized the motorist.'

Kate was already at the door. Dalgliesh said, 'Put her in the small interview room, will you, Kate? I'll see her at once and with you.'

BOOK FOUR

The Third Victim

Thursday 7 November–
Friday 8 November

I

The police had said that the SOCOs would need the rest of Wednesday and half of Thursday to complete their search of the museum. They hoped to be able to return the keys by late afternoon on Thursday. The trunk had already been removed. After the inspection of Caroline Dupayne's flat by Commander Dalgliesh and Inspector Miskin it seemed to have been accepted that there was no justification for taking her keys and keeping her out of what essentially was her home.

Getting up early on Thursday as usual, Tally was restless, missing her early morning routine of dusting and cleaning. Now there was no shape to the day, only a disorientating sense that nothing was any longer real or recognizable and that she moved like an automaton in a world of horrifying fantasy. Even the cottage no longer offered a refuge from the prevailing sense of disassociation and mounting disaster. She still thought of it as the calm centre of her life, but with Ryan in residence its peace and order had been destroyed. It wasn't that he was being deliberately difficult; the cottage was just too small for two such discordant personalities. One lavatory, and that in the bathroom, was more than an inconvenience. She could never use it without the uncomfortable knowledge that he was waiting impatiently for her to come out, while he himself stayed in it for an unconscionable time, leaving wet towels in the bath and the soap messily congealing in the dish. He was personally very clean, bathing twice a day, so that Tally worried over the fuel bills, but he dumped his dirty working clothes on the floor for her to pick up and put in the washing machine. Keeping him fed was a problem. She had expected him to have different tastes in food but not that he would get through such quantities. He didn't offer to pay and she couldn't bring herself to suggest it. He had gone to bed early each night, but only to switch on his stereo. Loud pop music had made Tally's nights intolerable. Yesterday night, still in shock from the discovery of Celia Mellock's body, she had asked him to turn it down and he had complied without protest. But the noise, although more muted, was still an irritating nerve-racking beat which even tugging the pillow over her ears couldn't silence.

Immediately after breakfast on Thursday, when Ryan was still in bed, she decided to go to the West End. Uncertain how long she would be away, she didn't pack her rucksack but took only a commodious handbag and an orange and a banana for lunch. She took a bus to Hampstead station, went by Underground to Embankment, then walked up Northumberland Avenue, across the confusion of Trafalgar Square and into the Mall and St James's Park. This was one of her favourite London walks and gradually, as she circled the lake, it brought her a measure of peace. The unseasonable warmth had returned and she sat on a bench to eat her fruit in the mellow sunshine, watching the parents and children throwing bread to the ducks, the tourists photographing each other against the sheen of the water, the lovers strolling hand in hand, and the mysterious dark-coated men walking in pairs who always reminded her of high-ranking spies exchanging dangerous secrets.

By two-thirty, refreshed, she wasn't ready to return home and, after a final circle of the lake, decided instead to walk to the river. It was when she reached Parliament Square and was outside the Palace of Westminster that she decided on impulse to join the short queue for the House of Lords. She had visited the House of Commons, but not the Lords. It would be a new experience and it would be good to sit in peace for half an hour or so. The wait was not long. She passed through the rigorous security, had her bag searched, was issued with her pass and, as directed, climbed the carpeted stairs to the public gallery.

Pushing open the wooden door, she found herself high above the chamber and gazing down in amazement. She had seen it on television often enough, but now its sombre magnificence came splendidly alive. No one today could possibly create such a legislative chamber, the wonder was that anyone had thought to do so at any time. It was as if no ornamentation, no architectural conceit, no workmanship in gold and wood and stained glass could be considered too grand for those Victorian dukes, earls, marquises and barons. It was certainly successful – perhaps, thought Tally, because it had been built with confidence. The architect and the craftsmen had known what they were building for and had believed in what they knew. After all, she thought, we have our pretensions too; we built the Millennium Dome. The chamber reminded her a little of a cathedral, except that this was a purely secular building. The gold throne with its canopy and candelabra was a celebration of earthly kingship, the statues in the niches between the windows were of barons not saints, and the tall windows with their stained glass bore coats of arms, not scenes from the Bible.

The great golden throne was immediately opposite her and it dominated her mind as it did the chamber. If Britain ever became a republic, what would happen to it? Surely even the most anti-monarchist government wouldn't melt it down. But what museum room would be large enough to house it? What could it possibly be used for? Perhaps, she thought, a future president, lounge-suited, would sit in state under the canopy. Tally's worldly experience of state was limited but she had observed that those who had risen to power and status were as keen on their perquisites as those who had acquired them by birth. She was glad to be sitting down, grateful to have so much to occupy mind and eyes. Some of the anxieties of the day fell away.

Busy with her thoughts and obsessed with the chamber itself, she at first hardly noticed the figures on the red benches below. And then she heard his voice, clear and to her unmistakable. Her heart jolted. She looked down and he was standing in front of one of the benches that ran between those of the Government and the Opposition, his back towards her. He was saying, 'My Lords, I beg to ask the question standing in my name on the Order Paper.'

She almost clutched at the arm of a young man sitting

next to her. She whispered urgently, 'Who is that, please? Who is speaking?'

He frowned and held out a paper to her. Without looking at her, he said, 'Lord Martlesham, a cross-bencher.'

She sat stiffly, leaning forward, her eyes on the back of his head. If only he would turn! How could she be certain unless she saw his face? Surely he must somehow sense the intensity of her downward gaze. She didn't take in the Minister's reply to the question or the inter-vention of other peers. And now Question Time was over and the next business was being announced. A group of members was leaving the chamber and, as he rose from the crossbenches to join them, she saw him clearly.

She didn't look at Lord Martlesham again. She had no need to verify that moment of instant recognition. She might possibly have been mistaken in the voice, but voice and face together brought an overwhelming conviction which left no scintilla of doubt. She didn't believe; she knew.

And now she found herself on the pavement outside St Stephen's entrance with no memory of how she had got there. The street was as busy as in the throes of the tourist season. Churchill, from his plinth, gazed in bronze solidity at his beloved House of Commons across a street jammed with hardly moving taxis, cars and buses. A policeman was holding up pedestrians to direct Members' cars into the courtyard to the House of Com-mons and a stream of tourists, cameras slung across their shoulders, were waiting for the traffic lights to change before making their way over the crossing to the Abbey. Tally joined them. She had become aware of an insistent need for quietness and solitude. She needed to sit and think. But there was already a long queue waiting at the north door of the Abbey; it would be difficult to find peace there. Instead she entered St Margaret's Church and sat in a pew half-way down the nave.

There were a few visitors, walking and speaking quietly as they paused before the monuments, but she neither noticed nor heard them. The stained glass eastern window, made as part of the dowry of Katharine of Aragon, the two niches with the kneeling Prince Arthur and Princess Katharine and the two saints standing above them, had been a source of wonderment on her first visit, but now she gazed at them with unseeing eyes. She wondered why she was overcome by this tumult of emotions. After all, she had seen Dr Neville's body. That charred image would revisit her in dreams all her life. And now there was this second death, multiplying horror, the corpse more vivid in imagination than if she had actually lifted the lid of the trunk. But in neither case had she been required to take responsibility until now. She had told the police all she knew. Nothing more was asked of her. Now she was intimately involved in murder, as if its contamination were running in her veins. She was faced with a personal decision; that it was one where her duty was clear provided no relief. She knew she had to act – Scotland Yard was only half a mile up Victoria Street – but she needed to face the implications of her action. Lord Martlesham would be the chief suspect. He had to be. Her evidence made that clear. That he was a member of the House of Lords didn't weigh with her; it scarcely entered her mind. She wasn't a woman to whom status was important. Her problem was that she didn't believe that the man who had bent over her with such anguished concern was a murderer. But if the evidence couldn't be found to exonerate him he might well stand trial, might even be found guilty. It wouldn't be the first time that the innocent had been convicted. And suppose the case were never solved, wouldn't he be branded a murderer all his life? And she was troubled by a less rational conviction of his innocence. Somewhere in the recesses of her mind, inaccessible either by racking thought or by quiet meditation, was something she knew, a single fact which she should have remembered and told.

She found herself reverting to an old device of her youth. When faced with a problem, she would conduct an internal monologue with a silent voice, which she sometimes recognized as that of conscience, but more often as a sceptical common sense, an uncomplicated *alter ego*.

You know what you have to do. What happens afterwards isn't your responsibility.

I feel as if it is.

Then if you want to feel responsible, accept responsibility. You saw what happened to Dr Neville. If Lord Martlesham is guilty, do you want him to go free? If he's innocent, why hasn't he come forward? If innocent, he may have information that could lead to the killer. Time is important. Why are you hesitating?

I need to sit quietly and think.

Think about what, and for how long? If Commander Dalgliesh asks where you've been since leaving the House of Lords, what are you going to tell him? That you've been in church praying for guidance?

I'm not praying. I know what I have to do.

Then get on and do it. This is the second murder. How many deaths do there have to be before you find the courage to tell what you know?

Tally got to her feet and, walking more firmly now, pushed her way through the heavy door of St Margaret's and walked up Victoria Street to New Scotland Yard. On her previous visit she had been driven there by Sergeant Benton-Smith and had journeyed in hope. But she had left feeling that she had been a failure, had let them all down. None of the photographs shown to her and no features cunningly fitted together had borne any resemblance to the man they sought. Now she was bringing Commander Dalgliesh good news. So why did she come with such a heavy heart?

She was received at the desk. She had thought out carefully what she would say. 'Can I see Commander Dalgliesh, please? I'm Mrs Tallulah Clutton from the Dupayne Museum. It's about the murders. I have some important information.'

The officer on duty showed no surprise. He repeated her name and reached for the telephone. He said, 'I have a Mrs Tallulah Clutton to see Commander Dalgliesh about the Dupayne murders. She says it's important.' A few seconds later he replaced the receiver and turned to Tally. 'One of Commander Dalgliesh's team will come down for you. Inspector Miskin. Do you know Inspector Miskin?'

'Oh yes, I do know her, but I'd rather speak to Mr Dalgliesh, please.'

'Inspector Miskin will take you to the Commander.'

She sat down on the seat indicated against the wall. As usual she was carrying her handbag slung over one shoulder, the strap across her chest. Suddenly she felt that this precaution against theft must look odd; she was, after all, in New Scotland Yard. She slipped the strap over her head and held the bag tightly in her lap with both hands. Suddenly she felt very old.

Inspector Miskin appeared surprisingly quickly. Tally wondered whether they were afraid that, left to wait, she might change her mind and leave. But Inspector Miskin greeted her calmly and with a smile, and led the way to the bank of lifts. The corridor was busy. When the lift arrived they crowded in with half a dozen tall and largely silent men and were borne upstairs. They were alone when the lift came to a stop but she didn't notice what button had been pressed.

The interview room which they entered was intimidatingly small, the furniture spare and functional. She saw a square table with two upright chairs each side, and some kind of recording equipment on a stand at the side.

As if reading her thoughts, Inspector Miskin said, 'It's not very cosy I'm afraid, but we won't be disturbed here. Commander Dalgliesh will be with you directly. The view is good though, isn't it? We've ordered some tea.'

Tally moved over to the window. Below her she could see the twin towers of the Abbey and, beyond, Big Ben and the Palace of Westminster. Cars cruised like miniature toys and the pedestrians were foreshortened manikins. She watched it all without emotion, listening only for the door to open.

He entered very quietly and came over to her. She was so relieved to see him that she had to restrain herself from running towards him. He led her to a chair and he and Inspector Miskin sat down opposite.

Without preamble, Tally said, 'I've seen the motorist who knocked me down. I've been to the House of Lords today. He was there on the crossbenches. His name is Lord Martlesham.'

Commander Dalgliesh said, 'Did you hear him speak?'

'Yes. It was Question Time and he asked a question. I knew him at once.'

'Can you be more specific? Which did you recognize first, the voice or the appearance? Crossbench peers would have their back to the public gallery. Did you see his face?'

'Not when he spoke. But it was the end of Question Time. He was the last one. After he'd been given an answer and one or two other peers had spoken, they went on to other business. It was then that he got up and turned to go out. I saw his face.'

It was Inspector Miskin, not Commander Dalgliesh, who asked the expected question. 'Are you absolutely sure, Mrs Clutton? So sure that you could stand up to hostile questioning in the Crown Court and not be shaken?'

It was to Commander Dalgliesh that Tally looked. She said, 'Absolutely sure.' She paused, then asked, trying to keep the note of anxiety out of her voice, 'Will I have to identify him?'

Commander Dalgliesh said, 'Not yet, and possibly not at all. It will depend on what he has to tell us.'

She said, looking into his eyes, 'He's a good man, isn't he? And he was concerned about me. I couldn't be mistaken about that. I can't believe . . .' She broke off.

Commander Dalgliesh said, 'He may have a perfectly innocent explanation for what he was doing at the Dupayne and why he hasn't come forward. He may have useful information which can help us. It was very important to find him and we're grateful.'

Inspector Miskin said, 'It's lucky you went to the Lords today. Why did you? Was the visit planned?'

Quietly Tally gave an account of her day, her eyes on Dalgliesh – the need to get away, at least temporarily, from the museum; the walk and picnic lunch in St James's Park; the decision on impulse to visit the House of Lords. There was no triumph in her voice. It seemed to Dalgliesh, listening, that she was seeking his reassurance that this confession wasn't an act of treachery. After she had finished her tea, which she had drunk thirstily, he tried to persuade her to accept a lift home in a police car, gently assuring her that she wouldn't arrive with a blue light flashing. Equally gently but firmly she refused. She would make her own way back as usual. Perhaps, he thought, it was just as well. For Tally to arrive chauffeur-driven would almost certainly have attracted comment at the museum. He had asked for her silence and could be sure that she would keep her promise, but he didn't want her bothered by questions. She was an honest woman for whom lying would be repugnant.

He went down with her and said goodbye outside the building. As their hands clasped, she looked up at him and said, 'This is going to be trouble for him, isn't it?'

'Some trouble, perhaps. But if he's an innocent man he'll know he has nothing to fear. You did the right thing in coming, but I think you know that.'

'Yes,' she said, at last turning away. 'I know it, but it isn't any comfort.'

Dalgliesh returned to the incident room. Piers and Benton-Smith were put in the picture by Kate. They listened without comment, then Piers asked the obvious question. 'How certain was she, sir? There'll be one hell of a stink if we get this wrong.'

'She said there was no doubt. The recognition came as soon as Martlesham got to his feet and spoke. Seeing him full-face confirmed it.'

Piers said, 'Voice before face? That's odd. And how can she be so sure? She only saw him bending over her for a few seconds and under a dim streetlamp.'

Dalgliesh said, 'Whatever the sequence of her thought processes, whether what determined the identification was appearance, voice or both, she is adamant it was Martlesham who knocked her down last Friday night.'

Kate asked, 'What do we know about him, sir? He's some kind of philanthropist, isn't he? I've read about him taking clothes, food and medical supplies to where they're most needed. Didn't he go to Bosnia driving a truck himself? There was something about it in the broadsheets. Tally Clutton may have seen his photograph.'

Piers went over to take *Who's Who* from the bookcase and brought it over to the table. He said, 'It's a hereditary title, isn't it? Which means he was one of the hereditaries elected to remain in the House after that first botched reform, so he must have proved his worth. Didn't someone refer to him as the conscience of the crossbenchers?'

Dalgliesh said, 'Hardly. Aren't the crossbenchers a conscience in themselves? You're right about the philanthropy, Kate. He set up that scheme whereby the rich lend money to those who can't get credit. It's similar to the local credit unions but the loans are interest-free.'

Piers was reading aloud from *Who's Who*. 'Charles Montague Seagrove Martlesham. Quite a late peerage, created 1836. Born third October 1955, educated usual places, succeeded 1972. His father died young, apparently. Married a general's daughter. No children. So far conforms to type. Hobbies – music, travel. Address – The Old Rectory, Martlesham, Suffolk. No ancestral house it seems. Trustee of an impressive number of charities. And this is the man we are about to suggest is guilty of a double murder. Should be interesting.'

Dalgliesh said, 'Contain your excitement, Piers. The old objections still apply. Why should a man fleeing from the scene of a particularly hideous murder stop to check that he hasn't hurt an elderly woman knocked off her bicycle?'

Kate asked, 'Will you warn him, sir?'

'I'll tell him I want to see him in connection with a

current murder investigation. If he feels the need to bring his lawyer with him, that's his decision. At this stage I don't think he will.' He seated himself at his desk. 'He's probably still at the House. I'll write a note asking him to see me as soon as possible. Benton-Smith can deliver it and escort him here. Martlesham's almost certainly got some kind of London address and we could go there if he prefers, but I think he'll come back with Benton.'

Kate walked over to the window and waited while Dalgliesh wrote. She said, 'He's an unlikely murderer, sir.'

'So are all the others – Marcus Dupayne, Caroline Dupayne, Muriel Godby, Tally Clutton, Mrs Faraday, Mrs Strickland, James Calder-Hale, Ryan Archer. One of them is a double murderer. After we've heard from Lord Martlesham we might be closer to knowing which.'

Kate turned and looked at him. 'But you know already, don't you, sir?'

'So I think do we all. But knowing and proving are two different things, Kate.'

Kate knew that he wouldn't speak the name until they were ready to make an arrest. Vulcan would remain Vulcan. And she thought she knew why. As a young detective constable, Dalgliesh had been involved in a murder investigation which had gone badly wrong. An innocent man had been arrested and convicted. As a new DC he had not been responsible for the mistake, but he had learned from it. For AD the greatest danger in a criminal investigation, particularly for murder, remained the same. It was the too easy fixing on a prime suspect, the concentration of effort to prove him guilty to the neglect of other lines of inquiry, and the inevitable corruption of judgement which made the team unable to contemplate that they might be wrong. A second principle was the need to avoid a premature arrest which would vitiate the success both of the investigation and of the subsequent court proceedings. The exception was the need to protect a third person. And surely, thought Kate, with this second murder Vulcan was no longer a danger. And it couldn't be long now. Sooner than she had thought possible, the end was in sight.

After Benton-Smith had left for the House of Lords, Dalgliesh sat for a minute in silence. Kate waited, then he said, 'I want you to drive to Swathling's now, Kate, and bring back Caroline Dupayne. She's not under arrest, but I think you'll find that she'll come, and it will be at our convenience, not hers.' Then, seeing Kate's look of surprise, he said, 'I may be taking a chance, but I'm confident that Tally Clutton's identification is right. And whatever Martlesham has to tell us, I have a strong feeling that it will be concerned with Caroline Dupayne and her private flat at the museum. If I'm wrong and there's no connection, I'll try to reach you on your mobile before you get to Richmond.'

2

Lord Martlesham arrived at the Yard within thirty minutes and was escorted up to Dalgliesh's office. He came in, composed but very pale, and seemed at first uncertain whether he was expected to shake hands. They sat opposite each other at the table in front of the window. Looking across at the bleached features, Dalgliesh had no doubt that Lord Martlesham knew why he had been summoned. The formality of his reception, the fact that he had been shown into this bleakly functional room, the bare expanse of pale wood between them, made their own statement. This was no social call and it was obvious that he had never supposed that it was. Looking at him, Dalgliesh could understand why Tally Clutton had found him attractive. His was one of those rare faces for which neither the word handsome or beautiful is entirely appropriate, but which show with a guileless vulnerability the essential nature of the man.

Without preamble, Dalgliesh said, 'Mrs Tallulah Clutton, the housekeeper at the Dupayne Museum, has this afternoon recognized you as the motorist who knocked her off her bicycle at about six twenty-five on Friday the first of November. On that night two people were murdered at the museum, Dr Neville Dupayne and Miss Celia Mellock. I have to ask you whether you were there and what you were doing.'

Lord Martlesham had been holding his hands in his lap. Now he raised them and clasped them on the table-top. The veins stood out like dark cords and the knuckles shone, white marbles under the taut skin. He said, 'Mrs Clutton is right. I was there and I did knock her down. I hope she wasn't more hurt than I thought. She did say she was all right.'

'She was only bruised. Why didn't you come forward earlier?'

'Because I hoped this moment would never happen. I was doing nothing illegal but I didn't want my movements to be known. That's why I hurried away.'

'But later, when you knew about the first murder, you must have realized that your evidence was material, that you had a duty to come forward.'

'Yes, I think I did know that. I also knew I had nothing to do with the murder. I didn't even know that the fire was deliberate. If I thought anything it was that someone had lit a bonfire and it had got out of control. I convinced myself that coming forward would only complicate the investigation and cause embarrassment to myself and to others. When I learned this morning of the second death, things became more complicated. I decided that I would still keep silent, but if I were identified, then I would tell the truth. I didn't see this as obstructing the course of justice. I knew I had nothing to do with either death. I'm not trying to defend myself, just explaining how it happened. It seemed unnecessary to come forward after Dr Dupayne's murder, and that decision affected what I did subsequently. With every passing hour it was more difficult to do what I accept was right.'

'So why were you there?'

'If you'd asked me that question after Dupayne's death, I would have told you that I was using the museum to get off the road and rest, and then I woke and realized I was late for an appointment and needed to hurry. I'm not a practised liar and I doubt whether it would have been convincing, but I think it might have been worth a try. Or, of course, I could have challenged Mrs Clutton's identification. It would have been her word against mine. But the second death has changed all that. I knew Celia Mellock. I went to the museum that night to meet her.'

There was a silence. Dalgliesh said, 'And did you?'

'No. She wasn't there. We were to meet in the car-park behind the laurel bushes to the right of the house. The time arranged was six-fifteen, the earliest I could manage. Even so, I was late. Her car wasn't there. I tried ringing her on her mobile, but there was no reply. I decided that she had never intended to be there, or had got tired of waiting, so I drove away. I wasn't expecting to meet anyone and I was driving faster than I should have been. Hence the accident.'

'What were your relations with Miss Mellock?'

'We had briefly been lovers. I wanted to break off the association and she didn't. It was as brutal as that. But she seemed to accept that it had to end. It should never have begun. But she asked me to meet her for the last time at the museum. It was our usual place of assignation, in the car-park. It's utterly deserted there at night. We'd never felt at risk of discovery. Even if we'd been seen, we weren't doing anything illegal.'

Again there was a silence. Martlesham had been looking down at his hands. Now he shifted them again and replaced them in his lap.

Dalgliesh said, 'You said you were here to tell the truth, but that isn't the truth, is it? Celia Mellock was found dead in the Murder Room of the museum. We believe she was killed in that room. Have you any idea how she got into the museum?'

Martlesham looked hunched in his chair. Without looking up, he said, 'No, none. Couldn't she have arrived earlier in the day, perhaps to meet someone else, and then hidden herself – in the basement archive room, say – and been trapped there, perhaps with her killer, when the doors were locked at five o'clock?'

'How do you know about the archive room and that the doors of the museum are locked at five?'

'I've been there. I mean, I've visited.'

'You're not the first person to put that forward as an explanation. I find that an interesting coincidence. But there's another way Celia Mellock could have got into the Murder Room, isn't there? Through the door from Caroline Dupayne's flat. Isn't that where you and she had arranged to meet?'

And now Lord Martlesham lifted his head and met Dalgliesh's eyes. It was a look of utter despair. He said, 'I didn't kill her. I didn't love her and I never told her I did. Our affair was a folly and I did her harm. She thought she'd found in me what she needed – father, lover, friend, support, security. I gave her none of these things. She wouldn't be dead if it weren't for me, but I didn't kill her and I don't know who did.'

Dalgliesh said, 'Why the Dupayne museum? And you didn't make love in the car-park, did you? Why on earth should you have sex in discomfort when you had her flat and the whole of London available to you? I'm suggesting to you that you met in Caroline Dupayne's flat. I shall ask Miss Dupayne for her explanation, but now I'd like yours. Have you been in touch with Miss Dupayne since Celia Mellock died?'

He said, 'Yes, I phoned her when the news broke. I told her what I would say to you if I were identified. She was derisive. She said I'd never get away with it. She wasn't worried. She sounded harshly, almost cynically, amused. But I told her that, if pressed, I would have to come out with the whole truth.'

Dalgliesh asked almost gently, 'And what is the whole truth, Lord Martlesham?'

'Yes, I suppose I'd better tell you. We did meet occasionally in the flat over the museum. Caroline Dupayne got two sets of keys for us.'

Dalgliesh asked, 'Although Celia had a flat of her own?'

'I did go there once, yes. It was only once. I didn't feel secure and Celia didn't like using her flat.'

'How long have you been an intimate friend of Caroline Dupayne?'

Lord Martlesham said unhappily, 'I wouldn't say that we were intimate.'

'But you must be, surely. She's a very private woman, yet she lends you her flat and hands out keys to you and to Celia Mellock. Miss Dupayne told me that she had never met Celia since the girl left Swathling's College in 2001. Are you saying that she's lying?'

And Martlesham looked up. He paused and said with a brief rueful smile, 'No, she isn't lying. I'm not very good at this, am I? Not much of a match for a skilled interrogator.'

'We're not playing games, Lord Martlesham. Celia Mellock is dead. So is Neville Dupayne. Did you know him, intimately or otherwise?'

'I've never met him. I hadn't heard of him until I read of his murder.'

'So we go back to my question. What is the truth, Lord Martlesham?'

And now, at last, he was ready to speak. There was a carafe of water and a glass on the table. He tried to pour a glass but his hands were shaking. Piers leaned over and poured it for him. They waited while Lord Martlesham drank slowly, but when at last he began speaking his voice was steady.

'We were both members of a club which meets in Caroline Dupayne's flat. It's called the 96 Club. We go there for sex. I think it was founded by her husband but I'm not sure. Everything is secret about it, even the membership. We can introduce one other member, and that's the only other person whose identity we know. The meetings are arranged on the internet and the website is encrypted. We went there for that one reason, to enjoy sex. Sex with one woman, two, group sex, it didn't matter. It was – or seemed – so joyous, so free of anxiety. Everything fell away. The problems we can't avoid, the ones we impose on ourselves, the occasional blackness of despair when you realize that the England you knew, the England my father fought for, is dying and you're dying with it, the knowledge that your life is based on a lie. I don't suppose I can make you understand. No one was being exploited or used, no one was doing it for money, no one was under-age or vulnerable, no one had to pretend. We were like children – naughty children, if you like. But there was a kind of innocence there.'

Dalgliesh didn't speak. The flat, of course, had been ideal. The concealed entrance to the drive, the trees and bushes, the space for parking, the separate entrance to the flat, the total privacy. He asked, 'How did Celia Mellock become a member?'

'Not through me. I don't know. That's what I've been trying to explain. It was the whole point of the club. No one knows except the member who first brought her.'

'And you have no idea who that was?'

'None. We broke all the rules, Celia and I. She fell in love. The 96 Club doesn't cater for that dangerous indulgence. We met for sex outside the club and that is forbidden. We used the museum for a private meeting. That, too, is against the rules.'

Dalgliesh said, 'I find it strange that Celia Mellock was taken on. She was nineteen. You can hardly expect discretion from a girl of that age. Had she the maturity or the sexual sophistication to deal with that kind of setup? Wasn't she seen as a risk? And was it precisely because she was a risk that she had to die?'

This time the protest was vehement. 'No! No, it wasn't that kind of club. None of them ever felt at risk.'

No, thought Dalgliesh, probably they didn't. It wasn't only the convenience of the flat, the sophistication of the arrangements and the mutual trust that made them feel secure. These were men and women who were used to power and the manipulation of power, who would never willingly believe that they could be in danger.

He said, 'Celia was two months pregnant. Could she have believed that she was carrying your child?'

'She may have believed that. Perhaps that's why she wanted to see me urgently. But I couldn't have made her pregnant. I can't make any woman pregnant. I had a bad attack of mumps when I was an adolescent. I can never father a child.'

The look he gave Dalgliesh was full of pain. He said, 'I think that fact has influenced my attitude to sex. I'm not making excuses, but the purpose of sex is procreation. If that isn't possible, never could be possible, then somehow the sexual act ceases to be important except as a necessary relief. That's all I asked of the 96 Club, a necessary relief.'

Dalgliesh didn't reply. They sat for a moment in silence, then Lord Martlesham said, 'There are words and actions which define a man. Once spoken, once done, there is no possible excuse or justification, no acceptable explanation. They tell you, this is what you are. You can't pretend any longer. Now you know. They stand unalterable and unforgettable.'

Dalgliesh said, 'But not necessarily unforgivable.'

'Not forgivable by other people who get to know. Not forgivable by oneself. Maybe forgivable by God but as someone said, *C'est son métier.* I had such a moment when I drove away from that fire. I knew it wasn't a bonfire. How could it be? I knew that someone could be at risk, someone who might be saved. I panicked and I drove away.'

'You stopped to make sure Mrs Clutton was all right.'

'Are you putting that forward in mitigation, Commander?'

'No, merely stating it as a fact.'

There was silence. Dalgliesh asked, 'Before you drove away, did you enter Miss Dupayne's flat?'

'Only to unlock the door. The hall was in darkness and the lift was on the ground floor.'

'You're quite sure of that? The lift had been brought down to the ground floor?'

'Quite sure. That convinced me that Celia wasn't in the flat.'

After another silence Martlesham said, 'Like a sleepwalker, I seem to have followed a path others have set out for me. I founded a charity because I saw a need and a way to meet it. It was obvious really. Thousands of people driven to financial despair, even suicide, because they can't get credit except from sharks who set out to exploit them. But the ones who need money most are those who can't get it. And there are thousands of people with money to spare – not much, just pocket money to them – who are prepared to provide funds at a moment's notice, interest-free but with a guarantee that they will get the capital back. And it works. We organize it with volunteers. Hardly any of the money goes on administration and gradually, because people are grateful, they start treating you as if you're some kind of secular saint. They need to believe that goodness is possible, that not everyone is driven by greed. They long for a virtuous hero. I never believed I was good, but I did believe I was doing good. I made the speeches, the appeals, expected of me. And now I've been shown the truth about myself, what I really am, and it appals me. It can't be concealed, I suppose? Not for my sake, but I'm thinking of Celia's parents. Nothing could be worse than her death but I wish they could be spared some of the truth. Will they have to be told about the club? And there's my wife. I know it's rather late to be thinking of her but she isn't well and I should like to spare her pain.'

Dalgliesh said, 'If it becomes part of the evidence before the court, then they will know.'

'As will everyone else. The tabloids will see to that even if I'm not the one in the dock. I didn't kill her but I am responsible for her death. If she hadn't met me she'd be alive today. I take it I'm not under arrest? You haven't cautioned me.'

'You're not under arrest. We need a statement from you and my colleagues will take that now. I shall need to talk to you again. That second interview will be recorded under the provisions of the Police and Criminal Evidence Act.'

'I suppose you would advise me at this stage to get myself a lawyer.'

Dalgliesh said, 'That's for you to decide. I think it would be wise.'

3

Despite the heavy traffic, Kate, with Caroline Dupayne, got back to the Yard within two hours of Kate setting out. Caroline Dupayne had spent the afternoon riding in the country and her car had turned into the Swathling drive a minute before Kate's arrival. She had not waited to change and was still wearing her jodhpurs. Dalgliesh reflected that, had she brought her whip, the impression of a dominatrix would have been complete.

Kate had told her nothing on the journey and she heard of Tally's identification of Lord Martlesham with no more emotion than a brief rueful smile. She said, 'Charles Martlesham rang me after Celia's body was discovered. He told me that, if he were identified, he would try to dissemble, but in the end he thought he'd have to tell the truth both about what he was doing at the Dupayne last Friday and about the 96 Club. Frankly I didn't think you'd find him but, if you did, I knew he'd be an ineffectual liar. It's a pity Tally Clutton didn't confine her political education to the House of Commons.'

Dalgliesh asked, 'How did the 96 Club start?'

'Six years ago with my husband. He set it up. He killed himself in his Mercedes four years ago. But you know that, of course. I don't suppose there's much about us you haven't snouted out. The club was his idea. He said

478

that you make money by looking for a need not catered for. People are motivated by money, power, celebrity and sex. The people who get power and celebrity usually have the money too. Getting sex, safe sex, isn't so easy. Successful and ambitious men need sex; they need it regularly and they like variety. You can buy it from a prostitute and end up seeing your picture in the tabloids or fighting a libel case in court. You can pick it up by cruising round King's Cross in your car, if risk is what turns you on. You can sleep around with the wives of friends if you're prepared for emotional and matrimonial complications. Raymond said that what a powerful man needed was guilt-free sex with women who enjoyed the activity as much as he did and had as much to lose. Mostly they would be women in marriages they valued, but who are bored, sexually unsatisfied or needing something with an edge of secrecy and slight risk. So he set up the club. By then my father had died and I had taken over the flat.'

He said, 'And Celia Mellock was one of the group? For how long?'

'I can't tell you. I didn't even know she belonged. That's how the club was run. Nobody – and that includes me – knows who the members are. We have a website so that members can check the date of the next meeting, whether the premises are still safe, but of course they always are. After Neville's death all I needed to do was put a message on the website that all meetings were suspended. It's no use asking me for a list of members. There is no list. The whole point was total secrecy.'

Dalgliesh said, 'Unless they recognized each other.'

'They wore masks. It was theatrical, but Raymond thought that added to the attraction.'

'A mask isn't concealing enough to hide an identity when people are having sex.'

'All right, one or two of them may have suspected who their temporary partners were. They come from much the same world after all. But you're not going to be able to find out who any of them are.'

Dalgliesh sat in silence. She seemed to find it oppressive and suddenly burst out, 'For God's sake, I'm not talking to the local vicar! You're a policeman, you've seen all this before. People get together for group sex and the internet is one way of arranging it, more sophisticated than tossing your car keys into the middle of the floor. Group consensual sex. It happens. What we were doing isn't illegal. Can't we keep a sense of proportion? You haven't even got the police resources to cope with paedophilia on the internet. How many men are there – thousands? tens of thousands? – paying to see young children sexually tortured? What about the people who provide the images? Are you seriously proposing to waste time and money hunting down the members of a private club for consenting adults held on private premises?'

Dalgliesh said, 'Except that here one of the participants has been murdered. Nothing about murder is private. Nothing.'

She had told him what he needed to know and he let her go. He felt no particular disapproval. What right had he to be judgemental? Until now, hadn't his own sexual life, conducted with more fastidiousness, been a careful separation of physical satisfaction from the commitment of love?

4

Ryan said, 'You'll be all right, won't you, Mrs Tally? I mean, you're used to being here. You don't think I ought to stay?'

Tally had reached home at last after a Tube journey in which there had been no hope of a seat and in which only the crush of bodies had kept her upright. It had been to find Ryan in the sitting-room with his rucksack packed and ready to leave. A note written in capital letters on the back of an envelope lay on the table.

Tally sank into the nearest chair. 'No, I don't think you ought to stay, Ryan. I'm sorry it hasn't been comfortable for you. The cottage is so small.'

'That's it!' he said eagerly. 'It's everything being so small. But I'll be back. I mean, I'll be coming to work as usual on Monday. I'm staying with the Major.'

Relief was clouded with anxiety. Where, she wondered, was he really going? She said, 'And the Major is happy to have you?'

He didn't look at her. He said, 'He says it's OK. I mean, it's not for long. I've got plans, y'know.'

'Yes, I'm sure you have, Ryan, but it's winter now. The nights can be terribly cold. You need to have shelter.'

'I've got shelter all right, know what I mean? Don't you worry, Mrs Tally, I'm OK.' He lugged the heavy pack on to his shoulders and turned to the door.

Tally said, 'How will you get home, Ryan? Perhaps, if she's still here, Miss Godby will give you a lift to the Tube.'

'I've got my new bike, haven't I? The one the Major bought.' He paused, then said, 'Well, I'll be off then. Goodbye, Mrs Tally. Thanks for having me.'

And then he was gone. Tally was trying to summon enough energy to move when there was a ring at the front door. It was Muriel. She was wearing her coat and was obviously ready to go home. She said, 'I've seen to the locking-up; I couldn't wait any longer for you to get back. I saw Ryan cycling down the drive. He'd got his rucksack with him. Is he leaving?'

'Yes, Muriel. He's going back to the Major. It's all right, Muriel. I'm used to being alone. I'm never nervous here.' She repeated, 'It's perfectly all right.'

'Miss Caroline won't think so. You ought to phone her and see what she advises. She might want you to stay with her, Tally. Or you could come to me if you're really frightened.'

The offer could not have been less gracious. Tally thought, *She feels she has to make it but she doesn't want me. She could offer to come and stay here, but she won't, not after what happened yesterday.* She thought she could read fear in Muriel's eyes and the realization gave her a small spurt of pleasure; Muriel was more frightened than she.

She said, 'It's very good of you, Muriel, but I'm perfectly all right. This is where I live. I've got the window bolts, a double lock on the door, and the phone. I don't feel I'm at risk. Why would anyone want to murder me?'

'Why did they want to murder Dr Neville or that girl?

Whoever it is must be mad. You'd be much better to ring Miss Caroline and ask her to come for you. She could find a bed somewhere in Swathling's.'

Tally thought, *If you're so concerned, why not just insist I pack and go home with you?* But she didn't blame Muriel. Muriel would have thought it all out very carefully. Once Tally moved in with her it could be for weeks, perhaps even for months. There would be no reason for her to go back to the cottage until the murders were solved, and there was no knowing how long that would take. Perhaps they never would be solved. She had a conviction, which she knew was hardly rational but which was too strong to be ignored, that if she left the cottage now she would never return. She could see herself desperately searching for a bed-sitting-room or being given house-room by one of the Dupaynes or by Muriel, a perpetual source of anxiety and irritation to them all. This was her place and she wouldn't allow a murderer to drive her out of it.

Muriel said, 'Well, it's your responsibility. I've made the suggestion. I came to give you your keys to the museum. We got them back by two o'clock and I told Sergeant Benton-Smith that I'd hand them over. And I'd better take the cottage keys that you lent to Ryan. They're the only spare set and they belong in the office.'

Tally said, 'Oh dear, I'm afraid Ryan forgot to give them back and I didn't think to ask him. But he'll be back on Monday.'

Muriel voiced her usual reprimand, but somehow as if her heart wasn't in it. She had certainly changed since the second murder. She said, 'You should never have let

484

him have the keys. He could perfectly well have kept normal hours and relied on you to let him in. If you see him on Monday before I do, make sure you get them from him.'

And then at last she had gone. Tally locked and bolted the door behind her and then moved to a chair before the fire. She felt sick with tiredness. The trauma of discovering Lord Martlesham, her visit to New Scotland Yard, worry about Ryan and now the brief skirmish with Muriel had increased her exhaustion. Perhaps she would have been sensible to have accepted Commander Dalgliesh's offer of a lift home. But gradually the tiredness became almost pleasurable and the peace at the end of the day, which she always felt when sitting alone, returned and calmed her. She indulged in this mood for a moment and then, refreshed, got up and began putting the cottage to rights.

Upstairs Ryan hadn't bothered to strip his bed and the air was fusty. She took the key to the window from the small hook on which it hung and opened the double panes. Sweet autumnal air came in. She stood for a moment savouring it and looking out over the dark void of the Heath before closing and locking the window again. Then she stripped the bed, shoving the sheets and pillowcases into the linen basket. She would wash them tomorrow; tonight she felt she couldn't tolerate the noise of the washing machine. Next she removed Ryan's wet towels from the floor of the bathroom, cleaned the basin and flushed the lavatory. She had a half-guilty feeling that she was washing him away with the mess he had left. Where would he sleep tonight, she wondered? She was tempted to ring the Major and ask whether Ryan was really expected, but Ryan hadn't given her the number, only the Maida Vale address. She could look up the number in the directory, but to telephone would surely be seen as an unforgivable intrusion. Ryan was nearly eighteen, she was neither his grandmother nor his keeper. But the small weight of guilt and responsibility couldn't be lifted. Somehow she had failed the boy, and it had been a failure of tolerance and kindness. The cottage was her sanctuary and her beloved home, but perhaps her solitary life was making her selfish. She remembered how she had felt at Basingstoke. Was that how she had made Ryan feel?

She began to give thought to her supper, but although she hadn't eaten since her picnic lunch she was beyond hunger and was tempted by none of the pre-packed meals stacked in the refrigerator. Instead she made herself a mug of tea, pouring boiling water on to a single teabag, opened a packet of chocolate digestive biscuits and settled at the kitchen table. The sweetness revived her. Afterwards, and almost without conscious thought, she put on her coat and, unlocking the door, walked out into the darkness. This, after all, was how she always ended the day. This evening was no different. She needed that short walk on the Heath, the shimmering vista of London spread beneath her, the cool air on her cheeks, the smell of earth and greenness, a moment of loneliness which was never complete loneliness, of mystery which was without fear or regrets.

Somewhere in that stretch of silence and darkness lonely people might be walking, some in search of sex, companionship, perhaps of love. A hundred and fifty years ago a maidservant in the house had crept down the same path, passed through the same gate, to meet her lover and her appalling death. That mystery had never been solved, and the victim, like the victims of those murderers whose faces looked down from the walls of the Murder Room, had become one of the great army of the amorphous dead. Tally could think of her with transitory pity but her shade had no power to disturb the peace of the night, and it could not make her afraid. She armoured herself with the blessed assurance that she wasn't in thrall to terror, that the horror of the two murders couldn't keep her captive in her cottage or spoil this solitary excursion under the night sky.

It was when she had left the Heath and had closed the gate behind her that, looking up at the black mass of the museum, she saw the light. It shone from the south window of the Murder Room, not brightly as if all the wall lights had been left on, but with a faint diffused glow. She stood for a few seconds regarding it steadfastly, wondering whether it could be some reflection from the lights in the cottage. But that, of course, was impossible. She had only left on lights in her sitting-room and hall and they shone out now through the narrow slits between the drawn curtains. They could have no power to light up any part of the museum. It looked as if only a single light had been left on in the Murder Room, probably one of the reading lamps by the armchairs in front of the fireplace. Perhaps one of the Dupaynes or Mr Calder-Hale had been in the Murder Room to study some of the documents and had neglected to turn off the reading lamp. Even so, it was surprising that Muriel, on her final checking of the rooms, hadn't noticed that one light.

Tally told herself firmly that there was no need to be afraid and that she should act sensibly. It would be ridiculous to phone Muriel, who must be home by now, or either of the Dupaynes, without checking that there had been a simple mistake. To phone the police would be even more ridiculous. The sensible thing would be to check that the front door was locked and the alarm on. If so, she could be confident that no one was in the museum and that it would be safe to enter. If the door were not locked, she would return to the cottage at once, lock herself in and phone the police.

She went out again, torch in hand, and made her way as silently as possible past the black spars of the burnt saplings to the front of the house. And now no lights were visible; that pale glow could be seen only from the southern and eastern windows. The front door was locked. Making her way in, she switched on the light to the right of the door and moved quickly to silence the bleep of the alarm. After the darkness outside, the hall seemed to blaze with light. She stood for a moment thinking how strange and unfamiliar it suddenly seemed. Like all spaces that are usually filled with human figures, human sounds, human activity, it seemed mysteriously to be waiting. She felt reluctant to move forward as if to break the silence would release something alien which was not benign. Then that sturdy common sense which had seen her through the last few days reasserted itself. There was nothing here to fear, nothing that was strange or unnatural. She had come for a simple purpose, to switch off a single light. To return to the cottage without moving another step, to go to sleep knowing that the light still burned, would be to give way to fear, to lose – perhaps for ever – the confidence and peace which this place and the cottage had given her for the last eight years.

She moved resolutely across the hall hearing the echo of her feet on the marble and mounted the staircase. The door to the Murder Room was shut but not sealed. The police must have completed their search sooner than they had expected. Perhaps Muriel, still traumatized by the horror of finding Celia's body, hadn't even dared to open the door. It was unlike her, but then Muriel had been unlike herself since that awful discovery in the trunk. She might not admit to being afraid but Tally had seen fear darken Muriel's eyes. It was possible that she had dreaded that final checking of the building, particularly as she had been alone, and had done it less conscientiously than usual.

She pushed open the door and saw at once that she had been right. The reading lamp by the right-hand chair had been left on and there were two closed volumes and what looked like a notebook on the table. Someone had been reading. Moving to the table she saw that it had been Mr Calder-Hale. The notebook was his; the small almost unreadable writing was in his well-known hand. He must have come to the museum to collect his keys as soon as the police were ready to return them. How had he been able to sit there so calmly working after what had happened?

It was the first time she had been in the Murder Room

since the finding of Celia's body, and she knew at once that something was different, something odd, then realized that it was the missing trunk. It must still be in police custody, or perhaps at the Forensic Science Laboratory. It has been such a dominant feature of the room, at once so ordinary and so portentous, that its absence was more ominous than its presence.

She didn't immediately go across to turn out the light, but stood for a full half-minute in the doorway. Photographs were not frightening to her, but then they never had been. Eight years of daily dusting, of locking and unlocking the cabinets, of polishing the glass above the exhibits, had robbed them almost of interest. But now the soft half-light of the room produced a new and unwelcome sensation. She told herself that it wasn't fear, merely unease. She would have to get used to being in the Murder Room; she may as well begin now.

She walked over to an eastern window and looked out into the night. Was this where Celia had stood on that fateful Friday? Was that why she had to die, because she had looked down at the blazing trees and seen a murderer bending down at the tap washing his gloved hands? What had he felt as he'd looked up and seen her there, white face and long yellow hair, the eyes wide with horror? She must have known the implication of what she had seen. So why had she waited for those strong hurrying steps to reach her, those gloved hands to clutch her by the neck? Or had she tried to escape, fumbling ineffectually at the closed door to the flat or rushing downstairs only to fall into her killer's waiting arms? Was that how it happened? She had been told little by Dalgliesh or by his subordinates. She knew that, since the first murder, they had been constantly at the museum, questioning, examining, searching, discussing, but no one knew what was in their minds. Surely it was impossible that two murderers should choose to kill on the same day, at the same time, in the same place. They had to be related. And if they were related, surely Celia had died because of what she had seen.

Tally stood for a moment thinking of the dead girl, of that earlier death, of Lord Martlesham's face bending over her and the look of terror and compassion in his eyes. And then it came to her. She had been told by Dalgliesh to ponder carefully every moment of that Friday, to tell him everything, however trivial, that later occurred to her. She had tried to do so conscientiously and nothing new had come to mind, nothing untold. But now in one second of complete certainty she remembered. It was a fact and it had to be told. She didn't even question whether morally she should tell, whether it might be misunderstood. None of the uncertainty she had felt in St Margaret's Church after recognizing Lord Martlesham afflicted her now. She turned from the window and went over briskly to switch off the fireside lamp. The door of the Murder Room was ajar and the light from the hall and upper gallery streamed in and laid a golden burnish on the wooden floor. She closed the door behind her and hurried downstairs.

In the excitement of the discovery she didn't consider waiting to telephone until she got back to the cottage. Instead she lifted the receiver on the counter of the reception desk and dialled the number which Inspector

Miskin had given her and which she knew by heart. But it was not Inspector Miskin who answered. The voice said, 'Sergeant Benton-Smith.'

Tally had no wish to give the message to anyone but Commander Dalgliesh. She said, 'It's Tally Clutton, sergeant. I wanted to speak to Mr Dalgliesh. Is he there?'

'He's tied up at the moment, Mrs Clutton, but he should be free shortly. Can I take a message?'

Suddenly what Tally had to tell seemed less important. Doubts began crowding in on her tired brain. She said, 'No, thank you. There's something I've remembered, something I need to tell him, but it can wait.'

The sergeant said, 'Are you sure? If it's urgent we can deal with it.'

'No, it's not urgent. Tomorrow will do. I'd rather speak to him personally than on the phone. I expect he'll be at the museum tomorrow, won't he?'

The sergeant said, 'I'm sure he will. But he could see you tonight.'

'Oh that would be a trouble to him. It's only a small thing and perhaps I'm making too much of it. Tomorrow will do. I'll be here all the morning.'

She replaced the receiver. There was nothing else to do here. She switched on the security system, moved swiftly to the front door, unlocked it and went out, double-locking it carefully behind her. Two minutes later she was safely back in the cottage.

After the front door had closed the museum was for the moment utterly silent. Then the door of the office slowly and soundlessly opened and a dark figure moved through the reception area and into the hall. No lights were switched on but the figure moved with delicate but confident steps across the hall and up the stairs. The gloved hand reached out for the knob of the Murder Room door and opened it slowly as if fearful of alerting the watching eyes. The figure moved towards the William Wallace display. The gloved hand felt for the keyhole and inserted a key, then lifted the lid of the display cabinet. The figure held an ordinary plastic bag and, one by one, the chess figures were taken from the cabinet and dropped into its depth. Then the hand moved along the bottom of the display case until it found what it sought: the iron bar.

5

It was just after seven-thirty and the team were together in the incident room.

Dalgliesh said, 'So now we know the who, the how and the why. But it's all circumstantial. There isn't a single piece of physical evidence directly linking Vulcan to either of the victims. The case isn't yet good enough. The CPS might be willing to take a chance on an over fifty per cent hope of conviction, but given a competent defence lawyer the prosecution could fail.'

Piers said, 'And one thing's certain, sir. There'll be a more than competent defence counsel. He could make a case for Dupayne's death being suicide. There's evidence enough that he was under acute stress. And if Dupayne wasn't murdered, then the link between the two deaths fails. Celia Mellock's death could be a sexually motivated murder or manslaughter. The uncomfortable fact remains that she could have got into the museum last Friday afternoon undetected and her killer could have left unseen. She could have arrived any time in the day intending later to meet Martlesham.'

Piers went on, 'If she arrived by taxi it's a pity the driver hasn't yet come forward. But it's early days. He could be on holiday.'

Kate turned to Dalgliesh. 'But it hangs together, sir. It may be circumstantial but it's strong. Think of the salient

494

facts. The missing handbag and why it had to be taken. The palm prints on the door to the flat. The fact that the lift was at ground floor level when Martlesham arrived. The broken violets. The attempt to make the murders look like copycat killings.'

Benton-Smith spoke for the first time. 'Only the second death, surely. The first was almost certainly coincidence. But whoever killed Celia could have known – probably must have known – about the first killing.'

'So it's too early, sir, for an arrest?'

'We need to go on with the questioning, and now under PACE and with a lawyer present. If we don't get a confession – and I'm not expecting one – we might with patience get a damaging admission or variation of the story. Meanwhile there's this message from Tally Clutton. What exactly did she say?'

Benton-Smith said, 'That she had some information that she wished to give to you, sir, but not over the phone. She was anxious to see you personally, sir. But she said it wasn't urgent. She said tomorrow would do. I got the impression that she regretted having rung.'

'And Ryan Archer? He's still in the cottage?'

'She didn't say he wasn't.'

Dalgliesh was for a moment silent. Then he said, 'Tomorrow won't do. I want to see her tonight. I'd like you with me, Kate. I don't want her to be in that cottage tonight with only the boy for protection.'

Piers said, 'But you don't think she's in danger, surely? Vulcan was forced into that second killing. We've no reason to suppose there'll be a third.'

Dalgliesh didn't reply. He turned to Kate. 'Would you

mind, Kate, staying the night with her? The boy will presumably be in the spare room so it'll probably mean sitting up in the armchair.'

'That'll be all right, sir.'

'So let's hear what Mrs Clutton has to tell us. Ring her, will you, Kate, and let her know we're on our way. Piers and Benton, unless I call we'll meet here tomorrow morning at eight.'

6

Normally Tally would be thinking now of what to have for her early supper, setting out the tray if she planned to eat while watching television or, more usually, covering the centre table with a cloth. She preferred to eat with some formality, having an obscurely guilty feeling that too many meals in the armchair with a tray on her knees was a slide into slovenly self-neglect. Sitting at the table was both more comfortable and made her evening meal, over which she usually took trouble, a pleasure to be anticipated and enjoyed, one of the comforting rituals of her solitary life.

But tonight she was still unable to summon up any interest in even the simplest preparation. Perhaps that snack of tea and biscuits had been a mistake. She found herself walking restlessly round the table, a pointless perambulation which she seemed unable to control. The revelation that had come to her at the museum was so simple but so extraordinary in its implication that she had thoughts for nothing but astonishment at the discovery. Commander Dalgliesh, on one of his many earlier visits, had asked her to think over what had happened on the day of Dr Neville's death and write down any detail, however small, which she hadn't previously remembered to tell him. There had been none. This was, she supposed, a detail, but she wondered why it hadn't occurred to her earlier. Certainly careful thought hadn't brought it back. There must have been some fusion of ideas, of sight, sound and thought co-existing, which had sparked off memory. Sitting at the table, her two arms stretched out on the surface, she was as still and rigid as a dummy placed there ready to receive some imaginary plate of food. She tried to reason, to ask herself whether she could have been mistaken in the time or the sequence or the implication of what she remembered. But she knew that there was no mistake. The realization had been absolute.

The ring of the telephone made her jump. It was rare for anyone to ring her after the museum closed and she lifted the receiver with some dread. It might be Jennifer ringing again; she was too tired to cope with Jennifer's questions and badgering concern. She sighed with relief. It was Inspector Miskin to say that Commander Dalgliesh wanted to see her tonight. He and Miss Miskin were on their way.

And then her heart leapt and she clutched the edge of the table in terror. The air was rent by an unearthly screaming. At first she thought it was human, then realized that this screech of agony came from the throat of an animal. It was Tomcat! She lurched over to the bureau for her door keys and made for the door. She reached for her torch from the ledge in the porch and seized the nearest coat – her mackintosh – from its peg. Flinging it over her shoulders, she tried to fix the keys into the two locks. They slithered against the metal. By an effort of will she managed to steady her hands and the keys slid home. And now for the bolts.

At last the door was open and she ran into the darkness.

It was a night of low cloud, almost starless and with only a glimpse of the sickle moon. The only light came in a shaft from the door of the cottage which she had left ajar. There was a low wind. It moved among the trees and grass like a living thing and touched her face with its clammy hands. The shrieking was closer now; it came from the edge of the Heath. Running down the path, she pushed open the wicker gate and swept the torch in an arc over the nearest trees. At last she found him.

Tomcat was hanging from one of the low branches, a belt slung round one hind leg with the other end tied to the branch. He was swinging as he screamed, his three unfettered paws ineffectually scrabbling at the air. Instinctively she ran and reached up, but the branch was too high and she gave a cry of pain as his claws slashed at the back of her hand and she felt the warm trickle of blood. She said, 'I'm coming, I'm coming', and ran back into the cottage. She needed gloves, a chair and a knife. Thank God the sitting-room chairs were strong enough to take her weight! She seized one, took a carving knife from the knife block and within seconds was again under the tree.

It took a little time to wedge the chair in the soft earth so that she could mount it in safety. She was murmuring reassurance and endearments but Tomcat didn't heed them. Holding her mackintosh before her she wrapped it round his body and with a sharp shove managed to raise him so that he could perch on the bough. Immediately the yowling stopped. The belt was more difficult.

The easiest way of releasing Tomcat would have been to loosen the buckle round his hind leg, but she couldn't risk his claws. Instead she inserted the blade of the knife under the belt and sawed away. It took a full minute before at last the leather broke and, enveloping Tomcat entirely in the mackintosh, she managed to reach the ground. Immediately she released him and he shot away onto the Heath.

Suddenly she was overcome with a terrible weariness. The chair seemed to have become too heavy to carry and, with the raincoat draped over her shoulders, she dragged it behind her up the short garden path. She found that she was quietly crying and the tears, once started, flowed over her cheeks, icy as winter rain. All she wanted now was to get back to the cottage, to lock the door behind her and wait for the police. Whoever had done that to Tomcat was evil and there was surely only one evil person at work in the Dupayne Museum. She dragged the chair through the porch. The key was still in the lock and she turned it, then reached for the bolts. The door to the small hall was open and, without trying to lock it, she almost staggered into the sitting-room. She managed to push the chair back in its place and then stood for a moment bending over it in utter exhaustion.

And then – but too late – she heard the footsteps crossing the hall. In her weariness she was too late even to realize her danger. She had half turned when the iron bar crashed down and she fell on to the carpet, her head within a foot of the gas fire, the mackintosh still round her shoulders. She saw, without surprise, her assailant's face, then heard and saw nothing more, as the chess pieces fell in a shower over her body. Seconds passed before consciousness finally seeped away. There was time to think how simple and easy it was to die, and to say thank you to the God in whom she had always believed and of whom she had asked so little.

7

They took Dalgliesh's car and he drove without speaking. Dalgliesh was given to these periods of silence and Kate knew him too well to break them. He was an experienced and skilful driver and they made as good time as was possible. It would have been pointless to fume at the inevitable delays, but Kate sensed Dalgliesh's increasing anxiety.

When they reached Hampstead, he said, 'Ring Mrs Clutton again, Kate. Tell her we're nearly there.'

But this time there was no reply.

And now they were turning into the Dupayne Museum drive. The Jaguar surged forward, the headlights seeming to consume the darkness. They silvered the grass verges and the encroaching bushes. And when Dalgliesh turned the final corner the house was lit up in the glare as if for *son et lumière*. They saw that the barrier had been raised. The car lurched round the eastern flank of the house, past the blackened ruin of the garage and jerked to a stop on the gravel path. There were no lights from the cottage but the door was open. Dalgliesh ran in first, through the hall and into the sitting-room. His hand found the light switch. The gas fire was lit and turned low, and Tally lay on the hearthrug, her head facing the flames. A mackintosh was bunched round her shoulders and the blood from her head was flowing fresh and red. Over her body the black and ivory chess pieces were scattered as if in a final gesture of contempt.

It was then that they heard, faintly but unmistakably to their keen ears, the sound of a car. Kate made for the door but Dalgliesh grasped her arm. 'Not now, Kate. I need you here. Let Piers and Benton-Smith make the arrest. Ring for the ambulance, then ring Piers.'

As she tapped out the number, he knelt by Tally Clutton's body. The flow of blood had stopped, but as he put his fingers to her throat, the pulse suddenly ceased. Quickly he rolled up the mackintosh and put it under her neck, opening her mouth and checking that she had no false teeth. He bent his head and, fastening his mouth over hers, began resuscitation. He wasn't aware of Kate's urgent words or the hiss of the gas fire, only of his own rhythmic breathing and the body he was willing to come alive. And then, it seemed by a miracle, he felt the beat of a pulse. She was breathing. Minutes later she opened her eyes and fixed on him an unseeing gaze, and with a little moan, as if of contentment, turned her head to one side and lapsed again into unconsciousness.

The wait for the ambulance was interminable but Dalgliesh knew it was pointless to phone again. They had received a call; they would come as soon as they could. It was with a sigh of relief that he heard it arrive and the paramedics come into the cottage. Expert help had at last arrived.

One of the paramedics said, 'Sorry about the delay. There's been an accident at the end of the drive. The traffic's down to a single stream.'

Kate and Dalgliesh looked at each other but neither spoke. There was no point in questioning the paramedics; their concern was with the job in hand. And there was no hurry, no need to know immediately. By the time they got back to the Yard Piers could have reported whether or not he had made an arrest. Whether Vulcan was alive or not, this was the end of the case.

Dalgliesh and Kate watched as Tally, wrapped in blankets and strapped to the stretcher, was loaded into the ambulance. They gave her name and a few details and were told where she would be taken.

The keys to the front door were in the lock. Kate turned off the gas fire, checked the windows upstairs and down and they left the cottage, turning out the lights and locking the front door.

Dalgliesh said, 'Take over the driving, will you, Kate?'

He knew she was happy to do so. Kate enjoyed driving the Jaguar. When they reached the drive, he asked her to stop, then got out, leaving her waiting in the car. He knew that she would neither join him nor question what he was doing. He walked a little way and gazed up at the black mass of the museum, wondering whether he would ever visit it again. He felt both sad and exhausted but the emotion was not strange to him; this was often what he felt at the end of a case. He thought of the lives which his life had so briefly touched, of the secrets he had learned, the lies and the truths, the horror and the pain. Those lives so intimately touched would go on, as would his. Walking back to rejoin Kate, he turned his mind to the weekend ahead and was filled with a precarious joy.

8

Thirty-five minutes earlier Toby Blake, aged nineteen years and two months, rode his Kawasaki into Spaniards Road on the last lap of his journey home. It had been a frustrating drive but Thursday night usually was. Weaving with cunning expertise between the almost stationary cars and buses and getting ahead of expensive cars with their disconsolate drivers had its satisfactions, but that was not what the Kawasaki was for. Now for the first time he saw the road gleaming pale and empty ahead. It was time to see what the machine could do.

He opened the throttle. The engine roared and the bike leapt like a tiger. His eyes glinted under the visor and he grinned with delight as he felt the rush of air, the giddy excitement of speed, the power of being in control. Ahead a car came out at speed from a driveway. The boy had no time to brake, no time even to register that it was there. He had one second of appalling realization and then the Kawasaki banged into the right side of the bonnet, spun across the road and slammed into a tree. He was hurled upwards, arms flailing, and then crashed to the side of the road and lay motionless. The car spun out of control and ploughed on to the verge.

There were ten seconds of absolute silence and then the headlights of a Mercedes lit up the road. The Mercedes stopped, as did the car following. There were hurried footsteps, exclamations of horror, urgent voices speaking into mobile phones. Anxious faces looked at the driver of the crashed car, slumped over the wheel. Voices conferred. It was agreed that they should wait for the ambulance. Other cars drove up and stopped. The procedure for rescue was underway.

At the side of the road the boy lay very still. There was no sign of injury and no blood. It seemed to the watching eyes that he was smiling in his sleep.

9

This time the hospital was modern and for Dalgliesh
unfamiliar territory. He was directed to the right department and eventually found himself in a long windowless
corridor. There was no hospital smell but the air was
different from any other, as if it had been scientifically
cleansed of any taint of fear or illness. There was no
doubt which was the right room. Two uniformed police
constables were seated at the door and got up and saluted
him as he approached. Inside was a WPC who rose and
greeted him quietly, then left closing the door. He and
Vulcan were alone together face to face.

Muriel Godby was in a chair at the side of the bed.
The only sign of injury was the plaster cast on her left
arm and wrist, and a livid bruise across the left cheek.
She was wearing a checked cotton dressing-gown which
looked institutional and she was perfectly calm. The
gleaming, extraordinarily-coloured hair held back by
a tortoiseshell slide had been carefully brushed. The
greenish-yellow eyes stared into his with the half-
concealed resentment of a patient receiving yet one more
unwanted visitor. They held no trace of fear.

He didn't go up to her. He said, 'How are you?'

'Alive, as you see.'

Dalgliesh said, 'I expect you know that the motorcyclist died. He broke his neck.'

'He was going too fast. I've told Miss Caroline many times that there should be clearer warning notices. But you haven't come to tell me that. You've got my confession and in my own handwriting. That's all I have to say.'

The confession was comprehensive but purely factual, making no excuses, showing no remorse. The murder had been planned in advance on the Wednesday after the meeting of the trustees. On the Friday of the murder Godby had come equipped with the bucket, protective overall, gloves, shower cap and long matches in the car boot, together with a large plastic bag into which she could thrust them after the deed. She hadn't gone home, but had returned to the museum after dropping Mrs Strickland at Hampstead Tube station. She knew that Tally Clutton would have left for her Friday evening class and she had that morning taken the precaution of disconnecting her landline telephone in case anyone should call. She had waited in the darkness of the garage until Neville Dupayne was seated in the Jaguar, then had stepped forward calling his name. Surprised, but recognizing her voice, he had turned his face towards her and had received the full force of the petrol. She had needed only seconds to light and throw the match. The last human sound he heard had been her voice. When Tally telephoned her later she had just reached home. There had been time to replace the receiver, put the protective clothing in the washing machine, scour out the bucket and wash herself thoroughly before setting off for the museum. During the weekend she had wrenched the handle from the bucket, cut up the gloves and shower cap and, under cover of darkness, shoved them among the rubble of a handy skip.

There was little in the confession that was new to Dalgliesh except one fact. Celia Mellock, when at Swathling's, had taunted her, resented her and had tried to get her sacked from her job. The girl had been a redhead then, only later dyeing her brown hair yellow, but from the moment Godby entered the Murder Room to dispose of her the recognition had been absolute on both sides. For Godby the killing had been a pleasure as well as a necessity.

Now she said, 'I don't know why you're here, Commander. You and I have finished with each other. I know I'll go to prison for ten years. I've served a longer sentence than that. And I've succeeded in what I wanted, haven't I? The Dupaynes won't close the museum to honour their brother's memory. Every day it's open, every visitor who arrives, every success will be due to me. And they'll know it. But leave my life alone. You're entitled to know what I did and how I did it. You know anyway, you worked it all out. That's your job and you're said to be good at it. You're not even entitled to know why I did it, but I didn't mind giving a reason if it made everyone happier. I've written it down and it's quite simple. Dr Neville Dupayne killed my sister through his negligence. She phoned him and he didn't come. She threw petrol over herself and set it alight. Because of him she lost her life. I wasn't going to let him lose me my job.'

Dalgliesh said, 'We've checked up on Dr Dupayne's life before he came to London. Your sister died fifteen

509

years ago, twelve years after you had left home. Did you ever meet Dr Dupayne at that time? How close were you to your sister?'

And now she looked at him full in the face and he thought he had never seen such a concatenation of hatred, contempt and – yes – triumph. When she spoke he was amazed that her voice could sound so normal, the same voice in which she had calmly answered his questions throughout the last week.

'I said you're entitled to know what I did. You're not entitled to know what I am. You're neither a priest nor a psychiatrist. My past is my own. I'm not going to get rid of it by making a present of it to you. I know about you, Commander Dalgliesh. Miss Caroline told me after you first arrived. It's the kind of thing she knows. You're a writer, aren't you, a poet? It isn't enough for you to meddle in other people's lives, to get them arrested, to see them sent to prison, their lives broken. You have to understand them, get into their minds, use them as your raw material. But you can't use me. You haven't the right.'

Dalgliesh said, 'No, I haven't the right.'

And then it seemed that her face softened and became touched with sadness. She said, 'We can never really know each other, you and I, Commander Dalgliesh.'

At the door Dalgliesh turned again to face her. 'No,' he said, 'we can't. But does that make us different from any other two people?'

IO

Tally Clutton's room, in another part of the hospital, was very different. Dalgliesh entered to an almost over-powering scent of flowers. Tally was in bed, her head was partly shaved and unbecomingly covered with a gauze cap beneath which a padded dressing was clearly visible. She stretched out her hand to him, smiling a welcome.

'How good of you to come, Commander. I was hoping you might. Pull up a chair, will you. I know you can't stay long but I wanted to speak to you.'

'How are you feeling now?'

'Much better. The head wound isn't too serious. She didn't have time to finish me off, did she? The doctors say that my heart stopped for a short time because of shock. If you hadn't come I'd be dead. Once I thought that death wouldn't matter very much. I feel differently now. I couldn't bear to think I wouldn't see another English spring.' She paused, then said, 'I know about the motorcyclist. That poor boy. They told me he was just nineteen and an only son. I keep thinking about his parents. I suppose you could call him the third victim.'

'Yes,' said Dalgliesh. 'The third and the last.'

She said, 'You know Ryan has gone back to Major Arkwright?'

'Yes, the Major rang to tell us. He thought we might wish to know where Ryan was.'

'It's his life, of course – Ryan's. I suppose it's what he wants. But I hoped that he would take more time to think about it, his future I mean. If they've quarrelled once they can again, and next time – well, it could be more serious.'

Dalgliesh said, 'I don't think it will happen again. Major Arkwright is fond of him. He won't let the boy come to harm.'

'I know Ryan is gay, of course, but wouldn't he be better off with someone nearer his own age, not so rich, not with so much to offer?'

'I don't think Major Arkwright and he are lovers. But Ryan's nearly of age. We can't control his life for him.'

She said, as if speaking more to herself than to Dalgliesh, 'I think he might have stayed with me longer, long enough to be sure what he wanted, but he knew I didn't really want him in the cottage. I'm so used to living alone, having the bathroom to myself. It's something I've always hated, sharing a bathroom. He knew that, he's not a stupid boy. But it wasn't just the bathroom. I was afraid of getting too fond of him, letting him into my life. I don't mean seeing him as a son, that would be ludicrous. I mean human kindness, taking trouble about him, caring about him. Perhaps that's the best kind of loving. We use the same word for such different things. Muriel loved Caroline, didn't she? She killed for her. That must have been love.'

Dalgliesh said gently, 'Perhaps that was an obsession, a dangerous kind of love.'

'But all love is dangerous, isn't it? I suppose I've been frightened of it, of the commitment of it all my life. I'm beginning to understand now.' She looked up straight into his face. 'You're only half alive if you're afraid to love.'

She continued looking up at him, as if seeking some wisdom, some reassurance, but it was impossible to know what he was thinking. He said, 'There's something you wanted to tell me.'

She smiled. 'It doesn't matter now but it seemed to at the time I rang. It was something I remembered. When Muriel arrived shortly after the fire, the first thing she said was that we ought to have locked up the petrol. I didn't tell her that Dr Neville had been doused with petrol. I couldn't have told her, I didn't know it myself then. So how did she know? At first I thought that remembering this was important, then I told myself that she could have guessed.' She paused, then said, 'I suppose there's no news of Tomcat?'

'I haven't been to the museum this morning but I haven't heard that he's back.'

'I suppose he's not really important while there's so much else to worry about. If he doesn't come back I hope he finds someone to take him in. He's not an engaging cat. He can't rely on charm. It was horribly cruel what Muriel did to him. And why? She could have knocked on the cottage door and I'd have let her in. And she wouldn't have had to worry about my recognizing her. After all, I'd be dead. I would be now if you hadn't come.'

He said, 'She had to kill you in the sitting-room to

make it look like a copycat murder. And she couldn't be sure that you'd open the door to her if she had knocked. I think she may have overheard you ringing us from the museum. Knowing what you did, you might well have refused to let her in.'

Hoping to turn her mind to other things, he said, 'Your flowers are lovely.'

Her voice brightened. 'Yes, aren't they? The yellow roses are from Mr Marcus and Miss Caroline, and the orchid from Mrs Strickland. Mrs Faraday and Mr Calder-Hale have telephoned and they're coming to visit me this evening. The news got round quickly, didn't it? Mrs Strickland sent me a note. She thinks we ought to get a priest to visit the museum. I'm not sure what exactly for, to say some prayers, sprinkle some holy water or carry out an exorcism. She writes that Mr Marcus and Miss Caroline are happy about it provided they don't have to take part. They say it won't do any good but it can't possibly do any harm. That's a surprising thing for Mrs Strickland to suggest, isn't it?'

'A little surprising, perhaps.'

She was looking very tired now. He said, 'I think I'd better go. You mustn't exhaust yourself.'

'Oh, I'm not exhausted. It's such a relief to talk. Miss Caroline came in to see me early this morning and she was very kind. I don't think I really understood her. She wants me to stay on in the cottage, and to take on part of Muriel's job. Not the reception or the accounts, of course, they're advertising for someone qualified to do that. We're going to need a lot of extra help now. No, I'm to help by cleaning the flat for her. She says she may be there more often in future. It's very light work, mostly dusting, clearing out the refrigerator, putting sheets in the washing machine. She has a number of friends to stay, people who need a bed for the night. Of course I'm happy to take it on.'

The door opened and a nurse came in. She looked at Dalgliesh. 'There's a few things I need to do now with Mrs Clutton,' she said. 'Perhaps you'd like to wait outside.'

Dalgliesh said, 'I think it's time to leave anyway.'

He bent to shake the hand lying limply on the coverlet, but her clasp was firm. Under the bandages the eyes which met his had none of the questioning anxiety of old age. They said goodbye and he walked back down the anonymous sterile corridor. There was nothing he had needed to say to her, nothing that would have helped. To tell her what the job could really entail would almost certainly mean she wouldn't take it. She would risk losing her cottage and her livelihood, and for what? Already she was falling under Caroline Dupayne's extraordinary spell. But she wasn't as naïve as Muriel Godby. She was too secure in her own personality to become besotted. Perhaps in time she would realize what was going on in the flat. If that happened she would make her own decision.

He met Kate coming down the corridor towards him. She was there, he knew, to arrange for the transfer of Muriel Godby.

She said, 'The consultant thinks she's perfectly fit to be moved. Obviously they'd like to get rid of her as soon as possible. Public Relations have phoned, sir. They'd like a press conference later today.'

'We can issue a press statement but, if they want me there, the conference can wait until Monday. There are things I have to do in the office and I need to leave early this evening.'

She turned her face from him, but not before he had glimpsed the cloud of sadness. She said, 'Of course, sir, you told me. I know you need to leave early this evening.'

By half-past eleven the backlog of urgent matters awaiting Dalgliesh's attention had been dealt with and he was
ready to write his report on the investigation. It was one
that both the Commissioner and the Minister of State
had asked to see. It was the first time that he had been
asked to submit a detailed report on an investigation to
the Minister and he hoped that it wouldn't set a precedent. But first there was some still unfinished business.
He asked Kate to ring Swathling's and tell Caroline
Dupayne that Commander Dalgliesh wished to see her
urgently at New Scotland Yard.

An hour later she arrived. She was dressed for a formal
luncheon party. The dark green coat in a heavy silk hung
in dramatic folds and the winged collar framed her face.
Her lipstick was stark against the pale skin. She took the
proffered chair and looked at him. The eyes which met
his were frankly appraising, as if this were their first
meeting and she was assessing him sexually, toying with
possibilities.

She said, 'I suppose I should congratulate you.'

'That's neither necessary nor appropriate. I've asked
you to come here because I have two more questions.'

'Still on the job, Commander? Ask, and if I can I'll give
you an answer.'

Dalgliesh said, 'On or after last Wednesday, did you

tell Muriel Godby that you were sacking her, that you no longer wanted her at the museum?'

He waited. She said, 'The inquiry is over, Muriel is under arrest. I'm not trying to be offensive or un-cooperative, but is that any longer your business, Commander?'

'Please answer.'

'Yes. I told her on Wednesday evening after we'd been to the flat. Not precisely in those words, but I told her. We were in the car-park together. I consulted no one before I spoke and the decision was mine alone. Neither my brother nor James Calder-Hale thought she was the right person for the reception desk. Earlier I'd fought to keep her – efficiency and loyalty count for something. By Wednesday I'd decided they were right.'

One more piece of the puzzle clicked into place. So that was why Godby had returned to the museum on Thursday night and was in the office when Tally made her call to the police. When questioned, Godby had said that she wanted to catch up on the backlog of work; but if that were true, why leave and return, why not just stay on?

He said, 'She'd gone to clear her desk. She couldn't do it while people were around. For her that would have been an intolerable humiliation.'

Caroline Dupayne said, 'To clear her desk and some-thing else: to leave me a list of outstanding things to be done and to tell me how the office should be run. Conscientious to the last.'

She spoke without pity, almost with contempt.

He said, 'Your colleagues may have thought her

unsuitable for the job, but that wasn't the reason you sacked her, was it? By Wednesday night you knew beyond doubt that she had killed your brother and Celia. You didn't want her on the staff of the museum when I made the arrest. And then there was the link with Swathling's. It's always been important, hasn't it, to keep the school unsullied by association with murder?'

'These were minor considerations. With any luck I shall inherit Swathling's. I've built up the school. I don't want it to begin the downward path before I get the chance to take over. And you're right about the museum. It was expedient to get rid of Muriel before you made the arrest. But that wasn't the main reason why I told her to go. When the truth comes out, neither Swathling's nor the Dupayne can escape some contamination. The school won't be much harmed; she left too long ago. I doubt whether the museum will be harmed at all. Already people are clamouring to know when we plan to reopen. The Dupayne Museum is at last on the map.'

'And when did you come to the conclusion that she was responsible?'

'About the same time as you did, I imagine, when I learned that someone had bolted the door from the flat into the Murder Room. Only Godby and I had keys. The difference between us was that you had to find the evidence, I didn't. And now I have a question for you. As she's confessed, we're spared a trial, but how much of my private life is likely to come out? I'm talking, of course, about the 96 Club. It isn't relevant to how either victim died. Isn't that what a coroner's inquest is concerned with, the cause of death? Need it be mentioned?'

The question was as calmly asked as if she were inquiring about the date. She showed no concern and this was no appeal. He said, 'Much will depend on which questions the coroner decides to ask. There are still the two adjourned inquests.'

She smiled. 'Oh, I think you'll find that the coroner will be discreet.'

Dalgliesh said, 'Did you tell Muriel Godby that you knew the truth? Did you challenge her?'

'No. She knew about the 96 Club of course, or at least had her suspicions. After all, she dealt with the bed linen; she put out the empty champagne bottles. I didn't challenge her and when I got rid of her I made no direct mention of the murders. I merely said that I wanted her to clear her desk and be gone as soon as our keys were returned. In the mean time she should keep out of my way.'

'I want to know exactly what was said by both of you. How did she take it?'

'How do you think? She looked at me as if I were condemning her to life imprisonment. I suppose it's possible that I was. I thought for a moment that she was going to faint. She managed to speak but the words came out as a croak. She said, "What about the museum? What about my job?" I told her not to concern herself, she wasn't indispensable. My brother and James Calder-Hale had been wanting to get rid of her for months. Tally would take over the cleaning of my flat.'

'And that was all?'

'Not quite. She cried out, "What will happen to me?" I told her that her best hope was that the police would see the deaths as copycat killings. That was my only reference to the murders. Then I got into my car and left.'

And with those last words, thought Dalgliesh, Tally Clutton was condemned to die. He said, 'The murder of your brother was her gift to you. It was for you she wanted to save the museum. She might even have expected you to be grateful.'

And now her voice was hard. 'Then she didn't know me, and neither do you. You think, don't you, that I didn't love Neville?'

'No, I don't think that.'

'We Dupaynes don't show emotion. We were trained not to and in a hard school. We're not sentimental about death, our own or anyone else's. We don't go in for that neurotic hugging and slobbering which people use as a substitute for the responsibilities of real compassion. But I did love Neville. He was the best of us. Actually he was adopted. I don't think anyone knew who the mother was except our father. Marcus and I have always assumed that the child was his. Why otherwise would he adopt? He wasn't a man given to generous impulses. My mother did what he wanted; that was her function in life. Neville was adopted before I was born. We quarrelled often. I had little respect for his job and he despised mine. He may have despised me but I didn't despise him. He was always there, always the accepted elder brother. He was a Dupayne. Once I knew the truth I couldn't bear to have Muriel Godby under the same roof.' She paused, and asked, 'Is that all?'

Dalgliesh said, 'All I have a proper right to ask. I'm

wondering about Tally Clutton. She says you've offered her Muriel's job looking after the flat.'

She got up and reached down for her handbag, then smiled. 'Don't worry. The job will be strictly limited. A little light dusting, vacuuming the floors. I know how to value goodness even if I don't aspire to it myself. And if the 96 Club is reconstituted, it won't meet at the Dupayne. We don't want the local fuzz breaking down doors and roaring in on the excuse that they've been tipped off about drugs or paedophiles. Goodbye, Commander. It's a pity we didn't meet in different circumstances.'

Kate, who had remained silent, left with her and the door closed behind them. Within minutes she was back. She said, 'My God, she's arrogant. And then there's the family pride. Neville was valued because he was half a Dupayne. Do you think she was telling the truth about the adoption?'

'Yes, Kate, she was telling the truth.'

'And the 96 Club, what was she getting out of that?'

'Some money, I imagine. People would have left gifts on the excuse they were helping to pay for the cleaning or the drinks. But mostly she enjoyed the power. In that she and Godby were alike.'

He could imagine Godby sitting there at the reception desk secretly hugging the knowledge that, except for her, the museum would have closed, wondering perhaps if and when she might dare to confess to Caroline what she had done for her, that exorbitant gift of love.

Kate said, 'Caroline Dupayne will keep the club going, I imagine. If she takes over Swathling's they could meet there safely enough, particularly in the holidays. Do you think we ought to warn Tally Clutton?'

'It isn't our business, Kate. We can't put people's lives in order for them. Tally Clutton isn't a fool. She'll make her own decisions. It's not for us to face her with a moral decision she may never have to resolve. She needs her job and the cottage, that much is plain.'

'You mean she might compromise?'

'When there's a lot at stake people often do, even the virtuous.'

12

It was five o'clock and the final seminar of the week was over. The girl student sitting opposite Emma beside the fire had been on her own. Her companion had gone down with flu, the first victim of the new term. Emma devoutly hoped that it wasn't the beginning of an epidemic. But Shirley seemed reluctant to leave. Emma looked across at the girl, huddled in her chair, eyes down, the small, rather grubby hands twisting in her lap. She could read distress too clearly to ignore it. She found herself silently praying, *Oh God, please don't let her ask too much of me, not now. Let this be quick.*

She had to catch the six-fifteen train and Adam was to meet her at three minutes past seven at King's Cross. She had dreaded the telephone call to say that he couldn't make it, but he hadn't rung. Her taxi had been ordered for five-thirty, early enough to allow for heavy traffic. Her case was packed ready. Folding her night-dress and dressing-gown, she had smiled, thinking that Clara, if watching her, would have said she was packing for a honeymoon. She wrenched her mind away from the mental picture of his tall dark figure waiting for her at the barrier, and said, 'Is anything worrying you?'

The eyes looked into hers. 'The other students think I'm here because I went to a comprehensive school. They think the government paid money to Cambridge to take me. That's why I'm here, not because I'm clever.'

Emma's voice was sharp. 'Has anyone said this to you?'

'No, no one. They haven't said anything but that's what they believe. It's in the newspapers. They know it's happening.'

Emma leaned forward and said, 'It doesn't happen here in this college and it didn't happen with you, Shirley, it's just not true. Listen to me, this is important. The government doesn't tell Cambridge how to select its students. If it did, if any government did, Cambridge wouldn't take any notice. We have no motive for selecting anyone except on the basis of intelligence and potential. You're here because you deserve to be.'

Shirley's voice was so low that Emma had to strain to hear her. 'I don't feel I am.'

'Think about it, Shirley. Scholarship is international and highly competitive. If Cambridge is to hold its place in the world, we need to select the best. You're here on your merits. We want to have you and we want you to be happy here.'

'The others seem so confident. Some of them knew each other before they came up. They've got friends here. Cambridge isn't strange to them, they know what to do, they're together. Everything's strange to me. I feel that I don't belong here. It was a mistake coming to Cambridge, that's what some of Mum's friends back home told me. They said I wouldn't fit in.'

'They were wrong. It does help, coming up with friends. But some of the students who seem so confident have much the same worries as you. The first term at university is never easy. All over England now new students are feeling the same uncertainties. When we are unhappy we always believe that no one else could ever feel the same. But they do. It's part of being human.'

'You can't feel like that, Dr Lavenham.'

'Of course I can, sometimes. And I do. Have you joined any societies?'

'Not yet. There are so many. I'm not sure where I'd fit in.'

'Why not join one in which you're really interested? Don't just do it to meet people and make friends. Choose something you'll enjoy, perhaps something new. You will meet people and you will make friends.'

The girl nodded and whispered something which might have been 'I'll try.' Emma was worried. This was the kind of problem brought to her by students which caused the most anxiety. At what stage, if any, ought she to advise that they ask for professional counselling or psychiatric help? To miss the signs of serious distress could be disastrous. But to overreact could destroy the very confidence she was trying to build up. Was Shirley desperate? She didn't think so. She hoped that she was judging rightly. But there was other help she could offer and which she knew was needed.

She said gently, 'When we first come up, it's sometimes difficult to know how to work most effectively, how to make the best use of our time. It's easy to waste it by working hard on inessentials and neglecting what is important. Writing academic essays takes a lot of practice. I'm out of Cambridge this Saturday and Sunday but we can have a talk about it on Monday, if you feel it would be helpful.'

'Oh it would, Dr Lavenham, it would. Thank you.'

'Shall we say six o'clock then?'

The girl nodded and got up to go. At the door she turned to whisper a final thank you, then disappeared. Emma looked at her watch. It was time to put on her coat, pick up her case, and go down to await the taxi. She was on Cambridge station before she realized that she had left her mobile in her room in College. Perhaps, she thought, this had been less an oversight than a subconscious dread of hearing it ring on the journey. Now she could travel in peace.

13

At last Dalgliesh was ready to leave. His PA put her head round the door. 'It's the Home Office, Mr Dalgliesh. The Minister would like to see you. His private office rang. It's urgent.'

When a call came on a Friday afternoon it usually was. Dalgliesh said, 'You told them I'm leaving for the weekend almost immediately?'

'I did tell them. The private office said it was lucky they caught you in time. It's important. Mr Harkness has been called as well.'

So Harkness would be there. Who else? Dalgliesh wondered. Even while dragging on his coat he looked at his watch. Five minutes to cut through St James's Park Underground station and to get to Queen Anne's Gate. Probably the usual delay with the lift. At least he was well known and, with his pass, wouldn't get held up by security. So, six minutes in total, if he were lucky, before he was in the Minister's room. He wasted no time checking whether Harkness had already left, and ran for the lift.

It was seven minutes exactly before he was shown into the private office and into the Minister's room. He saw that Harkness was already there, as was the Permanent Under-Secretary of State, Bruno Denholm from MI6 and the PUSS from the Foreign and Commonwealth Office, a suave young-looking middle-aged official whose air of calm detachment made it plain that he held merely a watching brief. All present were used to this kind of urgent summons and practised in reducing the unexpected and unwelcome to the manageable and innocuous. Even so, he was aware of an air of unease, almost of embarrassment.

The Minister waved a hand and made brief and largely unnecessary introductions. He was a man who had adopted good manners, particularly to officers, as a working policy. Dalgliesh reflected that on the whole it served him well. It had at least the merit of originality. But now his offer of sherry – 'Unless you gentlemen think it too early; there's tea or coffee if preferred' – and his scrupulous attention to their seating seemed wilful delaying tactics and Harkness's acceptance of the sherry, apparently on behalf of them all, an indulgence amounting to incipient alcoholism. God, would they never get started? The sherry was poured – excellent and very dry – and they seated themselves at the table. There was a folder in front of the Minister. He opened it and Dalgliesh saw that it held his report on the Dupayne Museum murders.

The Minister said, 'Congratulations, Commander. A sensitive case solved speedily and efficiently. It raises again the question of whether we shouldn't extend the Special Investigation Unit to cover the whole country. I'm thinking particularly of recent distressing child abductions and murders. A national squad with particular expertise could have an advantage in these notorious cases. I imagine you have views on the suggestion.'

Dalgliesh could have retorted that the question wasn't new and that views on it, his included, were already known. He said, carefully restraining his impatience, 'The advantages are obvious if the investigation needs to cover the whole country rather than clearly being a local crime. But there are objections. We risk losing local knowledge and contact with the local community which can be important in any investigation. There's the problem of liaison and co-operation with the force primarily concerned, and there could be a loss of morale if the more challenging cases are reserved for a squad which can be seen as privileged both in recruitment and facilities. What we need is an improvement in the training of all detectives including those at DC level. The public are beginning to lose confidence in the ability of the police to solve local crime.'

The Minister said, 'And that, of course, is what your committee is at present considering, the recruitment and training of the detective force. I'm wondering if there could be an advantage in our taking on this wider issue, the creation of a national squad.'

Dalgliesh didn't point out that it wasn't his committee, merely one on which he served. He said, 'The chairman would probably agree to a late extension of the terms of reference if that's what the Secretary of State wants. If it had been included from the beginning we might have had a rather different membership. There are problems in co-opting members at this late stage.'

'But in future it could be taken on board?'

'Certainly, if Sir Desmond is happy.'

But this reiteration of an old issue had, Dalgliesh

realized, been only a preliminary. Now the Minister turned his attention to the report on the murders. He said, 'Your report makes it plain that the private club – or perhaps I should say the meetings of friends of Miss Caroline Dupayne – was not responsible either for the death of Dr Neville Dupayne or of Celia Mellock.'

Dalgliesh said, 'There was only one person responsible, Muriel Godby.'

'Exactly, and that being so, it seems unnecessary to distress her mother further by any reference publicly as to why the girl was at the museum.'

Dalgliesh reflected that an ability to believe that all people were less intelligent and more naïve than oneself was a useful quality in a professional politician, but it wasn't one he was prepared to accept. He said, 'This hasn't anything to do with Lady Holstead, has it? She and her second husband were well aware of her daughter's lifestyle. Who exactly are we protecting here, sir?'

He was tempted mischievously to suggest some names but resisted. Harkness's sense of humour was rudimentary and the Minister's untested.

The Minister looked across at the official from the FCO. He said, 'A foreign national, an important man and a good friend of this country, has sought an assurance that certain private matters will remain private.'

Dalgliesh said, 'But isn't he being unnecessarily worried? I thought only two sins attract opprobrium in the national press: paedophilia and racism.'

'Not in his country.'

The Minister took over quickly. 'Before we give that assurance, there are details on which I need to be satisfied, particularly that there will be no interference with the course of justice. That doesn't need saying. But justice surely doesn't demand the stigmatizing of the innocent.'

Dalgliesh said, 'I hope my report is clear, Minister.'

'Both clear and detailed. Perhaps I expressed myself clumsily. I should have said that I would like to have your assurance about certain matters. This club, the one run by Miss Dupayne, I take it that this was a purely private club held on private premises, that no members were under the age of sixteen and that no money was involved. What they were doing may have been reprehensible in some eyes, but it wasn't illegal.'

Dalgliesh said, 'Miss Dupayne wasn't running a bawdy house and no member of her club was concerned with the death either of Neville Dupayne or Celia Mellock. The girl wouldn't have died if she hadn't been in the Murder Room at a particular time and she wouldn't have been there if she hadn't been a member of the 96 Club but, as I have said, only one person was responsible for her death: Muriel Godby.'

The Minister frowned. He had been meticulous in omitting the name of the club. He said, 'There's no doubt about that?'

'No, Minister. We have her confession. Apart from that, we would have made an arrest this morning. Tallulah Clutton recognized her assailant before she lost consciousness. The bloodstained iron bar was found in Godby's car. The blood has yet to be analysed but there's no doubt that it's Clutton's.'

The Minister said, 'Exactly. But to return to the activities in Miss Dupayne's flat. You suggest that the girl, who had an arrangement with Lord Martlesham to meet him that evening, did in fact go to the flat, entered the Murder Room by unbolting the door, motivated perhaps by curiosity and by the fact that entry to the museum that way had been specifically forbidden, and saw from an eastern window Muriel Godby washing her hands under the garden tap. Godby looked up and glimpsed her at the window, entered the museum, strangled her victim who was unable to escape to the flat through the closed handleless door, and put the body in the trunk. She was certainly powerful enough to do this. She then entered the flat by the outside door to which she had a key, switched off any lights in the flat, finally brought down the lift to the ground floor and left. Lord Martlesham arrived almost immediately afterwards. The absence of Celia Mellock's car which was being serviced, the absence of a light in the hall and the fact that the lift was on the ground floor persuaded him that the girl had not kept the appointment. Then he saw the flames from the garage fire, panicked and drove off. The following morning Godby, arriving early as usual, had time and opportunity to break off the stems from the pot of African violets in Calder-Hale's office and strew them on the body. The object, of course, was to make the second murder look like a copycat killing. She also re-locked and bolted the door from the flat into the Murder Room and checked that Mellock had left no incriminating evidence there of her presence. Neither that nor the ploy with the African violets could have been done immediately after the murder. Once the fire became visible she had to get away, and quickly, before the alarm was raised. I can see why Godby needed to take the handbag. It was important that the key to the flat wasn't found on Mellock's body. Quicker to grab the bag than to waste time searching for the key. There are, of course, ancillary details but that is the nub of the case.'

He looked up with the satisfied smile of a man who has again demonstrated his ability to master a brief.

Dalgliesh said, 'That's how the case presented itself to me. From the beginning I believed the two murders were connected. This view was confirmed when we had the evidence set out in my report that the trunk was empty at four o'clock on that Friday. That two completely unconnected murders should be committed at the same time and in the same place beggars belief.'

'But – forgive me – the girl could have come to the museum earlier and with another lover, met him in the basement archive room and then stayed hidden in the museum once it was closed. And if she did get into the museum other than from the flat, then the fact that she was a member of Miss Dupayne's private club was totally irrelevant to her murder. There need, therefore, be no reference to the club.'

Dalgliesh said, 'I was asked for a full report, sir, and you have it. I'm not prepared to alter it or to sign another. As Godby has signed a confession and proposes to plead guilty, there will be no trial. If a shortened version of the investigation is required for internal use, the department could no doubt provide it. And now, sir, I would like to leave. I have an urgent private appointment.'

He saw Harkness's look of surprise and the Minister's

534

frown. But he said amiably enough, 'Right. I have the reassurance I was seeking, that neither law nor justice requires that evidence of Miss Mellock's private life should be made public. I think, gentlemen, that our business is finished.'

Dalgliesh was tempted to point out that he had received no such assurance and that no one in the room, including himself, was competent to give it.

Harkness said, 'Lord Martlesham may, of course, speak out.'

'I've spoken to Lord Martlesham. He has an overdeveloped conscience which causes him some inconvenience, but he has no wish to cause inconvenience to others.'

'And there have been two adjourned inquests, Minister, and now there will be one other.'

The Minister said easily, 'Oh I think you'll find that the coroner will confine his questions to what is relevant in establishing the causes of death. That, after all, is what a coroner is required to do. Thank you, gentlemen. I'm sorry to have kept you, Commander. Have a pleasant weekend.'

14

Hurrying to the lift, Dalgliesh looked at his watch. Three-quarters of an hour to get to King's Cross. It should be more than enough. He had planned the journey well in advance. To drive from Victoria Street to King's Cross on a Friday in the rush hour would be to court disaster, particularly with the Mayor's retiming of the traffic lights, and he had left his car in his usual parking lot at his flat. The quickest, indeed the obvious route was to take the Circle or District line from St James's Park station the one stop to Victoria then change to the Victoria Line. Five stations only and, with luck, he would be at King's Cross within fifteen minutes. The plan to spend the waiting time at the British Library had been dropped. His summons to the Minister had put out all earlier calculations.

The journey began well. A Circle Line train arrived within three minutes and there was no wait at Victoria. Once in the northbound Victoria Line train he began to relax and was able to free his mind from the complications of the day to contemplate the very different complications and the promises of the evening ahead. But then, after Green Park, came the first intimation of impending trouble. The train slowed to an almost imperceptible speed, stopped for what seemed to Dalgliesh an interminable wait, then jerked into sluggish activity. They were hardly moving. Minutes dragged past in which he stood in a press of warm bodies, outwardly calm, but with his mind in a tumult of frustration and impotent fury. At last, they drew into Oxford Circus station and the doors opened to the shout of 'All change!'

In the chaos of discharging passengers surging through those who had been waiting to board, Dalgliesh heard a man call out to a passing guard, 'What's wrong?'

'Line blocked ahead, sir. A defective train.'

Dalgliesh waited to hear no more. He thought quickly. There was no other direct line to King's Cross. He would try for a cab.

And now he was lucky. A passenger was being set down at the corner of Argyll Street. Sprinting, Dalgliesh was at the cab door before she had time to alight. He waited impatiently while she fumbled for change, then said 'King's Cross, and as quickly as you can.'

'Right, sir. We'd best take the usual route, Mortimer Street, then Goodge Street and up to Euston Road.'

He had already moved off. Dalgliesh tried to sit back and discipline impatience. If he were late, how long would she wait? Ten minutes, twenty minutes? Why should she wait at all? He tried to ring her mobile but there was no reply.

The drive as he expected was tediously slow and, although their speed improved when they got to Euston Road, it was still little more than a crawl. And then disaster. Ahead a van had collided with a car. It wasn't a serious accident but the van had slewed across the road. Traffic was at a standstill. There would be an inevitable delay before the police arrived to direct the stream and get things moving. Dalgliesh thrust a ten-pound note at the cabbie, leapt out and ran. By the time he raced into King's Cross station, he was twenty minutes late.

Apart from the uniformed staff, the small concourse serving the Cambridge line was deserted. What would Emma have done? What would he have done in her place? She wouldn't want to go to Clara's flat and spend the evening listening to her friend's anger and condolences. Emma would go back to where she was at home, to Cambridge. And that is where he would go. He had to see her tonight, had to know the worst or the best. Even if she didn't want to listen to him he could hand her the letter. But when he enquired of a station officer the time of the next train, he learned why the concourse was so empty. There was trouble with the track. No one could give any idea when it would be put right. The train arriving at three minutes past seven had been the last one in. Were all the gods of travel conspiring to thwart him? The official said, 'There are the slow trains to Cambridge from Liverpool Street, sir. You'd be better to try there. That's what most passengers are doing.'

There was no chance of getting a taxi in a hurry, he had seen the length of the queue as he sprinted past. But now there was another and, with luck, quicker way. Either the Circle or the Metropolitan Line would take him to Liverpool Street in four stops if by some miracle it didn't break down. He ran through the mainline station to the Underground and tried to weave his way through the mass of people passing down the stairs. Finding coins for the ticket machine seemed an intolerable inconvenience, but at last he was on the platform and within

538

four minutes a Circle Line train arrived. At Liverpool Street he ran up the wide steps, past the modern clock-tower and stood at last on the higher level looking down at the wide blue departure board which stretched across the lower concourse. The train to Cambridge with its list of ten stopping stations was showing as departing from platform six. He had less than ten minutes to find her.

Because of the closure of the King's Cross line there was a bulge of humanity shoving and pushing at the barrier. Joining them and working his way through, he called to the woman on duty: 'I have to find someone. It's urgent.' She made no move to stop him. The platform was crowded. Ahead of him was a mass of people moving alongside the train, jostling at the carriage doors, looking hopelessly for a vacant seat.

And then he saw Emma. She was walking, he thought a little disconsolately, bag in hand, towards the head of the train. He took the letter from his pocket and ran up beside her. She turned and he had time only to see her start of surprise and then, miraculously, her quick involuntary smile, before thrusting the envelope into her hands. He said, 'I'm no Captain Wentworth, but please read this. Please read it now. I'll wait for you at the end of the platform.'

And now he was standing alone. He turned away because he couldn't bear to see her stuffing the letter into her pocket and entering the train. And then he made himself look. She was standing apart from the thinning crowd and she was reading. He could remember every word he had written.

I have told myself that I am writing this because it will give
you time to consider before you reply, but that may only be
cowardice. To read a rejection will be more bearable than to
see it in your eyes. I have no reason to hope. You know that
I love you, but my love gives me no claim. Other men have
said these words to you and they will again. And I can't
promise to make you happy; it would be arrogant to assume
that such a gift lay in my power. If I were your father, your
brother or merely a friend I could find plenty of reasons to
argue against myself. But you know them already. Only the
greatest poets could speak for me, but this is not a time for
other men's words. I can only write what is in my heart.
My only hope is that you may care enough to make you
wish to risk this adventure together. For me there is no risk.
I can hope for no greater happiness than to be your lover
and your husband.

Standing there alone and waiting, it seemed to him
that the life of the station had mysteriously vanished as
if it had been part of a dream. The uneven stamp of
marching feet, the waiting trains, the meetings and partings, the clamour, the closing of carriage doors, the shops
and the cafés of the wide concourse beyond and the
distant hum of the city all faded. He stood under the
magnificent vault of the roof as if no other two persons
existed but his waiting self and her distant figure.

And now his heart leapt. She was coming purposefully
towards him and breaking into a run. They met and he
took her outstretched hands in his. She looked up into
his eyes and he saw that hers were brimming with tears.
He said gently, 'My darling, do you need more time?'

'No more time. The answer is yes, yes, yes!'

He didn't take her in his arms, nor did they kiss. For those first sweet intimacies they needed solitude. For the moment he was content to feel her hands in his and let the extraordinary fount of happiness well up through every vein until it broke and he threw back his head and laughed his triumph aloud.

And now she too was laughing. 'What a place for a proposal! Still, it might have been worse. It could have been King's Cross.' She looked at her watch and added. 'Adam, the train goes in three minutes. We could wake to the sound of fountains in Trinity Great Court.'

Releasing her hands, he bent and took up her case. He said, 'But I have the Thames running under my windows.'

Still laughing, she tucked her arm in his. 'Then let's go home.'